Praise for Jeannie Watt

"Watt brings her complex,
wonderful characters to life."
—*RT Book Reviews*

"Jeannie Watt's stories are always vivid, heartfelt
and, simply put, an unforgettable experience."
—*USATODAY.com*'s *Happy Ever After* blog

"[A] good contemporary romance
between two adults that didn't rely
on a higher concept other than falling in love
to provide the conflict in the story."
—*Dear Author* on *Once and for All*

"*Crossing Nevada* is a finely detailed and
interesting tale with a touch of suspense, added
to very real animals and sympathetic people."
—*Fresh Fiction*

"A very engaging tale."
—*The Romance Reader* on *Undercover Cook*

JEANNIE WATT

lives in rural Nevada with her husband, horses and ponies, and she teaches high school in a small combined school close to the Nevada-Oregon border. When she's not teaching or writing, Jeannie enjoys sewing retro fashions and reports on her new projects regularly on her blog, *Retro Sewing Romance Writer*. She also makes mosaic mirrors, ignores housework as much as possible and is thrilled to be married to a man who cooks. Visit her online at www.jeanniewatt.com.

JEANNIE WATT

Home on the Ranch: Nevada

⟨H⟩ HARLEQUIN® THE COWBOY COLLECTION

Recycling programs
for this product may
not exist in your area.

ISBN-13: 978-0-373-60656-6

HOME ON THE RANCH: NEVADA

Copyright © 2014 by Harlequin Books S.A.

The publisher acknowledges the copyright holder
of the individual works as follows:

THE HORSEMAN'S SECRET
Copyright © 2007 by Jeannie Steinman

THE BROTHER RETURNS
Copyright © 2008 by Jeannie Steinman

This edition published by arrangement with Harlequin Books S.A.

For questions and comments about the quality of this book, please contact us at CustomerService@Harlequin.com.

Printed in U.S.A.

CONTENTS

THE HORSEMAN'S SECRET

To the Rays and Mr. Stein,
the best principals ever,

To my headstrong children,

To my parents,
who raised their own headstrong children,

To my mother, a true horsewoman,

I dedicate this book.

Thanks so much for everything.

CHAPTER ONE

THE CALL WILL BISHOP had been dreading came at 2:45 in the afternoon, just when he was beginning to think he was home free. As soon as he hung up the phone, he grabbed his hat and headed for the truck. True to form, his daughter Kylie had started junior high with a bang.

Will knew the way to the office by heart—he'd visited the place a time or two during his own scholastic career at Wesley Junior and Senior High. He pulled off his hat and stepped inside.

"Hi, Will." The secretary was the same woman who'd kept him company years ago, only a little grayer now and sitting in front of a computer instead of a typewriter. "Long time, no see."

"Mrs. Serrano."

"You can go in."

Will wondered how many more times he was going to hear those words over the next few years.

He pushed the door open. Four faces turned his way. Kylie, of course, looking defiant as only Kylie could; Mr. Bernardi, the principal; Pete Domingo, the PE teacher; and a lady he didn't know.

"Have a seat, Will."

At least Bernardi had refrained from making any comments about old times. The last thing Will needed was for Kylie to think she was carrying on a family tradition, even if she was.

"This is Miss Flynn," Bernardi said, indicating the dark-haired woman who was now regarding Will with an inquiring expression. "Miss Flynn is Kylie's science and social studies teacher."

Miss Flynn acknowledged the introduction with a nod and a smile that stopped short of her striking green eyes. She seemed cool and professional, exactly the kind of teacher that Kylie—and Will, back in the day—always butted heads with. In fact, Kylie was glaring at her now from under her lashes. Will sensed a long school year ahead.

"Will, Kylie has engaged in some questionable behavior that needs to be addressed immediately." Bernardi sounded as if he was reading from a cue card.

"I see." Will was an old hand at translating teacher speak. He'd heard enough of it over the years. "What did Kylie do that was questionable?"

Mr. Bernardi was about to respond when he was interrupted by Pete Domingo. "Let's let Kylie tell her father what she did."

"Good idea," Bernardi agreed. "Kylie?"

Kylie sent Pete a smoldering look. "I got caught."

No kidding. "Caught doing what?"

"Caught smoking after PE," Pete Domingo said, forgetting his intention of letting Kylie fess up.

"Smoking!"

Kylie nodded slowly. If Will hadn't been so utterly ticked off, he would have noticed his daughter trying to send him a message.

He glanced at Bernardi. "I'll be taking care of this at home. What happens here?"

"We know there are others involved, but Kylie won't name names."

"I was the only one," she said.

"We know that's not true." Bernardi sounded tired.

Kylie stubbornly shook her head, her straight dark hair shifting over her shoulders. She was no longer meeting anyone's gaze. Instead, she stared down at the floor tiles.

Principal Bernardi let out a sigh. "We've already discussed this with Kylie. If she won't tell us who else was there, then she'll have to bear the brunt of the punishment alone."

Will gave Kylie a long look. Her jaw was locked and she looked so much like his ex-wife at that moment that it almost frightened him. But even if she resembled Desiree, she mostly took after him.

"I understand why Pete is here, but…" Will glanced over at Miss Flynn. She hadn't said a word and she didn't appear as though she particularly wanted to be there. Unlike Domingo. The little general was enjoying this.

"They were outside my room," she said. "There was a group of at least three, but Kylie was the only one I recognized."

Will gave Kylie one last chance, even though he knew it was futile. "Kylie?"

She shook her head. Will stood. "Unless she needs to stay now, I think we'll go home and discuss this."

"This means an automatic three-day suspension, Will. School-district policy."

"I understand," Will replied. "Come on, Kylie. We're going home." Kylie got up from the wooden chair and headed for the door.

"If I get any names, I'll let you know," he told Bernardi, and followed his daughter out of the room. He was almost at the main entrance when he heard quick footsteps behind him. What now?

"Go to the truck," he told Kylie, who went out the door without a word. Will turned to face Miss Flynn, fast approaching with purposeful strides, the expression on her face that of someone about to give helpful hints on how to handle his child. Well, he'd had enough input from educators for one day.

"Don't worry," he said, "I'm not going to beat her."

"That's happy news," she replied mildly, and Will felt somewhat ashamed of himself. "I actually wanted to talk to you about another matter."

"Like...?"

"I'm looking for a horse. A pleasure horse, and I heard you have some for sale."

This was not what Will had expected. Not even close. He gave a slow nod of acknowledgment. "I did have some horses for sale, but they went fast. I only have one left at this point, and I'm afraid he won't do for you."

Miss Flynn's eyebrows edged upward. "Why? I'm an experienced rider."

"He's a man's horse."

She regarded him for a moment. "There's no such thing."

"He was abused by a woman and now he doesn't like women—not even Kylie. Some horses are like that."

She looked as though she'd like to argue the point with him, but she didn't. "Well, do you know of any other horses for sale around here?" She pushed her hair behind an ear, mussing the layers.

"Not right now." It was true. There weren't many suitable horses for sale in Wesley, Nevada, and he wasn't going to direct her to the Taylors, who always had a horse for sale at some ridiculously high price. "You might try closer to Elko."

One corner of her mouth tightened in obvious frustration and suddenly she didn't look so teacherlike.

"I'll let you go." She rubbed the back of her neck in a

way that made Will think he wasn't the only one who'd had a bad day. "I knew this wasn't a good time to ask, but I really want a horse. And since I was going to call about your newspaper ad anyway…." She shrugged. "Bad judgment on my part."

She turned then, walked back down the hall, leaving Will staring after her. He felt like a jerk.

He debated for a moment, then decided to rebuild his burned bridges later. Right now he needed to nudge the truth out of his daughter.

"So who are you covering for this time?" Will asked as he put the truck in gear. Kylie waited until they were officially off school property before she answered.

"Mark. You know what his dad would do to him."

Will knew. Mark's dad was a bully, but somehow Mark not only survived, he was a likable kid.

"What happened?"

Kylie gave a brief description of events, which played out pretty much as Will had expected. Mark, the geek, had been proving he wasn't a geek by smoking, with Kylie watching his back. The part where Kylie had got caught and Mark hadn't was still hazy, but Will let that slide for the moment.

"If you're suspended, I can't exactly let you go to the horse show this weekend, can I?"

Kylie's jaw dropped. "But I didn't do anything."

"You were there."

"But…"

"Smoking is wrong, and you were there," Will replied, holding firm.

"I was there because of Mark. People pick on him because they can. It's not right." Kylie let out a huff of breath to emphasize the remark.

"Well, I really don't think smoking was the answer. Do you?"

"No, but I couldn't talk him out of it."

"Then you should have walked away. You can't go through life protecting people, Kylie. And I don't see Mark standing up for you. He left you twisting in the wind."

Kylie gazed at her father earnestly. "He doesn't know. They got me after science and I didn't have time to see him. I totally missed my last class while we waited for you."

"And now you're going to miss three days."

"And the horse show," she muttered sullenly.

"You aren't going to be riding or working with your horse, either. I need some help fixing the pole corral and I think there's some housework that needs attending to. We'll stop by the school tomorrow and pick up your work."

They drove a few miles in silence and then Kylie asked, "How come the new teacher knew you?"

"What makes you think she knows me?"

"The way she was looking at you."

Kylie didn't elaborate and Will decided it was best not to ask. "She doesn't know me. She knows we have horses for sale and she's looking to buy a horse."

"But all we have left is the paint gelding."

"I know."

"He won't do for her."

Will smiled in spite of himself. "That's exactly what I told her."

"Miss Flynn?"

Regan turned to see Pete heading down the hall toward her, his whistle bouncing on his belly.

"Yes?"

"Look, I don't know how they handled things down in

Las Vegas, but frankly, I'd appreciate a little more support."

"I'm not sure I follow you."

"A united front."

Regan frowned, wishing he'd given her enough information to enable her to respond. His expression shifted toward impatience.

"I really think you could have backed me when I pointed out the other two boys that had probably been with Kylie."

"But I wasn't sure it was them."

"Well, I was."

In spite of not having seen them.

Regan forced a smile and refrained from pointing that out to him, in the interest of maintaining a peaceful work environment. She liked her new school. A lot. It had a small staff, nice-sized classes and one of her best friends from college worked there. Actually, when all her carefully made plans had blown up in her face, thanks to Daniel, her former colleague and jerk of an ex-boyfriend, it had been Tanya who'd encouraged her to move four hundred miles north.

"I'll try to be more observant next time."

Pete gave a curt nod. "It would help."

REGAN'S NEW PRINCIPAL lasted less than a week.

Bernardi experienced chest pains on Thursday. On Friday it was announced he was taking an indefinite leave of absence. Pete Domingo, the only person on staff with administrative certification, would become acting principal in the interim.

"Pete Domingo?" Tanya moaned on the day of the big announcement. She flicked her smooth blond hair back over her shoulder. "Do you know what we're in for?"

"A united front, I gather." Regan perched on the edge

of a student desk, waiting for her friend to finish her lesson plan.

"I'd rather have a monkey as an administrator. No, make that a baboon. Pete's ego is entirely too big and he's not concerned with learning. He's a do-or-die coach. He just wants to *dom-i-nate*."

"So do you, only in the academic sense."

"Yeah, yeah, yeah. Come on, let's go." Tanya closed her book. "I can finish up tomorrow. Oh, by the way, my landlord knows a guy who's selling a horse. Some kind of fancy quarter horse. He told me about it, but I can't remember much. I think it's female, has four legs and a tail."

"Funny, but that's exactly what I'm looking for."

Tanya reached for the phone book on the edge of her desk. "I'll find the number."

TANYA WAS BUSY on Saturday, so Regan drove to the landlord's friend's place alone. She was greeted by a man in cowboy gear who introduced himself as Charley. He led her to a panel corral, where a stocky bay mare stood.

"Her name is Bonita Bar Santos, but I call her Broomtail."

"Broomtail?"

"She rubs her tail on the fence in hot weather and makes a mess of it," Charley explained as he entered the corral with a halter. The mare lifted bored eyes and stood, docile, while he slipped the halter over her head and buckled it. Regan opened the gate and Charley led Broomtail out.

"Did you bring your saddle?"

"No." Her saddle was English and it was still at her mother's house. She'd have to send for it.

He dropped the lead rope and went inside the tack shed without tying up the mare. She cocked a hind leg and waited, ears at half-mast. After much clunking and banging, the guy came out carrying a dusty saddle in his left hand. "Only small one I have." With his right hand, he put a blanket on the mare and smoothed it, then settled the saddle into place. He cinched it up. "Just let me get the bridle and you can take her for a spin."

Regan rode for almost an hour, happy to be back in a saddle after too many years out of it. The horse moved slowly—pleasure rather than performance material. But she knew her stuff. She sluggishly picked up her leads, turned on the forehand and side passed. As Regan worked her, the mare gradually became more responsive, quicker in her movements. She tossed her head impatiently a few times on the way home and started to jig, but after her slow beginning, Regan took it as a good sign. Maybe the mare had life in her after all. Maybe all she needed was to lose weight and get some exercise.

"I hope I haven't kept you from something," Regan said after dismounting and handing the man the reins. He'd been looking at his watch when she returned and she felt bad for taking so long.

"Not at all." He smiled hopefully. "Well?"

"I'll think about it and let you know."

His face fell. "Just a word of warning. There will be some people coming to see her tomorrow morning."

"I'll let you know," Regan said firmly. "Thanks for showing her to me."

IT WAS NOT a call Will wanted to make, but Zero Benson from the feed store had seemed pretty certain of his information. Zero wasn't exactly the sharpest person in the world, but Will figured he'd better check things out anyway. He dialed Charley Parker's number. The conversation lasted almost a minute before Charley hung up on him.

"Is Charley trying to sell Broomtail?" Kylie asked without looking up from her math book. Her collie pup, Stubby, lay at her feet, his chin resting on her shoe.

"When is he not trying to sell Broomtail?" Will went to the old-fashioned enamel sink and rinsed the coffeepot, then wiped down the counter.

"Charley'd probably be happy if someone stole her, then he wouldn't have to feed her anymore." Kylie erased part of an answer, then rewrote a few numbers.

"That would only work if he had her insured, and I'm pretty sure he doesn't."

"So, did the Martinezes have insurance?"

"Hardly anyone insures their horses around here, kiddo, except for maybe the Taylors. Too expensive."

"So when their horses got stolen…" Kylie made a gesture with her pencil.

"They're out of luck, unless we find them." And it wasn't looking good. Most stolen horses ended up in an out-of-state auction within days of being taken. The Martinez horses had been gone for three days.

"Should have freeze-branded them," Kylie murmured before turning back to her homework.

"Ever hear that saying about the barn door and the horse?"

"Only when you say it," she replied in a way that made him feel very old and out of touch.

Will settled in the kitchen chair across from his daughter and pulled his account books closer. He'd developed the habit of doing his paperwork while Kylie worked on her homework, finding that it kept them both on track. He now had a set of books he was proud of and Kylie was proving to be a much better student than he'd been.

Now if she could just stay out of trouble for a day or two.

THE MARE WAS no longer on the market. Charley called early Saturday morning to give Regan the news.

"Did you sell her?" she asked, thinking that if he had, he'd sold her within the past twelve hours.

"Not exactly. I just…changed my mind."

Regan hung up the phone with a frown. Weird. The guy'd seemed anxious to sell the horse less than a day ago. She decided to chalk it up to small-town eccentricity.

She gathered her purse and car keys, ready to start phase two of her horse hunt.

Madison White operated the indoor riding arena at the edge of town and, according to people at school, if she didn't have a horse, she at least had the connections to find one. Regan had already decided to see what the woman had to offer before making a decision on Broomtail, which was fortuitous, since the mare was now mysteriously off the market.

As it turned out, Madison had a horse for sale that was stabled at the arena. A nice, big horse with a nice, big price tag. A Thoroughbred that had been purchased as a jumper and had proven to be too hot for the girl who'd bought him.

Regan borrowed a saddle and mounted what felt like a bundle of dynamite. But once she got him moving, she found that he was smooth and smart. He just needed work, and Regan was looking for a project to fill her free time.

She did a quick calculation, decided to eat less for a few months and told Madison she wanted the gelding. She managed to dicker the price down by a couple of hundred dollars, but the purchase was still going to eat a hole in her budget. Regan didn't care. She had a horse.

She made arrangements to continue boarding him at the arena until she got her pasture properly fenced, and then drove home, feeling richer rather than poorer.

Now all she had to do was hire a fencer, buy a water

tank, arrange a vet check, send for her saddle and watch her pennies for a few months. Okay, maybe a year. But it didn't matter, she had a horse.

CLAIRE TRIED TO be excited for Regan when she called to share her news. But since Claire had never owned an animal in her life, Regan knew her sister was having a hard time relating. Claire soon turned the topic to her primary concern.

"I can't believe you left me alone in this city with Mom."

"How're your classes going?"

"I'm not wild about them. I mean, they're easy enough, but...I don't know. Something's missing."

Only Claire would say that engineering classes were "easy enough." She was accidentally brilliant, according to their mother. She could do upper-level math with ease, but she found the things she was good at boring. She liked to dive into subjects she knew nothing about, learn what she could and then move on. An attention-deficit engineer. Probably not what the world needed.

"What's missing?"

"I don't know. Passion?" Claire must have sensed Regan's smile. "Hey, you feel passionately about your job. Why shouldn't I feel the same about mine? And you put your foot down when Mom wanted you to go to law school."

"Yes, and you can do the same."

There was a slow intake of breath on the other end of the line, followed by a long exhalation. "I'm not quite ready for that."

KYLIE STAYED LATE on the day she returned to school, making up the science lab she'd missed the day before. Regan attempted to initiate a conversation once the girl was finished—*attempted* being the key word. In the wake of the smoking incident, Kylie wasn't exactly warming up to Regan.

"Do you ride?" Regan asked after a string of frustrating monosyllabic replies to other questions. The conversation was becoming a battle of wills, but Regan wasn't ready to give up.

"Yes."

"Does your dad ride?"

"It's his job."

"Riding?"

"He starts colts for people."

"I see." Regan was beginning to feel as if she were starring in an episode of *Dragnet*.

"That's what I'm going to do, too."

Ah, progress. Two answers with more than two words. Regan decided to press on. "Has your dad always been a horse trainer?"

"Pretty much."

"What did he do before he started training horses?"

"I think he's always trained horses. He used to ride rodeo, before he got hurt. I do junior rodeo in the summer." Kylie pushed back the dark strands of hair that had escaped from her ponytail.

"You're a lot like your dad, then."

"Yeah." Kylie gave a wry twist of a smile. "Even in ways he doesn't get."

Regan cocked her head. "Like how?"

"Like he keeps telling me I can't be rescuing things, but he does it all the time."

"He rescues things?"

"Horses. People."

"People? How does he rescue people?"

Kylie shrugged nonchalantly. "He saved you from buying Broomtail, didn't he?"

Regan just managed to keep her jaw from dropping. That was the end of twenty questions and Kylie knew it. Regan gave the girl a tight you-win smile and went to tidy up the lab equipment. She would be discussing the Broomtail matter further, but it would be with the father and not the daughter.

About a minute later Will's big diesel truck pulled into the school parking lot. Good timing. Regan would just as soon get this over with while she was still annoyed.

"I'd like to talk to your father alone."

"I'll wait here." It sounded like a procedure Kylie was familiar with.

"We're not going to talk about you," Regan assured her with a half smile.

Kylie couldn't quite erase the "yeah, sure" look from her face.

Regan stepped out into the hall, pulling the door shut behind her, and met Will at the glass entryway a few feet from her room.

"Are you trying to keep me from buying a horse?" she asked without bothering to say hello.

Will tilted his black hat back, allowing her to see his eyes without the shadow of the brim. And they were nice eyes—not Kylie's deep brown, but blue-gray.

"That would be rather presumptuous of me."

Regan let out a snort. "Yes. I agree."

"Been talking to Kylie?"

"Yes."

Will's gaze shifted to the door of the room behind her. He paused before he brought his attention back to Regan.

"I am not trying to keep you from buying a horse. I am trying to keep you from making a mistake."

Incredible. "And who are you to decide whether or not I'm making a mistake?"

"I know the horses in this community. But more than that, I know the people selling them." His expression was impassive. "I know a mistake when I see one."

Regan narrowed her eyes. "And just why do you know so much?"

"Because I'm a deputy brand inspector. If it has four legs and eats hay, I'm probably involved in the sale." His eyes went back to the door. "Do you think I could have my daughter?"

Regan didn't budge. "Why was Broomtail a mistake?"

"She's a very unpleasant mare most of the time."

"Most of the time? But she seemed…" Regan's voice trailed off as several aspects of her experience with Broomtail began to make more sense—the mare's lethargic attitude, followed by a display of impatience. Charley glancing anxiously at his watch….

Will saw that she'd caught his meaning.

"He gives her enough tranquilizer to make her less cranky and more salable. We had a chat the other night. I don't think he'll be doing it again in the near future." He gestured to the classroom. "My daughter?"

Regan moved to her door and pulled it open, her mind still working over the Broomtail issue. Kylie stumbled out a bit too fast, but the brand inspector didn't seem surprised by his daughter's sudden appearance.

"Let's go," he said. He met Regan's eyes for a brief moment as he pushed the glass door open. Kylie slipped out under his hand and Will followed, letting the door swing shut behind him.

Regan gave her head a slow shake. It sounded as if Kylie was right. Her dad had rescued her.

"WERE YOU EAVESDROPPING on us?" Will asked as he put the truck in gear.

"I couldn't hear through the door.

"I'll take that to be a yes."

"Dad," Kylie said seriously. "I like to know what's going on, if it concerns me."

"It didn't concern you."

"Yeah. I figured."

"How?"

"You guys didn't even look at me when I went by."

Will told her to knock off the eavesdropping, but he was impressed. His kid was observant, which was why she was good with horses. She could read cues. It was a valuable skill, one she seemed to be more talented at applying to people than he was. A bit of her mother coming through there.

"Something wrong, Dad?"

Will shook his head, keeping his eyes on the road.

"What are we eating tonight?"

He gave the standard answer. "Beef…"

"It's what's for dinner." They spoke in unison, mimicking an old ad slogan from the Beef Council.

One of these days she'd probably grow tired of the games and routines they'd started when she was younger, but he still had a few years left. He hoped. Kids seem to grow up so fast.

"Anything else?"

"No," he said facetiously. "Just beef."

"Good. I was tired of vegetables, anyway."

"How was school?"

"You didn't hear from anyone, did you?" It would have been funny, if she hadn't been serious.

"No."

"Then it was fine."

"Kylie."

She grinned. "Gotcha."

He rolled his eyes, wondering if he was ready for the approaching teenage years. Somehow he didn't think so. He was still debating how to handle certain matters that would have to be cropping up soon. He wasn't squeamish about girls' growth issues, just uninformed. Okay, maybe he was a little squeamish. He was hoping he could get Beth Grant, Kylie's best friend's mom, to help with that part of Kylie's upbringing. It wasn't exactly fair, but neither was growing up without a mother. Father and daughter both had to do the best they could.

He pulled to a stop in front of the house and reached over the back of the seat for the bag of groceries.

"I see carrots."

"There's worse stuff below that. Spinach, beets, spuds and corn."

"I liked the just-beef plan better."

"I'm sure you did, but veggies are a fact of life."

A STORM WAS moving in. A full moon was in the offing. In Regan's experience, those were usually the best explanations for the off-the-wall behavior of her classes on such a day.

Jared, the new guy, Pete's long-term PE sub, stood in the hall with her. "I'm whipped," he said. "I usually teach elementary. Now I know why."

"This age grows on you."

"When?"

Regan smiled at his comeback and he returned the smile crookedly. The bell rang and Jared exhaled and headed for his class.

Regan managed to keep a lid on things until sixth period, near the end of the day. Kylie's class. Regan was teaching observation skills and since kids love nothing better than something gross and slimy, she'd invested in several calamari. The lesson was good—she'd simply picked the wrong day to teach it.

The trouble started as soon as the students were released to start their lab.

"Hey, Sadie," one of the boys called, holding up his squid. "Doesn't this look a lot like a *spider?*"

The girl immediately turned pale and stared straight down at the table. The boy wiggled the squid and a few students laughed, until they saw the look of death in Regan's eyes. It had been a long day and she was not going to put up with this. She walked over to the offending student, took his books, led him to a desk and told him to read chapter two of his textbook, outline it and then answer all questions at the end.

She moved back to Sadie, who was still staring down at the floor with Kylie beside her, and discovered that the girl did indeed have a major fear of spiders. Regan assured her that the squid was not a spider and that she could observe it from a comfortable distance. *"No one will bother you."*

A quick look around the class told her that everyone had gotten her message—or so she'd thought—until the students filed out after the quietest lab of the day and she realized that one of her specimens was missing.

She didn't need it—her final class was social studies—but she couldn't have an unauthorized squid floating around the school. She hated to think of what might happen if it fell into the wrong hands. She had to find that cephalopod.

Then a shriek in the hall gave her a good of idea of where to look. She hurried to the door and pushed her way through a throng of kids to see three people in the center of the hall—Pete Domingo, Sadie and Kylie. The missing squid lay on the floor near Pete's feet.

"Pick it up." He was talking to Sadie.

Sadie's face was ashen. She shook her head, looking as if she was about to be sick. Domingo's face grew red.

"I. Said. Pick. It. Up."

The girl was close to tears. She didn't move.

"Joseph threw it at Sadie. So Joseph should pick it up." Kylie said hotly. Sadie was Kylie's best friend and Kylie was bent on protecting her.

"I distinctly saw it in Miss Grant's hand just before it hit me in the face."

"I was just getting it off me." The girl's voice was shaky. Her entire body was trembling, but Pete didn't seem aware of that. He'd just been hit in the face with a squid. The world was about to end.

"I'll pick it up," Kylie snapped. She started to reach for it, but Pete stopped her.

That was when Regan stepped into the center of the circle, calmly stooped down and grabbed the slimy creature. "I was wondering where this had gotten to," she said evenly, looking Pete in the eye. "I'm glad you found it." She turned and the crowd parted as she walked back to her room.

There was a silence and then— "Anyone who is not in class when that bell rings will have three days' detention."

The crowd broke up, leaving Kylie and Sadie standing silently in the center of the hall, uncertain whether they were supposed to go or stay. The bell rang and Regan paused at her door to see what was going to happen.

Domingo shook his head. "Three days, ladies."

His voice was clearly audible in Regan's classroom. She let out a breath and, knowing the kids were watching her reaction, carefully kept her face expressionless as she walked to the front of the class and started taking attendance. Inwardly she was seething.

Tanya was right. A baboon would be better.

CHAPTER TWO

"Dad, do you think you'll ever get married again?"

Will managed to flip the hotcake he was cooking without muffing it. "Not anytime soon."

"Good."

"Why?"

"Mark's dad and stepmom are breaking up. He says it sucks."

It did suck. No argument there. "Marriage is serious business, Kylie. Not something to be entered into lightly."

"How about you and my mother?"

My mother. The shadow figure. Kylie rarely spoke of her, although she did keep a photo of her in her hope chest. The last Will had heard, Des had hooked up with a rodeo stock contractor and was living in Florida. He hoped she'd finally matured enough to try to stick it out in a relationship.

"We were young."

Kylie speared a hotcake off the plate her father had set in the middle of the table. "That matters?"

"A lot of times it does. You can't have a grown-up relationship if you're not grown up."

"Marriage must be a lot of work."

"A good one is," Will said as he poured more batter into the pan.

"Then how do parents have time for kids?"

Will didn't know, since he'd never had a wife and a

child at the same time. He winged it. "They work together to raise the kids."

"How do they have time for each other?" Kylie slathered butter on the hotcake and started to eat, not bothering with syrup.

"They make time."

"Mark's parents didn't."

"How so?"

Kylie gestured with her fork. "He said his stepmom was always complaining that his dad paid more attention to Mark than to her."

"So Mark's feeling guilty?"

"He doesn't like his stepmom, but he feels bad about his dad being so unhappy."

"Well, I don't think you have to worry. There aren't any women knocking down my door."

The phone rang. Kylie answered it and then wrinkled her nose as she held out the receiver. "It's Madison… I think *she'd* like to knock down your door."

Will took the phone with a mock scowl.

"Will? Madison here." Madison always spoke as if she were slightly out of breath. "Did you get the contract for the clinic?"

"It came this morning."

"Thanks for stepping in."

It had been the third time in a year and a half he'd "stepped in." He was beginning to suspect she wasn't getting cancellations, "Are you sure you're really booking a second trainer for these clinics?"

Madison laughed. "Honest, I am. Del cancelled the first time and Mike the second. I'm just lucky you're close."

"And agreeable."

"That, too." She still had a smile in her voice. "Think

of all the good you're doing for those horses whose owners don't have a clue."

"Hey, you already have me. You don't need to sell me."

"Actually, I'd like to get you to present on a regular basis. Two, three times a year—it wouldn't be that bad."

"I'll get this contract signed and back to you tomorrow."

Madison was enough of a trainer herself to know when to stop pushing. "Just think about it, Will."

"Goodbye, Madison."

Will turned down the burner under the pan and poured the last of the batter. He hated crowds and he hated talking, but Madison had a point about the horses. Most people who came to a training clinic were genuinely concerned about their animals, although there were always a few who thought bigger bits and spurs would solve most of their problems. Which was why Will often had more work than he could handle rehabilitating damaged horses.

REGAN HAD SUSPECTED her sister's four days of phone silence were a sign of impending disaster and she'd been correct. Claire called early Saturday morning with a classic case of stress overload. She'd had an argument with one of her professors, followed by a fight with her boyfriend, then her roommate had spilled wine on her new cashmere sweater. *But,* Claire assured Regan, the biggest problem was their mother, who was having a hard time butting out of Claire's life. Arlene had already lost one daughter to public service, and now the other one was damn well going to live up to her potential.

Regan listened patiently for almost fifteen minutes, letting Claire talk herself out. Finally, her sister wound down and asked Regan how she was doing.

Regan responded with a simple, "Fine." It seemed easiest. "Do you want me to call Mom and see what I can do?"

"Would you?"

Regan always did, but she had been hoping when she put some miles between herself and her family that Claire and Arlene would somehow learn to deal with each other without getting a mediator involved.

Regan called her mother a few minutes later, negotiated a truce and then parried a few thrusts aimed in her direction.

Yes, she did like the smaller community she'd moved to. No, there wasn't much opportunity for advancement in this school district. No, she wasn't going to keep in touch with the Education Development Authority (EDA), a private curriculum-development company that she'd hoped to work for only months before. There was no way she would work for them now that Daniel had taken a job there. Besides, she had a job she liked.

Unfortunately, Arlene was not convinced. By the time Regan hung up, she was exhausted. And she was thinking about Daniel again. She made herself stop. It was bad for her blood pressure.

THE MUSTANG MARE circled the round pen at a floating trot, her nose high in the air, her attention outside the rails, on anything but Will, who stood near the center. Her objective was fundamental. Escape.

Will kept her moving, using his body language to propel her forward, to control her direction. Finally, she shifted an eye toward him as she trotted by, flicked an ear back. Will's gaze immediately dropped from her head to her hindquarters and he took a backward step. She slowed, uncertain, then decided she would rather ignore him and escape. Will upped his energy, moving the mare forward again.

A few circles later, another glance, another ear flick.

Will stepped back. The mare slowed, both eyes on him now. He took another step back, rewarding her attention by reducing the pressure on her. She slowed still more, eventually coming to a stop, her eyes on Will. They stood and studied one another. Will took a single slow step forward and the mare made her decision—no one was going to control her. Will set her moving again.

Will had made some major headway with the mare by the end of the session. Sometimes with mustangs, especially older ones, it took almost twice as long to teach a concept, but once they got it, the knowledge was deeply engrained. He had yet to saddle her, but he *had* been able to rub her all over, desensitize her body, pick up her feet. He'd start again tomorrow and see what she remembered.

It had been a good day, made better by a phone call from the head brand inspector late that evening. Trev's laid-back voice actually held a note of excitement. "We located Martinez's horses."

"You're kidding. Where?" Kylie, who was settled at the kitchen table with her homework, glanced up, a hopeful expression in her dark eyes.

"Idaho. A total fluke, but, hey, we have them."

"How about the thieves?" Will gave Kylie a thumbs-up and she grinned.

"We don't have them."

"Does Martinez know?"

"He's already on his way north. I thought you'd want to know that we're no longer batting zero." No, but they were close to it. Six incidents of horse stealing in the past six months and this was the first recovery. Trev filled in the details and then said, "Heard about Kylie today. Pretty funny."

"Yeah." Funny if it wasn't your kid who'd popped the school bully in the eye. Fortunately, she'd lived to tell the tale. Kylie'd always been a pretty good sprinter. "Hey, I need a favor. I'm looking for a pleasure mount. Would you let me know if you hear of anything?" Will scuffed his boot along the floor as he spoke. Kylie'd forgotten to sweep again.

"For Kylie?"

"No. I have a friend who's looking." Or, more accurately, he wanted to make peace with his daughter's teacher and this seemed like a good way to do it.

"I'll let you know. I think McKirk might have some horses for sale. He was talking about reducing his herd, now that his kids are in college. What price range?"

"Not a clue. Just let me know if you find anything." Will hung up a few seconds later and turned to face an incredulous daughter.

"Is it *Miss Flynn?* Is she the *friend* who's looking for a horse?"

"It's an expression."

"Good. I don't want you to be friends with my teachers." Kylie gave a shudder.

"I'll try and be careful about that."

ALL OF THE squid were missing.

Instead of creating a hot-weather biohazard in the school Dumpster, Regan had stored them in the staff freezer on Tuesday, planning to throw them out on trash day. And now they were gone.

Regan shut the freezer and tried to ignore the sinking sensation in her midsection. Perhaps the custodian had seen the gross creatures and disposed of them. Or Pete had found them and tossed them before another one hit him in the face. There could be no other explanation.

Regan caught sight of Tanya's distinctive blond hair through a crowd of students moving down the hall to their class. With some careful maneuvering, she managed to catch up with her friend.

"Do you think eight missing squid are a problem?"

Tanya stopped dead, forcing the current of students to flow around them. "Here at school?" Her blue eyes widened. "No, Regan. No problem at all."

But the morning passed without any strange incidents and Regan was able to convince herself that the custodian had indeed cleaned out the freezer. Kylie had initially aroused her suspicions by being uncharacteristically subdued, but as the class wore on, Regan decided that the girl was merely distracted.

"Are you all right?" Regan asked after the bell.

"I'm fine." Kylie's expression was not friendly. "Did you know that my dad is trying to find you a horse?"

"He is?" If Kylie had thrown out the statement to sidetrack Regan from thinking about squid, the strategy had worked beautifully.

"Yeah. But I don't think you should read anything into it."

Regan cocked her head at the kid. "What could I possibly read into it?"

"Maybe that he was doing it because he likes you. That isn't why he's doing it."

Regan managed not to laugh and say, *I'll try not to get my hopes up.*

"I expect he's doing it because he knows the horses around here," she suggested instead.

"Yeah. And he doesn't like it when people get horses they can't handle. That's how horses get hurt and ruined, you know."

Regan gritted her teeth. *Thank you for the vote of confidence, Mr. Bishop.*

She drew in a sharp breath. "You can tell your father

that I'm buying a horse from Madison White and that I'll do my very best not to ruin him."

Kylie nodded gravely, missing Regan's irony. She picked up her books and left the room.

Regan gathered her materials for the next class. She wasn't going to think about Will right now. No sense taking her frustrations out on an innocent social studies class.

At the end of that class Regan discovered her overhead projector was no longer working. A quick investigation revealed that the bulb was missing.

A strange day was getting stranger. Someone had stolen it, and quite recently, too, since she'd used the machine just before lunch.

Who would want to steal an overhead projection bulb?

Regan rushed to the office between classes to get the key to the supply room. The student aid looked at her with surprise. "Mr. Domingo doesn't give out the key. He opens the supply room himself."

Regan let out an exasperated breath and set off to find Mr. Domingo, the supply Nazi. He was in the gym, counting uniforms.

"There's only one more period," he said when she explained that she needed a projector bulb. "Can't you make it?"

"No. I need my overhead to teach the lesson." She stared at the uniforms. "Are you putting those in numerical order?"

"It's easier to keep track of them that way," he muttered. "Come on." Pete marched out of the gym and down the long, dark hall that led to the supply closet. He turned the final corner ahead of her and then let out a sharp cry and swatted wildly at something that appeared to be attacking his head.

Regan gasped as Pete reeled backward, cursing and

thrashing, until he finally tripped over his own feet and ended up flat on his butt in front of her.

Several of the…things…seemed to fly off him as he landed, and then a familiar smell hit Regan's nostrils. Squid. Quite possibly freshly thawed.

Domingo glared up at her. A limp tentacle was stuck to his shoulder. Another was attached to his back. Several other squid parts were suspended from the door frame above him.

He flicked the tentacle off his shoulder, radiating fury. Regan tried to think of serious things—SATs, mortgage payments, the nightly news. It wasn't working.

"Who had access to these squid?" he demanded, wiping a smear of slime from his face.

"I don't know. I was keeping them in the staff freezer and planned to throw them out on trash day, but…they were missing this morning."

"Why didn't you report this?" His face was dangerously red.

"You want me to report missing squid?"

"This wouldn't have happened if you had. *You* are responsible for this."

The bell rang. Regan pulled in a deep breath. "No, Pete. I'd say you're responsible. Maybe if you weren't so over-the-top with your discipline policy, you wouldn't be covered with squid parts right now."

"You can't talk to me like that."

Regan flicked a piece of slippery cephalopod off the wall. "I need to get to class. Are you all right?"

She was rewarded with a furious look, which she took as a yes.

"There will be no more seafood in this school!" Domingo shouted as she rounded the corner without her lightbulb. She decided then and there she'd bring shrimp salad for lunch every day for the rest of the month.

The next day, the Wesley staff and students discovered that hell had no fury like a principal who'd been punked.

Pete Domingo had no evidence, no suspects. All he had was a head full of possibilities, a school packed with smirking students and staff who'd heard about what had happened and had thought it funny, too.

Student after student was called down to the office to be grilled. All had returned to class looking shaken, but also vaguely satisfied. Kylie and Sadie were subjected to a longer inquisition than the other kids called from Regan's class, but they came back unscathed. No one confessed and, at the end of the day, Pete was no closer to solving his crime than he'd been when he was sitting on the floor in front of the supply-closet door, flicking tentacles off his clothing.

The staff avoided being seen gossiping in groups. No one wanted to be accused of conspiracy and no one wanted to relight Pete's very short fuse.

"You've been a good sport about this," the librarian whispered, late in the afternoon, as she scanned Regan's reference book. "I hope you didn't get into too much trouble."

"I'm fine," Regan whispered back. "But I wish I knew who did it. I'd kind of like to shake their hands."

The woman winked and then nodded toward a table of three geeky eighth-graders who had been thoroughly reamed out by Domingo a few days before for some petty infraction.

"You're kidding," Regan mouthed.

The librarian gave her an arch look and disappeared into the stacks.

A few long hours later Regan was in her kitchen making tea, peppermint tea, to help combat the stress head-ache she'd acquired.

A windstorm had started brewing late that afternoon and was now in full force, bending the trees and rattling the windows, and at first Regan thought the noise at the front door was a blast of wind. When she heard it again, during a lull, she realized someone was knocking.

She glanced down at her after-work wear—a tank top, sweat bottoms and fuzzy socks. Short of ignoring the door, there wasn't much she could do about her appearance and she couldn't exactly leave someone standing outside in a windstorm.

Or could she?

Will Bishop was out there, his shoulders hunched as the wind whipped at his clothing.

A gust caught the storm door as she pushed it open, and Will caught it just before it hit him. "Do you want to come in?" She raised her voice to be heard.

"For a minute."

Okay. She could deal with a minute. He'd barely gotten inside when another blast hit.

"Does the wind do this a lot?"

"We get some good storms here."

She wondered if she should ask him to sit down, offer him something to drink. Then she glanced at him and de-cided no. He had some reason for coming and it wasn't social, so she'd skip the niceties.

"I'm sorry to barge in like this," Will said, getting right to the point, "but I'd like to know… Do you think Kylie is involved in this squid thing?"

Those damned squid again. She'd had it up to here with squid—especially when they brought parents to her house.

"Have you asked her?" she asked with a touch of im-patience.

"She says she's innocent." The *for once* went unspoken.

The house shook with the force of the wind. Twigs and pebbles bounced off the windows, but Regan's attention was focused on Will and the deep concern she saw on his face. This man was worried about his daughter and she owed him an honest answer.

"I don't know if she was involved, but my gut feeling is no. I've heard that it was actually some eighth-grade boys, but I'm not sure."

Will put a hand on the back of Regan's recliner. "Domingo harassed Kylie twice today. The second time he came on pretty strong, trying to force her to confess." His expression became stony. "If he starts again tomorrow… Well, I wanted an independent opinion before I went in to have a, um, chat with Pete."

"Everyone's a suspect, including the staff."

Will let out a breath and dropped his hand, ready to leave now that he had his answer. "Thanks. This helps."

"Would you like some tea or something before you go?"

He'd started for the door, but now he turned back, looking surprised. Regan was a little surprised herself. Her mother had hammered manners into her, but she hadn't realized to what degree. "Since you're here," she said lamely.

"I need to be getting home. Kylie's supposed to be starting dinner and I need to make certain the vegetables don't get burned mysteriously. But thanks. Especially after, well, everything."

She followed him to the door. He stopped before going out. "I would have called, but you don't seem to have a number."

"Unlisted. I like to avoid irate parents at report card time."

"Irate parents tend to show up on the doorstep around here."

She smiled. "I noticed."

Their gazes held for a second and then he smiled. And, oh, what a smile.

Regan blinked and then Will ducked his head and stepped out into the bad weather. Regan grabbed the storm door, fighting the wind to latch it shut. It shook, making an odd noise, but it held.

She settled into her chair with her lukewarm tea and unsettled thoughts, listening to the house try to blow down around her, hoping she would remember her vow to stay away from damaged men.

APOLOGIZING HAD BEEN the right thing to do.

Realizing that his daughter's teacher was attractive was a guy thing to do. But it had been a long time since Will had felt such a gut-level draw toward a woman and it perplexed him. Well, it didn't matter, because he wasn't going to do anything about it. Wrong time. Wrong circumstances. Probably the wrong woman.

Will propped a foot on the lower rail of the pole corral and watched his horses graze as his daughter rode bareback at the far end of the pasture. The windstorm had blown out as rapidly as it had blown in, leaving the air oddly still. Will had zillions of branches to collect around the place, but he'd start tomorrow while Kylie was at school. It was a good way to stay close to the house and the phone, in case that jerk Domingo called.

Kylie started cantering a pattern, practicing her flying lead changes and probably winning big trophies in her head. It was almost dark and a school night, but Will was glad his daughter was enjoying the things a kid should be enjoying, things he'd never gotten enough of at her age. He'd been too busy dealing with his old man. The phone rang and he jogged to the house, scooping up the receiver on the eighth ring.

"Hey." It was Trev. And he sounded stressed.

Will made a guess as to what was coming next. "More livestock stolen?"

"No." There was a silence, and then he said, "I saw your brother in Elko today."

Will stilled. "Brett was in Elko?"

"Yeah. He's working for the Friday Creek Ranch. I thought you'd want to know."

"Thanks." Will pressed his lips together. He couldn't think of anything else to say. He was having a hard time thinking at all.

"I didn't talk to him, but I thought you'd want to know," he repeated.

"Yeah, Trev. Thanks again."

CHAPTER THREE

THE NEXT MORNING Will drove Kylie to school in a haze. She'd missed the bus, but he'd skipped the usual lecture on responsibility and simply told her to hurry so he could get back home and start working the horses. He was fully booked and it took a good part of the day to put in his contracted time on each animal; after which he still had to clear the windfall branches and conduct a brand inspection for a horse sale.

"You okay, Dad?" Kylie asked when they reached the school. "I mean, you didn't yell at me about the bus."

"I'm fine. Just tired. I didn't sleep very well."

"Too much coffee, probably."

"Probably. Behave, kid. *And don't miss the bus!*"

She grinned and got out of the truck, oblivious to the fact that her jeans were getting too short and totally unaware that her father's heart was squeezing tight as he watched her join a group of friends.

He pulled out of the lot and drove at the posted snail's pace to the end of the school zone. He passed Kylie's bus going in the opposite direction. The driver waved and Will forced himself to wave back, although he didn't think it would have killed the driver to wait a few seconds while Kylie found her history book.

Right behind the bus was Regan's small car.

So Kylie wasn't the only one having time issues that morning.

He accelerated as soon as he was out of the safety zone, then made a conscious effort to slow down. With only a couple hours of troubled sleep, he wasn't as alert as he should be.

Couple of hours? Probably more like thirty minutes. He'd finally dozed off just before the alarm rang. And then he'd been instantly awake and the worries had come crashing down on him.

Why the hell was Brett back?

It had been more than ten years since he'd last seen Brett and it had not been a happy parting. In fact, someone had had to call the sheriff and Will had barely escaped a night in jail. Brett had not.

They hadn't spoken since that night. Brett had left town the next morning and that had been the last Will had seen or heard of his brother.

Now he was back. Why?

The thing that really set Will on edge was that he wasn't quite sure about the legalities of his situation. He might be better off if he did know, but looking into those things meant opening a can of worms he was inclined to leave firmly closed. He wouldn't do it—not unless he absolutely had to. Brett was a good eighty miles away at the moment and he'd better *stay* eighty miles away. If he didn't, he'd be a sorry man.

REGAN PARKED IN the only available staff space, some distance from the back door. She grabbed her work bag off the passenger seat and made a dash for the teachers' entrance just as the bell rang. Flinging the door open, she ran smack into Pete.

"Ah, Miss Flynn," he said, looking a bit like a satisfied bullfrog.

"Sorry I'm late." She tried to speak calmly, even though

she was winded from her sprint. "I had a problem this morning." As in, an enormous elm branch on top of her new fence had stretched the wire and popped the staples; another large branch lay across her driveway, too big for her to do anything about. It had taken her almost fifteen minutes to work the first leafy monster free of the drooping fence wire. Even then she could have made it to work on time by driving around the branch that was blocking her drive, if her mother hadn't called just as she was walking out the door. Claire she could put off, but not her mother.

"You do know it's district policy to phone when you're going to be late?"

Regan nodded and refrained from telling him she had called, but Mrs. Serrano had been away from her desk. No sense having Pete jump all over the secretary, too.

He gave Regan a stern look, then abruptly turned and stalked off on his standard morning hunt for marauding pranksters. Regan secretly wished the pranksters success as she unlocked her classroom.

It might have been the aftermath of the squid inquisition, or it might have been that the students were hoping for the appearance of new slimy specimens to use for various nefarious purposes, but, whatever the reason, they paid close attention to Regan's lesson on classification. And she'd wisely opted to use an utterly benign material for this lab: leaves.

At first the kids seemed disappointed, but as the lab progressed the general mood became lighter—to the point where Regan began to wonder if Pete was going to find his car full of foliage when he left work that day. Once the thought had occurred to her, she issued a stern warning about the misuse of lab materials. The kids looked as if they were listening and a few even nodded after she spoke, but she'd taught for long enough to know that kids could look as if they were listening attentively and still not hear a word she said. All she could do at this point was hope for the best.

"Regan, what are you doing?" Tanya asked as she walked into the teachers' lounge several hours later.

"Watching Pete's car."

"Do I want to know why?"

Regan turned back to the copy machine, which was happily churning out ninth-grade history work sheets.

"I'm trying to avoid trouble not of my own making."

"I knew I didn't want to know." Tanya, a one-woman cleaning machine, went to the sink and started rinsing and drying coffee cups. "So why were you late this morning?"

"The wind blew a branch down on my fence and I had to get it off."

"It couldn't wait?"

"I needed to call the fence man, if it was damaged. He's kind of a slow worker and I want to get Toffee home this weekend."

"Was there that much damage?"

"Yes. I can't tighten the stretched wire myself, so I called him. He's going to try to get out there before the weekend." She tightened one corner of her mouth. "Emphasis on *try*."

Tanya gave her a sympathetic look just as Karlene, the girls' PE teacher, came in and flopped down in a chair, blowing a few of her short brown curls off her forehead. "Ever have the feeling that you wanted to kill your boss?"

"Shh." Tanya said. Pauline Johnson walked into the room just then, her high heels clicking on the tiles with metronomelike precision, the hem of her skirt hitting exactly midknee and her pale hair carefully lacquered into a French twist. She gave her colleagues a professional smile and went to check her mail. After sorting it, she marched over to the copy machine.

"Do you have many more?" she asked, indicating the masters Regan held in her hand.

"Two more sets."

"We really need to have a schedule for this machine."

"We pretty much have one," Tanya pointed out. "We're supposed to use it during our prep periods."

"I'm talking about before and after school." She gave a sniff as Regan positioned another master copy in the machine. "I'll talk to Pete about this. I think it's important."

Regan stubbornly went on with her copying, in spite of Pauline's impatient gaze boring into her back. Every school seemed to have a Pauline on its staff and Regan had plenty of practice dealing with them—her last school had had no fewer than three. One Pauline was no problem at all.

WILL DIDN'T GET any sleep that afternoon, though he'd promised himself he would. The day was simply too jam-packed. He put in an hour on each of the horses he was starting and he got the biggest branches piled up and ready to burn, the smaller ones left for Kylie to stack after school. Then Will got his inspection book out and headed to the Taylor ranch.

The Taylors had sold yet another overpriced horse, this time to a first-time horse buyer from Elko. The buyer seemed pleased as punch to pay double what the animal probably was worth. Will silently documented his inspection, noting the horse's brand, sex, age, color and markings. He handed the book to Todd Taylor to sign, then peeled off the copies.

At least the animal was well trained, so the new owner wasn't buying trouble. Todd paid the inspection fee, grumbling about the recent increase, which amounted to about one fifth of a percent of the purchase price. Will felt bad for him. Especially when he watched Mrs. Taylor drive up in her gleaming new SUV, waving as she eased the big machine into a three-car garage.

"So, how does Kylie like her teachers?" Todd asked after the garage door had closed.

"So far, so good."

"Great." Todd smiled. He continued to smile until Will gritted his teeth and asked the question he knew Todd wanted him to ask. "How's Zach doing in football?"

Todd launched into a ten-minute spiel. Will nodded. A lot. And then finally managed to sidestep his way to his truck and reach for the door handle.

"Oh, you probably have to be going. Well, anyway, be sure to go to the game next Friday. Zach will be starting and I think you'll see what I've been talking about."

Will gave a noncommittal nod and got into his truck.

On the way home he took the loop, even though it added a couple miles to the trip, passing by Regan Flynn's house to see what havoc the windstorm had wrought, wondering if she had a hole in her roof or other major damage that had caused her to be late that morning.

He didn't see much wind damage—just a few scattered branches—and then he wondered just what the hell he was doing driving by her house in the first place.

Looking at the wind damage. Right.

He was curious about Regan Flynn.

Shit. As if he didn't have enough trouble without adding to it in a way he'd promised himself he wouldn't—at least not while Kylie was still living at home.

REGAN LIKED WORKING in Madison's arena, even if it was a little pricey. It was well kept and in addition to the large covered arena there were several paneled work areas outside. Today she chose to work inside, since the wind was starting to blow again. She'd managed to drag the big branch off the drive before she left and was hoping there wouldn't be another branch in its place by the time she got home.

"That's quite an improvement," Madison called almost an hour later, after Regan finished her last training pass of the day.

Regan eased Toffee to a halt and dismounted as Madison walked toward her, carrying a sheaf of papers in one hand and a cell phone in the other.

"He's coming along," Regan agreed, rubbing the gelding's forehead. She'd spent a good forty-five minutes working him over both ground poles and a series of foot-high jumps, talking to him with her hands and her body and teaching him to yield to her cues.

"He likes the work," Madison commented. "You used to show jump, didn't you?"

"How'd you know?"

"After watching you ride a few times, I figured you had to have been in competition somewhere, so I Googled you."

"I see." Regan wasn't sure that she liked being Googled.

"Do you have any plans to compete again?"

Regan smiled as she slipped the reins over Toffee's head. He pushed her with his nose, nearly knocking her off balance. It was getting to be a habit. She put her hand on his nose and firmly pushed his head away before turning her attention back to Madison.

"Those days are long gone. I just want to ride for my own pleasure." She started leading the horse toward the gate as she spoke, fighting to keep him from crowding her space. "Kind of a sanity saver, you know?" she said through gritted teeth, wishing Madison wasn't there to witness the power struggle. When she was on Toffee's back, there was no question as to who was in control. On the ground, he had both the height and the weight advantage, and he used them. He was very disrespectful.

"You might consider teaching a jumping class," Madison said, eyeing the horse as she opened the gate for Regan, but saying nothing about the obvious. "People would be interested and I like to offer a variety of classes here at the arena."

Regan gave a brief nod. She wouldn't mind teaching a class, once she was settled into her real job. It would be a good way to meet people who didn't have kids in school.

"All you have to do is book the times with me, charge the fees set on the arena rate chart and give the arena thirty percent of the proceeds."

"Is that all?" Regan replied, thinking it sounded like highway robbery, since she'd seen the rate schedule.

"You'd have access to the jumps and all the other equipment, and I'd put you on the calendar of events, which goes out in the newspaper and over the radio."

"I'll think about it."

"You know," Madison said as they reached the stall, "I'm putting on a training clinic next weekend. You've seen the advertisements, haven't you? Del Gilbert and Will Bishop?"

It was impossible not to see them. They had appeared that morning and were plastered all over town—the grocery store, the post office, even the school.

"You, uh, might consider going." Madison shoved the cell phone into her pocket and handed Regan yet another paper advertising the event. "I give a ten percent discount to people who board with me. All you have to do is bring this paper with you. There's a discount code stamped on the bottom."

"Thanks," Regan said. "I had planned on going." She'd

never seen anyone start a horse from the ground up and she'd heard enough about Will's abilities to be curious.

"It's worth the fee," Madison replied. Regan had a feeling she could have said she'd like to watch the tractor till the arena and Madison would have told her it was worth the fee.

"There's something else. I was wondering how much longer you plan to board Toffee here. I'm getting calls from people who want a stall and I'm full up."

"The fence was finished yesterday—just in time for the windstorm to bring a big branch down on top of it. I need to have the wire tightened again before I can bring him home."

"Well, it shouldn't take long to do that." Madison spoke confidently, making Regan believe she'd never worked with contractors. "I'll call Trev or Will about doing a brand inspection and make arrangements for one of them to haul Toffee to your house whenever they're available." Madison waved at a person who'd just walked in the stable door and then turned her attention back to Regan. "You don't have a trailer, yet. Right?"

"Not yet. Do you think they'd mind hauling for me?"

Madison shook her head no.

"Great. I'll pay them, of course. But I won't be available on a weekday until after school hours."

"When is that? Three o'clock?"

"Better make it four." She knew Pete wouldn't bend the rules for her and let her leave a little early.

"I'll give you a call."

"Thanks."

Madison smiled a nice-to-do-business-with-you smile before walking down the aisle between the stalls, slipping clinic discount flyers under each of the nameplates.

Regan pulled her stall door open and Toffee all but

walked over her in his hurry to get to his hay. She firmly smacked his chest with the flat of her hand. "No," she told him. He stopped and let her take off the halter. As he walked away, Regan leaned against the edge of the door frame, admiring his lines and gleaming coat and wondering how on earth she was going to get him to respect her. She'd never handled a horse with no manners before and she knew she needed to do something about it.

With luck, the clinic would give her a place to start.

BY THE NEXT DAY it was obvious that, although Pete hadn't fully given up on his squid-related prankster hunt, he was winding down. He stalked around the school scowling, almost a defeated man. But then, just after lunch, he received an ego boost of such massive proportions that it had to be shared with the staff in an emergency after-school meeting.

"This feels bad," Tanya murmured behind Regan, as they entered the meeting room.

Pete did look remarkably smug, rocking on his heels at the podium and waiting for the staff to straggle in, most of them showing signs of irritation at having been pulled away from their after-school prep time. And most of them seemed to have an idea of what was coming.

Mr. Zeiger, the school superintendent, stepped to the front of the room. "I wanted to tell you, in person, that although Mr. Bernardi is doing better, he has decided to retire. The board met last night and rather than commence an employment search now, we're going to continue with the current situation. Mr. Domingo will continue as acting principal until the end of the school year."

Karlene raised her hand. "When will you advertise this job?"

"We'll fly it in February and interview in March. The position officially begins in July. That'll give the successful candidate a chance to tie up loose ends." Zeiger gave Pete a small nod. "Unless, of course, he's local."

Pete's chest swelled so much that Regan began to wonder how his buttons held. "Thank you, Mr. Zeiger."

The superintendent smiled and then turned his attention back to the group. "On a more serious note, the Renshaw family is still dealing with some huge medical bills and they're trying to avoid bankruptcy. Our schools are in good shape, financially, so the board has agreed that a percentage of the proceeds from our independent fall fund-raisers can be donated to this cause. Also, the high school's FFA club is organizing an auction to be held in October, and there'll be various bake sales and car washes, too. I know you'll support these events as best you can."

There was a general murmur of approval. Even Pete looked supportive.

"Who are the Renshaws?" Regan asked Tanya.

"They work for the district. Mr. Renshaw in the bus garage, and Mrs. Renshaw in the district office. Their daughter had to have a kidney transplant, and the insurance hasn't covered everything."

"I'll want the individual faculties to vote and decide what percent of their fund-raisers, if any, to donate. And now I'll turn things over to your principal."

Pete took his place behind the podium as the superintendent stepped away. "That'll be all for this afternoon," he said, "but we'll be having another short meeting tomorrow at 8:00 sharp, to discuss our own fund-raiser."

"Scary." Regan said to Tanya, as they walked back to their classrooms. "He looked orgasmic."

"He was orgasmic. He's wanted this for a long time."

"Maybe he'll relax once he has the position." Tanya rolled her blue eyes and Regan sighed. "I guess we'll just muscle through this year and hope the board is smart enough not to make the appointment permanent."

"We can hope, but never discount the good-old-boy network. I think Pete has a shot at this. Heck, I wouldn't be surprised if they'd already decided to shoehorn him in."

"Because of his charismatic personality?"

"Because of the eight state football and basketball championships. School boards and ex-athletes in positions of power like that kind of stuff."

WHEN REGAN ARRIVED at the arena on Friday afternoon to pick up her new horse, she found Madison preoccupied, anxious about some problem with the upcoming clinic and ready to take it out on the first innocent person who crossed her path. And then, as if that wasn't enough, Toffee made it clear he had no intention of getting into a small two-horse trailer.

Regan had just spent a long day trying to keep more than 150 adolescents under control and she was in no mood to deal with either of these two. Fortunately, though, the brand inspector, a man named Trev Paul, had a way with both horses and women.

He was a good-looking man, dark and lean, with an easy smile, but it was his patience and the sense that he saw more than he acknowledged that most impressed Regan. Both Madison and Toffee responded well to his combination of easy humor and quiet determination, and in a surprisingly short amount of time, Regan was following his truck and trailer back to her place.

Once they were there, Trev unloaded Toffee and led him around the house to the pasture. It was obvious the gelding had no more respect for Trev than he did for Regan, but Trev was big enough to do something about it. He elbowed the horse out of his space more than once on the walk from the trailer.

"This boy needs some groundwork," Trev commented, as he released the horse into the knee-high grass.

"Amen to that," Regan muttered.

"Are you going to Madison's clinic?" Trev pushed his ball cap back and Regan found herself staring into a pair of stunning hazel eyes.

"Sure am."

"You might talk to Will or Del. I'd suggest Will, since he lives here and you won't have to skip a rent payment to pay him."

Regan laughed. "Speaking of payment, you're sure you won't take anything for hauling Toffee?"

"Nope."

"Are you sure you can get your trailer out of this narrow driveway?"

"Yep." He grinned. "See you around."

Trev effortlessly reversed down the drive and made the tricky backward turn onto the county road in one shot. Regan hoped she'd be that competent once she bought a trailer, which would be in two years or so, the way things were going.

She had grading waiting for her, but instead of doing what she was supposed to be doing, she walked to the pasture to take another look at her horse. After all, how many times did a person get her first horse?

Her horse. Not a leased horse or a borrowed horse or a schooling horse.

He stood almost exactly where he'd been released, pulling up big mouthfuls of fresh grass, his dark coat shining in the late afternoon sun. Every now and then he would raise his head to look around, as if he couldn't believe he had all this space, all this freedom—all this grass!—to himself.

With the exception of the grass, Regan knew exactly how he felt. She loved her mother and sister, but she was glad to be several hundred miles away from them and no longer required to act as a handy referee. And although dating Daniel had not put a crimp in her freedom, the aftermath of their relationship had given her an an even deeper appreciation of independence.

Too bad it had been such a hard lesson.

Regan settled her forearms on the gate, telling herself to focus on the present, forget about the past, but she hated the fact that she'd been conned so masterfully—personally and professionally. She'd even broken a number of personal rules for him—don't date a colleague, don't let anyone get *too* close.

But after working with the guy for a year, team teaching a math and science pilot program at a middle school, she thought she knew him well enough to break those rules. They'd started dating and it had seemed a perfect relationship. They were close both personally and professionally, yet Daniel understood and respected Regan's need to have her own space. He was supportive and attentive, generous. Almost perfect. Or so she thought.

Her professional goal at the time, heartily endorsed by her mother, Arlene, since it involved getting out of the classroom and into a power suit, was to secure a position with the Education Development Authority.

Over the course of that school year, she developed a package of innovative interactive lesson plans, which both she and Daniel used in their classes. With Daniel's input, Reagan had fine-tuned the material. When EDA had announced a job opening, Regan was ready. But so was Daniel.

He'd been up front about the fact that he was applying for the job, as well. Regan had been a bit surprised, but she knew that was the way things were in the professional world. She convinced herself she didn't have a problem with it. However she did have a problem with the fact that when it was her day to be interviewed, to present her materials and teach a demonstration lesson, it soon became apparent the interview committee had seen quite similar material before. The day before. During Daniel's interview.

Maybe, if life was fair, neither of them would have gotten the job. But life wasn't fair. Daniel had set the stage nicely, talking about his junior teaching colleague, Regan, who'd helped him tweak the lessons he'd spent so much time developing. It was only fair, after all, that she get a tiny portion of the credit.

At least Daniel had been smart enough to know that Regan would no longer be sharing his life after he'd accepted the job, so there had been no nasty breakup. Just a painful case of self-recrimination for trusting him, for almost convincing herself that she loved him.

She wouldn't be making that mistake again.

WILL WENT THROUGH his equipment, setting aside the few things he planned to bring with him to the clinic. He didn't need much. The horse would be there. All he needed was a sturdy halter, a rope, a saddle and a clear head. Three out of four wasn't bad.

"Hey, Dad." Kylie strolled into the barn, yawning but fully dressed and ready to go. The only time she got up willingly was when the day involved horses.

"Hey."

She had on her good black cowboy hat, her T-shirt with a barrel racer emblazoned on the back and her new jeans, which were already getting too short. Shopping time again. He'd have to see if Sadie's mom had a trip to Elko planned in the near future. No, maybe he'd take her himself. He didn't want her in Elko without him just now.

"You look ready."

She grinned at him. "So do you. Are you up first today?"

"Nope, second." Del liked to go first. He was the head-liner.

"Can Stubby come?" Both Kylie and the young border collie looked at Will hopefully.

Will shook his head. "Not yet."

"He'll behave."

"He'll eat the interior of my truck."

"He didn't eat much the last time."

No. Just the gearshift knob, but Will wasn't taking any chances. "Not this time."

Kylie bent down to explain to the collie that he had to stay home, then she got into the truck as the pup slunk to the porch steps to watch them leave without him.

Will waited as Kylie fastened her seat belt and the surge of protectiveness he felt as he watched her small hands work the latch was almost overwhelming. He knew logically there was probably nothing to worry about, that Brett had been in the area for more than a month and he'd made no attempt to contact them, but paternal instinct and logic did not always jibe. In fact, in Will's experience they rarely did.

"Ready?" Kylie's dark eyes were shining with excitement. She loved any and all horse events—especially those that involved her dad. He smiled.

"Ready as I'll ever be, I guess."

Kylie gave him a patient look. "I know you hate having all those people looking at you, but just imagine them in their underwear."

"That's a frightening thought, considering some of the people who will be there."

Kylie grinned. "I'd never thought of it that way. Do you think old Grandpa Meyers wears boxers or briefs?"

"Stop now."

Kylie started giggling and Will put the truck in Reverse. The day was actually off to a decent start.

REGAN WAS THERE.

He'd been scanning the crowd, while Madison introduced Del, looking for his brother, just in case, when he spotted her on the opposite side of the arena. And then, since it kept his mind off his upcoming performance, he continued to watch her. He'd never seen her in jeans before, but they suited her. And he liked the way her chestnut hair was pulled back in a haphazard non-teacherish ponytail.

She had a notepad balanced on one thigh and from the moment Del stepped into the ring with his horse, her attention was focused on his performance. She jotted notes every couple of seconds, it seemed.

Will watched her as she wrote, wondering if she'd take notes on him, too. He told himself he'd check, but he knew that, once he was in the round pen with the mustang, all his attention would be focused there. It was the only way he ever got through public performances—by pretending the audience wasn't there. Kylie's classic underwear strategy didn't work, primarily because of people like old Grandpa Meyers.

Lunch was the usual free-for-all, with the high school's FFA club flipping burgers and people hustling Will and Del for free advice.

Just before it was Will's turn to begin his afternoon performance, he eased away from the person he was talking to and approached Kylie and Sadie in the audience.

"Hey, would you guys do me a favor and stay here during the demonstration? In the front row?"

"Why?"

"I need some feedback and I want you to watch in order to give it." He pulled the reason out of thin air, but it sounded good and he could see that Kylie liked it.

"Okay."

"You won't get bored and wander off?"

"Nope."

"Good. I expect something constructive."

"Be careful what you ask for," Kylie quoted one of his favorite sayings. Will reached out, tapped the brim of her hat down and she laughed.

"Stay put," he repeated.

WHEN MADISON ANNOUNCED the start of the final demonstration, Will walked to the center of the arena, his short chaps flapping just below his knees, his gaze down, so that it was impossible to see his face under the brim of the cowboy hat. But when he reached Madison, he tilted his hat back, gave a tight-lipped, well-here-I-am smile and looked as if he'd dearly love to be anywhere but where he was.

Madison talked about Will, his background and training strategies, but Will's eyes were on the chute through which the mare would enter the round pen. There was some banging on the rails, as the horse was pushed into the paneled runway, then she emerged, her eyes round and wild.

She circled the round pen at a full gallop several times before coming to a stop at the side farthest away from the crowd. The rails were too high to jump, but she bunched up as if she was going to try. She continued to dance at the edge of the pen, desperately looking for a way out.

Will stood quietly until the mare threw him a wild glance over her shoulder and snorted. He took a slow step forward and the mare took off, galloping furiously around the pen, her hind feet kicking up divots and her attention outside the rails. Will moved to the center, pivoting as she circled, keeping his eyes on her, waiting for her to slow. When she did, he stepped forward quietly to get her moving again. This time her canter wasn't quite as wild and every now and then she looked at the man in the center of the pen, trying to read him.

"What Will's doing is controlling the mare's movements—showing her that he is the lead animal, the boss," Madison explained. Will also had a microphone clipped to his collar, but Regan wondered if he even had it turned on. "Horses want to know their place in the hierarchy of the herd and that's what Will is establishing now. He'll keep her moving, then give her an opportunity to stop when he wants her to stop."

The demonstration continued, the crowd watched attentively as Will eventually approached the mare and then touched her. When she turned away from him, he set her moving again, repeating the pattern until she understood that he wouldn't hurt her but if she didn't hold still for him she'd have to run. And running was work.

Will continued approaching and backing off, asking her to allow him to do as much as she could tolerate, then releasing pressure by backing away for a moment. In the end, he was able to rub her all over, halter her and saddle her. Madison kept up a running commentary throughout the entire procedure.

Finally, Will stepped away from the mare and walked to the edge of the round pen. The mare followed. He ran a hand over her neck when she stopped, facing him.

"I'm not going to get on her," he said, speaking for the first time since the start of the demonstration. "She's done enough for one day. I hope I've been able to show you guys something during this demonstration. If there are any questions…?"

Several hands shot up and Regan leaned back in her seat as Madison began fielding the questions.

After the demonstration, Will was surrounded by people—mostly women, Regan noticed as she gathered her notebook and purse—and although he was polite, she had a feeling that like the mustang mare, all he wanted to do was escape.

WILL WATCHED REGAN leave the arena over the head of a woman who was outlining her horse's behavior in a rather long-winded manner. He redirected his attention and listened, thinking that this woman's only problem was that she babied her animal. When he told her that, she wasn't happy with the answer. She wanted her horse to mind her because he loved her, not because she was the boss. Will opened his mouth to tell her that horses were not wired that way, but instead he just nodded. If she'd sat through both his and Del's presentations and hadn't yet picked that up, then she was only going to hear what she wanted to hear. Some people couldn't understand that affection and boundaries could actually go hand in hand.

When he'd answered his last question, he found Kylie in the front row where he'd left her. Sadie was gone, but another girl had taken her place.

"Honest," she was saying to Kylie as Will approached. She suddenly noticed that Will was there. "I gotta go. See you tomorrow."

"What's that all about?" Will asked after the girl left.

Kylie frowned. "She said that she saw a guy who looked just like you in Elko yesterday."

Will felt an instant tightening in his midsection, but

before he could think of something to say, Kylie screwed up her forehead and said, "Gee, Dad. You don't suppose it's Uncle Brett, do you?"

CHAPTER FOUR

"WELL, DO YOU think it was him?" Kylie repeated a few seconds later.

"Might have been."

"Aren't you curious?"

Kylie was certainly curious. She always had been and the older she got, the more curious she'd become. He didn't blame her. The kid hardly had any relatives and the few she did have were not part of her world. So far, they'd only had a few brief discussions about Brett and the fact that Will and his brother hadn't been in contact for more than a decade. She'd eventually stopped asking, but he knew she still wondered about her uncle.

"Get your stuff together."

"Dad." He frowned down at his daughter's perplexed expression. "Don't you ever want to see him again? I mean, was what happened really bad?"

"It wasn't good." Will made an effort to sound matter-of-fact. "And maybe someday Brett and I will get together and hash things out, but I don't think it's going to be any time soon."

Kylie bit her lip and let the subject go, even though Will knew she wanted—deserved—answers. He couldn't give her answers just yet. And he didn't know if he ever could.

They started toward the truck, Will carrying the saddle and blanket and Kylie carrying the halter and rope.

"You know, Dad, you did really good in your demonstration."

"Thanks, kid." He appreciated her changing the subject, but he knew they'd be facing it again one of these days.

"You might try talking a little, you know, like Del does. Madison does all right, but I think people'd like to hear you explain more of it."

"All right," he said. "I'll try. Anything else?"

"Nope." She flipped the end of the rope as she walked. "Sadie was kind of weird today. She kept looking around, instead of watching the performance. And she asked me if I wanted to buy makeup with her when we go to Elko. I said okay, but," she puckered her forehead, "whenever we put on her mom's stuff, I forget and rub my eyes and it gets all over."

"You're pretty just the way you are," Will said gruffly. "And I'm thinking maybe I'll take you to Elko myself. All my jeans are worn out. I need to replace them."

"All right," Kylie said hesitantly.

"Come on." He took the halter and rope from her. "I'll buy you a milk shake."

"You're on." Kylie scrambled into the truck. "And maybe a hamburger?"

"And maybe a hamburger."

PETE BREEZED INTO Regan's room on Monday just after the final bell rang, dismissing the students. "A moment, Miss Flynn?"

"Sure." She'd seen this expression before. It was his taking-care-of-business face and it had yet to bode well for her.

"I'm concerned about some of your students' grades."

"Really?" Regan'd had a feeling this was coming. Some of her ninth-grade football players were not meeting their academic commitments and therefore were flirting with ineligibility.

"These three, in particular." Pete held out a short list of names.

"Those boys owe makeup work from last Friday. It was an important assignment, but they can still turn it in. I'm accepting it until tomorrow."

"They have practice tonight."

"So does everyone else on that list."

"Most of those kids could have finished their work on the bench at last Friday's game. But these three," he flicked the paper for emphasis, "are starting players."

"The assignment is due tomorrow."

Pete sucked in a breath, obviously taking issue with her attitude, but Regan spoke before he had a chance to. "Look, I'm not heartless. I don't mind giving a student a break, but it bothers me when they expect it."

"How so?" Pete asked.

"Those three didn't turn in last Friday's makeup work, either. I excused those assignments and now look at the result. They expect me to do it again."

"Miss Flynn…"

"At what point do these boys learn responsibility?" Regan asked, shaking the pencil she held at Pete.

"They are learning that on the football field."

"Life is not a football field."

"The lessons apply," Pete replied sternly. "These boys will do their makeup work, but if they require extra time, I expect you to give it to them."

"Yes, sir."

Pete eyed her, trying to decide if she was being insubordinate or properly respectful. Finally, he gave her a curt nod.

"Thank you. Have a good evening, Miss Flynn."

"Same to you," Regan muttered as he left.

She pressed her lips together as she shoved homework papers into her tote bag. Damn, but she hoped those three would turn in their work tomorrow. This was not an issue she wanted to press, but if she had to, she would. The boys were more than capable of getting their work done *and* attending football practice. They weren't doing their work simply because they thought they could get away with it.

The phone was ringing when Regan walked into her house, half an hour later. Her sister. What now?

"Mom is driving me crazy!"

"Don't let her, Claire."

"Oh, very helpful, Reg."

"What's she doing?"

"You name it."

"Let's narrow it down to one or two specific issues."

After listening to her sister unload, Regan waited a moment to make certain Claire was finished and then said, "Just do what you want."

"And listen to Mom harangue me?"

"Claire, I've seen you stand up to everyone else in authority. You may as well give Mom a shot."

"I'd like to give Mom a shot," her sister said darkly.

"You're going to have to do this on your own or it isn't going to work, you know. You can't keep depending on me to run interference."

"It's so much easier when you do."

"Just ask yourself, what's the worst that could happen if you did take a stand with Mom?"

"She could move in with me as a punishment."

"DAD, SHE IS S-O-O-O PRETTY."

"Yeah," he said and she had a look in her eye, too.

Will knew, the minute that Kylie had dragged him over

to the holding pen outside the auction barn, that he was in trouble. The mare was poor, but her conformation was excellent and she had that dark gold palomino coat that Kylie particularly favored.

"She looks so much like Skedaddle. Maybe we could stay and see what she goes for."

Will had already bought a two-year-old roping prospect for one client, a brood mare for another and a Welsh pony that Kylie was going to tune up for a younger neighbor kid. He'd also spent the day on the edge of paranoia, wondering if Brett would show up at the sale, and he was not in the best mood because of it.

"We only brought the three-horse," he said, referring to his trailer.

"You know that we've put four in there before."

"They knew each other. These are strangers."

"Hey, I bet Trev would haul her home. He hauled Miss Flynn's horse to her house just a few days ago. She told the class. And he didn't buy any horses today, so his trailer is empty."

"Kylie, this mare has not had a good life." It showed in the way she was watching them.

"I know," his daughter said softly. She reached through the panel bars. The mare moved away. Kylie pulled her hand back and leaned her forearms on the panel.

"Maybe we could just give her a try. You said I could get a new horse pretty soon." She smiled up at him. "You've turned some really scared horses into good horses, Dad. Couldn't we just try? And if she doesn't work out, we can sell her."

Will felt himself bending and he had to decide fast whether to keep going or not.

"Just because she looks like Skedaddle, it doesn't mean she'll act like her, you know." Kylie's beloved first horse had died the previous summer, and Kylie still hadn't quite gotten over it.

"No one will ever replace Skedaddle," she said firmly. "But I like this mare and I have money saved up. How about we go halves?"

Will looked the mare over. She had the potential to be a stunning horse—one that show judges would give a second look. And it was late in the day, raining to boot. The sale prices had been low across the board and it was possible she wouldn't go for much, unless someone wanted a palomino bad. "What's the most you can afford, without draining your account?"

Will knew exactly how much she had and was surprised when the price she named was half her money, instead of all of it. He gave a slow nod. "But, if it turns out that she's too much for us to handle, she goes. Right?"

"Right." She suddenly waved. "I see Trev. Let's ask him to haul her."

"We might wait until we see if we've actually bought her."

Kylie gave him a "details, details" smile and hurried off to talk to Trev.

"This may not have been your wisest move," Trev said later, as they stood in the drizzling rain next to his horse trailer. The mare had been terrified when they loaded her, and she obviously expected to be beat when she balked at the trailer door. When she finally went in, it had been with a huge bounding leap and then she'd immediately tried to back out again.

If he'd been at home, Will would have let her exit and that would have been the beginning of a lesson, but in the rain, miles from home and late in the day, he'd shoved his shoulder against the door, absorbing the impact of the horse's hindquarters as he latched it shut. The mare immediately stepped forward and started pawing the front wall.

"I think Dad will be able to do something with her," Kylie told Trev in a serious tone, as the banging grew louder. "He's handled worse."

Trev grinned. "He's handled you, I guess."

"Yeah, and look how good I turned out."

THE BRASS BELLS tied to the feed store door jangled as Will walked in. He'd seen Regan's car outside and he figured she was buying things for her new gelding. Sure enough, there she was reading labels on nutritional supplements for horses. She looked up at the sound of the bells and their gazes connected for a moment. She smiled briefly, impersonally, before she looked down at the label again.

Every time he saw her, Will was struck by how pretty she was, with her delicate cheekbones, wide green eyes and chestnut hair. It was the kind of pretty that crept up on a guy, but then, once it hit you, there was no going back. And surprisingly, the day he'd realized just how attractive she was, was the day her hair had been tousled by the wind and she'd been wearing big, fuzzy socks.

Will headed for the order counter, where Maggie Benson was going over invoices.

"I need senior equine food. Better make it four bags."

"Have you taken in an old horse?" she asked as she wrote the ticket.

"Nope. More of a starved horse. I'm supplementing."

"Should do the trick. I'll have Zero load you."

Will tucked his change into his wallet while Maggie called her husband on the intercom. Regan came to stand behind him, a rope halter in one hand and a vitamin supplement in the other. She met his gaze squarely, the way teachers tend to do, but she didn't look at all teacherish today. Her hair was pulled back in a short ponytail at the nape of her neck, but most of it seemed to have escaped around her face. He noticed for the first time that she had freckles. She looked nothing like the polished educator he'd first met in Bernardi's office. He moved aside so she could put her items on the counter.

"I liked the clinic. I learned a lot. Do you do many?"

"Madison usually has me do two a year."

"Do you ever give clinics elsewhere?"

He shook his head.

"You don't like the crowds, do you?"

"Is it that obvious?"

"Only to the trained eye."

Maggie rang up Regan's total. As Regan dug through her purse for her checkbook, Will heard the distinctive growl of a hungry stomach. She gave him a sheepish grin. "I'm starved."

"So's his horse," Maggie said, cackling at her own joke. Regan frowned at Will.

He shook his head. "I'll explain later." The last thing he wanted to do was to encourage Maggie—especially in front of an audience.

"You want to explain over pizza?" Regan asked, gathering her purchases. He must have looked startled, because she gave him a wry look. "Come on, Will. Live dangerously."

"Yeah, Will," Maggie chimed in. "When's the last time you…" Her words became a cough as he shot her a quick look.

"You don't have to," Regan said mildly. "I had some horse questions, but I can catch you another time."

"I'll come."

He saw Maggie smirk out of the corner of his eye, but

he ignored her. A few minutes later he and Regan left the feed store together.

"How about this?" he said as he held the door open. "We could pick up the pizza and go someplace where we could talk in private."

"Afraid to be seen with me?"

"No, but…."

"But what?" she asked.

"You're Kylie's teacher." *And I haven't been seen out with anyone in about a hundred years—even for pizza.*

"Let's make people talk," Regan said as she started across the parking lot to the pizza place. "I'm too hungry to wait."

Will hesitated, then jogged a few steps to catch up. He had to admit he was intrigued by this side of Regan—open, totally human. And he had to admit he'd like to see more.

"Pretty good for a guy in boots," she said.

"I'm a man of many talents."

Heads turned when they walked into the busy restaurant.

"What's with these people?" Regan whispered as they took a seat in the back booth. A thirtysomething woman had been craning her neck to watch them.

"I, uh, don't go out too often."

It took her a second to get his drift.

"What? Are you like a monk or a hermit?"

"Not exactly." *Yes, exactly.*

"Not *exactly?*" She regarded him for a moment; when he didn't clarify, she slowly shook her head. "That's sad, Will."

"I think it's important to keep my life on an even keel while Kylie's still at home, so I just focus on being a parent." To Will, the words came out sounding as if he'd practiced them in front of a mirror, but they must have been okay because Regan nodded.

"I wish more parents put their kids ahead of their social lives," she said, pushing the napkin-wrapped cutlery aside to lean her elbows on the table. She rested her chin in her hands. "I think we'd have a more stable population of students."

"Uh, yeah." And if she'd known the real direction of his thoughts at that moment, she'd have called him a damned hypocrite. Here he was expounding on putting parenthood first, while he was pretty much undressing her in his mind. Damn, how long had it been since he'd really been attracted to someone?

A long time. And it had not ended well.

The waitress showed up then to take their order. She took her time and wrote it out word for word, taking little peeks at them over the top of her order pad. Finally, after the third furtive look, Regan folded her hands together and spoke in her teacher voice.

"As I mentioned earlier, Mr. Bishop, I think Kylie would benefit from the accelerated-tutor program. Every student who's been on it has jumped at least one grade, usually more..." She grinned at Will after the waitress trudged off to the kitchen a few seconds later. "There. Your reputation is safe."

He knew she was underestimating the determination of the local gossips, but he felt his mood lifting for the first time in days. "What horse questions did you have?"

"Okay, first of all, where can I buy hay? I cannot afford to keep getting it at the feed store."

"It's pretty late in the season, but Charley Parker is your best bet."

Regan let out a breath. "Will he cheat me?"

"Not if you have him weigh the truck and bring you the slip."

"All right." Two Cokes plopped down between them. Regan gave the waitress a quick nod of thanks, then focused on Will. "Statistics show that students who do online studies outperform their peers by…"

"Anything else?" Will asked with a grin as the waitress disappeared. He leaned back, stretching his arm along the top of the seat, feeling surprisingly relaxed. Regan dropped a straw into her glass. She took a long sip and it occurred to Will that it had been a long, long time since he'd done anything so, well, spontaneous.

As it turned out, there was plenty she wanted to know: from techniques for correcting Toffee's rolled-out hoof—call Trev, and he'll show you—to his opinions on specific nutritional supplements, including the one she had just purchased.

"There's one more thing.…" She sounded as if she was about to make a guilty confession, which instantly piqued Will's curiosity. "I'm having some trouble with Toffee. I thought maybe you could give me some advice."

"What kind of trouble?"

"He's pushy—he walks on me. Neither of my previous horses did that." She stirred the ice in her glass. "I don't put up with it, but he keeps doing it. I'm tired of elbowing him. And if I drop my guard he walks right up over the top of me."

"I *can* help you with that," Will said. "You want to ride him over to my place on Saturday and work with him?"

"I won't be able to pay you until payday, so maybe we should wait until then."

"Or maybe I could just help you."

She cocked her head. "Really?"

"You've never had anyone just help?" he asked.

She shrugged. "Of course I have." But there was something in her expression that made him wonder if she was telling the truth.

"Will Saturday work, then?"

"It would work fine." She gave him a smile that made the volunteering feel worthwhile. "Should I bring anything other than the horse?"

He shook his head. "I have everything you'll need."

The pizza arrived a few minutes later. "I was wondering," Regan said, as she carefully lifted a slice onto a paper plate, "what exactly a brand inspector does?"

"I'm a deputy brand inspector, so I only work part-time. We deal with livestock sales, making certain that an animal being sold doesn't belong to someone else. Or that animals in someone's custody actually belong to them."

"Kind of like an animal cop?"

"Exactly. We've been having a rash of thefts in the northern part of the state and we're the guys who deal with that, too. It's mainly Trev's headache, but we're all involved."

"Is it dangerous?"

"It can be, but I've never seen any trouble. I pretty much look an animal over, record markings and brands and collect a fee for the government. Trev actually stops vehicles transporting animals and looks at the paperwork."

"Interesting. So what's this about a starving horse?"

"Kylie and I went halves on a horse yesterday. She resembles Kylie's first mare and, well, the kid wanted her and I caved."

Regan's lips curved, but she didn't say anything.

"What?" he asked with a half smile.

"I don't know many dads who would cave on a horse. A new phone, maybe. An iPod…but a horse?"

He shrugged. "It's kind of in my line of work."

"My dad never caved. I had to lease my horses. I hated not owning them. I'm so glad to finally have a horse of my own." She bit the edge of her full lower lip as she gave him a conspiratorial look. "Someday, I'd like to have two horses. Toffee is already lonely being by himself all day."

"Well, I know a cranky palomino mare you can go halves on...."

It was six o'clock when they walked back to their cars. Regan smiled at him over her door. "Thanks for the pizza, Will."

"Anytime," he replied and, surprisingly, he wished they *could* do it anytime. Too bad real life had that way of rearing its ugly head.

CHAPTER FIVE

"I CAN'T WAIT for you to see her."

Regan clearly heard Kylie whispering during what was supposed to be silent reading time. She sent a warning glance in Kylie and Sadie's general direction, hoping it would be enough to quiet Kylie down. But she had a new horse and she was excited. The girl probably wouldn't believe it, but Regan knew exactly how she felt.

"I named her Skitters, because she's skitterish right now, but Dad is working with her."

Obviously, the warning glance was not enough to stifle Kylie's enthusiasm.

"Uh, Kylie?" Regan said in her no-nonsense teacher voice, "would you mind saving this for later, so other people can concentrate?"

"Yes, Miss Flynn." Kylie's shoulders slumped in frustration and she rummaged through her notebook for paper. Regan had a feeling the girl was about to commit her excitement to paper and pass it along. She decided not to notice. Sadie had been absent earlier in the day due to a doctor's appointment, so this was Kylie's first chance to see her, but something was amiss. Sadie wasn't as engaged in Kylie's whispered asides as usual. She smiled politely, but she didn't offer any comments in return.

Regan sensed Kylie's frustration. Especially when Sadie looked away from Kylie midsentence, shifting her attention to a boy who sat two rows over, smiling shyly when he glanced her way.

Hoo, boy.

Kylie looked as if smoke was about to come out of her ears. Regan focused on her papers. Junior high dynamics were exhausting and she was glad when the final bell rang and she no longer felt compelled to watch Sadie simper and Kylie fume. As soon as the kids left, Regan gathered her materials and headed for the teachers' workroom.

The copy machine was clear, for once. Regan figured Pauline must have just finished, since the top was still hot.

"Please, baby, just eighty copies of each," she murmured to the machine, which had a penchant for jamming when it was overheated.

"Miss Flynn, can I have a word?"

"Certainly, Mr. Domingo." Regan adjusted her face to be pleasant and turned around. She'd been trying, really trying—in spite of the athletes' grade problem—to maintain a professional attitude around Pete. It soothed his ego and made life easier for both of them. And he was her acting principal, technically her boss, even if he didn't have a clue about what he was doing.

"I'd like you to speak to the Taylors. They seem to think that Zach is ineligible for this week's football game."

"Right now, he is." Because in spite of being warned last week that she would not accept work at the very last minute again, he still hadn't handed in his makeup assignments. Regan had learned through the grapevine that Zach was a football marvel—a freshman starting quarterback—and apparently that made him feel that rules didn't apply to him. And Pete wasn't helping matters.

"No. He's not. His missing work will be handed in before the game."

"That's fine. And I'll accept his work, just like I told

you, but until I get it, it's automatically a zero in the computer." Which made him ineligible.

"I told you—" Pete fought to maintain his composure "—his work will be in before the game and that's good enough for me. You take that zero out of the computer and mark the assignment excused."

"Fine." The word slipped out from between clenched teeth, as she tried hard to maintain a professional demeanor. This was not district policy. She'd read up on the matter.

"Now, let's go talk to the Taylors."

Oh, boy. Let's. Regan dropped her copying with a thud and followed Pete out of the room.

Pete walked, in scowling silence, as far as the office and then began to smile broadly as he opened the door.

"I've spoken to Miss Flynn. Zach needs to get his work in by tomorrow morning, then he can play."

"My concern is that this will happen again," Mrs. Taylor said. Regan felt a surge of relief, at least the mother understood that her son needed to be held accountable. "Zach doesn't need this kind of *stress* on top of everything else he's juggling. It's just too much."

"And it's affecting his playing," Mr. Taylor added sternly.

So much for accountability.

Regan sat in a chair across from the Taylors and met their cool gazes dead-on. She made it a point to never show weakness in front of bullying parents.

"Zach is a very capable student. He's bright and personable. I enjoy him in my class." *When he's not looking down his nose at me.* "But school district policy is clear on this matter. Athletes have two school days to make up work they miss due to sports-related events. I believe the board made this policy with the students' best interests in mind." Regan paused. The Taylors did not appear to be impressed by her opening remarks. They stared at her stonily. She was afraid to look at Pete, so she simply didn't.

"It would be confusing to both students and staff if we had different policies for different students. Therefore, if I give Zach a week, I have to give everyone a week. And if I'm giving my kids a week, then other teachers would have to give a week. And then district policy would have to be rewritten. You can see what a can of worms this would open?"

"Yes," Mr. Taylor finally responded, but the look he sent Pete was deadly.

Regan plunged on. "Now, if Zach needs additional help with anything he misses in class, I'm available at lunch and before school, so it wouldn't interfere with football practice. In fact, he's welcome to come into my room at those times and work on his makeup."

She paused to draw in a breath before she hammered the final nail into her coffin. "I just want everyone here to understand that I will be following written district policy from this point on. Two days for makeup work. Regardless."

There was a heavy silence. Regan waited for a reaction. Any reaction. Mr. and Mrs. Taylor exchanged glances and then Mrs. Taylor spoke.

"Thank you for your time, Miss Flynn."

There was no doubt Regan was dismissed. Mr. Taylor's eyes were on Pete, who in turn was staring at Regan, his jaw rigid.

Regan stood and excused herself. She thought she heard Pete say her name just as the office door swung shut behind her, but she didn't slow down. She was officially off the clock and she needed time to think before her next confrontation with the man.

She wasn't going to get that time. He caught up with her.

"How dare you make me look like I don't know my job?"

"*Do* you know your job?" Regan snapped. Pete went scarlet.

"You do understand that I'll be doing your evaluations?"

Since she was a new teacher in the district, Regan would have the pleasure of not one, but two observation sessions with Pete.

"Yes, and I'm certain they'll be conducted in a professional manner, or you'll be looking at a grievance."

Pete narrowed his eyes. "Do you know who the Taylors are?"

"No. Who are they?"

"Todd Taylor's brother is on the school board."

"Then Mr. Taylor should know district policy and respect it."

"This isn't Las Vegas, Miss Flynn. We run a more 'personalized' district here."

"Are you saying that some people are exempt from rules and others aren't?"

Pete's face became even redder. "I am saying," he said in a deadly voice, "that we handle things on a case-by-case basis."

"I didn't see that in the policy manual."

"It's understood!" Pete looked as if he would burst a blood vessel and Regan found she was holding her breath, possibly in anticipation of the big event. She slowly exhaled as he turned and stomped down the hall, apparently too angry to speak.

Keep breathing, Regan told herself as she went into the teachers' room to finish the copying Pete had interrupted. *Deep steady breaths.* She wanted to go home, but she knew she'd be dealing with a line at the copier in the morning. Better to do it now.

"Guess what?" Tanya said, when she walked in a few minutes later.

"Pete's been made superintendent," Regan replied without looking up from the jammed copy machine.

"You already heard." Tanya flipped her hair over her shoulder.

Regan carefully tried to ease a sheet of paper free from the interior, biting her lip as she worked. The paper tore and Regan dropped her shoulders in defeat. Now she would have to retrieve every little bit that had been left behind or the machine would remain inoperable.

"Hey, what's wrong?"

Regan knew full well that Tanya wasn't talking about the copy machine. "I made the mistake of trying to make the same rules apply to everyone."

"This doesn't sound good."

"Not good at all." Regan briefly described her encounter with the Taylors, as she pulled little scraps of paper from between the roller bars. "So," she concluded as she finally dug out one particularly stubborn piece, "I know what I did was right. Zach is intelligent and capable. He's working the system and feeling entirely too safe doing it."

"And that drives you crazy."

Regan glanced over at her. "Yes. It does. No one's doing this kid a favor by convincing him the world revolves around him. But maybe I should have ignored my conscience and played along. I don't know."

"Why should you have done that?" Tanya asked softly.

"I don't want to endanger my job and I am first-year probationary in this district."

"You did the right thing. I can't see anyone trying to

punish you for following policy." She paused. "Except maybe for Pete."

"The Taylors didn't look all that friendly, either."

"Zach is their last child and their only boy."

"That explains things." Regan pulled out yet another sliding drawer. "What were you going to tell me before I sidetracked you?"

"We're in charge of the dessert table at the school fund-raiser."

"We're what?"

"In charge of the dessert table at the Harvest Dance. No one ever wants the job so they always foist it off on the newcomer. And," she cleared her throat, "the newcomer's friend, which is me. Our first committee meeting is Thursday after school in the library."

Regan pulled out what was possibly the last sheet of misfed paper, shut various compartments and the main housing door of the copier. The control panel lit the all clear.

She checked her hands for toner smudges, then gathered up her copies. She was ten papers short, but she was not going to risk another tussle with the machine. She gave Tanya a weary smile. "Let's try to have fun with our dessert table?"

"Sounds good to me. Are you going to be all right? I mean, do we need to have a wine-cooler night?"

Regan shook her head. "I'm going home to ride my horse. And I am not going to think about a single school-related issue."

WILL WAS TIGHTENING the gates when the bus pulled up and Kylie trotted down the steps, skipping the last one entirely. He wanted to get all his pre-snow maintenance done early this year. In Nevada, winter was anyone's guess—early, late, warm, cold, wet, dry. He wanted to be ready for all possibilities.

Gravel crunched as Kylie marched toward him instead of heading to the house to drop off her backpack. Stubby met up with her and poked his nose into her hand.

"Did you and Miss Flynn go out?" she demanded before she'd even reached him.

Will's eyebrows went up in surprise. He hadn't expected this. "We ate a pizza."

"Why?" Kylie crossed her arms. In another second, she'd be tapping her toe.

"She needed answers to some horse questions."

Kylie's expression shifted, edging toward relief. "So you weren't talking about me?"

"Any reason we should be?"

"No," she responded quickly. "But it's kind of weird to hear that your dad was out with your teacher."

"I imagine that would be weird."

"You have no idea." She went to the edge of the corral, leaving her backpack next to Will. Skitters moved closer and Kylie climbed up onto the fence to stroke her. "Hey," she straightened up so she was balancing on the bottom rail as she pointed toward the county road, "is that Miss Flynn?"

"Looks like it."

"She's riding English!" Kylie couldn't have sounded more shocked if she'd seen her teacher riding naked.

"Yeah. I see that." Regan had the horse nicely gathered as she rode past the house. Hard to believe this was the same horse he'd watched terrorize a jumping class at the 4-H horse show only a year ago.

"I don't like posting."

They'd had this discussion before. Kylie thought post-ing looked dumb and she really wanted Will to agree with her, but he stuck to his position that posting had a purpose.

"It's easier on your butt and the horse's back if you can't ride right," he reiterated.

"You don't post."

"I said if you can't ride right."

"Are you saying Miss Flynn can't ride right?" Kylie asked hopefully.

"No. Watch her." Regan was rounding the bend and al-most out of sight. "She knows what she's doing."

Kylie's mouth twisted. "Yeah. I guess."

"If people can't sit a trot, they'd better post, whether they're riding English or Western. It's better than bounc-ing around, jarring the horse's back."

"Why do English riders always post?"

Will drew in a breath. "They don't." He cocked his head at an angle. "Maybe you should ask Miss Flynn some of these questions. She probably knows more than I do about English riding."

"I might."

"Don't misquote me." Will could only imagine what his daughter might do with the posting comment he'd just made.

Kylie smiled and jumped down off the fence. "I think I'll groom Skitters now."

She headed for the barn, whistling under her breath, leaving her backpack on the edge of the driveway.

Will kept on eye on the road as he finished tightening the cables that helped suspend the gate, but Regan did not ride back past him. She'd obviously taken the loop that ran past his house and ended near her own. Too bad. He kind of wanted to watch her ride by on that big horse again.

KYLIE WAS AT a 4-H MEETING when Regan arrived for Toffee's tune-up on Saturday.

"Hi." She pushed her dark hair away from her forehead as she looked down at him from atop her horse.

"Hi, yourself." He tipped the brim of his ball cap up. "Let's get the saddle off him and warm him up in the round pen."

"He's warm."

"No, I mean, get him used to being moved where I want him to go. Do you lounge him?"

"Yes," she said as she dismounted. "At least a couple times a week. More, if I can."

A few minutes later Regan's saddle was perched on a lodge pole rail and Will had Toffee circling the round pen at a relaxed canter. He stopped him, turned him, started him going again. As he'd expected, the horse was an old hand at traveling in a circle, picking up gaits on command.

Now to see what he did when he was on a lead line. Will snapped on the rope and started to lead the horse. In two seconds the gelding all but walked up the back of Will's leg. Will instantly turned, told the horse no and began vigorously shaking the lead rope.

Toffee took a few backward steps and looked at Will curiously. Will started walking again and the horse was on top of him in an instant.

Will whirled around, only this time he started taking giant stamping steps at the horse as he shook the rope. Toffee quickly reversed, but Will kept coming at him until the horse had backed up a good ten feet. Then Will stopped. Toffee blew through his nose, but he kept his distance.

Will chanced a look over at Regan, who was watching with her mouth open. She quickly closed it.

Will quietly walked to the horse and rubbed his forehead and then his neck. "It's all right, son. You just gotta stay out of my way. Got it?" After a moment the big gelding began to chew, a sign that he was relaxing.

"Okay, let's try again."

It took several more tries before Toffee realized that Will was serious—he was not going to allow the horse to get too close. For a horse who had probably spent most of his life walking wherever he pleased, even if it happened to be on someone's foot, it represented a major shift in attitude.

Will gestured at Regan and held out the rope. "Your turn."

She took the rope. "I feel kind of bad scaring him."

"You aren't so much scaring him as you're teaching him respect. What do you do to control your classes?"

"I set boundaries," Regan replied, knowing that was the answer she was supposed to give.

"That's what you'll do here. When Toffee crosses that boundary, you want to make him so uncomfortable he doesn't want to cross it again, but you don't want to frighten him. When horses are frightened, they're not thinking. They're reacting, trying to save themselves. That's when people and animals get hurt."

"How do you decide how aggressive to be?"

"You take it horse by horse. Toffee's bullheaded. It's going to take more to teach him who's in control. Now that little filly over there—the tobiano?" He pointed to a young black-and-white pinto in a corral near the barn. "I barely have to make a move and she's trying to figure out what I want and how to do it. She's a much more sensitive horse."

"Well, here goes." Regan took the lead rope out of his hand, tightened her mouth in an expression of resignation. He smiled a little. "I won't tell anyone if you don't do it perfect the first time." And the look she sent him told him he'd hit the nail smack on the head. Regan wanted to be perfect the first time.

REGAN WALKED A few steps and Toffee followed at a respectful distance until she turned toward the gate. At that point he crowded close, pushing against her in his hurry to leave the round pen.

Regan turned and tried to do exactly what Will had done, shaking the rope and stamping her foot as she moved toward him. She felt awkward, self-conscious with Will watching and, as always, she could hear her mother demanding a more accomplished performance. She forced herself to ignore it.

Her stamping left a little to be desired, but Toffee understood. He stood at the end of the rope and cautiously regarded Regan, as if to say, *Where did you come from and what did you do with the nice lady I could walk all over?*

"Good," Will said quietly. "Praise him and try again."

She moved close to stroke the horse, then started walking again. The gelding followed her without hesitation, keeping out of her space. She continued to lead him around the pen. He started to encroach again near the gate, but she gave a sharp, no, and flipped the rope. The horse immediately moved to the proper position.

"Good boy." She stopped after a complete circle around the pen and rubbed his neck. Then she smiled over at Will. "He holds no grudges."

"He shouldn't. He just needs to know his place. He's used to being the dominant animal. *You* need to be the dominant one. Once he understands who's boss, he'll accept his place."

"Hmm. I think that's what Pete's trying to do with me."

Will's expression was deceptively mild. "Is he bothering you?"

"Nothing too extreme," Regan replied. "Do you know Pete well?"

"We went to high school together. Graduated the same year."

Regan couldn't resist. "Did you get along?"

"No one gets along with Pete unless they're wearing a jock strap."

"So that's my problem," Regan said. "I left mine in Vegas. How about you? Were you a jock?"

"I was in high school rodeo, so, no, not in the traditional sense, anyway. We competed in the southern part of the state in the fall and the northern part in the spring. That took care of all the athletic seasons except for basketball, and I was never that good at dribbling." He grinned. "But Pete was."

"I bet he was. I hear he's a good coach."

"Yes, if you're all right with the win-at-all-costs philosophy, and a lot of people in this town are."

"I take it you're not?"

"I like winning." Will dropped the rope and started moving his hands over Toffee's body in a massaging motion. The gelding stiffened, but as Will continued, his head began to come down. Regan could almost hear an equine sigh as Will worked the muscles in the horse's neck. She found herself wondering what those hands could do to her.

"Tight spot," Will murmured. "Oh, there we go." He smiled a little as Toffee's head went even lower. He started toward the withers and shoulder area. "Anyway, I like winning and, yeah, Pete is good at putting together winning teams. But sometimes I think he loses sight of the big picture, focuses on the big names and ignores the less spectacular kids. Some of those kids eventually develop into reasonable athletes, but he's missing the boat with them."

"How do you think he'll be if he makes principal?"

"I wouldn't want to work for him if I wasn't one of his star players." Toffee suddenly shifted his weight and switched his tail as Will touched a spot on his hindquarters. "Little bit of a sore spot here."

Regan approached. "Where?"

"Here." Will took her hand and put it on the spot. "Press lightly." He kept his hand over hers as she pressed. "Can you feel the knot in the muscle?"

Yes, she could feel the knot, but she was more aware of the work-roughened hand that was covering hers. And of how close she and Will were to one another. She could feel the warmth of his body, smell sweat and soap and leather— a surprisingly heady mixture. Will suddenly seemed to become aware, too. He took away his hand, running it casually over the horse's rump as he stepped backward. Regan cleared her throat.

"What causes a knot like that?"

"Could be an old injury. Or overuse. Or compensating for some other injury. You might want to massage it every day and see if you can get it worked out. He'll move better if you do."

"I will." Regan moved toward Toffee's neck and started stroking his mane. "I guess I've neglected a big part of my equine education. I did a lot of work in the saddle, but maybe I ignored the groundwork." She smiled. "You know, the respect part?"

"How old were you when you started riding?"

"Older than Kylie. I was fourteen the first time I got on a horse."

His eyebrows went up. "You must have been a natural."

"I guess I was. Also, my riding teacher took me under

her wing. She's the one who groomed me for competition. I rode for hours every day in the summer. She arranged to let me ride other people's horses for exercise and she took me on the jumping circuit with her." Regan twisted her fingers in the gelding's dark mane. "I never thought about it, but I guess she was my Pete. I was good, so she paid more attention to me than her other students." And she had quite possibly sensed that Regan needed to have ownership of something that had nothing to do with her mother.

"Maybe we all need a Pete in our lives," Will said sardonically.

"Easy for you to say when you don't have a Pete in your life." Regan pulled her saddle off the fence. "Well, I guess I should be heading home."

"All right." Will took the saddle from her and settled it on Toffee's back.

It almost sounded as if he didn't want her to go, which Regan found interesting. And what she found even more interesting was that at the same time she felt an impulse to stay—which was exactly why she needed to get on her horse and head home. Once Will had tightened the girth, Regan led Toffee to the fence and used the bottom rail as a mounting block.

"Thanks for the lesson, Will. I'll keep this big guy in line."

"If you need any more help, just yell."

She met his gaze and found herself getting lost in a storm cloud of bluish-gray. "I will," she said softly. "I promise."

CHAPTER SIX

REGAN GAVE CLAIRE a call after she'd returned home and settled a more respectful Toffee back in his pasture. It had been several days since she'd heard from her sister and she was beginning to wonder what the deal was. Claire never went that long without moral support.

"Wow, you must have ESP," Claire said in her best California-girl voice. "I was just going to call. Guess who I ran into?"

"Not a clue."

"Daniel. And," Claire's voice took on a gleeful note, "he asked me out! Just for coffee, mind you, but he actually had the gall to pretend that everything was peachy."

"He is such a jerk," Regan stated flatly. And he had such a need to look like a good guy.

"Well, if he wasn't aware of that fact before, he's aware of it now. In fact, I asked him if he was looking for a new job and needed some help getting ready for his interview. He turned red up to his ears."

"Good for you." Regan put the kettle on the stove. "Where did you run into him, anyway?"

"The, uh, UNLV College of Education."

Regan's hand stilled for a moment before she twisted the burner knob and lit the flame. She had an ominous feeling about this. Not for Claire, but for their mother, who was determined that at least one of her girls would follow the career path she'd chosen for them. "Why were you at the College of Ed?"

"Oh, just checking out options," Claire said quickly. "So how's life in Smallville?"

"Good." Regan recognized a blatant redirection when she heard one and she decided this was a good sign. Claire, in spite of her fiery nature, had always depended on Regan to steer her through the big decisions in her life. And the small ones. Claire would blithely tackle any and all problems with no thought to the possible consequences, then drag Regan in to help her clear up the mess. Teamwork was what Claire called it. A headache was what Regan called it.

Yes, the redirect was definitely a good sign and Claire was rather good at it. Regan was laughing by the time she hung up the phone ten minutes later. About the only reason she missed living in Las Vegas was her sister.

WHEN REGAN WENT into the office first thing Monday morning, Jared-the-Sub was checking out the job board.

"Any luck?" she asked.

"Only if I want to go deeply rural. There's an opening in Barlow Ridge next semester."

Regan wrinkled her nose. "Where's that?"

"About seventy miles from here. I think the teacher is either pregnant or just coming to her senses."

"Would you take it?"

"I might. It would get me employed with the district, then maybe I could transfer to Pete's PE job here next fall."

Regan felt her stomach tighten. Jared was a Wesley native and he probably had a good sense of which way the wind was blowing. "You don't think the board'll put Pete in as principal, do you?"

He didn't answer out loud, but his expression told the story.

Regan blew out a breath as Jared walked away. She consoled herself with the thought that it hadn't happened yet.

"You ride English, don't you?"

Kylie'd dropped by to pick up a notebook she'd left under her desk during sixth period and then, to Regan's surprise, she'd hung around, watching her redo the bulletin board.

"Sure do." Regan punched another staple into the cork as she hung photographs of the different biomes the class would soon be studying. She wondered if Sadie was off boy watching again, leaving Kylie at loose ends, because the girl rarely, if ever, stayed a minute longer in class than she had to.

"We saw you the other night."

Regan figured they might have.

"I think English saddles are weird."

"Do you think jumping is weird?"

"No."

"You need an English saddle to jump properly."

"I know." Kylie spoke with an air of wistfulness. "Do you jump?"

"I used to." A long time ago. She'd loved being involved in something that was hers and hers alone, with no input from her mother, but she was happy to just pleasure ride now.

"I jump low ones bareback. Dad won't let me jump in a Western saddle."

"That's because the horn will poke your belly."

"I know," Kylie said in a tone that made Regan think that she'd learned that lesson the hard way.

"You must be pretty good if you can jump bareback."

"I am," the girl replied matter-of-factly.

"Want to get better?"

"How?"

"I'm giving jumping lessons." She and Madison had firmed up the deal the day before. In fact, Madison had all but signed up three students before Regan had even agreed.

"Really?" Kylie's eyes widened and then she caught herself. "That might be interesting, but I don't have an English saddle and I don't think my dad'll buy one unless he knows I'm serious."

"Madison has a couple she'll rent."

"Does that mean you're giving lessons at the arena?" Kylie picked up a photo of the polar region and handed it to Regan, who stapled it next to the steppe region.

"That's the plan. I have to charge the arena rate for the lessons, but Madison has nice equipment and it'll keep us out of the weather." And the wind, which was blowing once again.

"How will you get your horse there?"

"I won't need him. I teach from the ground."

"You know, you really should buy a trailer. If your horse gets sick or something, you'll need to take him to the vet."

"Yes, well, I do have a trailer on my wish list." Right under a few other things, like something to pull it with. "In the meantime, I'll just have to find a vet who makes house calls."

"That'd be Dr. Martin," Kylie said. "He charges the least for mileage and he's a good horse vet."

"Thanks for the tip."

"No problem. When will lessons start?"

"I still have to iron out a few details, but it would be pretty soon. Two weeks maybe."

"I think I'll go and tell Sadie. She might want to do it, too, and I think her grandma has an English saddle."

Kylie practically skipped to the door and Regan hoped, for her sake, that Sadie was equally enthusiastic.

"Okay. It's all set." Pauline Johnson walked in as Kylie exited. Kylie gave the woman a wide berth and a look that Pauline fortunately missed. "We leave next Friday."

"We leave for where?" Regan asked, surprised to find she was going anywhere, much less with Pauline.

Pauline frowned and gave her head a small shake, as if she couldn't believe her ears. Her lacquered hair refused to move. "Standards training in Elko, of course. You're covering science and I'm covering math."

This was the first Regan had heard of it and she said so.

"Well, I don't know why you haven't. Pete met with me this morning and told me to handle the arrangements." She gave Regan a dubious look, as if she thought Regan was trying to pull a fast one—or worse yet, was kidding her. "We have reservations. Government rate, of course."

"It's not that far." Regan closed the stapler she still held and set it aside. "Why don't we just drive?"

"It's more convenient and less expensive to stay at the hotel than drive both days."

"Government rate?"

"Exactly." Pauline held out a sheath of papers. "These are the materials we need to familiarize ourselves with prior to the training."

Regan took the papers, but didn't look at them. She'd been wondering if Pete would find a way to get back at her for the Taylor incident and now she had her answer. "Do I have any say as to whether I go or not?"

"We have to have a representative from both science and math. I volunteered to represent math," Pauline added importantly.

"But I didn't volunteer to represent science," Regan protested.

Pauline smirked. "No one volunteered from *your* department, so Pete decided to send the person with the least seniority. That's you."

No arguing that.

"I'll be picking up the car from the motor pool the night before, of course. If you'd like, I can pick you up at your house in the morning."

"That would be nice," Regan murmured.

"I'll let you know the time closer to our departure."

And since the departure was almost five days away, Pauline had plenty of time to figure it down to the minute. Regan looked at the stack of freshly copied papers, then back at Pauline. And she'd thought she was detail oriented.

"Thanks, I think."

First, the dessert table and now standards training. No doubt about it—Pete was getting his licks in. Well, Regan would go to standards training with Pauline and she would do her best to get something out of it.

Besides a headache.

THE DAY WAS PERFECT, as early October days tended to be. Warm and golden. Skitters had her ears pricked forward as Will guided her through the waist-high sage.

He rode the mare every day in the late afternoon. As soon as Kylie got off the bus, she demanded to know if the horse was ready for her. So far the answer had been "not yet," but Will was starting to think the day was getting closer. The mare'd been cranky the first few times he'd ridden her, shying and giving the occasional crow hop if she thought she had an excuse, but recently she'd settled a bit.

Kylie'd been spending extra time with the mare lately, grooming and bonding, and Skitters was beginning to show signs of affection toward the kid—so much so, that Will was thinking he'd let Kylie ride this weekend and see how it went.

The sun was warm on his back, the wind cool on his face and Regan Flynn was on his mind. Again. He wasn't paying as much attention as he should have been when a rabbit suddenly darted out of a bush at Skitters's feet. She shied violently and then began some serious bucking.

Will had ridden rodeo for years and he could ride a bronc, but Skitters'd had more recent practice than he had. She went high, flipped her hind legs to the right, twisted her body to the left, then lost her footing as she came down. Will kicked his feet free of the stirrups and managed to dive before she crushed his leg beneath her. He smacked his head pretty good on a big rock. The next thing he knew, the mare was a blur in the distance.

But at least she was headed for the ranch, so he didn't have to try to cut her out of the mustang herd, and because Kylie was in school, she wouldn't worry when Skitters came home without him.

He dusted himself off and tried to convince himself on the walk home that this was an isolated incident, but his gut was telling him differently. The mare had been waiting for him to stop paying attention, then had taken her opportunity.

Skitters was waiting calmly for him in the yard when he got home. She'd broken the reins, but other than that, his gear was unscathed. She let him catch her, as if nothing had happened.

He unsaddled her and was leading her back to her pen when the bus rolled to a stop at the end of the drive and his daughter emerged.

"Not yet," Will said before Kylie could ask her question.

"You sure?"

"I'm sure."

Kylie went to the edge of the corral and Skitters came

over to her, nudging her with her nose. Kylie smiled as she stroked her.

Will watched for a moment, then decided to give Skitters a cautious benefit of the doubt. But he was going to spend a lot more time on her before Kylie got on her back. One more incident like today's and the mare was gone, no matter how much Kylie loved her.

REGAN GATHERED HER newly acquired pile of materials and dumped them into the official State of Nevada educational standards tote bag that each participant of the class had received. She hoped that her substitute had had a better day than she had. Even Pauline was looking slightly cross-eyed from the pedantic blathering of the alleged trainer, but that didn't slow her down from organizing an evening fete.

"We'll meet for dinner at six o'clock," she announced on her way out the door.

"Um, all right," Regan said, but an hour later, when she met Pauline in the hotel lobby after a long, relaxing and well-deserved shower, she found that they were looking at a forty-five minute wait for a dinner table.

"There is some kind of a conference going on," Pauline explained with a frown. "I never dreamed we'd need reservations here."

"Do you want to go somewhere else?" Regan asked, trying to be a team player. "Or maybe we could have a glass of wine here while we wait. I'll buy." She had changed into jeans and a long-sleeved red T-shirt for a casual dinner, but Pauline was still wearing her dress-for-success conference wear. No matter where they went, one of them was going to look out of place, so she decided to let Pauline make the call.

Pauline considered. "Let's have a drink."

A few minutes later they were seated at a small table

in the bar area waiting for their drinks—Picon Punch for Pauline and white wine for Regan.

"I've never had a Picon before," Regan said in the hope of starting a noneducational conversation. Maybe if she got to know Pauline, the woman would ease up a little. Become more human, less like Regan's overly perfect mother. Maybe. It was worth a shot.

"It's a Basque drink," Pauline explained with her customary touch of superiority.

"Are you Basque?"

"No. But I like to absorb the culture of the place I'm in and it's part of Elko's heritage."

Absorbing culture in Elko was a novel idea. Regan kind of liked it.

"How is it?" she asked.

"Interesting. It's a little strong, but interesting."

Pauline was practically sliding out of her seat half an hour and two Picons later. Regan finally convinced the woman to let her help her to her room.

"Yes," Pauline agreed, leaning heavily on Regan's shoulder. "I'm not very hungry anymore." She yawned noisily, bringing her hand up and accidentally popping herself in the nose. "I'm really more tired."

"It's been a long day," Regan agreed. She was glad she wasn't sharing a room with the woman. The suggestion had been made, in order to save the school district a little money, but Regan had shot it down. She'd do her part, but she was not rooming with Pauline.

"I think I'll just stretch out for a minute." Pauline crawled onto the bed on her hands and knees, her pink pencil skirt riding up around her thighs before she collapsed on her stomach. Seconds later she began to snore. Regan tiptoed out of the room, closing the door softly.

Her stomach rumbled. She was hungry and still had a dinner reservation. If she hurried.

Her table was ready. She ordered the special, without looking at the menu, and settled back to wait for her solitary meal. The table was at the edge of the bar area, so she amused herself watching the patrons as she sipped her lemon water.

And then she sat up a little straighter. Standing at the end of the bar was…Will Bishop?

No, it wasn't.

But the guy could have been Will's twin and he appeared to have radar, because he raised his head to look directly at her, catching her midstare. There was no graceful way to look away, so Regan didn't even try. A moment later she wished she had, because the man had pushed away from the bar and started across the room toward her table.

Now you've done it.

Regan pulled in a breath as he came to a stop. "You caught me staring."

He smiled, a carbon copy of Will's. "Well, now that you mention it…"

"I know this sounds lame," Regan bit the edge of her lip, hoping he'd buy her story, which was, after all, true, "but I thought you were someone else."

"Really." He didn't seem all that surprised.

"Are you related to Will Bishop?"

"I'm his brother."

"You'd almost have to be," Regan replied softly. So there were two Bishops. Both attractive, but this one was slightly younger, leaner, more chiseled. He swirled his drink, made no move to leave. Regan let curiosity get the better of her. "You want to sit down?"

"Sure." The pirate's smile came a lot easier to him than it did to Will.

"I'm Regan Flynn." She held out her hand in the automatic gesture of politeness that her mother had engrained in her.

"Brett Bishop." His fingers were warm, work-roughened.

"Are there any more of you? Bishops, I mean?" Regan asked.

"Just Will and me."

"I'm Kylie's teacher." She took a sip of water, then set the glass on the table, keeping hold of the stem. "Are you a horse trainer, too?"

"No. I'm a roving cowhand."

"I didn't know there still was such a thing."

"I spent the last ten years managing a ranch in Montana, but when the owner died the kids wanted to cash in the real estate, so I was out of work for a while. When I got a job offer here, I took it."

Regan tilted the glass, wishing the waitress would come and refill it, so she'd have something to do while she talked. For some reason, talking to Brett Bishop made her feel slightly unsettled. "Have you been here long?"

"A month or so."

"It's nice you could get a job closer to your family."

"Yeah." There was subtle irony in his voice.

All right. We'll leave the family issue alone.

"I moved to Wesley from Las Vegas," Regan said.

"That's a bit of a change."

"A good change." She smiled and let go of the glass, settling both hands in her lap.

"Not a big-city girl?"

"Born and raised there. But no. I'm not." And she hadn't realized the extent to which she was not a big-city girl until she'd moved to the relative peace and quiet of Wesley.

"Good for you." He rattled the ice in his glass, then

drained the last few amber drops. "Would you like a drink?"

Regan thought of Pauline and shook her head. "I'm waiting for my dinner." And she wanted to keep her wits about her, here with this guy who was so much like Will, yet wasn't Will.

"So what are you doing in Elko on a school night?"

"I'm taking a two-day class."

"I figured you probably weren't a pipe fitter." He nodded toward the raucous group shoving tables together at the opposite end of the dining room.

Regan smiled. "No. I bend young minds."

"Hi." The waitress set Regan's salad in front of her, then refilled her water glass. "You want to order?" she asked Brett.

He shook his head. "I'm good." The waitress smiled and moved to the next table. "Do you know Will well?" he asked as Regan mixed the dressing into her salad.

"I didn't know he had a brother," she pointed out.

"Well, we haven't seen each other in a while."

"You didn't come home much when you were in Montana?"

"No," he replied softly.

She smiled politely and then focused on her salad, wondering what was going on between the two brothers. Definitely a chasm there and she wondered if it was mutual or one-sided.

"So you're a teacher."

She glanced up. "Yes. And you're a cowboy."

"Roving cowhand."

"Ten years in one place doesn't qualify as roving."

"I was roving at heart." He idly tilted his glass, clinking the cubes against the side. "What made you go into teaching?"

"My mother didn't want me to," Regan replied, only half joking.

"What did your mother want you to do?"

"Oh, something high profile. Doctor, lawyer, CEO."

"What does your mother do?"

"She's a CEO."

Regan's meal arrived. She expected Brett to leave, but he didn't. They talked for almost half an hour while Regan ate. He asked her questions about her job, how she liked it, what kind of student his niece was, whether there was much of a difference between urban kids and rural kids. He laughed, disbelievingly, when she told him that Pete was her boss.

"I thought he'd be polishing trophies for the rest of his life."

"Well, we can all hope he goes back to it." Regan set her napkin on the table. "I need to get to bed, so I don't sleep through class tomorrow."

"Yeah, and I need to go and catch up with my friends." Brett got to his feet. He glanced down for a moment, frowning as though making a decision, then he looked back up at her. "I was wondering…if you're ever back in Elko, maybe we could have dinner or something. A real dinner. You know, where we both eat?"

"You had your chance," Regan pointed out with a smile.

"I didn't realize how much I'd enjoy the company," he replied sincerely.

Regan felt her color rise a little, even though she knew it was a line. Brett was obviously much more practiced with lines than his brother was. "Do you ever make it to Wesley?" She'd rather be on her home turf if she did see him again.

Again the subtle blanking of his expression. "Not often."

"I don't know if I'll be coming back to Elko anytime soon. It could be a while."

"Well, if I ever do get to Wesley, can I call you?"

Regan agreed and wrote her number on a napkin. Brett folded it into his pocket and buttoned the flap. As he walked away, Regan figured that was that. If he didn't forget her as soon as she was out of sight, he'd almost certainly wash that napkin the next time he did laundry.

CHAPTER SEVEN

ALTHOUGH WILL HAD great faith in his daughter's abilities, he would have bet on substitute teacher Mary Burkey in a fair fight. And he would have bet wrong.

The first details were sketchy, but Will received an invitation by telephone to discuss the details at greater length with Pete Domingo, ASAP.

He wiped the corral dust off his face, refrained from checking for new gray hairs and took off for the school. Kylie'd been acting differently lately. She'd been quieter, more introspective and, to tell the truth, part of him was almost glad she was acting like her old self again.

Will entered Pete's office with his hat in his hand, as a token gesture of respect. A principal was a principal. Will was going to be polite and open-minded as long as both parties observed the rules.

There'd been changes in the office since the previous time he'd visited. The place was definitely Pete's, now. An ornate nameplate stood on the desk and pictures of Pete's winning teams hung on the walls. There was even a photo of Pete himself in his high school baseball uniform circa the early nineties.

"Where's Kylie?"

Will had expected to see her sitting on the uncomfortable straight-back chair next to the wall where he himself had sat a time or two while waiting for someone to come and pick him up—when someone *could* be found to pick him up.

"Washing desks." Pete leaned back in his chair. He was holding a spring-loaded hand-strengthening device, which he squeezed and released, squeezed and released.

Will watched for a few seconds, allowing the little general his wordless power play, before he said, "What's up, Pete?"

Pete leaned forward. "Your daughter is insubordinate."

Will took a wild guess. "She tried to take advantage of the sub?"

"Mrs. Burkey reported her for a disturbance in the hall, but that's not why you're here today." He leaned back and began to squeeze his athletic gizmo again.

Will waited. This time he'd let Pete break the silence. He counted the repetitions, wondering if Pete would end on a multiple of five. Gym teachers loved multiples of five. Fifteen push-ups. Thirty sit-ups.

Ten squeezes later, Pete spoke. "I will not tolerate disrespect."

"Neither will I. Kylie knows better." Will tapped the brim of his ball cap on his knee. "Out of curiosity, how do *you* treat *her?*"

"Like any other student."

"What about the squid incident, Pete? You threatened her."

When Will had found out about it, he had seriously considered challenging Pete on the issue, but then he'd decided that since Pete was temporary, it wasn't worth it. Now that Pete was looking less temporary, Will was rethinking things. "Did you threaten all the students?"

"She did it."

"She did not."

"How do you know?"

"I asked her."

Pete sneered. "And you believed her."

"Yes." Will could see Pete thought that was part of the problem and it ticked him off. "She's never lied to me."

"Never?"

By omission maybe, but never directly—and Will had asked her point-blank about the squid. "What did my daughter do to you?"

"She was openly rude—in front of other people. I can't have that."

"I agree, Pete. She knows better than to disrespect adults." But he had a strong feeling that this adult must have done something to provoke her. "Would you mind telling me what she said?"

Pete waved the hand that held the exercise device. "That isn't important. What is important is that she receives a consequence for her behavior."

Will disagreed. He wanted to know what she said, so he could deal with it, but he decided for Kylie's sake not to press matters. He had other ways of finding out what was said. As he'd told Pete, Kylie had never lied in response to a direct question and she was about to be on the receiving end of some very direct questions.

"What do you suggest?"

"Working detention. After school. One week."

Will had a feeling Pete wasn't going to kick her out of school, because then he'd have to share whatever it was Kylie had said that so infuriated him.

"All right."

"I have an appointment in ten minutes, so I'll speak to her myself in the morning. You'll find Kylie with Mrs. Burkey."

"I'm sorry about this, Will," the substitute teacher said a few minutes later. They'd left Kylie washing desks in another classroom. "I had to report her because of the ruckus in the hall. I hadn't expected Pete to come down so hard."

"I think it has something to do with another incident."

"Well, she wasn't the only one involved. She was with that friend of hers, Mark, and that Taylor kid said something about Mark's weight—he is a bit pudgy, you know." Will was glad the school was empty. He was certain that Mark didn't want everyone to hear about his pudginess, and when Mary spoke in her normal voice, just about everyone heard.

"Anyway," she continued, "there was a bit of a tussle. Mark actually got a pretty good swing in at the kid before I broke it up. I marched everyone involved to the office, where Pete took over."

"Then what?"

"He gave everyone a good talking to, then when they were on their way out, Pete told Mark that he could stand to lose a few pounds—that there was no excuse for being heavy at his age. That was when Kylie said it."

"What did Kylie say?"

Mary looked both directions and leaned closer. "She told Pete that he shouldn't be picking on kids who were heavy, when he was such a lard ass himself."

Will almost choked.

"All of our jaws just dropped," Mary said, laughing merrily at the memory, "and then Mrs. Serrano, bless her heart, saved Kylie's life. She bustled in there, and while Pete was still doing his impression of a carp out of water, she took Kylie by the arm and hauled her out, saying, 'Well, I'll just get Kylie started washing desks to keep her busy, while you call her father.' That's when I called you. Good thing you got here fast."

"Thanks, Mary."

"Lard ass," she chuckled. "Where'd she pick up such a term?"

"I don't know," Will muttered as he started down the hall, thinking it was time to give his fat, lazy stud horse a different name.

KYLIE MISSED THE first of Regan's jumping lessons because she was grounded. Realistically, Will knew Pete had gotten what he deserved for picking on a kid like Mark, but Kylie could not spend her life disrespecting authority, even if she was standing up for someone else. Will wasn't doing her any favors condoning behavior that would only get her into more trouble.

In other words, Kylie needed to learn to choose her battles.

Father and daughter spent a mutually miserable Saturday afternoon cleaning out the tack shed during the time that Kylie should have been learning the basics of riding with an English saddle and Will should have been working with a horse. And Kylie had been quiet again. Not pouting quiet, preoccupied quiet. She'd been that way for more than a week and Will was starting to get concerned. Was this a passing stage or was it something he should be dealing with?

As soon as they were finished, Will sent Kylie in to do her homework and the dishes in whichever order she chose, while he saddled Skitters. He tossed a flake of hay into the feeder for Laredo—formerly Lard Ass—as he went by, then mounted and headed around the loop in the reverse direction to the one Regan usually rode. She rode on a pretty regimented schedule and by his calculations she should be coming around the far bend in a matter of minutes.

He was not disappointed.

"Hi," Regan said as she brought Toffee to a halt a few yards away from Skitters. "Is that Kylie's new horse?" Will nodded. "She's pretty."

"Yeah," Will agreed, but he wasn't thinking of Skitters. He turned the mare so she was pointing in the same direction as the gelding.

"What are you doing out so late?" Regan asked as she nudged her horse forward and the two of them started riding side by side.

"I was helping my kid do penance and it put me behind on my schedule."

"We missed her at jumping class. I hear she made a comment on Pete's physique while I was in Elko."

"Yes, and it didn't go over well. She'll be apologizing to everyone involved on Monday."

Regan laughed. "Well, she doesn't need to apologize to Mary or Mrs. Serrano. They're both highly amused."

Will sucked in a long breath. "Yeah." He paused for a moment, then dived into the question he'd been hoping to ask Regan. "I was wondering. Lately, there's been something going on with Kylie. Something other than being in trouble with Pete. She's been quiet. Thoughtful. I guess I was wondering if you had any clues as to what's going on, because I sure don't." Which was hard to admit.

"She and Sadie have been having some ups and downs over the past week or two." She glanced over at him. "Were you aware?"

No. "Now that you mention it, there haven't been as many phone calls as before."

"Sadie has a crush on a boy and I don't think she and Kylie are communicating on the same plane."

"A crush?" Will let out a snort. "Her parents are going to love that."

"I don't think she's had any success yet. The boy is more interested in football than girls right now."

"I am not looking forward to the boy thing."

"No father ever does."

"How'd your father handle it?"

"From a great distance."

Will sent her a sidelong glance and Regan cleared her throat. "My father didn't have anything to do with my childhood, except for paying for my riding lessons and leasing my horse." Guilt money, her mother had always said. Regan knew she was probably correct. He'd also paid for the modeling and acting lessons that Claire had wanted. Claire had eventually grown tired of acting, but Regan had ridden right up until the time she'd had to choose between horse expenses and college expenses. Her mother had not yet hit the big time and money had been tight in those days.

"I think he got his money's worth," Will said.

"Thanks."

She focused straight ahead.

"How was the Elko class?"

"Not a lot of fun. But there was one interesting thing."

"What's that?"

"I met your brother."

Will's heart jumped, but he managed to ask offhandedly, "Did someone introduce you?"

"We ran into each other in the hotel restaurant. He was waiting for friends and I thought he was you."

Will was still waiting for the day when he could hear mention of his brother and not feel a knee-jerk reaction of panic. Tentatively, he'd come to the decision that Brett really was in the area only for a job. It made sense. Jobs in ranch management were rare and Brett would have to take one wherever he could. And he'd made no move to get in contact.

"We talked for a while."

Will nodded, because he couldn't think of a reasonable response. Somehow, *I hope he keeps the hell away from here* didn't seem appropriate for casual conversation.

"He seemed like an okay guy."

"He is." Except in the ways that counted. Such as loyalty.

"Are you going to the Harvest Dance?" Mercifully, Regan changed the subject.

"We'll go if Kylie manages not to get herself grounded again. Are you going?"

"I'm working at the dessert table. I'll be serving pie for an hour and a half."

"You'll be busy."

She tilted her head curiously. "Why?"

"They only serve homemade pies and a lot of people go all out in terms of their pie consumption. Kind of a competition. Some people wait all year just to sample those pies."

Regan grinned. "How folksy."

"You'll certainly think it's folksy after you've spent a good hour shoveling pie onto plates." He pulled Skitters to a stop as they reached his driveway. "Thanks for letting me know about Sadie and Kylie. It helps."

She smiled. The breeze tousled the layers of her hair, giving her a just-tumbled-out-of-bed look that stirred thoughts Will knew he probably shouldn't have. But there was no denying the fact he was thinking them. And he was beginning to wish he could do something about them.

ZACH TAYLOR HAD drawn his final line in the sand. He'd fallen behind in his assignments again and Regan, fed up with his assumption that he was bulletproof, not only put zeroes into the computer, but called the athletic director and told him why Zach was ineligible. And the man backed her up. Two days later, Wesley lost its first regional football championship in eight years. Zach Taylor, starting quarterback, had not played.

Regan found herself in the unusual position of being in deep trouble with her boss, even as she approached folk-hero status with her coworkers.

"No one has ever taken on the Taylors successfully before," Karlene told her, with a look of awe, the morning after the game. "Way to go. Maybe he'll behave now, even if it is kind of a shame about the game."

Regan had not intended to cause the football team to lose. In fact, she didn't think she had. It wasn't her fault the second-string quarterback had been injured on the first play. Or that Zach was lazy and had a sense of entitlement. But Pete seemed to think so.

He didn't say anything to Regan. Not one word. But he glowered coldly whenever she was near. The reason was obvious. Zach's uncle was on the school board and had a lot of clout. The school board had the power to hire Pete. Pete had failed in his mission to keep Zach eligible. The team had lost.

Regan couldn't understand why no one on the board could see that Zach could have prevented all this simply by following through with his responsibilities. Her fellow teachers seemed to see it plain as day.

"Because they need a scapegoat and a new teacher is a lot easier to blame than a star athlete or a veteran athletic director," Jared told her over lunch.

Both Tanya and Karlene had assured her the issue would blow over and the district would be better because of it.

Regan just hoped she'd be there long enough to see the improvement.

THE HARVEST DANCE was a big event—big enough that Will made certain Kylie wasn't grounded for it. She put her horse away early that day, got into her newest jeans, pulled her hair back into a ponytail and put a glittery doo-dad over the elastic. Will also wore new jeans, since they were the only ones he owned with no work-related wear and tear; a white cowboy shirt and his good belt with the trophy buckle.

They got there early and Kylie immediately started searching the crowd, as did Will. He told himself he was looking for Trev, but really he was looking for Regan. He thought maybe he'd go and give her a hand setting up the dessert table, when Kylie burst out with an incredulous, "Whoa."

At the entry, a pretty girl with long blond curls had just paused in the doorway.

"I don't believe it," Kylie muttered.

Neither did Will. The pretty girl was Sadie, wearing makeup, a short dress and heels. She looked about three years older than the last time he'd seen her. His daughter was staring opened mouthed at her friend.

"She didn't *tell* me," Kylie finally growled, her gaze following Sadie as she headed across the room to a group of eighth graders. The cool group.

"Maybe she didn't think it mattered."

Kylie sent him a look that said it mattered very much, then brushed past him, walking out of the gym.

Will followed, emerging into the hall in time to see his daughter disappear into the girls' restroom. He let out a frustrated breath. What now?

He had no idea how serious this was, but Kylie was definitely pissed.

He waited in the hall, trying to look nonchalant. He nodded at a couple of women as they emerged from the ladies' room. Neither looked concerned in any way.

Okay, that probably meant she was all right. Maybe he should just leave her alone.

If this was any other kind of emotional situation—a lost dog, a failed test, a white ribbon in a horse show—he would let her work it out and be available when she was ready to talk. But this was her best friend and it was new territory for both of them.

He needed advice.

Feeling a little desperate, he headed back into the gym and straight for Regan, the one person who might have an inkling about handling girl dynamics who wouldn't gossip about it with everyone in the county.

"I think I have a situation on my hands."

"I saw." She untied the official dessert-table apron she'd been wearing over her jeans and sparkly green top. "Where'd she go?"

"Ladies' room."

"You want me to check on her?"

Will nodded. "She was pretty mad. I don't want her heading home on foot or anything."

"Would she do that?"

"This is Kylie we're talking about."

Regan handed Will the apron and headed for the restroom.

KYLIE'S FACE WAS RED, but if she'd been crying she'd managed to shut off the waterworks before Regan entered the washroom.

Regan made no pretense as to why she was there. "Your dad is worried about you."

"Tell him I'll be out in a minute."

"He's afraid you might take off."

"Tell him not to worry."

"Kylie…" Regan touched her shoulder.

"I won't take off."

"Maybe you should talk to…"

"I'm not talking to her."

"I guess I don't blame you." Kylie glanced up, suspicious of empathy from a teacher and obviously wondering if this was some kind of trick. "But do you honestly think she did this to hurt you?"

"It doesn't matter, because she did. We've always told each other everything."

"There are other kids out there to be friends with, you know." Even as she said it, Regan knew it was lame advice. It didn't matter how many kids were out there if your best friend had just betrayed you.

Kylie gave a sullen nod.

A group of girls came giggling in and Regan turned away to the sink and started the water running. Kylie walked out as soon as Regan's hands were wet. Regan reached for a towel and followed, catching site of Kylie going back into the gym as she stepped into the hall.

Okay, at least the kid hadn't started walking home.

Regan returned to her post and tied on the apron Will had left folded over a chair. A few minutes later he casually made his way back to the dessert table.

"How is she?" he asked.

"Mad. Confused." Regan carefully peeled plastic wrap off the top of a pumpkin pie beautifully decorated with pastry leaves.

"I never saw this coming."

"Neither did Kylie. That's the problem."

"Excuse me…" Mrs. Serrano edged by the two of them to get some disposable coffee cups. "You might want to get out of here while you can, Will."

"Sure thing." He smiled politely at Mrs. Serrano and

then leaned close enough to Regan that she could smell the spicy scent of his aftershave. "Thanks."

"Anytime." She fumbled with the latch on an old-fashioned metal pie carrier and Will automatically reached over to snap it open for her.

"Maybe I'll see you later."

"Maybe."

A line of people began to form at the dessert table, despite Mrs. Serrano's attempts to shoo them away until the coffee was ready. For the next hour and a half Regan wasn't aware of much of anything other than hungry people wanting to buy dessert.

By the time Tanya came to take her place, Regan was more than ready to hand over the pie server and apron. "Have fun," she murmured to Tanya, who grinned.

"The second shift is never as bad as the first."

"I love being the newcomer," Regan said with a grimace, but the truth was she didn't really mind.

Pete was holding court nearby, far enough away from the speakers and the dance floor that he could talk. From the number of mock basketball shots he took as he talked, Regan assumed he was reliving some championship game. The men surrounding him seemed fascinated by his story.

Kylie sat in the same general area, with Mark and a few other kids. Another girl joined them as Regan watched and Kylie said something to her that made her laugh. They all looked at Sadie, who was standing close to her crush and his friends, then they looked at each other, before laughing again. Sadie pretended not to notice, but Regan saw her back stiffen at the sound of Kylie's laughter.

Will was leaning against the wall several yards away, holding a glass of cider and looking as if he needed something stronger, watching his kid pretend not to be miserable. Regan went over to him.

"How're you doing?"

"I'm foreseeing a long adolescence ahead of me."

"It's only another five or six years."

Will made a face. "My gut instinct is to haul her away from all this right now."

"And protect her from everything that might hurt her?"

He nodded. "And maybe buy her a new horse, to make it all better."

"It would be nice if it was that easy."

"Hi, Miss Flynn." A seventh-grade boy suddenly appeared next to Regan, almost as if he'd been shoved, which Regan strongly suspected was the case. "You wanna dance?" he squeaked.

A group of boys were huddled nearby, nudging each other as they watched their friend.

"I'd love to," she told the kid with a straight face, letting her shoulders slump with disappointment, "but I don't two-step."

"Thanks, anyway!" The kid made his escape as his friends collapsed into fits of laughter. Will grinned at her.

"Welcome to my world," Regan said wearily.

"The next dance isn't a two-step. They play a slow one every fourth song. Like clockwork." Sure enough, a soulful country ballad came through the speakers a moment later.

"Thank you for not pointing that out to Romeo." Regan said dryly, then her eyes widened as she saw Pete heading toward her. "What now?" she muttered.

"Come on," Will said, gesturing to the floor. He held out a hand and Regan took it, liking the way it felt when his warm fingers closed around hers and experiencing a surge of satisfaction at the look on Pete's face as she made it onto the dance floor before he reached her.

"Thank you," she said, setting a light hand on Will's shoulder.

"I was going to ask you anyway," he said.

"Were you?" She looked up at him, surprised.

He shrugged. "I thought I might ease out of monk status just a little."

Regan smiled. "You'll probably want to take it slow, so you don't hurt yourself."

He held her with a chaperone-approved space between them. "I'm setting a good example." He said with a smile in his eyes. "This is the way I expect Kylie to dance when the bad days come and boys start asking her out."

"She's a very pretty girl, Will. It may not be too long."

"Her mom was pretty, too."

It was the first time Will had ever mentioned Kylie's mother and Regan found that she really didn't like it much. She wondered what their relationship was now, Will and Kylie's mom.

"Does Kylie have contact with her mom?"

"No." It was quite clear that was all that was going to be said on the matter, but Will pulled her just a little closer, as if to make up for the abrupt answer. Regan's hand tightened on his shoulder. It'd been a while since she'd touched anyone so rock solid. It'd been a while since she'd felt a deep physical attraction like this—and she was torn as to how to respond. She knew what she *should* do. And she knew what she'd promised herself she'd do. She just didn't know what she was going to do.

It's only a dance. With an attractive man. You swore off unhealthy relationships, not men. As long as you keep it light, as long as everyone knows what's what, there was no danger.

Yeah, and there's this bridge for sale in Brooklyn.

Will gestured toward his daughter with a nod of his head. Kylie was looking seriously unhappy.

"Any words of advice on how to handle a girl whose

best friend has just abandoned her?" he asked softly. She wondered if he was aware of the fact that the chaperone-approved distance was slowly disappearing, that her thighs were now touching his. She didn't know how he couldn't be aware of it.

"Patience. It'll work out. The thing is, Kylie honestly doesn't get it. She doesn't understand why Sadie has suddenly changed on her."

"I'm glad she doesn't get it."

"She will soon enough."

"I know." He pulled her closer still and they danced without talking. Karlene and Jared-the-sub were also dancing nearby and there was definitely no chaperone-approved distance between them. Karlene's brown curls rested against Jared's shoulder and his arm was firmly clamped around her back. Regan closed her eyes, forgot about chaperones and enjoyed the rest of her dance.

When the music wound to an end, Regan eased herself away from Will. It was funny how safe she'd felt in his arms, as if nothing in the world could touch her. Speaking of which, Pete was trolling the edge of the crowd. He was watching her surreptitiously. But why?

"Thanks for the dance, Will." She nodded in Pete's direction. "I think I'll head home now, before my boss has a chance to ruin my evening."

"I'll walk you to your car. You know, run interference, just in case."

"Thanks."

They wound through the crowd to the coat room. Regan found her jacket and then followed Will out of the gym, watching for Pete the entire way.

The breeze lifted her bangs as Will held the door and she stepped out into the much cooler night air, inhaling deeply. A few more people tumbled out behind them, laughing.

She felt like laughing herself. It was good to escape.

"What do you think he wanted?"

"I have no idea. I worked my shift. I didn't make any athletes ineligible. I left the squid at home."

Actually, Regan did have an idea. He'd been talking to Zach's father earlier and she had a feeling that'd had something to do with his interest in her. But she was surprised he was approaching her in public. Usually, he was sneakier.

Regan was parked around the corner of the building in her usual parking spot. It was darker there. The Vegasite in her was instinctively on the alert and she was glad Will was with her, even if she was only in sleepy Wesley. He was walking close beside her—close enough that their shoulders bumped companionably every now and then, but the feeling Regan was getting didn't exactly belong in the companion category. In fact, it was pretty much at the opposite end of the spectrum.

When they reached her car she unlocked it, but she didn't open the door right away. Instead, she turned and leaned back against it, looking up at Will, knowing she was probably going to regret her decision, but really wanting to see how this played out. She had a feeling that Will was venturing into uncharted territory with her and that he was as curious and conflicted about it as she was. He confirmed the suspicion a second later when he moved so close that she had to tilt her head back to look up at him.

Her eyes had adjusted to the darkness and she could see the intensity of his expression as his hands settled gently on her shoulders. And once again their thighs were touching.

"I haven't danced in a long time."

"It's that monk thing," she said softly, acutely aware of the pressure of his fingers as they stroked the curve of her neck and ran through her hair. "They don't dance much."

"They don't kiss people good-night, either."

"How long's it been for that?" she asked, trying for the casualness she kept telling herself she should be feeling. That's all this was—the causal flirtation of two lonely people.

"Long enough," he said, as he lowered his lips to hers.

His mouth was warm and firm. Inviting. Tantalizing. He didn't pull her nearer, but from the way he deepened the kiss, she suspected it had been a while since he'd kissed someone good-night. And from her response, he was probably thinking the same thing.

A loud hoot of laughter sounded nearby at about the time Regan thought her knees were going to buckle, followed by a car horn, bringing them back to earth.

Regan stepped back, putting some space between them, pressing her fingers against the cool metal of her car door so she wouldn't be tempted to wrap them back around Will.

"I guess I'll be going." Her voice was uncharacteristically husky.

"Yeah." So was his. He pushed his thumbs through his belt loops. "I'd better get back and collect my kid."

She nodded, but neither of them moved.

"I probably shouldn't have done that."

"It was just a kiss, Will." At least that was all it should have been. She couldn't figure out why it felt like so much more. Why everything with Will felt like so much more.

"I guess I was thinking more along the lines of, now that I've done it once, I'll want to do it again."

"And you can't?" Regan asked softly, almost hopefully.

"I want life to be stable for Kylie, so it's not so much that I can't, but rather that I need to proceed with caution."

Regan glanced down for a moment, choosing her words before she looked back up. "I have to tell you, Will, the last thing I'm looking for is anything resembling a relationship, so I think it's a good thing this happened."

"A good thing?" She sensed his frown. "How's that?"

"We were both obviously wondering what this would be like, with each other. Now we know and now we can move on." She sounded like a teacher conducting a lesson. Oh, well. Whatever it took.

"Just like that?"

She shrugged with an apparent nonchalance that she was far from actually feeling. "Just like that."

She had a feeling she'd just hit his male ego pretty hard, but after that kiss—which had been about a hundred times hotter than she'd expected—she wasn't taking any chances.

Will took a step backward. "You're right. Good night, Regan. I'll see you around." He started back toward the gym, leaving Regan wondering whether she'd just dodged a bullet or been hit by one.

CHAPTER EIGHT

ON SATURDAY, REGAN rode Toffee cross-country, making a big loop behind Will's place and several other ranches. She'd been riding for almost an hour when she came to a fence. She followed it for at least a mile before deciding she wasn't going to find a gate and turned back. Toffee immediately pricked his ears and raised his head. A horse and a small rider topped the hill she'd just come down and headed directly toward them.

It was Kylie on an older sorrel gelding. Even though the girl seemed surprised to see her, Regan had an idea that the meeting was not quite as spontaneous as Kylie was pretending.

"Is there a gate in this fence?" Regan asked, pushing windblown hair out of her face. Kylie was wearing a blue ball cap that Regan had seen Will wearing a few days earlier. It was pulled low over Kylie's eyes, keeping her hair from whipping around her cheeks the way Regan's was.

"Not for a long way, but if you follow the fence far enough, you'll be close to the mustang hole."

"The mustang hole?" Somehow that sounded wrong.

"The place where the mustangs water."

"As in wild horses?"

"Mmm, hmm." The girl seemed pleased that Regan was impressed.

"How far?"

Kylie squinted her eyes. "About half an hour."

"I've never seen a mustang in the wild."

"They're neat and a lot of them are pretty but," the girl wrinkled her nose, "some of them are kind of ugly up close. Big heads and skinny necks. Not everybody likes them, but I do."

"I think I'd like them, too."

"You wanna see if they're around?"

Regan thought about the history tests she had to grade. "Yes. That sounds like fun." And she was still wondering how accidental the meeting with Kylie was. She wondered if the girl wanted to talk.

"How's your new horse?" she asked after almost twenty-five minutes of silent riding. During that time they had crossed two low hills separated by half-mile-wide valleys, each with its own dry streambed. If Kylie had something to say, she was taking her time getting to it.

"Dad doesn't think she's trustworthy yet, but he's making progress. She bucked him off one day and he wants to make sure she's done with that before I get on."

"Has Sadie seen her yet?" Regan asked as she zipped her jacket the rest of the way up to her chin. The wind was getting stronger and the sky was clouding up.

"Who?" Kylie asked coolly.

"Is that the way it is?"

"It's the way it is now."

"Think it'll be that way forever?"

"Maybe." Kylie adjusted her ball cap as a gust of wind lifted the brim, keeping her attention firmly ahead of her as she rode.

"People grow up at different speeds, Kylie."

"I know all about that. We had that stupid video at school."

"I mean, some people like to stay kids longer than others and there's nothing wrong with that. If you're not ready to put on a party dress and hang out with boys, then fine."

"Who said I wasn't?"

"Are you?"

Kylie snorted through her nose.

"When you're ready, you're ready. Sadie feels ready. Maybe you don't. But one of these days you'll be at the same place again—for a while, anyway."

"What do you mean?"

Regan smiled. "I mean maybe you'll be ready to do some other things before Sadie, then she'll wonder what's up with you."

Kylie smiled a little, but it faded fast.

"You just might have to be patient with her for a while."

"I'll try." Her mouth tightened for a moment and then she said, "There's something else."

"Yes?"

"I think my Dad might kind of like you."

"What?" Regan unconsciously tightened the reins and Toffee bobbed his head in response. She let them slide back through her fingers a few inches.

"He kind of likes you. You know. As in, *likes you*." She spoke slowly, enunciating carefully, just in case Regan didn't get her drift.

"Um…"

"And I don't think that's a good idea."

"Oy," Regan muttered in a low voice.

Kylie pulled her horse to a stop at the top of the hill they'd been climbing. "He's been hurt before, you know."

Regan didn't know and she didn't want details from a kid. "Don't worry about me and your dad, Kylie. If he likes me, it's as a friend."

"You guys were looking friendly at the dance."

"Lots of people were looking friendly at the dance. It was a dance."

"My dad never dances much. He just goes to talk."

"And that's what we did. We talked while we danced." Except maybe at the end, when she'd let her imagination wander as she felt his hard body pressed up against hers. "Your dad and I are friends. That's all." Because she, for one, was not going to let the relationship move beyond that. For the first time in a long time, she was feeling at peace. In control. She wasn't going to jeopardize that feeling. Not even for a hot man.

Kylie regarded her for a moment, trying to decide whether Regan was being honest or just brushing her off. Regan could see the girl was on the edge of being convinced. She was about to reiterate her point when Kylie held up a hand, cutting her off.

"Look." She pointed to the bottom of the next valley. There, walking in a bunch through the grass, was a herd of fifteen or twenty horses.

The lead horse stopped suddenly and perked its ears, staring at the two strange horses on the horizon. For a long time the herd stayed stock-still, noses in the air, studying the riders and their mounts across the half mile of sage that separated them.

Toffee caught the scent. He put his head up and whinnied. The lead horse called back.

The herd went on alert and then the lead mare suddenly spun and ran. The herd followed and Regan had to fight to control Toffee, who had begun to dance.

"We should go," Regan said, shortening her reins even more.

"Yeah." Kylie turned her placid gelding and Regan managed to spin Toffee around.

"He probably wants to race them. Have you ever let him just run?"

"Not yet."

"I bet he's fast."

"Yes," Regan said through clenched teeth, fighting the reins until Toffee finally settled and started walking, "but I don't want to find out how fast he is today."

Kylie sighed and urged her own horse forward. "Boy, I would."

As the fall livestock gathers were completed, it seemed that a few more cattle were missing than usual. Strays were common, but strays concentrated in a certain area were out of the ordinary. Mountain lions and accidents took their toll, but when one of Will's neighbors ended up missing fifteen head, Will started to wonder if something was up.

There'd been a case of a kid stealing newborn calves early last spring. With beef prices up and a calf being easy to toss into a truck, Will understood the temptation. But that young thief had been caught and loading full-grown cows required a little more expertise than maneuvering a calf into a truck.

Will decided to take a wait-and-see approach and Trev agreed. There wasn't much else they could do except keep an eye out for unusual activity, which wasn't easy in a part of Nevada where there were plenty of cows and not a lot of witnesses.

"Helping with the Renshaw auction?" Will asked. Trev was pushing his chair back from the kitchen table. He'd stopped by to drop off some paperwork, then had stayed so long talking shop that Will knew he'd be working late that afternoon to make up the lost time.

"I'm shipping cattle that day." Trev set his empty cup in

the old enameled sink. "But I'll be there when I'm done. I'm being sold."

"Me, too." Will was glad to do it. The Renshaws were nice people and it looked like this fund-raiser might help them finally get out from under their medical bills.

WILL BROUGHT KYLIE to her first jumping lesson on the day of Regan's first professional evaluation. She was not in the best of moods. She had a feeling that Pete had been waiting for the "proper" moment for his drop-in visit, and sure enough, he turned up during a lab that wasn't going well. One of her students had managed to spill vinegar all over Regan's new skirt and she'd looked up to see Pete smiling. Malignantly.

She'd smiled back, then helped the kid wipe the floor— just before the demonstration flask got knocked off the podium and shattered on the floor. Not a good day. Pete had loved every minute of it. He wrote so fast that Regan was pretty certain he'd have to ice his wrist that night.

But in spite of the stress of the school day, in spite of the low-grade headache building between her temples, when Regan saw Will enter the arena wearing his canvas jacket and those old blue jeans that hugged his hips and legs just right, her pulse jumped.

"It was just a kiss," she muttered to herself.

A kiss that she'd dreamed about.

Will started to leave after getting Kylie mounted, but Madison ambushed him—ignoring Regan's telepathic plea to just let him go—and he ended up staying for the entire session, leaning against the arena fence, watching, with Madison at his side.

Regan focused on her class, as she led her six students through a series of balancing exercises and then over low jumps, calling instructions and corrections. But she was

acutely aware of the man by the fence, which was not helping her mood one iota.

For the most part, Will kept his eyes on his daughter—
who was a natural at jumping—even when Madison was
making a concerted effort to talk his ear off. Sometimes
he smiled a little, but it seemed that whenever he did, his
eyes invariably strayed to Regan and then the smile disappeared.

When the class was over, Regan decided she was going
to face the situation with Will head-on and get it over with
so things could settle. She'd liked their old relationship and
she wanted it back.

She found Will sitting on the fender of his trailer, waiting for Kylie to finish cooling her horse.

"Hi."

"Hi," he echoed. He looked at her cautiously, maybe
wondering if she was going to hammer his ego again.

She began by sidestepping the real issue. "I was wondering if Kylie had a peppier horse that she might be able to
bring?" Kylie might be a natural, but the horse she was riding was not. He'd clipped his feet on even the lowest jumps.

"I thought we'd start with her old standby gelding, but,
yeah, we'll bring something with more pep next time." He
spoke politely, his expression distant.

Regan shoved her hands down into her pockets. "I also
hope that what happened the other night isn't going to affect us."

"I think you made it clear that it was just a matter of
curiosity."

"That's not exactly what I meant."

"Well, maybe…"

Kylie came around the trailer just then, leading her
horse. She scowled when she saw Will and Regan together,

but her voice was polite as she said, "Good lesson, Miss Flynn."

She moved her gelding directly in between Regan and Will and tied him to a metal loop on the trailer. "Dad, we need to take the saddle back to Madison. She has to keep them here, because she has another class using them."

"I'll take it over while you load." He met Regan's gaze over the horse's back as Kylie undid the girth, then he pulled off the saddle and walked toward the arena office.

And that was apparently the way they were going to leave matters. Not quite settled—exactly the way Regan hated things.

"See ya, Miss Flynn," Kylie said in a flat voice, before getting into the truck.

Regan pulled her keys out of her pocket and walked around the trailer to her car. As she was unlocking her door, Will walked over. He checked to make certain he was out of his daughter's field of vision before turning back to Regan.

"Maybe you can tell me what you did mean the other night?"

"I meant that I like being friends and I'd like to stay friends."

"Me, too."

"And to be truthful, that kiss was a lot more than I expected—for friends."

"Not just a kiss, then?"

Her composure took a dip as he focused momentarily on her mouth before letting his gaze travel slowly up to her eyes in a way that surprised her. She forced herself to rally, to remember her purpose.

"No. But I wanted it to be just a kiss and I was annoyed with myself for letting things go too far."

"Why did you let things go too far?" he asked.

She hesitated for a beat, then her mouth twisted wryly. "Because I was curious. Why'd *you* let it go that far?"

He grinned back and the tension between them began to dissipate. "I guess I was curious, too."

"Gee, where have I heard that?" She bit the edge of her lip. "So what do you think now?

"I think I'd like to do it again, just like I said."

"But," Regan said, with a touch of cocky bravado, "will you ever have the chance?"

He took a step back and Regan suddenly knew what a horse in the round pen felt like when Will released the pressure. "I guess time will tell."

HER SISTER, CLAIRE, hadn't phoned or emailed in almost five days, so when the phone rang late Sunday afternoon, Regan figured it had to be her.

It wasn't, however. It was Brett Bishop.

"You sound surprised," he said, in a voice very much like his brother's.

"A little." She was actually astonished.

"I'll be coming to Wesley in a week or so to look at some cattle, I was wondering if you'd like to go out? For dinner."

Regan pulled in a breath. She'd had enough one-on-one Bishop encounters for a while. They seemed to be ending unpredictably lately. "You know, Brett…"

"I thought we could talk," he said, when she hesitated.

"Talk?"

"Yeah. You know, as opposed to me hitting on you."

Regan laughed at his candor, but she wasn't entirely convinced. "Why don't you give me a call when you know for sure that you're coming?" That would give her some time to think things over and to decide whether she wanted to have another meeting with Brett Bishop or not.

"I'll do that," he promised.

Regan hung up after saying goodbye, only to have the phone ring again. Claire.

"Where were you a few minutes ago, when I needed you?" Regan said.

"What?"

"Never mind. How are things going with Mom?"

Regan could actually hear Claire's fingers drumming on some hard surface at the other end.

"I told her about some changes I'm making in my life. She's in a huff, but I'm weathering it. And I've made it a point not to call and ask you to be the referee." She stated this with exaggerated self-righteousness. "I'm going to do this on my own. I've been doing some internet research and, according to what I've read, if I hold my position long enough, Mom will buckle. It's called extinction. Unfortunately, I don't know which of us becomes extinct first."

"What kind of changes?" Regan had a feeling they involved the College of Education, but nothing was ever certain with her sister.

"I'd kind of like to wait before I talk about them. See if I survive Mom. It'll be embarrassing if I'm the one who crumbles."

"Don't crumble."

"I'll try not to. And actually, I'm calling to give you a heads-up."

Regan reached for a dishcloth and gave her counter a wipe. "What kind of heads-up?"

"Mom's pulling in favors. She's trying to finagle an interview for you with the Department of Education."

"No." Regan crumpled the cloth in her hand.

"It's killing her that you're, and I quote, 'wasting your talents in some backwater town.' Unquote. She wants you back in Vegas, babe."

"I like it here." Regan returned to polishing the counter, trying not to let her mother's actions get to her.

"Why?" Claire asked, genuinely curious.

"There's a sense of community here."

"That sounds nice," her sister replied in a way that told Regan she wasn't all that familiar with a sense of community. That was what came of moving and changing roommates every few months.

"The staff at my school is very supportive. No one leaves until they retire."

"That sounds better than the thirty percent turnover rate at your previous school," Claire agreed. "What else have you got?"

"My rent is half what it was in Vegas for twice the space, and I can take a walk at night if I want."

That seemed to impress her sister.

"Well," Claire said grudgingly, "I'm going to trust that you know what you're doing—even if you did abandon me to Mom. But I would truly love to know how you keep from dying from boredom on the weekends."

REGAN AND PAULINE were never going to be close friends, but after the Elko trip, Pauline had been much less prissy, which made Regan think she remembered more of her Picon adventure than she let on. Therefore, when Pauline flagged her down in the hall, wearing the same pink pencil skirt she'd had on when she'd collapsed on her hotel-room bed, Regan did not immediately assume the worst.

"I was wondering if you had anything you'd be willing to donate to the auction to help the Renshaws."

"Sure," Regan said, even though her bank account was still recovering from all the Toffee-related expenses. "How much?"

"Oh, no. Not money, unless you want to, of course.

We're all donating goods or services. For instance, Millie Serrano is donating one of her crocheted tablecloths and the high school art teacher is contributing one of her paintings."

"I have an opal necklace I'll donate." Regan had been wondering what to do with the necklace Daniel had given her for her birthday. It wasn't as if she'd ever wear it again and now it would go to help a good cause.

"That sounds lovely." Pauline penciled a note onto her clipboard. "Thank you very much."

"Glad to help."

"The auction is next Saturday at seven o'clock at the arena. Quite a few people have donated livestock."

"I'll be there."

"One more thing. Mr. Domingo was looking for you the last time I saw him."

"Oh. I've been in the library."

"Don't worry about it," Pauline said. "If it was important, he would have called for you on the intercom."

Unless he wants to bully you in private.

She'd never found out why he'd been stalking her at the Harvest Dance. He'd basically avoided her after that night, with the exception of her first evaluation, which had been barely acceptable.

Regan thanked Pauline and headed for her classroom. Pete was coming out as she was heading in.

"Can I help you?" she asked. She had the oddest feeling that he'd been on the edge of saying no before he said yes.

"I want to set up our next evaluation session."

"We just finished an evaluation."

"My schedule will be full, with wrestling and basketball, so I wanted to plan around the games and matches. I have a lot of evaluations to get through, you know."

"I understand."

They settled on a date in January—two months away—then Pete snapped his notebook shut and left without another word.

Regan stood staring at the door he'd just gone through. Something was up.

And then she noticed her computer screen. She'd left her email account accessible on the bottom toolbar. Pete had probably been reading her email. What a snake.

THE RENSHAW AUCTION was officially put on by the high school's agricultural club, but everyone in the community pitched in. Will spent most of the afternoon at Madison's arena, where the event was to be held, first setting up the auctioneering stand, then cataloging and tagging donated items while Kylie ran errands for Madison. Quite a few people donated livestock and the FFA club kids were kept busy setting up temporary pens and chutes just inside the doors at the far end. Soon the arena sounded like a petting zoo gone mad.

Will had gotten two cell-phone calls from Trev as he worked. Their horse thief was back. Or rather, *a* horse thief, but both he and Trev figured it was the same guy who'd been at it a few months before. This time the thefts followed the state highway, starting in Carlin and heading south.

Trev looked tired when he finally showed up late.

"Total of four thefts last night," he said, when he found Will behind the pens, making sure the numbers matched the animals. "Carlin, Eureka, Ely, Lund."

"Must be pulling a four-horse," Will commented darkly, handing his clipboard to the freckle-faced kid who was now in charge of making sure the right animal came out at the right time. "I'd love to know where he's unloading them. You know—meet him at the sale."

"Has to be some slaughterhouse. Have you…"

"Trevin." Madison's voice blared over the PA system and Trev grimaced as his proper name reverberated off the metal walls. "We're ready to start the auction and you're first."

"Better go sell yourself," Will said.

"Ladies and gentlemen. To start the night, Trev has offered two free shoeings or resets. That's all four feet, right Trev?"

"Yep." Trev called, as he walked through the gate into the arena. He went to stand next to Madison's podium and smiled at the audience. Will decided he was going to try to smile, too.

"So what am I bid for this service? You guys know what a decent farrier charges and it's all for a good cause."

Will listened as Trev's services went for double what he normally charged. Maybe this auction *would* put the Renshaw fund over the top tonight.

"Oh, Will," Madison called. "Will Bishop is item number two in your programs."

Will stepped into the ring as Trev walked out. "Geri Winters bought me."

"She doesn't have a horse."

"I know." He sounded grim.

"Will has offered thirty days on a horse," Madison announced. "He'll start a new one or tune up an old one. Let's start the bidding at two hundred."

"MAYBE YOU SHOULD buy him," Tanya murmured, close to Regan's shoulder. Will stood in the ring next to the auction stand, his hands on his hips. He was wearing jeans that had just the proper amount of fantasy-inducing wear and a plaid shirt rolled up over the elbows. He looked…good. And Regan was still processing their previous meeting.

"I don't need him. I can train my own horse."

"Pity." Tanya unfolded the auction list and perused it for the hundredth time, idly toying with the end of her blond ponytail. "I'm bidding on the housepainter."

"I'm bidding on the saddle rack."

"Regan, sometimes I worry about you."

"Sold!" Madison finally called, after a heated bidding war for Will's services, then Mrs. Serrano's lace tablecloth was brought out.

Regan and Tanya bid on a number of items, but the townspeople were feeling generous and after almost an hour, neither of them had ended up with anything. Regan's opal necklace had gone to a young newlywed, who happily presented it to his bride as soon as he'd paid for it. Regan hoped the girl would be far happier with it than she'd been.

Tanya excused herself to go to the concession stand just as a high school girl led a fat pony into the arena.

"Geri," someone called from the audience, "here's your chance to buy a horse to go with your farrier!"

Apparently the pony was a well-known fixture in the community, because no one met the starting bid. Madison grudgingly dropped the price by twenty dollars and Regan suddenly had a flash of inspiration.

She raised her card.

"I have one hundred." Madison pounced on the bid. "Now let's have one-twenty for this fine, um, piece of horseflesh." The pony swished his tail. "One-twenty? Anyone? Do I hear one-fifteen…one-fifteen? One-ten?" The crowd remained stubbornly silent. "Sold to number sixty for one hundred dollars."

Regan turned to see Tanya gaping at her, a drink in each hand.

"My horse is lonely," she explained.

"Your horse is lonely."

"Yes. And ponies don't eat much."

"Did you happen to notice that no one else was bidding on him? I mean, doesn't that worry you? A cute little pony and no one wants him?"

"I'm not going to be riding him, so, no." Regan picked up her purse. "I need to find some way to haul him, though. Madison will charge me if I try to keep him here overnight."

Four boys in FFA jackets came into the ring carrying a beautiful pieced quilt, which they unfolded for everyone to see. A gasp of appreciation sounded and the bidding was on. Tanya's card flashed into the air. Regan went to the sales table near the stands to pay for her purchase.

"I hope you know what you just did." Will's voice sounded behind her, just as she finished writing the check.

"What did I do?" she asked, taking her receipt and folding it.

"You bought Peanut Butter."

"I bought him to keep Toffee company," she said. "If he doesn't work out, I'll sell him."

"To whom?" Will asked innocently, leaning an arm on the arena fence.

Regan frowned. This did not sound good. "What…"

A whoop of excitement cut off her words. Startled, she turned to see Tanya jumping to her feet.

"I bought the quilt." Her friend was practically dancing.

"You could have got two ponies for that price," Regan pointed out.

"But quilts don't eat anything," Tanya replied smugly.

Two girls began dragging a bawling nanny goat into the ring as soon as Tanya's quilt was safely folded and taken away. All four of the goat's legs were locked, her splayed feet leaving furrows in the arena dust. As soon as the girls stopped, the nanny quit bawling, put her feet squarely beneath her and blinked at the chuckling crowd. The laughter grew louder when she gave her tail a few impertinent shakes.

Even Madison laughed. "All right, what am I bid for this fine animal? Goat tiers? *Cabrito* eaters? Anyone? Let's start the bidding at fifty dollars."

Trev strolled over and leaned on the rail next to Will, but his eyes were on Regan. "You bought Peanut Butter?"

Regan sighed at the doomsday note in his voice.

"How many people have owned old PB?" Trev asked Will.

Will pushed his hat back. "I can think of three sales I was involved in. No, four."

"I've seen at least that many."

"How would you feel about owning a goat?" Regan asked Will.

"I'd rather not."

"Then you'd better hope someone else bids, because I think your daughter is winning."

"What?" His gaze shot to the auction ring and then a colorful word escaped his lips. He pushed his way past Trev as Madison called "Going, going," but he was too late. The gavel came down.

"Sold to number seventy-eight."

Will quickly strode over to number seventy-eight and the two had a brief conversation. A few minutes later Kylie grudgingly approached the auction stand and whispered something to Madison.

"Ladies and gentlemen. Nanny is being donated back to us to auction again. Thank you, Kylie."

Kylie briefly stretched her lips into a good-sport smile before she turned and stalked back to her father, scowling the entire way.

She said something to him, he nodded, and the girl headed for the concession area.

Will watched her for a moment, then walked back to where Trev and Regan stood. Trev wore a wide grin.

"Yuck it up," Will muttered. "Here comes Geri to collect on her purchase."

Regan had to bite her lip to keep from laughing as Trev whirled to see a tall, curvaceous brunette striding toward him with a purposeful expression on her face.

"Geri," Will greeted the woman with a polite nod, as he edged past her. "See ya, Trev. I have to check the livestock."

"Regan," Trev said from between his teeth.

"I need to find a ride for Peanut Butter." And she did not want to get between a predator and her prey.

"Um, was it just me or was she licking her lips?" she asked Will as she caught up with him.

"I think Geri's had her sights on Trev for quite a while now."

"He doesn't seem too thrilled about it."

"Geri's known to be…hard on men."

"Oh."

Peanut Butter stood at the edge of his pen, looking adorable, his little ears tipped forward, his brown eyes wide and inquiring.

"So what's the matter with him?" Regan asked with a frown. "Is he mean?" He didn't look mean.

"No. He's smart. He's outwitted just about everyone who's owned him. People get tired of staying one step ahead of him."

"All I want him to do is to stand in the pasture and keep Toffee company."

"Well, since everyone else has expected him to either carry a kid or pull a cart, you may be all right—as long as he doesn't decide the grass is greener on the other side of the fence and figure out your gate latches."

"You're kidding, right?"

Will simply smiled. He leaned back against a pen, looking unaffectedly sexy as only a confident male could.

"I'd better go find whoever sold him and see if they'll drop him by my house."

"That'd be the Butlers. And if they can't do it, I'll haul him in the morning."

"I'd appreciate that," she said, stepping aside to let two kids with a rabbit cage go by. "Why'd you have Kylie donate her goat back?"

"Have you ever come out of your house to find a goat standing on the hood of your vehicle?" he asked.

"Just this morning as a matter of fact."

"Very funny," he muttered, but his smile was genuine.

"Why'd she buy the goat?" Regan went to lean on the rail next to him, smiling fondly at her pony.

"She was afraid someone would buy it to butcher."

"I hadn't thought of that."

"Kylie did, thanks to Madison. *Cabrito* means goat meat, you know."

She gave him a frowning glance. "I didn't."

"*Cabrito* or not, Kylie needs to understand she can't rescue everything."

"Isn't Skitters a rescue?" Regan asked candidly.

Will took his time answering. "When we bought her, I honestly thought I might be able to shape her up. Now it's not looking so good."

"What happens if you can't shape her up?"

"She'll probably go to the cannery."

"Oh." There didn't seem to be much else to say. She stared at her toes, thinking it was such a shame some animals got so beat up there was no saving them.

He reached out to tip up her chin, his fingertips warm, gentle. "Fact of life, Regan. Not all horses can be saved and few people can afford to feed a horse just because it's pretty."

"I'm curious. Why couldn't you just let her join the mustang herd, since it's so close?"

"Probably because it's illegal."

"Pretty good reason not to," Regan said softly.

"Yeah. I really wish I hadn't bought her, because I think I see heartbreak ahead. Kylie's getting too attached."

Speaking of whom…

"Dad. There you are. Ready to go?" Kylie gave Regan an I-thought-we-talked-about-this look as she approached. She did not seem pleased to see the two of them together.

"Any extra animals in the truck?" Will asked.

"No." Her mouth twisted and Regan could see the girl was in no mood to be teased. "I'm just glad the Andersons bought the nanny. They don't eat goats. They're going to milk her. I checked."

Regan wondered what Kylie would have done if their plans had been less goat friendly. A goatnapping, perhaps?

"Have you seen the Butlers?"

"They just left," Kylie said.

"Probably escaping while they can," Will said in a low voice.

Kylie looked at Regan with dawning understanding. "Did you…"

"Yes. I bought Peanut Butter."

Kylie gave her head a shake, as though trying to clear it.

"He's a *pony*," Regan said. "I'm going to see Madison and try to convince her to be charitable until I can find a ride for my pony."

"Give a yell if you need me to haul him tomorrow," Will called after her.

As it turned out, though, Madison was not only chari-table, she was helpful. She arranged a ride from a couple leaving with an empty trailer. Fifteen minutes later Regan watched as Peanut Butter walked into the trailer, the pic-ture of equine amiability. And he was so darned cute.

Will and Trev had to be exaggerating. He was just a pony.

How much trouble could one pony be?

CHAPTER NINE

KYLIE PULLED A booted foot up onto the seat and hugged her arms around her knee as Will turned out of the parking lot. "I can't believe Miss Flynn bought Peanut Butter."

"He is cute."

"Yeah." Kylie cast her father a sidelong glance. "What do you think of her? Miss Flynn, I mean."

"She's a nice lady."

"You act different around her."

Not exactly what Will wanted to hear.

"Do you ever want to, you know, go out with her or anything?"

Will had a feeling that even though she was making an effort to act nonchalant, Kylie was holding her breath as she waited for his answer.

"Would it bother you if I did?"

"Well," Kylie hesitated, then it all poured out. "I like Miss Flynn. She's pretty nice to me most of the time, but, it's kind of gross, you know? Guys your age. My dad and my teacher?" She made a face. "And when my friends' parents date something always goes wrong, then they're all unhappy. My friends say it sucks. They say I'm lucky that you don't do that. Mark's dad has been married three times! Mark says he's not ever getting married. And if he does, he isn't having kids."

"I get your drift," Will said.

"So you're not going to be dating her or anything? Even if she *is* nice to us?"

"I really doubt it."

Kylie sank back in her seat and stared straight ahead, but even in profile she looked relieved.

How much trouble can one pony be?

Regan discovered the answer the next morning when she got up just after dawn and found Peanut Butter standing belly deep in her neighbor's garden.

"Ohmigosh!" she muttered as she threw on a robe and shoved her feet into slippers.

She hadn't released the pony into the pasture the night before, since it was risky to put two horses together without giving them a get-acquainted period. So she'd tethered him on a picket line in her backyard, instead. The pony was able to get close enough to Toffee so that they could familiarize themselves with one another, but not touch or fight. Once they knew each other, Regan would put Peanut Butter in the pasture.

That had been the plan, anyway.

"That your pony?" Her elderly neighbor, whom she'd hoped would still be in bed, called to her from his porch.

"Uh, yes." She attempted a smile as she picked her way through his half acre of pumpkins and gourds—now marked by deep pony prints—and into the corn, where Peanut Butter had taken refuge. "I'll pay for the damage he caused." Not that there should be much, since most of the garden had been harvested.

The old guy harrumphed. "I called animal control, you know."

Regan could honestly say she'd never had cause to deal with animal control before. So what was she supposed to do now?

It didn't really matter, because she knew what she was going to do. She was going to take her pony and run.

"I'll, uh, just take him back to my place until they come."

And then what were they going to do? Impound Peanut Butter? Charge her with trespassing? Fine her?

She gritted her teeth as Peanut Butter tipped his fuzzy ears forward. "Cute isn't going to cut it this morning, bud. Come on."

She slipped the rope around his neck and pulled him out of the corn as carefully as she could. One of her slippers stuck in the muddy soil and water seeped through her sock. A colorful expletive escaped her as she took a backward step, slipped and fell flat on her butt.

The dry stalks of corn waved above her.

"You okay in there?"

"I'm fine," Regan said through clenched teeth as she got to her feet and wiped a muddy hand on her muddy robe.

She dragged Peanut Butter out of the corn with as much dignity as she could muster while wearing a robe with a wet, muddy butt impression on the back. The old guy started to cackle.

She could see a truck coming in the distance and decided to get Peanut Butter on her property ASAP, just in case it was animal control.

"Come on," she muttered. The little guy trotted companionably beside her. At any other time, it would have been cute.

She examined the halter, still snapped to the picket line, expecting it to be broken, but it was in one piece and still buckled together.

Regan scratched her head. It fit him too well for him to have slipped it off, and there was nothing he could have rubbed against to get it off. Weird.

She debated, then put the halter back on the pony and snapped the line onto it, hoping he'd stay put while she cleaned herself up. She wanted to be wearing something warmer than a wet robe when she introduced her two horses to each other. If Toffee decided to stomp Peanut Butter—and she wouldn't really blame him at this point— she'd have to rescue the little guy.

She tossed Toffee a flake of hay, just as the truck pulled into her neighbor's yard. It was Will. She jogged to her house, knowing full well that her place would be his next stop, kicked off the muddy slippers and wet socks, sloughed off the robe and quickly dressed in jeans and a sweatshirt. She'd barely zipped up when she heard the knock.

Will stood on the porch, yawning. He had a five-o'clock shadow and his shirt was buttoned crookedly. She pulled open the door and tried to appear nonchalant.

"Yes?"

He wasn't buying it. "Dispatch called me because there was a horse at large."

"Animal control doesn't take horses?"

"They figured it was lost and, since I live close, that I'd know who it belonged to. It would have saved everyone a lot of time, if your neighbor had mentioned it was a pony."

"Am I in trouble?"

"Not if you pay for some pumpkins."

Regan swung the door wider. "You want some coffee?" She felt bad that he'd been dragged out of bed. And since he'd negotiated a settlement with her neighbor, coffee seemed like the least she could do.

"Sure."

But he seemed hesitant. Something had changed since last night.

"Good," she said. "You can keep watch."

"Watch on what?"

"Peanut Butter. Somehow that little…" her mouth tightened as she searched for a polite word "…bugger managed to slip his halter and I want to know how he did it."

Will went to the window while Regan measured coffee and poured water into the reservoir.

"Come here," he said. "I've never seen this before."

Regan clicked on the brewer and went to the window. "I don't believe it," she said. The pony had his head turned back toward his rear end and was methodically working the halter off over his ears with one hind foot.

Regan headed for the door, with Will a few steps behind her.

Peanut Butter looked up, the picture of innocence even though the halter was now only over one ear.

Regan put her hands on her hips. "What do you think?" she asked Will. "Should I tether Toffee and put Peanut Butter in the pen, or should I go for broke?"

"It's a big pasture. Go for broke. They've spent the night within sight of each other."

"All right." Regan freed the pony while Will opened the gate. "I just don't want Toffee to hurt him."

As soon as he was released, Peanut Butter made a beeline for the hay.

"Look at that," Regan said as the pint-sized equine snaked his neck and pinned back his ears, threatening Toffee. "He thinks he's going to scare off a sixteen-hand horse."

"He appears to be doing it."

Sure enough, Toffee whirled and retreated. He stopped a respectful distance away, his ears pricked forward as he studied the pony.

Toffee edged forward toward his hay and Peanut Butter turned his butt and cocked a back foot. Will laughed.

Regan glared at him. "This isn't funny."

"No. It's not." But his eyes were still full of amusement. Regan let out a huff of breath that lifted her bangs, wishing she weren't so aware of how good the man looked when he laughed.

He put a companionable hand on her shoulder and Regan had to force herself not to lean into it. "They'll probably settle in together just fine."

The two watched as Toffee approached cautiously from a different angle. Peanut Butter swung his butt around again and Toffee stopped in his tracks.

"At least Peanut Butter hasn't hurt him yet." Regan went to the haystack and threw another flake of hay a good twenty yards away from the first. Toffee moved toward it, but Peanut Butter headed him off and claimed it for himself. Toffee went back to the original smaller pile of hay.

"I guess I won't worry about him getting fat when I stop riding him this winter."

"Meanwhile, PB will be approaching coronary status."

"Hey."

They both turned to see Regan's neighbor stomping down the driveway.

"When are you going to pay for my ruined pumpkins?"

"Just as soon as…"

"She'll trade you fertilizer for them."

The old man's eyes widened. "Hey, yeah."

"Yes," Regan agreed, quite happy with Will's sudden inspiration. She never would have thought of a trade. "You can have all you want. Bring your wheelbarrow over anytime."

"All right. That would be great." He started back down the drive, then stopped. "I have some beds to work. Mind if I start today?"

"Just watch the pony when you go in and out. He's a slippery little guy."

"You bet. I sure don't want him back at my place."

The timer on the coffeepot beeped. "I never thought horse manure would make someone so happy," Regan said as she headed for the back door. "Thanks for thinking of it."

"No problem." Will stopped at the back step. Their gazes connected for a moment.

He hadn't bothered with the hat this morning. His sun-streaked hair was rumpled. He needed a shave. And Regan was no closer to forgetting how talented he was with his lips than she'd been right after he kissed her. The reckless part of her wanted to take him by the hand, lead him into the house and find out what else he could do. And the sane part of her wasn't protesting as loudly as usual, which concerned her.

"What's wrong, Regan?"

"I… What do you mean?"

"I mean I can practically hear the wheels turning in your head."

"I was just planning my day," she murmured.

He glanced at his watch. "I hate to do this, but I think I'll pass on the coffee. I should get back before the kid starts wondering where I am."

"Will she be up this early?"

"Maybe not, but I'd like to be back when she gets up." He tapped the toe of his boot against the back step, gave her an uncomfortable look. "Kylie's afraid I'm going to start dating you."

"We've spoken."

Will stared at her for a moment. "You've spoken?" Regan nodded and Will rolled his eyes. "I probably don't want the details, but do I need to apologize?"

"She's just worried."

"I guess it's because I've spent more time around you than any other woman during her life."

"She's not buying the friendship angle?"

"I'm not sure *I'm* buying the friendship angle," he said in a low voice.

"It's the only angle we have."

"I know." Yet Regan wondered if he did when he reached out to take a strand of hair behind her ear. His touch was gentle. She could see why the horses responded to it. She was responding, too.

"I have to go."

She gave a silent nod. No question about it. He did have to go.

WILL MANAGED TO keep out of Regan's way for two weeks, thinking it would be beneficial to put some distance between them, to get perspective. It sounded good in theory, but in reality all it did was make him more aware of the empty feeling that had enveloped his life over the past several years.

Before he'd met Regan, he'd just lived with that feeling, never allowing himself to think about it too much. Now he not only thought about it, he wanted to do something about it.

But he had no idea what. Especially not when his daughter was so set against him dating—not that he blamed her for her attitude. His own father had brought a long line of women into his life after his mom had died, and it had seemed the quicker Will got attached to one, the quicker she took off. He never wanted Kylie to go through that. And she did have a tendency to get attached. Cranky, old Skitters was living proof.

But he was also damned tired of being alone.

Trev showed up at Will's house on a Wednesday morning, asking for both a cup of coffee and a favor.

"Are you riding the fence line for Meyers this weekend?"

"Sure am." Will cleared the kitchen table of his account books, then poured coffee into the last clean mug and set it in front of Trev. "I'm going on Saturday."

He usually checked the fence in the fall and spring for the older man, riding one of the young horses he had to put miles on and looking for stray cows at the same time.

"Would you, uh, keep an eye out for Geri's hound dogs? Two blueticks."

Will raised a brow. Trev looked away.

It was a long, solitary ride to the high country. Usually, Kylie went with him, but since she was doing volunteer work at the senior center with her 4-H group over the weekend, he was either going alone or... He debated briefly, then gave in.

He called Regan Thursday night.

"I have to ride out and check a fence on Saturday. I was wondering if you'd like to come along. It'll take most the day." The words seemed to fall out of his mouth without a lot of finesse. He was sorely out of practice.

There was a long silence and Will figured the answer would be no. It had been a long shot, after all; one he probably shouldn't have taken. She appeared to have had more common sense than he did.

"What time?"

A slow smile spread across his face. "Eight. You'll need to dress warmly."

REGAN HAD GIVEN up on trying to keep Peanut Butter in the pasture when she rode. He always managed to maneuver himself under the bottom wire of the fence and would suddenly turn up at a dead gallop somewhere along her route, invariably spooking Toffee. She either had to tie him to the fence high enough so that he couldn't pull his halter-slipping stunt or let him come with her from the start. When she rode cross-country, away from potentially disastrous encounters with vehicles, she let him come along, telling herself he needed the exercise.

Will had obviously not expected the pony to join them. He tipped his hat back when he saw him.

"I can't leave him home alone. Where's Kylie?"

"4-H." Will was still frowning in Peanut Butter's general direction. And then he looked at Regan in that half-direct, half-guarded way he had. "Thanks for coming. Sometimes this makes for a lonely day."

"I'm looking forward to it."

But she had thought Kylie was coming.

They rode directly into the mountains across the valley from Will's house. Peanut Butter would stop every once in a while to eat dry grass as they climbed, then race madly to catch up, his little hooves thundering on the hard ground. It had been a dry fall.

It was Peanut Butter who first spotted the cattle. He was off on one of his mad jaunts, when he suddenly stopped on the crest of a hill and perked his ears. Will urged his horse up to the top and reached into the pocket of his heavy canvas coat for a small pair of field glasses. He bit the corner of his lip as he frowned into the binoculars. He gave his head a shake.

"Is there a problem?"

"They're haired up."

"Pardon?"

"It's hard to read the brands when cattle have their winter coats and I don't want to ride down there unless we have to."

It was a steep hillside and Regan wasn't wild about the idea of riding Toffee down, either, since she didn't know much about his hill abilities yet. Steep hillside could be tricky for a horse who wasn't used to carrying a rider downhill.

"Okay, there's a Bar P on the Angus, and a Rocking O on those two and… Come on, turn around so I can see you. A Diamond Bar… Definitely a mixed bunch."

"Now what do you do?"

"Contact the owners." His voice trailed off and she could see him frown as he moved the glasses.

"Something wrong?"

"Probably not." He put the binoculars back in his pocket. "Are you hungry yet? I brought some food."

"You did?" Regan was starving and she'd been wishing she'd thought to throw something edible into a coat pocket.

"When you ask someone to work with you, you feed them."

"I didn't realize this was work."

He grinned at her. "Not everybody enjoys a long late-October ride."

"Do you?" She asked as he dismounted. She imagined it was second nature for him to spend long days in the saddle, regardless of the weather.

"When I have company, it's not bad." That surprised her, since Will struck her as a man who preferred his own company. "And I thought you might like to see some country."

He led his horse toward a granite outcropping and tied the gelding to a tree. Regan dismounted and followed, loosely looping Toffee's reins over the same gnarled tree, hoping the gelding wouldn't pull back and break them.

Will had already settled at the base of a cluster of big rocks, out of the wind, and Regan went to sit close to him.

They ate the sandwiches he'd packed in his saddlebags, then shared a bottle of water. The horses moved together as the wind picked up and the pony slipped in between them, using the two larger animals as a windbreak. Regan took her cue from them and moved toward Will, borrowing some of his warmth. He didn't seem to mind. In fact, he settled his arm around her, pulling her even closer. Regan rested her cheek against the rough canvas of his coat and stared out over the valley, feeling warm and secure in spite of the wind. She liked this place, so wild and isolated. And she liked this man. Maybe more than she should.

A large hawk glided on the air currents above them, lofting before slowly spiraling down. They watched the bird until he finally spotted prey and dove. It must have been a successful hit because he did not reappear in the sky.

Regan figured it was probably a sign that it was time to go, but she was reluctant to move out of Will's embrace, away from his warmth. Away from him.

"You know," Will said, his eyes still on the spot where the bird had disappeared, "I think we're edging closer to one of those moments that'll give us pause later." His arm tightened around her.

Regan smiled at his phrasing. She'd been doing some thinking and had come to some conclusions of her own. Will was a grown man. It wasn't her job to protect him from himself. Her only job was to set her own ground rules and pay attention to his.

"I can go with the moment just fine, as long as we understand that's what it is. Just a moment in time."

"Sweetheart, that's exactly what it is."

His mouth settled on hers, to punctuate the point. She sighed against his lips, wondered why she had expended so much energy trying to avoid this. His face was cold to the touch, but his mouth was wonderfully warm. Wet. Hot. For a guy who'd been out of circulation for a while, he had skills to be proud of. By the time they came up for air, she was practically lying on top of him. And she was not exactly in a hurry to get off.

"You've had me running scared, Will."

"Why?"

"Do you want the short list or the long list?"

"Your choice." He ran his hand up over her heavy coat, cradling her against him. His breath was warm against her face.

"Because we live in a small town and we can't exactly pal around without exciting comment. Heck, we couldn't even share a pizza without causing a stir."

"True."

"And because you have a daughter who doesn't want you to date just yet."

He nodded, his expression sobering a bit.

"And because I am serious about keeping my independence."

"So why is it you aren't looking to get involved with anyone?" he asked, lightly brushing her windblown hair away from their faces.

"I just don't want to deal with it."

"It's you or them?" he asked quietly.

She raised her head, her eyes widening a little as he put her exact sentiments into words.

"I have this habit of picking losers."

"I'm no loser, Regan."

"I know. That's why you kind of terrify me." But she didn't tell him the last man in her life hadn't looked like a loser, either.

He smiled, kissed her lips one last time, lightly, making

her want more, then eased her off. "I guess that may be a good thing. Come on. We'd better get going."

They rode back along a different route, following the fence line toward the valley. There was a rutted dirt track running parallel and the horses plodded down it, side by side, with Peanut Butter taking up the rear, keeping out of the wind. Suddenly, Will raised his chin, his eyes narrowing.

"What?"

"There's someone coming up the road."

Regan glanced down at the ground. "What road?" And then she, too, heard the whine of an engine.

"Let's get off to the side a bit." He walked his horse several yards off the track, with Regan, Toffee and Peanut Butter all following.

"Dismount, would you?"

Regan did as he asked, wondering what was happening as he, too, dismounted.

"Come here."

She stepped closer, holding Toffee on a loose rein.

He reached out and took her hand. "Walk with me."

"All right." She wondered what was up, but did as he asked.

They walked hand in hand, slowly, leading their horses, Toffee staying out of her space like the good boy he now was and Peanut Butter poking along at the rear. Will's grip tightened as the vehicle, a beat-up dually pickup, came up over the crest of the hill, its engine roaring with the effort, then his fingers relaxed slightly.

"Do you know who it is?" Regan asked

"I recognize the rig, but not the driver." Will lifted their interlinked hands to his lips and kissed her knuckles in an old-fashioned gesture. And Regan felt an old-fashioned tingle start in her toes and move upward.

"What are you doing?" she inquired through her teeth.

"I'm trying my best to look like I'm here for pleasure, instead of business, and I hope I'm far enough away from those cows for them to buy it."

Her gaze strayed to the pickup, which was moving steadily past. Will lifted a hand in casual greeting, then dropped his arm around Regan's shoulders as they walked on. She leaned into him.

"Where does the road go?"

"To the next valley."

"To the cattle?"

"Yep."

The pickup rolled out of sight and Will slowly released her.

"I'd like to get to where I can talk to Trev. I won't have service on my cell phone here."

"You'll need to give me a leg up." Toffee was so tall that the stirrup was too high for her to reach comfortably without a mounting aid.

"We need to get you a real saddle."

Regan smirked at him over her shoulder. He cupped his hands and she stepped into them, letting him boost her lightly into the seat. He mounted his own horse with that inimitably smooth motion that all good cowboys seemed to have.

"Forgive my denseness, but I don't understand what the big deal is. It isn't like they can steal a cow with a pickup."

"No, but they can feed them and hold them in one place until a trailer comes to get them. There were two bales of hay in the bed of that pickup."

"Oh."

KYLIE WAS ALREADY home by the time Will rode into the yard. He rubbed down his horse and put away the tack.

He'd managed to get hold of Trev a few miles from his house and broke the bad news that he hadn't spotted Geri's hounds, then said that a few people needed to ride out to Munson Creek and collect their animals before they disappeared.

"I don't know who was driving, but it was that truck Charley keeps behind the barn."

"Well, Charley was helping us ship cattle today, so it wasn't him. Maybe I'll give him a call and see if he sold that rig."

"Sounds good."

Kylie had dinner going, including a pot of simmering green beans. A vegetable! Will assumed that meant she was about to ask for something she probably wasn't going to get, but it turned out that she was simply celebrating.

"Sadie and Chad broke up," she said conversationally, before heading back to her room with Stubby at her heels.

"Too bad," Will called after her, playing the game even though he knew Kylie wouldn't be too upset over the downturn in her friend's love life.

"Yeah. It is." She came back down the hall a few minutes later, pulling her hair into a ponytail. "Sadie said she was sorry she ignored me. I think she meant it."

"I'm sure she did." Will checked the spuds, then drained the excess water into the sink.

"We made this deal. We won't put boyfriends ahead of us being friends."

Will couldn't say he liked the casual way she dropped the *B* word, but he kept quiet. Boyfriends were going to happen. But they would be well screened and well managed. And if that didn't work, he'd invest in a porch and a shotgun.

"How was the ride?" Kylie asked, as she put the plates on the table.

"It was good." He took a breath, came clean. "You should probably know that I asked Miss Flynn to come with me." Her hand hovered for a moment, then she put the forks next to the plates.

"Why?" The single word tugged at his heart.

"Because she likes to ride and I thought it would be nice to show her some country."

"Okay."

But Will had a feeling it wasn't.

CHAPTER TEN

REGAN COULDN'T BELIEVE IT. She'd been called to the office. Again. And this time it had nothing to do with squid.

Pete Domingo handed her a policy manual. Regan frowned at the booklet, then at Pete.

"I know you have one of these, but there is something in it I'd like to point out. Would you please turn to page forty-eight and read subsection four?"

Regan knew that whatever she found on page forty-eight was going to make her angry and she was correct. After reading the vaguely worded policy, she looked up, her expression clear.

"I'm not certain I understand what you're getting at here."

"It's extremely clear, Miss Flynn. You are not to become involved with the parent of a student, while that student is under your sphere of influence."

"Define *become involved*."

"I think you know exactly what it means."

"You'd better give me some specifics."

"Will Bishop was seen driving away from your house very, *very* early in the morning a few weeks ago."

Regan's temper jacked up another notch. "So what? He was visiting." And just who had reported this incident? Her manure-shoveling neighbor? Someone who'd been driving by? And why would anyone mention this to Pete, unless he'd asked?

"At six a.m.?"

"He was there in a professional capacity."

Pete smirked. "You two were seen kissing at a community event. Was that also done in a professional capacity?"

Regan felt an unpleasant jolt of surprise, but fought to keep her expression serene. "By whom?" she asked pleasantly.

He smiled. "By me."

"Engaging in a little voyeurism, Pete?"

"No," he sputtered. "It was hard to miss."

It had been dark. He had to have been following them, which was more than a little disturbing. It sounded as if Pete was doing surveillance on her. Apparently standards training and the dessert table had not been punishment enough.

"What I do during my free time in my own business."

Pete tapped the manual.

"Oh, come on. The date on that is 1980 and I have a feeling that board attitudes have changed since then."

He placed both palms flat on the desk and leaned forward, his expression belligerent. "The important thing is that the policy is in writing."

Regan took a moment to study the framed photo of a much younger and slimmer Pete wearing a baseball uniform, and compared it to the older, more full-figured Pete leaning next to it. Not a happy contrast.

"Frankly," she said, "this smacks of desperation. I don't appreciate you spying on me and you're not going to intimidate me with an out-of-date policy manual."

"And I'm not going to have a teacher on my staff who is not a team player."

Ah, yes. The united front. She remembered the pep talk he'd given her after their first meeting with Will and Kylie.

"It isn't officially your staff yet," Regan reminded him softly.

"It *will* be my staff. If you keep trying to make trouble for me, you'll wish you hadn't." The veins were starting to bulge in his forehead.

"You're threatening me," Regan stated flatly.

"I'm informing you of school policy."

Regan turned on her heel and walked out of the office.

THE MEETING HAD made her late for her jumping lesson. She went home and dressed in jeans and a heavy sweatshirt, fuming the entire time. The thing that really annoyed her was that she was taking such great pains *not* to get involved with Will, other than a little harmless kissing. It was like being accused of a crime she had yet to commit. Not that she thought Pete was actually going to follow through on the matter. If he brought the issue before the board he wouldn't accomplish anything other than making himself look foolish. Extremely foolish.

So why was he pursuing this?

Because he wants to get rid of you.

And then the second part of the answer came to her in a flash.

Because he's planting seeds.

If he put enough small things together, well, it wouldn't do her professional reputation any good. That was a certainty. The question was, could he do any major damage? Regan had a bad feeling that he could. Especially with Zach's uncle on the school board.

Pete Domingo was not a man who shrugged off embarrassment—especially the kind Regan had caused. Instead, he got even.

Regan pulled into the arena parking lot ten minutes late. Her students were waiting, including a new one—Sadie.

"I hope you don't mind," she said to Regan. "I, uh, well, my mom borrowed my grandma's English saddle, because Kylie told my mom it was fun and Mom thought…"

"I'm glad you could come," Regan said, pleased that Sadie and Kylie's friendship was apparently on the road to recovery. "We'll just have you work on some basics for a bit."

REGAN HAD TO pass Will's horse trailer on the way to her car and as she approached, she could see that Kylie was working on her father, trying to wheedle something out of him as she unsaddled her horse.

"Dad, maybe we could borrow Madison's saddle for the weekend?" Kylie was using her most persuasive voice. "She doesn't have a class and she says its okay."

"You mean rent a saddle, don't you?"

"I have allowance coming."

"You want to borrow my saddle for the weekend?" Regan asked. She wasn't going to be riding, due to an overload of grading. Kylie swung around excitedly.

"For real?" she asked. "Because Sadie and I were going to build some jumps of our own and practice. Low ones," she added with a glance at her father. "A whole jumping course out in the field. We could do different patterns."

"If you want to stop by my place on your way home, it's in the utility room. I'm going to meet Tanya—Miss Prescott—for dinner, but my back door is unlocked."

Kylie was practically bouncing. "Can we, Dad?"

Will met Regan's gaze over Kylie's head. Regan nodded and he gave her a half smile.

"Sure," he said. "And I imagine you'll have it oiled up, Kylie, before you return it?"

"You know I will. It's a long weekend. Can I have it until Monday?"

"I'll stop by Monday afternoon and pick it up."

"We'll drop it by your house," Will said.

"I have to shop sometime. I'll just swing by on my way home."

"Thanks for the loan," Kylie said, grinning broadly as she untied her horse. "This is going to be so cool."

Regan smiled and started for her car, glad at least one positive thing had come out of the afternoon. She waved at Will as she drove past the trailer, wondering how he'd react if he knew that Pete was spying on him, too. She had a feeling he might do something about it.

Brett phoned her early that evening, while Regan was still debating about Pete.

"I'm coming to Wesley this weekend. Are you interested in dinner?"

"That would be nice," Regan replied without hesitation.

"Great. Do you want me to pick you up or do you want to meet?"

"Let's meet."

"The Supper Club?"

"That would be perfect." Regan hung up with a feeling of satisfaction. There was no law against fraternizing with students' uncles and she hoped this might put a crimp in Pete's seed planting. How serious could she be about a parent, if she was going out with his brother?

A call from Regan's mother less than an hour later provided the perfect punctuation to the end of a weird day.

"Check your email."

"Why?" Regan asked, instinctively cautious.

"I think you'll find something interesting."

"Mom…"

"I forwarded a job bulletin. It's perfect for you. Exactly like the job you applied for last spring."

"I like the job I've got."

"Regan."

"Mom."

"At least take a look."

"I will," Regan promised halfheartedly, then changed the subject to her mother's newest project. Arlene allowed herself to be sidetracked, but they both knew it had been her decision. If she'd wanted to discuss Regan's future further, they'd still be talking about it.

THE PARKING LOT of the Supper Club was close to full when Regan pulled in. Brett got out of an older model pickup truck and crossed the lot to meet her, walking with the easy gait of a natural athlete.

"I'm glad you decided to come." He reached out to close her car door for her.

"It's good to see you, too," Regan replied as they started across the parking lot. He had the same good looks as Will, the same rugged sensuality, but he somehow looked more careworn. Regan had a feeling that life had kicked him around a bit.

Brett opened the heavy wooden door of the club, ushering her inside. "This place used to have decent steaks."

"It still does. I eat here every now and then." As in twice. With Tanya. On payday.

When they walked into the dining area, people noticed. It reminded her of the night she'd gone out for pizza with Will. Did the Bishops *never* go out?

They had a drink while they waited for their menus and Brett pretended not to notice that people were checking him out.

"How long since you've been here?" Regan finally asked.

"A long time."

Regan smiled wryly. Brett ordered another beer.

The meals came just as a three-piece combo started to play. Brett seemed to relax a little as the drinks kicked in and the patrons who'd been watching him earlier either left or lost interest. He started to tell stories about working in Montana, his rodeo days, his hopes of going to college someday, which were rapidly fading now that he was thirty.

He asked Regan about Las Vegas, and although he seemed interested in her response, she sensed something just under the surface. Something that was keeping him on edge.

After the waiter refilled Regan's coffee cup, toward the end of the meal, she decided to find out what it was.

"Why'd you ask me out, Brett?"

He didn't even try to hedge. "I wanted to ask you about my brother."

Regan's fork hovered over the last of her cheesecake. "Your brother?"

Brett peeled a thin strip of paper from the label of his beer bottle, twisting it between his fingers. "I was kind of curious about how he's doing."

"Why ask me?" Regan asked, genuinely perplexed. There were many town gossips who knew a heck of a lot more than she did.

"Because if I ask anybody else, it'll get back to him."

"Do you really care if it does?"

"Yeah." And it sounded as if he meant it.

Regan placed her fork on the dessert plate and pushed it aside. "I think he's doing all right, but I really don't know that much." Except that he punched her buttons in a way that Brett did not. "He's doing well with his horse business."

The answer was basic, but Brett seemed satisfied with even that small amount of information.

"Does he seem, I don't know... Happy?"

Regan thought this was an odd question, but she answered him. "Yes. He does." *In a lonely sort of way.*

Brett fiddled with the paper. "And Kylie? I was wondering, what kind of a kid is she?"

"A great kid."

He grinned tentatively. "Is she?"

"Yes. She's smart, outspoken, loyal and protective."

"Sounds like Will. Except for the outspoken part."

"I think she takes after him. A lot."

"Good grades?"

"Like I said, she's smart."

Brett was silent for a moment, as though he was going over what he'd just heard and was taking his time processing the information. Regan studied him over her coffee cup.

"So, what happened with you and Will?" she finally asked.

"We had a falling out a long time ago."

Well, there was a load of information. Almost as much as she'd given him.

"And you don't think you'll ever work things out?"

"I doubt it, since neither of us is likely to try."

Regan opened her mouth. She honestly thought that if Brett wasn't interested in trying, he wouldn't be sitting with her, asking questions about his brother and his niece. But instinct told her to close her mouth and keep her thoughts to herself. She changed the subject.

"To be honest with you, I'm here for more than one reason myself." Brett looked up and she continued. "My principal thinks I'm carrying on with the parent of a student. I thought that having dinner with you would muddy the waters a little." And from the way people had been staring at them since they'd arrived, she was certain word would get back to Pete in no time. She just hoped there wasn't a section of the policy manual that dealt with this situation. It was a pretty thick book.

Brett leaned back in his chair, eyeing Regan with new respect.

"Who's the parent?"

"Will."

He started twisting the label again. "Are you carrying on with him?"

"No." At least, not yet. She set her coffee cup back on the saucer and waited for Brett's next question.

He frowned. "Then why…?"

"It's a long story, but it boils down to the fact that Pete doesn't like me."

Brett fiddled with the twisted bits of paper for another moment, then pushed them aside. "You want to dance?" he asked with a conspiratorial smile. "Give those muddy waters a swirl?"

Regan put her napkin on the table. "As a matter of fact, I do."

True to his word, Brett didn't try to hit on her. They danced, they talked and they laughed. Two hours later, he opened her car door for her, offered his hand, then kissed her cheek.

Regan gave him a light kiss back and then drove home thinking about the brothers. Brett, who seemed to want to reconnect with his family, but had no idea how to do it; and Will, who'd never even let his daughter meet her uncle.

What on earth had happened between the two of them?

WILL WAS WORKING a horse when Regan drove into his yard on her way home from shopping. He glanced over his shoulder, then refocused his attention on the mare. Regan parked and got out.

She watched for a few minutes, letting him finish. Finally, Will patted the horse, then walked to the gate, glancing at her only briefly.

"Hi," Regan said. "I came to pick up the saddle."

Will nodded, barely meeting her gaze. Something was up. Bad morning with Kylie, perhaps, or a bad morning with a horse. He headed for the barn and Regan followed.

The tack room was clean, well organized. Will walked to a wall-mounted saddle rack and pulled down her saddle. Regan reached for it, but he said, "I'll take it to your car."

"I can manage." She took the saddle from him and headed for her vehicle.

He opened the door and she settled the saddle onto the backseat.

"Bad morning?" Regan asked as she straightened up. Will closed the car door.

"I've had better."

"So've I," Regan said.

"How was your evening?"

Regan stilled.

Innocent question; not so innocent tone. In fact, a person could read a lot into a tone like that—especially with Will looking at her with a stormy expression she'd never seen before. And there was no doubt which evening he was talking about.

"What's it to you?"

"Nothing."

Oh yeah. She believed that. Regan drew herself up straighter. She'd had enough judgment, meddling and passive-aggressive nonsense to last a lifetime, and she wasn't going to take any from a guy who had no right to comment on what she did or didn't do. If Will had a problem with her dating his brother… Well, it really wasn't any of his business.

"I think I'd better be going."

"Did he ask about Kylie?" The blunt question surprised her.

"In passing. He asked about you, too. Maybe you should put him on your Christmas-card list. You know, keep him updated?"

"Hey, Dad!" Kylie yelled from the porch. "Trev's on the phone. He says it's important."

Regan gave him a tight smile, opened her car door and stepped inside.

The last thing she saw in her rearview mirror was Will walking toward the house. She drove home with her jaw set so hard that it ached by the time she pulled into her own driveway.

Will told himself to stay home, to leave it alone, but he'd been a first-class jerk and he needed to explain—as much as he could, anyway. Or apologize. Or both.

He rapped on Regan's screen door.

"What?" she said, as soon as she opened the door.

"I came to apologize." But his tone did not sound apologetic. Even to his ears it sounded harsh, stressed.

"Thank you. I accept." She stared at him stonily, obviously waiting for him to leave. But he wasn't ready to go.

"We all have our knee-jerk responses, Regan. Brett just happens to bring out mine."

"Brett?" She said his brother's name with surprise.

He frowned. "Yes, Brett. What else?"

"Oh, I don't know. Maybe you thinking you had a right to comment on my life, because we've kissed each other a couple of times. I don't do well with possessiveness— or control."

She glanced away, but Will gently reached out to cup her chin in his hand, bringing her focus back to him. He was surprised she didn't pull away; her eyes were cold.

"This was about Brett, Regan."

"Maybe to you." She shifted her chin so that his hand fell away. Apparently, he'd hit a hell of a nerve.

Finally, she spoke. "Is there some reason I shouldn't go to dinner with your brother? I mean, is there some problem I don't know about?"

It was his turn to remain silent. He couldn't tell her the real reason going out with Brett bothered him and "I'm jealous" wouldn't cut it, either.

"So where do we go from here?" he asked. It had become more than evident he wasn't going to talk about Brett.

"I think, for right now, it would be a lot less complicated if you were a parent and I was a teacher."

"Regan…"

She started back inside the house. "Oh, and one more thing. If I want to go out with your brother, I will."

It was all Will could do not to kick something on his way to the truck.

IT REALLY WAS a dream job.

Regan had finally opened her mother's forwarded job bulletin at school. It was a curriculum-implementation position with an independent educational consulting firm, Learning Tech. She'd be able to go into classrooms, demonstrate curriculum, lead seminars, train teachers…. And one of her college friends, Cheryl Riscal, was the human resources director.

She couldn't believe how good it looked.

Kylie and Sadie walked into class together as Regan closed down her computer. They were whispering, and Regan watched as Sadie walked by her former beau without even noticing that he was now talking to another girl.

"Okay," Regan said to her class, "I hope you did your

genetic trait charts last night, because we're going to use that information today."

Teenagers loved anything that had to do with themselves, so Regan always started her genetics unit with a lesson on dominant and recessive traits and had the students record some of their own characteristics.

Regan collected the papers, then pulled out two charts at random. "Names will be withheld to protect the innocent," she said. "I'll read the traits of parent A and the traits of parent B and, assuming that they are not hybrids, you tell me what traits the offspring will have. First we have tongue roller and non-tongue roller."

Hands shot up. Regan pointed at Sadie.

"Tongue roller," Sadie replied, with a smirk at Tyler, who always tried to answer every question.

"Why?" Regan asked.

"Tongue rolling is a dominant characteristic."

"Next, parent A has blue eyes and parent B has blue…"

"Blue eyes!" Tyler blurted out.

"What makes you so sure?" Regan asked.

"Two recessives cannot produce a dominant characteristic. Blue is recessive."

"All right, let's shift the rules a little—and no yelling out the answers, Tyler. The parents *are* hybrid, both having one brown eye gene and one blue eye gene. What percentage of offspring will have brown eyes?"

Pencils scribbled across scraps of paper and then several hands went up.

"Seventy-five percent," Tyler announced.

Regan gave him the death ray.

"Sorry."

"Does anyone agree with Tyler—who will be in the hall, if he yells out again?"

Most of the hands went up, except for Kylie, who was

still scribbling on her scratch paper. She reached for her science book and opened it up to the chapter they'd just read.

Well, at least she was on subject, Regan thought. She read the next two characteristics and the class continued to chart the imaginary offspring of hypothetical parent A and parent B. Tyler managed to keep his mouth shut, thus remaining in the classroom, and Kylie eventually put away her book and joined in the discussion, but by that time Regan was practically done with the exercise. She handed out worksheets and started the students working in pairs. Kylie and Sadie not only paired up, they spent more time whispering than working.

And for once Regan just let it go.

REGAN'S MOTHER CALLED that evening, to see if she'd applied for the position with Learning Tech.

"Not yet," Regan replied, balancing the receiver on her shoulder as she shoved clothes into the dryer.

"Regan, you're crazy to let this slide by. You were the one who wanted out of the classroom and here's the perfect opportunity. *And* you're acquainted with the person who'll be hiring."

"I'm not so certain I want out of the classroom any more. I'm enjoying the kids this year."

There was silence on the other end of the phone, then her mother said, "At least apply, Regan."

"I'll think about it. No promises."

Regan held her ground for five more tiring minutes before her mother abruptly changed the subject—something she always did when she was losing. "Did Claire tell you about my holiday plans?"

"No," Regan replied, relieved to be on a different topic.

Arlene drew in a breath. "Stephen and I are going to Vancouver, British Columbia, for Thanksgiving."

It was obvious from her brittle tone that Arlene was not happy. She'd never been one to travel for pleasure, so Stephen must have given her a heck of an ultimatum.

"I'm glad you're going to be able to relax instead of working."

"Yes," Arlene murmured with dose of sarcasm. "We'll stay in Las Vegas for Christmas, though. I'll see you then."

WILL HAD TO attend two peace-officer training sessions during the month of November. The first was an overnighter in Ely. Thankfully, Kylie and Sadie had made up, so Kylie had a place to stay. But she didn't seem all that excited to go.

"You do want to go to Sadie's, right?"

Kylie nodded, but something was off. He'd sensed it for a few days now and was wondering if she and Sadie were having trouble again.

"Honestly."

"Honestly, Dad. I think I'll go brush Skitters."

The mare had developed a real bond with Kylie—possibly because, while ignoring Sadie, Kylie had spent a lot of time with her. But Will still didn't know if he would ever let Kylie ride the mare outside the round pen or arena. She was simply too unpredictable—quiet one moment and explosive the next. At least with him. He'd sacked her out in every possible way, worked at teaching her to shy in place and she could do it. When she chose to.

She'd pulled her buck-and-roll stunt on Will again, letting him know she hadn't accidentally lost her footing the first time. Kylie assured him it would be different with her, but Will wasn't ready to take a chance with his only child. A rolling horse could kill someone.

Will packed his duffel and even though he told himself that everything was fine with Kylie, he couldn't squelch the nagging feeling that something was wrong.

He hated leaving under these conditions, but he finally gave in and called Sadie's mom. The nice thing about Beth was that she'd already raised Sadie's two other sisters and she knew when to panic and when to step back.

Beth assured him that all was well between the two girls and hinted that maybe it was just hormones kicking in.

Hormones. Great. Well, he'd better get used to it. Hormones were pretty much a fact of life, and from what he'd seen, they were likely to get worse before they got better.

But Beth wasn't so positive about her hormone theory by the time Will came to pick Kylie up again.

"You know, Will…" There was something in her voice that alerted him. "You're right. Kylie is…well, distracted seems the best way to put it. She's not herself."

He absorbed her words. "Any idea?"

"She and Sadie seem to be thick as thieves again, but she's quieter than I've ever seen her. We had to make a trip back to your place to get a few things she forgot and— I don't know if this means anything, but she brought back her picture of Desiree."

"She did?"

"I saw it in Sadie's room." She tilted her head. "This might just be part of not having a mom at a time when a girl kind of needs a mom."

Will let out a breath. "Not much I can do about that right now."

"No. But maybe you could talk to her. I know it's hard for you to talk about Desiree, but Kylie might have questions and maybe she's afraid to ask."

"Kylie afraid?"

"Maybe."

"All right. I'll, uh, see what I can do."

Kylie was quiet on the way home. Too quiet. Usually, when Will picked her up after a trip she was bubbling with excitement.

He started to ask if everything was all right, but stopped himself. He'd asked that before and it had gotten him exactly nowhere.

He waited until they were in the house. "Hey, I'm feeling like popcorn. What do you say?"

"Okay."

"I'll make it. Why don't you take your stuff to your room? Grab an ice-cube tray from the back refrigerator on your way."

"Sure."

When they were settled at the sofa with the bowl of popcorn between them and a couple of sodas sitting on the coffee table, Will dove into a subject he generally preferred not to think about, much less talk about. But he'd do this for his daughter.

"Um, Kylie?"

She frowned at his odd tone and he didn't blame her. He pushed on. "I know you've been thinking a lot lately and I was wondering... Do you have any questions about your mom?"

Kylie's gaze flashed up at him and her mouth dropped open. For a moment they stared at one another and somewhere, deep down, Will had a feeling that he was about to walk a tightrope. He was right, but it wasn't the one he was expecting.

"Maybe." She pressed her lips together for a moment, then blurted out, "I'm adopted, right?"

CHAPTER ELEVEN

"Adopted?"

"Yeah," Kylie said softly, her dark gaze clinging to his.

He moved the popcorn to the coffee table. "Why would you think you were adopted?" His mouth was dry and he had a hard time getting the words out.

"I don't look like my mother."

Relief washed over him. "You look just like your mother."

She sent him an incredulous look. "I have her picture. She's beautiful."

"So are you." He pulled her close then and hugged her tight, rejoicing that this was easier than he'd thought it would be.

"My face is all roundish and hers isn't. She has cheekbones." She spoke against his chest.

"In that picture, your mother was about eight years older than you are now. Someday you're going to look so much like her you'll be amazed." He expected to feel her relax, but she didn't. She pulled away to look up at him.

"Then what about my eyes?"

He frowned. "What about your eyes?"

"They're brown. We learned in science class that two blue-eyed people can't have a brown-eyed kid."

For a moment he was speechless. Tears were welling up in those brown eyes and he automatically reached out to wipe them away, but they only came faster, running silently down her face.

Words jumbled together in his mind. He wanted to tell her there were exceptions to genetic rules, but it felt too much like a lie, so instead he gave her an undeniable truth.

"Kylie, I was there when you were born. My name and your mom's name are on the birth certificate. I'll show it to you."

"Really?"

He let out a breath, surprised at how shaky it was.

"Really."

"I don't need to see it."

"Maybe I'd like to show it to you. Wait here."

A few minutes later he came back with the colorful certificate, and sat beside her while she looked at it. It listed the hospital, the doctor, the parents—Desiree Rose Bishop and William Trenton Bishop. Time of birth, date of birth, baby's name—Kylie Marie Bishop. Will remembered how shell-shocked he'd been when he'd helped the nurse fill out the details. He hadn't wanted anything to do with the birth, but he'd been there for his wife's sake—still hoping that maybe, once they had the child, she would settle down and they could try to work through the mistakes they'd both made.

As to being a father? It was a concept he couldn't begin to fathom, especially under the circumstances in which he found himself. He'd assumed he'd play an emotionally distant role, as his father had played in his own life, and hadn't counted on falling in love with the squalling pink bundle the nurse placed in his arms. He hadn't known it was merely a reflex action that made Kylie clamp onto his thumb with those tiny fingers. To him it represented the beginning of a lifelong bond and he knew then that he would try his hardest to make his marriage work, if for no other reason than to give this little miracle a decent life.

Unfortunately, Des hadn't been able to make the same commitment.

He reached out now to stroke his daughter's hair as she held the certificate, intently reading every word. And then she handed it back.

"Thanks, Dad."

"No problem, kid."

"I, uh, don't really feel like popcorn."

"That's okay."

"I think I might just go to bed."

"Sure." She gave him a quick hug and started toward the hall. "Kylie?"

She turned back.

"You should keep that photo of your mom out where you can see it."

She shook her head. "Not yet."

As soon as she was gone, Will sank back onto the sofa, spreading his arms out along the back and tipping his head up to study the ceiling. He'd always had a feeling this day would come, but he'd tried to tell himself it wouldn't.

There was no denying what it said on the birth certificate, but there was also no denying the color of his daughter's eyes.

He just hoped, with all his heart, that Kylie would be satisfied by the birth certificate. He'd worked so hard to give her a stable life, to protect her. It would kill him if it all started to unravel now.

TREV SWUNG BY the next morning, just after the school bus had left. Kylie had been subdued as she got ready for school and Will was uneasy. He didn't know if he'd convinced her, didn't know what else he could do but ride out the storm and hope for the best.

"You want some coffee?" Will needed a healthy dose of caffeine after yet another long night.

"Are you all right?" Trev asked as Will started to dump generous scoops of coffee into a filter basket.

Will knew, if Trev felt the need to comment, he was looking bad, so he added one more scoop for good measure. "I'm fine."

Trev didn't say another word until Will finished making the coffee and turned to lean back against the pine cabinets. "What time do you want to leave?"

"I have to bring Kylie's horse home after jumping class, so I'll meet you at six."

"Sounds good. It'll give me time to trim that horse Madison just bought. His feet are a mess."

Kind of like my life, Will thought.

WILL STAYED FOR the jumping class. He watched for a while, then paced, watched, then paced some more, his hands shoved deep in his coat pockets. It was cold in the arena. Madison didn't have the blowers on, but Regan didn't think that was why Will was pacing. Something was wrong— something more than their small blowup.

Regan hugged her arms against her chest and walked over to give Sadie advice on her seat. Will turned and paced toward the door. Regan forced herself to focus on her class as they gathered their things and headed for the door themselves.

Her car was close to Will's trailer. Too close, really, but she'd parked there first. Will was opening the rear door as she approached.

"Cold today," she commented, refusing to let herself walk by without acknowledging him. Too small a community for that. And the weather was a safe topic for passing conversation—much better than anything else they'd discussed recently.

"Yeah." He didn't look at her as he led the horse inside.

She drew in a breath, debated. Common sense lost.

"What's wrong?" If he was still upset about the other day, she was ready to have it out again, and maybe—grudgingly—ready to make peace.

"Blue eyes," he muttered from inside the trailer, in such a low voice she knew she wasn't supposed to have heard. He exited and slammed the door shut, hooked the latch.

"Excuse me?"

"Nothing." He made an effort to sound civil as he edged between her car and his trailer. "Good lesson today. You have a knack with the kids." A cardboard speech, delivered to placate her and send her on her way.

Regan frowned after him as he walked to his truck and got inside. A second later the trailer was pulling away.

Two seconds later, Regan had an epiphany.

Blue eyes...

Will was unloading the horse when she pulled into his driveway. She parked beside his truck as he released the gelding into the pasture. She had no idea what to say, but she knew she had to say something.

He latched the gate as she stopped a few feet away from him. For a moment they stood staring at one another. "Is this a parent-teacher visit?" he finally asked.

"In a way."

He set his jaw. Waited. Regan felt a sense of trepidation.

"Does Kylie's mom have blue eyes?"

He didn't answer, which was confirmation enough for her. Kylie had dark eyes. Her parents both had blue eyes. Regan had really hammered on about blue eyes during her genetics lesson.

She felt sick to her stomach.

She should have told the class that it was possible in rare cases for two blue-eyed people to have a dark-eyed child. Kylie was obviously one of those cases. Regan could only imagine how upset the kid must be.

"I had no idea…"

"How could you have?" Will asked bluntly before she could tell him she'd rectify the mistake the first chance she got.

"I'd appreciate it if you didn't, you know, let on about this. I don't think too many people know, and, well, Kylie…" He broke off, glanced away.

Regan stilled. "What are you talking about, Will?"

A swirl of frigid wind hit them and Regan hunched her shoulders against it. Will was now staring at her, apparently oblivious to the cold until she shoved her hands deeper into her pockets. "You want to go in the house?" he asked gruffly.

"Yes."

He started across the drive and Regan followed, pulling her coat tightly around her.

"Trev'll be here soon. We're going to Reno for a peace-officers' training course." He held the door open and Regan stepped into the warm of house.

As soon as he closed the door she said, "First thing on Monday, I'll explain to the classes that blue-eyed people can have dark-eyed children. It's not a true brown, but…"

"Kylie doesn't have a blue-eyed father. She has a brown-eyed father." Will leaned back against the counter, looking at her with his blue-gray eyes. "You can see why I have issues with Brett and the fact that he's back?"

There was a long, uncomfortable moment of silence, then Regan nodded. She remembered how interested Brett had been in Kylie and suddenly it took on a whole new meaning. Will's reaction to her going out with Brett had a new meaning, too.

"Has Kylie figured it out?"

"She's working on it. I don't quite know how to handle this." Will looked up at the ceiling and she knew he was barely holding on. She took a step toward him, but he put up his hand.

"Parent-teacher," he said softly.

"Screw parent-teacher."

"You need to make up your mind here, Regan."

He had a point, but she didn't back away.

"I'm sorry," she said in a whisper. Then they both heard the sound of a truck pulling to a stop. "That's Trev."

The screen door squeaked as it opened a moment later.

"It'll be okay," Will said. He swallowed. "It'll work out."

"Yes," Regan agreed, as Trev gave a perfunctory knock before pushing the door open.

She wished at least one of them could believe that.

REGAN HAD A message waiting on her phone when she got home. It was from Cheryl at Learning Tech. She would appreciate it if Regan would return her call on Monday, concerning an opening they had. Regan exhaled as she hung up the phone. Her mother must have contacted Cheryl. Or, at the very least, somehow let her know that Regan was looking. Which she was not.

Regan went out to feed Toffee and fume a little. She liked being four hundred miles away from Las Vegas. Arlene was crazy if she thought Regan was going to move back.

She put Peanut Butter inside the fence before she started tossing hay. He no longer wandered over to the neighbor's place when he escaped, but instead seemed content to graze on the dry grass just outside the pasture. He and

Toffee had developed a bond and if the little guy wandered too far away, the Thoroughbred called until he came back.

The two now happily shared a pile of hay, PB only chasing the bigger horse away when it got down to the last bits. Regan leaned her forearms on the fence and watched them eat, but the usual sense of peace she felt was marred by her mom butting into her life and by what she had learned from Will that afternoon. Her heart ached for him—and she had a hard time with the fact that, in a backhanded way, she was responsible for Kylie being closer to a truth her father didn't want her to have to deal with.

All in all, it had been a rotten enough day that she decided it was a perfect time to call her mother, confront her about the job and tell her to back off. Tactfully, of course. Arlene liked nothing better than a full frontal assault, so Regan avoided that approach. But when Arlene answered the phone, she was using the strained tone of voice that indicated something—usually something major—was amiss. What had Claire done now?

"What's wrong, Mom?"

"Nothing."

"Nothing?"

"It's Stephen. He's being unreasonable."

Regan pressed her lips together, feeling the beginning of a headache coming on. This was worse than a disagreement with Claire. This was how things had begun the previous two times Arlene's marriages had disintegrated. Her husband had become "unreasonable." He wanted his wife to spend at least a portion of her time with him, instead of devoting one hundred percent of it to her career.

"Maybe counseling, Mom."

"Counseling? Why?"

Regan closed her eyes. "It might help you communicate

with Stephen. Then you can discuss your needs and his needs and actually hear what the other is saying."

"I'm hearing just fine, thank you. He wants me to delegate important decisions to underlings and I simply do not have anyone competent enough to take over right now."

"You might want to find someone, Mom. It might be important."

"You sound just like Claire."

"Because maybe Claire knows what she's talking about."

Arlene hung up a few minutes later, leaving Regan feeling even more unsettled than before.

She reached for the phone. Claire hadn't called with a problem in more than a week, but if she had one, Regan figured now was a good time to hear about it.

THERE'D BEEN FEWER participants than expected in Will's second peace-officer's training session, so by working through the meals, they'd been able to finish a good half day early. When Will picked up his truck from the USDA parking lot it was 8:30 p.m. and he was tired. He headed for the Grants' place.

It had been a long two days, made longer by the fact that he was worried about Kylie. He couldn't tell her the truth. He knew, in his gut, Kylie would feel hurt and betrayed beyond measure and it would forever change their relationship. He wasn't prepared to face that.

Especially when there was no reason for it.

Brett was aware Kylie was his, yet he'd never made a move to acknowledge the fact. It was the one decent thing he'd done in the years since their falling out.

When Will finally pulled into the Grants' driveway and knocked on the door a few seconds later, he was beat, physically, emotionally. All he wanted to do was pick up his daughter, go home and crash.

"Will?"

Beth seemed surprised to see him.

"Is Kylie still up?" It was a dumb question. Kylie was always up at nine.

Beth turned pale. "Kylie's not here, Will."

"What?"

"Is she supposed to be here? I mean, we assumed she was only staying Thursday night—last night."

Will shook his head, trying to get a grasp on the situation. "She was supposed to ride the bus home with Sadie this afternoon, too. Spend one more night. She'd told me it was all set up."

Kylie had always made the arrangements to stay with Sadie—Will hadn't even thought of double-checking. But then, he'd always been able to trust his daughter.

Maybe she was home. Maybe she'd misunderstood. But even as the desperate thoughts rattled through his brain, he knew she'd understood him perfectly.

Beth turned and shouted, "Sadie!"

The girl appeared, took one look at Will and turned white. "Hi. I thought you were coming back tomorrow afternoon."

"I finished early."

"Where's Kylie?" Beth demanded.

Sadie swallowed hard. "She…she went to find her uncle."

"She what?" Will's heart stopped for a moment.

"She had this idea… She just wanted to know the truth, without hurting your feelings. She thought her uncle might know."

"What truth?" Beth demanded, bewildered.

"When did she leave?" Will interrupted. "How did she go up there?"

"Bensons' cattle truck. She left this morning with Zero. She told him she was meeting you up there."

And Zero was just dumb enough to believe it. Will bit back a furious expletive. "How the hell did she plan to get back?"

"She checked the trucking schedule at the feed store," Sadie replied, tears spilling down her cheeks. "They're shipping from the Friday Creek Ranch tomorrow, too. She thought she could catch another ride with Zero either today or tomorrow. Tell him you hadn't made it, after all. She wanted to get back before you got home." The last word came out on a sob. "She figured if that didn't work, then her uncle would help her out."

"Of all the stupid…" Visions of what could happen to his child out there, who the hell knew where, alone and unprotected, blazed through his brain.

"I tried to talk her out of it," Sadie said, her voice quaking. "She told me I owed her."

"You should have told *me*." Beth sounded as if she was on the verge of hyperventilating.

"I didn't know she'd actually done it until she wasn't in class this morning. She called me when she got there."

Okay. Thank the Lord for that. She got there. Now all he had to do was get her back. "Do you have a phone book?"

Beth yanked open a drawer, pulled out a phone book and gave her daughter a furious tight-lipped look. Will flipped through the pages and found the main number for the Friday Creek Ranch. It rang and rang. He was about to hang up when someone finally answered.

"I need to talk to Brett Bishop."

"I was just going to call you."

"Brett?" He recognized the clipped tones now. "Is Kylie there?"

"She's here." Relief slammed into Will.

"Is she all right?" Any other time and he would have reflected on how odd it was to talk to Brett after so many lost years. Right now he didn't care, didn't feel anything except relief that Kylie was with someone he knew, not alone on the highway somewhere.

"She's fine."

"I'll come get her."

"We're already loaded up. I'll be there in an hour and a half."

"Brett…"

"Hour and a half." And then he hung up.

Will wanted to smash down the phone, but instead he set it carefully on the cradle and turned to see Sadie cringe a little.

"She's on her way back with my brother. I'll head home and wait for them."

"I'm sorry." Sadie's voice was little more than a whisper.

"I know," Will said. And he wished "sorry" was enough to fix things.

He walked to his truck, feeling numb. He could hear Beth lighting into Sadie as the door closed behind him.

It looked as if he and Brett were finally going to continue that discussion they'd started thirteen years ago—before the sheriff had broken it up and hauled Brett off to jail for drunk-and-disorderly.

Will wondered how Kylie was going to deal with this. Hell, he wondered what *this* was. He had no idea what Brett might have told her or not told her.

And he wondered, when it was all said and done, whether he'd still have any kind of a relationship with his daughter.

Will was on the porch pacing when the lights turned into the drive. He stopped and walked to the edge of the walk, his heart hammering.

The truck pulled to a stop. Both doors opened. Kylie got out of one side and Brett out of the other.

Will had no idea what to expect and so he just stood there, his heart thumping against his ribs, waiting for a sign from Kylie. He got it. In spades. She rushed for him and threw herself against his side, hitting him with a sturdy thud.

"I'm sorry," she mumbled against his shirt.

"It's okay," he said quietly, clamping an arm around her.

"I know I scared you."

"Yeah." She had no idea how much she'd scared him or how deeply grateful he was that she was there, hugging him, acting as if she still loved and trusted him.

He met his brother's eyes then.

"Brett…"

Brett shook his head, his expression set. He got back into the truck. The door slammed and he put the rig in Reverse.

Will's arm tightened around his daughter as he watched his brother drive away.

I still have my kid.

The thought tumbled through his mind.

"Don't ever do anything like that again."

"I won't. It was stupid."

Kylie pulled in a shaky breath, then eased herself away from her father.

"Dad, I'm so sorry I didn't believe you."

"Come on," he led the way in through the kitchen and down the hall to the sitting room. "Tell me what happened."

"I hitched a ride with Zero. I told him you were going to meet me at the Friday Creek to do the brand inspections. Once I got there, I told the guys at the corrals that I wanted to see my uncle."

"What happened then?"

"It took a while because he was out gathering, but when he got there I knew who he was because he looks just like you."

"He looked really surprised when he saw me. Like he knew who I was, too. Maybe he had pictures." She raised her eyes. "Did you send him pictures?"

He shook his head, knowing that Brett had recognized her simply because she looked so much like Des.

"And then he looked mad or scared or something and asked what I was doing there."

"What did you tell him?"

Kylie swallowed. "I— What I was doing seemed so stupid, once I was there. It was a lot easier in my head. In my head I thought he would be nice."

"What happened?" Will asked gently.

"Okay... Don't be mad?"

"I promise."

"I looked it up on the internet and I shouldn't have brown eyes, Dad. I just shouldn't. I thought maybe you were just trying to protect me or something." She dropped her gaze. "I thought maybe he'd tell me the truth and you'd never need to know. I tried to call him at the Friday Creek, but he never called back, so I decided to go see him, because I just had to know."

She bit her lower lip and Will held his breath, waiting for the rest of the story. "When I asked him if I was adopted, he got all pissed and asked me if this was the way to treat my father? To run away and ask stupid questions. He was really mad, Dad. *Really* mad."

Will didn't know what to say.

"He told me that my brown eyes were just a freak of

nature, and even if they weren't, it didn't matter where I came from. I had a home and I was loved and that was what was important. And then he told me to get in his truck, because he was taking me home."

Will laid his head back against the sofa cushion.

"I'm real sorry, Dad."

"Yeah."

"Uncle Brett is kind of scary. He talked a little on the way home, but it was mostly about my being grateful for what I have." She dropped her own head back against the cushions. "He did ask me whether I rode as well as you did."

"What'd you tell him?"

"I told him yes," she replied matter-of-factly. "That was the only time he smiled." She wiped the back of her hand over her forehead. "I'm tired."

"Me, too."

"How long am I grounded?"

"You know, I think we'll just let it go this time."

"You can ground me."

"I know. But I'm thinking that you won't be doing anything like this again."

"Never," Kylie agreed quietly. "Not ever." She looked him directly in the eye. "I love you, Dad."

"And I love you, kid."

WILL SAT UP late that night, sipping good whiskey, thinking about the past and feeling deeply grateful that Kylie was on the other side of her bedroom door, sleeping in her own bed. The greatest gift of his life had come from the same man who'd perpetrated the greatest betrayal of his life. A man Will had convinced himself he hated.

And now he didn't know how he felt. He and Brett had been close as young boys, but after their mother died, their old man had delighted in pitting them against each other. He particularly liked to hold Will's achievements up as a benchmark for Brett. No matter what Brett did, it wasn't as good as what Will had done. Will had hated being the favored son, but after a while it didn't do any good to talk to Brett, because Brett had stopped listening.

Maybe what had happened had been inevitable. If it hadn't been the deal with Des, it would have been something else. Brett had wanted desperately to show up his older brother.

It was done. It was past. He now knew, for certain, that Brett was not going to try to butt into their lives, claim his rights as Kylie's biological father. From what Kylie had described, it sounded as if Brett had been frightened at the mere idea of admitting paternity. Or felt guilty. Or both.

Will finally put the whiskey bottle back in the cabinet and went to bed, stopping on his way down the hall to look in on Kylie. Stubby was asleep across her feet. The collie opened one eye, then closed it again as he adjusted his chin over Kylie's ankles. Will felt a swell of emotion as he eased the door shut and continued down the hall to his own room.

He still had his kid.

The phone rang at four-thirty, beating the alarm clock by half an hour. Will half stumbled, half jogged out to the kitchen.

"Yeah." Early morning calls weren't always bad news, but somehow he knew this one was.

"Will?"

He recognized the sheriff's baritone. "Yeah, Ernest. What is it?"

"Your brother. We just found him."

CHAPTER TWELVE

WILL'S HEART STUTTERED. "What do you mean *found him?*"

"Lying in the road at the turnoff to Claiborne Canyon. He's in bad shape. From the tracks around there, it looks like he tried to intervene in a stock theft and someone beat the shit out of him. There's an ambulance in transit from Elko. You need to go to the hospital, Will."

"That bad?"

"Could be."

Will hung up the phone and glanced at the clock. He couldn't take Kylie with him and he wasn't going to take her back to the Grants—not unless he absolutely had to. They had a few issues to work out with Sadie, without Kylie being in the middle of things, making matters more tense.

He reached for the note card stuck to the fridge and dialed Regan's number. Too damn early, but not much he could do about it.

"I need a favor."

Less than twenty minutes later, he was steering his stubborn daughter up Regan's front steps. Regan held the door open for Kylie, but her eyes were on Will.

"Thanks for doing this." He set Kylie's small suitcase, still packed from her disastrous stay at Sadie's, just inside the door.

"I'm glad to help." Regan was pale. A small part of

him still wondered just how attached she'd become to his
brother.

"They've taken Brett to Elko. I'll call when I know
something." Kylie had flopped down on the couch and
was staring straight ahead. She'd insisted she should come
with him, but he wouldn't let her.

"Keep an eye on her, would you?"

"Don't worry."

But he knew he was going to. Even with the small
amount he'd told Kylie, he knew she was blaming herself for Brett being in the wrong place at the wrong time.

"She's thinking this is her fault."

"I'll take good care of her. Honest." Their gazes held
for a moment and then Regan stepped forward and put her
arms around him, pressing her cheek against his chest.
Will hugged her tightly, inhaling her scent and wishing
life weren't so damned complex.

"You'd better get going," she finally said, as she eased
herself out of his arms.

"I'll call when I know something."

"Do that."

He turned and jogged to his truck, getting in without
looking back. Kylie was in good hands. He'd deal with
everything else later.

Kylie sat on the sofa, her arms wrapped around her waist,
staring blankly. Regan had no idea what to say to her. She
was fine with kids, in a teaching capacity. But with this
kind of stuff… She decided to offer some hospitality.

"Would you like to get a little more sleep? I have a
guest room."

Kylie shook her head.

"Something to eat?"

"No, thanks," she murmured, hugging her arms a little tighter. Regan gave hospitality one last shot.

"Television?"

Another shake of the head.

"All right. Well, I'm going to have coffee. Let me know if you get hungry."

Regan kept an eye on Kylie through the doorway as the coffee brewed. The girl didn't move. Finally, Regan gave up and went to sit on the couch next to her. She figured they might as well be miserable together.

"This is my fault," Kylie said as soon as Regan sat down. The girl focused across the room, a pillow hugged tight to her middle.

"How could it be your fault?"

"If he hadn't brought me home…"

Regan had no idea what she was talking about, but she was relatively certain that Kylie was not responsible for Brett getting beat up.

"I've spent a lot of my life thinking that various things happened because of what I did or didn't do. And it's taken me a long time to figure out that just wasn't true."

"But this *is* true. My uncle would have been on the ranch if he hadn't driven me home."

Driven her home? Regan didn't like the sound of that.

"Why don't you tell me about him bringing you home?"

A few minutes later, Regan almost wished she hadn't asked. She was never teaching genetics again.

"So," Kylie said, misreading the expression on Regan's face as an indication of blame, "you see what I mean?"

"No," Regan said firmly. "This isn't your fault."

Kylie looked away.

"Kylie."

The girl refused to turn her head. A tear spilled down

her cheek. Regan went into the kitchen and got a box of tissues, which she set on the end table next to Kylie.

"I need to feed Toffee and Peanut Butter. Why don't you come with me?"

Kylie grabbed a tissue and wiped her eyes, then got to her feet without a word.

So far, so good. Regan led the way out the back door.

"Would you put the hose in the water tank?"

She got a mute nod in reply. Kylie submerged the end of the hose and Regan turned on the water.

"I think maybe we should cancel jumping lessons today."

"Yeah."

Regan cut the strings on a bale of hay. "Two flakes for Toffee and one for PB. Spread them far apart."

"Okay."

The feeding was done in no time. "You want to go grocery shopping with me? I usually go early."

"Can we stop by my place on the way back?"

"Why?"

"Dad didn't have time to feed the horses. Maybe we could do it."

"All right."

It took Kylie almost twenty minutes to feed all the animals. She saved Skitters for last, walking into the corral and wrapping her arms around the mare's neck before she went for the hay. The mare nuzzled her.

"Dad won't let me ride her, except in the round pen and the arena. She's blown up with him a couple of times out in the desert, but I know she wouldn't do it with me." She turned to look at Regan. "Maybe with Toffee...?"

Regan shook her head. "I'm not going to let you ride her, kiddo." Not even if it took her mind off her uncle.

Kylie pressed her cheek against the silvery mane. She

pulled in a deep breath. Her entire body shuddered when she let it out.

"I'm afraid we're going to have to can her," she said, her voice cracking. "Because she's not trustworthy."

"If your dad sold her as a riding horse, she might hurt someone."

"She wouldn't hurt me. She makes me feel better."

"Maybe he could sell her as a broodmare."

"Can't. She has a tipped uterus." The clinical assessment sounded odd coming from someone Kylie's age.

Regan reached out and touched Kylie's shoulder just as the phone in her car began to ring. Kylie ran for it, barely getting the gate closed behind her.

Regan latched it. She tossed Skitters' hay into the feeder, then followed Kylie to the car.

"Really?" she heard the girl say. "Honest?" Kylie kept her gaze down, a frown of concentration drawing her dark brows together as she listened. "All right. Yes, I will. Okay, I'll tell her." She glanced up at Regan, then down again. "When? I'll tell her. Thanks, Dad. Thanks."

She pushed the end button.

"Uncle Brett is going to be okay. Dad says he'll call later, but right now he and Trev have to do something." The smile suddenly faded and her mouth started to quiver. She squeezed her eyes shut, pressed her lips together. Regan couldn't hold back any longer. She stepped forward and pulled the girl into her arms. Kylie collapsed against her, choking on deep sobs of relief. Regan held her until the sobs had turned to hiccups, by which time Regan's shirt was soaked.

"I'm sorry," Kylie said at last. She pulled back and Regan smoothed her hair away from her damp forehead. "I was really afraid."

"So was I."

"You didn't act like it."

"It's an adult trick."

"I usually figure those out."

"I know, but you're working at a disadvantage today." Regan steered Kylie over to her car. "Come on. Let's go back to my place for now. We can make some lunch, and you can tell me what your dad said."

Kylie sniffed and wiped her nose on her sleeve. "All right."

"WHAT ARE YOU doing for Thanksgiving?" Kylie asked half an hour later, after helping Regan make turkey sandwiches for their lunch.

"I'm going to Vegas to visit my sister and my mother." Or actually just her sister, since Arlene would be off on a reluctant vacation. If she and Stephen were still together.

"It's funny thinking about a teacher having a mother."

"Well, we're not hatched from eggs."

Kylie smiled. "I was kind of thinking that you could have spent Thanksgiving with us, but I guess you gotta go see your mom."

Gotta being the keyword there. "Trust me, I'd much rather spend it with you guys." Regan was more than a little surprised at the offhand invitation, after Kylie had warned her away from Will more than once.

"Really?"

"Really," Regan replied adamantly.

"What's your mom like?"

Regan almost said "stressful," but she caught herself. "She's…nice. She's successful in business. She wears clothes I hate. Blouses with bow ties and suits—things like that." Kylie giggled and Regan left it there.

"I think I did okay without a mom."

"You have a terrific dad."

"I know."

Kylie hesitated, then said, "You want to see a picture of my mom?"

"Yes. I would." She wanted to see the woman Will had married. The woman who'd had Will's brother's baby.

Kylie went to her suitcase and pulled a framed photograph from under her clothes.

Regan's first thought upon seeing the picture was that Kylie's mom was young. Very young and very beautiful. Kylie was almost a clone.

"How old was she here?"

"Dad said, when this photo was taken, she was eight years older than I am now, so I guess about twenty. She was a year older than Dad." Her mouth tightened. "Maybe that's why it didn't work out."

"I doubt that," Regan said softly. "It was probably just the fact that they were so young."

"That's what Dad says."

"Do you miss her?"

"No. It's like she's not real. She's just this…picture."

Regan thought that was sad, but it showed what a job Will had done, being both mother and father to the girl.

REGAN SETTLED DOWN to grading later that afternoon, even though her concentration was nil. Kylie amused herself going through the bookshelves.

Will had called again, this time to talk to Regan. He reported that Brett had been beaten almost beyond recognition. He had a battered, swollen face, a fractured wrist, a couple of cracked ribs and a helluva concussion. He was being kept in the hospital for another two days, to be monitored for possible internal injuries, but he was expected to recover. Kylie didn't know the extent of his injuries—

only that he was going to pull through—and she was feeling much better.

"Look at your hair." She pulled Regan's junior high yearbook closer, wrinkling her nose as she studied a picture.

"Don't rub it in."

"If the kids saw this…"

"I'll know who showed it to them. I'm going to count my yearbooks when you leave."

"Yes, but you have a scanner on your printer."

"And I also have your grade under my control." Regan got to her feet. She was antsy and so was Kylie.

"Let's make cookies."

Regan wrinkled her brow at the suggestion. "I don't have any dough."

"That's probably because you have to make it first," Kylie replied.

"From scratch?" Regan bought her dough ready-made. Less chance for error that way.

"Yeah. Dad taught me. We make Christmas cookies in the summer sometimes. His mom used to do it with him, before she died."

"I don't know about Christmas cookies, but if we're going to make any kind of cookies, we'll have to go to the store again."

Kylie looked at her as if she were from Mars. "You don't have flour and butter and eggs and baking powder and salt?"

"I have eggs and salt and butter."

"No flour?"

"Get your coat. We'll go buy some."

They'd just returned from the store when Sadie's mother called. They had been shopping in Elko when they heard about Brett, and so they'd stopped by the hospital and offered to let Kylie spend the night with Sadie. Will had agreed.

"We're on our way home now. I think we should be there by six or so."

"I'll call before I bring her over."

"We'll stop by and pick her up."

Kylie was blatantly eavesdropping. "I was kind of hoping to stay here," she said when Regan hung up.

Regan was touched—and just a little concerned. It probably wouldn't be good if Kylie got too attached—although Regan sensed she was stepping over that line herself. "Well, I wouldn't mind, but I really think this is important to the Grants. I think they want to prove they're trustworthy, and that they won't lose you again."

"I guess I can see that."

"They *won't* lose you again, will they?"

Kylie smiled ruefully and shook her head.

Kylie and Regan spent over an hour making cookies. Kylie'd found a recipe on the internet, but then had to scold Regan for not having the proper baking supplies. Regan talked about the beauty of improvising, though in reality the ability to improvise was one of her weaknesses. She liked things planned and wanted to know exactly where she was going, exactly what was expected of her. Then she could deal with things and relax.

Unfortunately, she couldn't think of many aspects of her life that fit those parameters at the moment.

Almost seven hours later, she pushed aside her grading. Kylie had gone home with the Grants and the house was quiet without her. Regan was no longer able to focus and she was ready to call it a night, when headlights swung into her driveway. Her pulse jumped. It had to be Will. Who else would be stopping by her place so late?

Pete.

Totally mystified and more than a little wary, Regan went out onto her porch, shutting the door behind her. It was close to ten o'clock and extremely chilly, but she had no intention of letting the man into her house. And the look on Pete's face when he stepped on the illuminated walkway told her that she could dispense with the pleasantries.

"Pete." She acknowledged his presence with the single word.

"Miss Flynn."

"What brings you here?"

"I want to give you some career advice."

At ten o'clock. This couldn't be good.

"What kind of career advice?" Regan hugged her arms around her midriff as a gust of wind blasted them. Pete didn't seem to notice the wind. Or maybe he had so much insulation that it didn't bother him.

"They're desperate for warm bodies in the classrooms down in Vegas and you're homesick. I suggest you apply for one of the many semester openings there. If you do, I have it on good authority the school board will release you from your contract with no hard feelings."

Regan had to fight to keep her jaw from dropping. Talk about putting the cards on the table.

"You seriously think I'm going to do that?"

"If you don't, you'll wish you had."

"Another threat?"

"Another threat?" he echoed mockingly. "Think about it. If you transfer out of here, your career is intact. If you don't, well, you might not be the only one hurt when I bring my concerns before the board. This is a small community. Word travels."

She must have reacted then, because Pete smiled.

"Kylie Bishop," he said softly. "Don't you think she's going to find this embarrassing?" His expression hardened.

"Although, frankly, the kid could use a little embarrassment. Maybe it would shut her up."

"Get off my property."

Pete bowed his head in a condescending salute. "Make a careful choice, Miss Flynn. It could affect your career, as well as a little girl's peace of mind."

It was all she could do not to chuck one of her empty clay flowerpots at the back of Pete's fat head as he walked down the dimly illuminated path. Instead, she pulled in a deep breath then blew it out as she stood. She watched until the jerk reversed out of her driveway. She wanted to make certain he was truly on his way and not setting up surveillance cameras before he left.

And speaking of which, a movement in the window of her neighbor's house caught her eye. The place was dark, but the yard light lit up his place like daylight and the curtain had definitely moved.

Was her manure-toting neighbor spying on her for Pete? Or was he just a nosy old man?

WILL WAS ON his way out of the hospital for the night, when Trev showed up.

"How's Brett?" Trev looked patently uncomfortable, though he'd barely set foot in the foyer. He hated hospitals.

"Better. They may move him out soon."

"Good." Trev waited a moment before he said,

"I think I have something."

"What's that?" They started moving toward the exit.

"I talked to the kid who found Brett. He didn't tell Ernest everything."

"Why?" Will pushed the door open and they stepped out into the cool night air.

"Because he's a Stanley. You know how they feel about any branch of law enforcement. Or government. Hell, we're lucky he phoned at all. Anyway, a truck passed him driving in the opposite direction just before he found Brett."

"Who was it?"

"Charley Parker. And there's something else. He says he saw Charley's truck carrying a load of panels up Claiborne Canyon a few days ago. Like he was going to gather."

"He doesn't have any cattle up there to gather. In fact, there shouldn't be any cattle on that allotment right now."

"But there were, according to the kid. Just ten to fifteen head that should have been somewhere else, but weren't—and I think that's why the kid talked to me. I have a feeling that he'd planned to do a little cattle thieving up there himself and he's torqued that Charley beat him to it."

"We might have to do something about this."

"We already are. I told the Stanley kid I'd make it worth his while, *if* we could catch old Charley in the act. He was agreeable."

"It takes a thief to catch a thief?"

"Yep."

BRETT WAS MOVED out of the ICU the next day. He gave a statement to the sheriff, who in turn passed it on to Trev, which was of no help since Brett didn't recall anything after turning onto Claiborne Canyon Road. And he flat-out refused to see Will.

Will wasn't surprised and didn't push the matter. He left the hospital after the last round of visiting hours, then came back the following morning. Brett remained stubborn. So did Will. He hung around until early afternoon, when he met up with one of the guys from the Friday Creek Ranch.

"Listen. Just tell him…" Will hesitated, not wanting to pour too much out to a stranger, then decided to hell with it. "Tell him that I kind of miss having a brother."

On the way home, he phoned the Grants, talked to Kylie

and asked her to stay put. She could ride the bus home from school the next day and, yeah, her uncle was fine.

As fine as he could be after having the daylights beat out of him, anyway.

Will really wanted to do something about that.

Trev called just as he was pulling back into Wesley. "Where're you at?"

"Main Street."

"Is Kylie with the Grants?"

"She is."

"Great. Meet me at the USDA office."

Ten minutes later they were on their way back down the highway in Trev's official SUV.

"Let's just say it was an abbreviated call," he said as they pulled out of town. Will understood. The Stanleys had never been big talkers. No one cared, because they were kind of scary.

"All he said was, 'Take a look at Willow Creek stone corral, and you'd better do it soon.' I don't know if he meant tonight, tomorrow or couple-of-days soon. And he hung up before I could ask."

"I'd like to check tonight." Will knew they might well get out there and find nothing, but he was glad to be doing something—anything—constructive. He was beyond edgy after spending so many hours cooped up in the hospital. He'd had too much time to think and now he needed to be doing something.

Willow Creek was forty miles out of town on a gravel road that spurred off the state highway. It was not a high-use area, so when they crested the last hill and saw tail-lights in the distance, Trev accelerated without saying a word.

Will propped his arm against his window as Trev negotiated the washboarded road, keeping his eyes on the rig ahead of them. The truck and trailer were at least two miles away, well past the Willow Creek Road, but it was entirely possible they had turned out of there.

The truck and trailer maintained a constant speed as Trev approached. Will's eyes narrowed as he got his first good look at the outfit.

"I think we should check paperwork. That's the same rig Regan and I saw in the high country." Will had a pretty strong hunch that this driver had no paperwork to prove that the cattle he was hauling were his own.

"Call Ernest, will you?" Trev turned on his light as he spoke.

It took a few seconds before the rig began to slow. It finally pulled to a stop and Trev parked at an angle behind it. The light on the top of the SUV was still flashing as Trev headed toward the driver's window, wearing his business face.

The road was raised a good two to three feet above the desert floor, in order to protect it from the spring floods. There was a steep gravel embankment on either side, and Will only had about eighteen inches of level ground between the trailer and the drop-off. He climbed up on the aluminum running boards and peered into the openings just under the roof.

The trailer was fully loaded, sagging on its springs. The cows inside were tightly packed, shuffling against one another, and the smell of urine was strong. It'd been a while since this trailer had seen a pressure washer. Will instinctively held his breath and jumped down. Fifteen head. He started edging his way toward the passenger side of the truck when the trailer suddenly started rolling backward.

"Hey!" Will shouted, automatically stepping back to the edge of the road.

The driver hit the accelerator hard.

Will jumped sideways, losing his footing and falling down the steep embankment as the trailer jackknifed. He looked up in time to see it smash into Trev's vehicle, crumpling the hood and pushing it almost completely off the road. Radiator fluid sprayed from the SUV, coating the back of the trailer, whose rear wheels had slid just far enough over the edge of the embankment to bring it to a grinding halt. The cows bellowed and smashed against the sides as the trailer tilted.

The truck lurched forward again, its tires spinning as it strained to pull the loaded trailer back up onto the road. Gravel flew, but the trailer didn't budge. Suddenly the passenger door of the truck swung open and a man jumped out. He dashed to the back of the trailer and started yanking on the latch of the damaged door, which was now slick with green radiator gunk.

The bastard was trying to let the cows go, dump the evidence, lighten the trailer and make an escape.

"Trev!" Will shouted as he scrambled up the embankment. He could hear sounds of a struggle on the far side of the trailer over the noise of the cattle—grunts and thuds, followed by a crash as something hit the side of the truck hard.

A woman started screaming and Will moved faster. He couldn't see what Trev was up against. The worst-case scenario was two against one, possibly with weapons, but then it became obvious he had his own problem. The guy at the back of the trailer abandoned the latch when he saw Will coming and charged straight at him, growling with rage.

Will dodged sideways and grabbed the man's coat as he made contact, pulling him off balance and somehow managing to block a wild punch in the process. He hung on, hindering the man's movements until they both lost their footing and tumbled back down the embankment.

Will made a lunge for his opponent, who'd broken free during the fall. He managed to get hold of the coat again, but the other guy twisted free, scrambling away on his hands and knees. A split second later he sprang to his feet and charged, tackling Will and taking him down.

But he hadn't counted on the number of years Will and Brett had spent attempting to beat each other to death. Will shifted into fighting mode.

His opponent was wiry and strong. He got in a couple of good body shots before Will finally connected with a solid fist to the jaw and the man toppled back, collapsing on the ground. He lay on the half-frozen mud, moaning.

The cows were still thrashing inside the trailer, as Will slowly straightened, working to catch his breath. With the exception of the cattle, there was now an ominous silence.

Will cautiously started for the embankment, half-afraid to call Trev's name. He could see the woman working on the damaged trailer door, trying to free the jammed handle, but he had no idea where the driver was. He was almost to the top of the berm, when a bullet zinged over his shoulder.

Instantly, he froze, his brain refusing to acknowledge what had happened.

The driver, a man Will did not recognize, stood in the middle of the roadway with a gun in his shaking hand. Trev was on his hands and knees, gasping, a few feet away. The driver's chest was heaving. Will took a slow step backward. The man lifted the gun and coolly fired again, barely missing him. "Hold still," he screamed, and then he glanced at Charley Parker's wife, who was also standing frozen, her mouth gaping open. "Get that damn door open," he growled. The words were barely out of his mouth when Trev executed a crouching tackle that even Pete would have been proud of. The driver's head hit the edge of the trailer with a sickening thud and he lay still.

"You bastard," Charley's wife shrieked, stumbling forward toward the fallen man. Will pulled her back.

"Look," Trev said, still gasping for air. He pointed in the general direction of Wesley, and there in the distance, they could see headlights.

"Damn," Will muttered. "I hope those are good guys."

CHAPTER THIRTEEN

IT WAS LATE when Will left the sheriff's office. He took the loop to Regan's house without pausing to think or analyze.

He wasn't going back to a lonely house. He'd spent too much time alone. Today. Yesterday. The past decade.

He pulled into the drive on autopilot. If Regan was awake, he wanted to be with her. He could still feel the sensation of that bullet whizzing past and see the man he now knew to be Charley's brother-in-law pointing that gun at him again. He was no coward, but confronting your own mortality did have a sobering effect.

He drew in a deep breath and got out of the truck, his sore muscles protesting the move. His boots felt as if they weighed fifty pounds each and clunked hollowly as he walked up the front steps.

Regan opened the door, a quizzical expression pulling her brows together. Then the color drained from her face as she got her first good look at him. "What happened?"

"Long story." He tried for flippant but just ended up with weary.

She took him by the arm without another word and steered him toward the open door. "You look like hell," she muttered, pushing the door shut behind them.

"You should see the other guy."

There was a fire burning low in the woodstove. She led him closer to the warmth, then bent to open the damper so that the flames grew brighter.

"What happened?" she repeated.

He gave her an overview, which consisted of "We found some people stealing cows and arrested them." He left out the part where he could have died.

"Do I know them?"

"Charley Parker's wife, her brother and one of his friends. We still don't know if Charley was involved."

He turned back to the stove, watching the light play through the little glass window. Regan stood a few feet away, watching him watch the flames.

"It was bad, wasn't it?"

"Yeah."

For a long moment the only movement in the room was that of the flames, twisting and curling; the only sound was the pop of the log as the heat intensified. Will put his fingers to his temples. His face was sore. Dirt flaked off his sleeve when he dropped his hands back to his sides. He stared down at his filthy clothing, surprised at how dirty he was.

The fire popped again.

"I wish you would come over here."

He looked over at her. "Dirt and all?" he asked quietly.

"Dirt and all."

He moved toward her. When he got close, he awkwardly put an arm around her pristine blue robe, aware of how grimy he was. She brushed at his chest, flaking more dirt off onto the hearth tiles.

"It's hopeless."

"Yeah." In many ways. But he was alive and he was here with her.

Regan leaned her head against his chest. He managed not to wince as she came upon a bruise. And then the pain evaporated as other sensations began to take its place.

He touched her face lightly with his free hand. She

glanced up and he bent his head to touch her lips. Softly. Savoring the sensation of tasting her.

She was the one who deepened the kiss, pushing her fingers into his hair, dislodging bits of mud and debris before letting her hand slide back down to grasp the edge of his shirt as she pressed her body against his. And this time he felt no pain, at all.

His breathing was unsteady when their lips parted. "Should I go home?" he asked. Because if he didn't go soon, he didn't think he'd make it out the door.

"Why'd you come here?"

"So I wouldn't be alone."

"Then, don't go. Just for tonight, Will. Don't go." Her expression was so serious that he knew she meant it. A brief sidestep from reality. A celebration of being alive, when he very easily could have been dead.

Damn, but he wanted her.

He pulled her against him, kissing her hard. She cupped his sore face in both hands.

"The shower is back here. Come on."

He followed her down a short hall, knowing there would be no going back. But deep down, he'd known that from the second he pulled into her driveway.

She snapped on the bathroom light. When he saw himself in the mirror, he was shocked that she had let him into her house, much less kissed him.

When he turned away from his reflection, Regan reached up and undid the top button of his shirt, biting the edge of her lip in concentration. He didn't move. She undid another button. His hands came up to cover hers. She raised her eyes.

"Regan…"

"Yes?"

"I don't have anything to wear after I shower."

"I'll wash your clothes."

And it would probably take a while for them to dry.

She went to the shower and turned on the water.

He eased out of his clothes, extremely aware of her standing there still dressed, watching, and of the fact that he was almost fully erect. Pushing the shower curtain aside, he stepped into a blast of blessedly hot water. Mud spiraled around his feet.

Regan picked up his clothes and he heard the bathroom door close as she slipped out. A few minutes later the water pressure bumped, telling him she'd started the washing machine. Then the door opened again. The curtain shifted a second later, sending a draft of cold air swirling in as Regan stepped into the far end of the tub. She held a net scrubber in one hand and a bar of soap in the other.

"I thought maybe I could help."

As Will ran his gaze over her, almost-erect became fully, enthusiastically erect. He was certain that teachers hadn't looked like that when he'd been in school. If they had, he would have paid a lot more attention.

"Turn around," she murmured after a perusal of what he had to offer. He turned and a moment later she was soaping down his back and shoulders, her touch light enough not to hurt too much, her strokes long and sensual. She rubbed down to the small of his back. His erection pulsed.

"I think you understated the extent of your activities tonight. You are on your way to becoming one solid bruise."

He was surprised he had enough blood left to even make a bruise. It all seemed to be ending up in another part of his body.

He ducked and let the water pour straight onto his head, but it didn't help him think any more clearly.

The scrubbing stopped. Will felt a moment of disappointment, until she put her palms flat on the muscles of his back and began to slowly rub circles in the lather. She slid her hands around Will, over the muscles of his chest where the cascade of water instantly rinsed the suds away. And then she pressed herself against him, her breasts flattening against his back.

He closed his eyes. It had been way too long since he'd done this.

He took her hand and pushed it lower, so that her fingers could encircle him. She sighed as she took hold of him. He was astonished he didn't come right then. But what a waste that would have been.

He turned, pulling her close. She lost her balance and he caught her, his hand cupping her buttocks, pressing her more firmly against his erection.

"This is dangerous," she said with a laugh.

In many, many ways. But he was not interested in assessing the danger. For once in his life, he was going to go with the moment. And to celebrate the decision, he kissed her again. And again.

"The water is getting cold," she pointed out a few minutes and many deep kisses later. "I have a small water tank."

"You should see about getting a bigger one."

She smiled, water streaming down her face. "I'll talk to the landlord."

He turned off the water, and Regan pushed the curtain open to reach for the one towel on the bar. A few seconds later she led him to her bedroom. She turned at the doorway to touch her finger to his lips in a soft caress.

"Last chance for sanity," she murmured with a raise of her eyebrows.

He was not surprised that she knew exactly what he was thinking.

"Screw sanity," he said gruffly. "At least this once."

ONCE WAS NOT ENOUGH. They made love twice. The first time was wild and needy—a long overdue release for both of them. The second time was languid and tender. Afterward, Will held Regan against him, their bodies pressed almost as closely together as they'd been while making love.

And Regan was dealing with the aftermath. Making love to Will was different than making love to anyone else. She didn't know why. She was afraid of knowing why.

"You all right?" Will murmured.

She laughed softly against his chest. "I'll survive."

"Me, too." And his voice was just intimate enough to spark her desire yet again.

This could easily become a habit, making love with him. She needed to get her feet back on the ground. Work her way back to reality.

"Where'd you meet your wife?" she asked softly, thinking this was about as real as she could get.

"Rodeo circuit. She was a barrel racer." He spoke matter-of-factly, so she chanced another question.

"And you married young?"

"Too young, but neither of us really had any family left. Her mom had dumped her with a cousin when she was just a kid. And my dad didn't have a lot to do with me after I had left home. Brett and I weren't too close, by then."

"Were you married long?" Regan propped herself up on one elbow. This was really none of her business, but she wanted to know what had happened.

"Almost three whole years," he said, with a measure of sarcasm. "We had issues from day one. Money was one of the biggest. It costs a lot to rodeo and I was tired of being broke all the time. I wanted to get a real job and try to buy a place of our own, but Des loved the rodeo. She wanted to stay on the circuit as long as we could." His lips curved humorlessly. "She wanted to party while we were young.

We agreed to do one more season before we decided anything, one way or the other, and then I got beat up pretty bad by a bronc halfway through. I came home to mend and Des kept racing. She was pissed about being alone on the road. And I was pissed she wouldn't come home with me."

Regan found herself holding her breath, knowing what was coming next and not really wanting to hear it because she knew how deeply it had hurt the man beside her. She lowered her head to the pillow.

"I started hearing rumors about her and Brett. And then," his mouth tightened, "she came home pregnant. There was no way the baby was mine." Will rolled on his side to face her, then, settling his arm over her and drawing her close. She snuggled against him.

"I don't understand how Brett could do that," Regan murmured, her voice a whisper.

"He was only eighteen, which was something I hadn't given a lot of thought to until I was pacing at the hospital the other night." Will brought a hand up to touch her hair, his fingers sifting through the layers. "Brett and I had a pretty bad fight after I found out Des was pregnant. He said she'd told him we were separated." Will let out a soft, scornful snort. "If she did, she was only referring to the distance between us. But I knew I'd screwed up by leaving her on the road. There's no doubt how she'd screwed up. We agreed we'd try to make things work, for the kid."

"It didn't work?"

He shook his head. "Des wasn't cut out to be a mother. It was almost as if she lacked the confidence to take care of someone other than herself. I think she was scared. One day she just left. She didn't sneak out or anything. She just told me she couldn't do it, handed me Kylie, walked to her truck and left."

"And that was that?"

"That was that. I hated her for a while. Okay, more than a while." A muscle worked near the corner of his mouth. "But I don't hate her anymore."

Regan pulled the blanket over them and cuddled closer to Will's side, telling herself to stop thinking.

REGAN WASN'T SURE exactly when they'd fallen asleep, but she had a feeling she'd been the first to succumb. She awoke when Will gently eased away from her.

"I've got to go," he said softly. His voice was intimate, stirring things inside her. He did a little more damage by pressing a kiss to her temple.

"What time is it?"

"Nearly five."

She pushed herself upright. He gently brushed the hair away from her cheek. "Stay here. I'll let myself out."

She heard him dressing in the clothes she'd put in the dryer after they'd made love the first time. A few seconds later, the front door opened and closed, then she heard the rumble of his truck's diesel engine. She pulled the blanket around her shoulders more tightly, missing his warmth. Missing him.

And once again she felt not quite in control, even though she'd made it clear they were only going to be together for that one night. It alarmed her.

She consoled herself with the thought that they both understood the situation. This was a one-time thing, meant to be healing. And that was that. She was not taking a lover.

Not even Will.

PETE'S LOOKING FOR YOU."

Regan had barely put her coat away when Tanya stuck her head into her classroom.

"Thanks." Regan opened her bottom drawer and put her purse inside.

"There you are." Mrs. Serrano peeked in next to Tanya. "Mr. Domingo would like to meet with you before classes." She gave a gentle, unreadable smile and disappeared.

"What do you think?" Regan asked Tanya.

"I think we'd better plan on a wine-cooler night."

"I hope not," Regan said, as she put on her professional face and headed down the hall.

Pete was waiting in his trophy-studded lair.

"Please close the door."

Regan closed it and moved to the chair, but she didn't sit.

"I'll need you to sign this," Pete said, pushing a student transfer form toward her. "You won't need to collect the texts. The next teacher will get them back to you at the end of the year."

Regan stared at the paper and then her gaze shifted to Pete.

"Why is Kylie being taken out of my classes?"

"For her own well-being."

Regan's mouth dropped open. Pete gave her that cold smile of his. "Miss Flynn, when you spend the night with someone, you shouldn't let him park his vehicle where everyone can see. It gives rise to speculation."

Regan had no defense.

"Please don't take Kylie out of my classes. She won't understand."

"I guess you should have thought of that before. I did warn you." He tapped his pen on the desk, next to the paper she had yet to sign. "You know, there are still quite a few semester openings in your old hometown. You may want to think about applying."

"Or maybe I'll just stay here and see how this all plays

out. You aren't principal yet. You're an interim." She managed to make the last word sound satisfyingly derogatory.

"I'm still writing your evaluations."

"Yes, and while you're doing your best to make me look bad here, you're also making it darned hard for me to go elsewhere. Think about it."

She could see he hadn't considered that point.

"I'm not signing that," she said. "Do whatever you do when a teacher refuses."

"So, HOW BADLY did I mess up?" she asked later, as she and Tanya and Karlene, who was still dressed in her gym clothes from teaching PE, settled into Tanya's overstuffed chairs with their wine coolers. Pete had written her up for professional insubordination, for refusing to sign the transfer request. He'd sent a copy to the superintendent, and she could only imagine what else he'd told the boss. Regan had a feeling her days in the district were numbered. She hadn't quite realized how much went on behind the scenes in a smaller district, how many people owed each other favors.

And then, to add insult to injury, word had come down that the school board had approved a district transfer procedure for administrative jobs. When the principal's job was announced in March, it would be open to transfer, prior to being advertised. The only reason they would have done that was if Pete had already been slated unofficially for the position. Regan knew, without a doubt, that her life would be a living hell if she stayed. Pete Domingo was not a forgive-and-forget sort of guy.

"How'd Kylie take being moved out of your classes?" Tanya asked, pushing her blond hair back over her shoulders. It immediately fell forward again.

"She thinks I had something to do with it. I never got the chance to explain. Not that I'd know what to say." There really wasn't much she *could* say, considering the situation, and she despised Pete for putting her in that position. "Has this ever happened before?"

Karlene and Tanya exchanged glances.

"It has, but never like this. If it was known that a parent and a teacher were…friendly, shall we say, then the registrar wouldn't put the kid in that teacher's class," Tanya explained. "To avoid conflict of interest."

"So they don't automatically enforce that rule Pete threatened me with? The one concerning parents and teachers?"

"I think the only morality thing they actually enforce, without exception, is the moral-turpitude clause and you have to get pretty wild for them to employ that."

"But," Karlene said carefully, "Pete could justify taking Kylie out of your class if he had to."

"How?" Regan asked, wanting to know Karlene's take on the matter. She was a native of Wesley and had worked in the district for more than ten years.

"By saying that being in your class is detrimental to Kylie. That it affects her academic performance. That she is embarrassed by the rumors and that he's only thinking of the good of the child."

Regan held up a hand. "I get the picture." Pete could very well say all those things—whether they were true or not—and look like a child advocate in the process. "You know this district, Karlene. Can Pete make much trouble for me? Concerning Will, I mean?"

Karlene wrapped one of her brown curls around her index finger. "Under normal circumstances, nobody would dream of saying anything about you and Will. It would be your own business. You know, like it is in real life. But if Pete decides to make a big deal of this…" She sucked air through her teeth and left the rest unsaid.

"The school board is conservative and it looks like they're impressed by Pete," Tanya said as she followed Karlene's line of reasoning. She leaned forward, her expression sober. "My feeling is that if Pete decides to push the matter and get loud about it in the name of protecting morality and decency and peace of mind, the board will do what looks best. As near as I can tell, appearances are more important than reality with public boards."

"And you did annoy the Taylor family and there's a Taylor on the board," Karlene pointed out with a tilt of her bottle.

"Thanks for reminding me," Regan muttered. "So what do you think they would do, if Pete made a big deal?"

"Probably give you an official reprimand and a warning," Karlene said. "They won't fire you or anything, but it would go on your record. And I'm sure they'd put a letter in your file, documenting the incident."

"That doesn't sound good." Prospective employers would want to read her file. Regan set aside her wine and slumped lower in her chair. She hadn't really thought about how much politicking she was up against.

"It's not good. Rumor travels fast. And sometimes one letter in your file can lead to another."

"And since Pete hasn't been laid in a decade," Karlene added, "he can make a big sanctimonious deal with no fear of repercussion."

Well, that didn't sound too good, either. Especially in light of the fact that the board had adjusted hiring protocol to make it easier for Pete to slide into the principal's position.

They sat quietly for a moment.

"So," Regan summarized, "what you're both saying is that Pete can definitely make trouble for me one way or another."

Both of her friends nodded.

"Lovely," she murmured. "So glad I got on his bad side." She picked up her wine, took a healthy swallow and set it back down on the table with a hollow thump.

Karlene shifted in her chair. "Do you want to stay? Here in the district?" she asked, reaching down to catch the lavender afghan that had started to slide off her chair when she'd moved.

"I like this district—except for Pete. I don't want to go back to Las Vegas." But she would, if she had to; in fact, she was already taking steps in that direction, just in case. She not only had herself to feed now, but her horse and pony, too, and she wasn't giving them up. She hoped. It would be expensive to board a horse and a pony in Las Vegas, unless she got roommates to help with her rent. Or moved in with Claire. She wasn't certain she could take that much drama. She seemed to be generating enough of her own lately.

"Well, I, for one, don't think we should let Pete push Regan around," Tanya said, draining the last drops of her wine.

"And what do you, for one, think we should do about it?" Karlene asked.

"I say we show a united front, make a point of the fact that our private lives are just that."

"That's the problem," Regan said softly. "If we do that, my private life won't remain private." And she wasn't going to put Kylie through the embarrassment. She'd been through enough lately. "I'm going to handle this alone, although I'm not sure how just yet. Pete's clever. Everything he does in public shows him to be a guy focused on fulfilling his administrative duties."

"Taking the hard line," Karlene muttered. "Running a tight ship."

"He has the board impressed," Tanya added, quietly.

"Because they aren't teachers. They don't have a clue." Karlene drained her glass, then looked at her watch. "I have to go meet Jared."

Regan and Tanya looked at her with surprise.

"Yes," she said briskly, picking up her jacket, "we're skirting the school fraternization rule, which is a real rule," she added with a glance in Regan's direction. "But, he's only a sub, so I'm not sure it applies."

"It will, if you annoy Pete," Tanya pointed out. "Is Jared still considering the Barlow Ridge job?"

"Too far away, but," Karlene smiled, "Mrs. Biggs is finally talking retirement and that would open up a third-grade job. That's what we're hoping for. That way we'd be at different schools and we could come out of the closet." She zipped her coat with a flourish. "Think good thoughts for us, okay?"

"DAD, IT WAS an accident." Kylie's lower lip was quivering. He leaned closer to look at the nasty bruise blooming just above the top of her cowboy boot. Skitters had come unglued when a loose paper had blown into the arena and even though Kylie had ridden her out nicely, the mare had smashed her leg against the arena rail.

Kylie gulped a breath. "Give her another chance."

His expression must have told the story. The mare could have broken Kylie's leg. Accidents happened in riding, but there was no sense helping them along. There were too many other good horses out there, to keep one that wasn't trustworthy.

"It isn't her fault," Kylie said from between her teeth. "She's reacting."

As if he didn't know that. The only problem was, Skitters' fears were so deeply ingrained that no matter how much Will worked with her, he knew he'd never trust her. Her self-protective instinct was too strong. Whatever had happened to her was too much a part of her.

"This stinks," Kylie muttered, before she turned and limped toward the house, her back stiff. "First Regan, now you."

Regan. No longer Miss Flynn after their days together, although Will was certain that she still called her Miss Flynn at school.

Or would have, if Regan had still been her teacher.

Kylie was damned upset over that one. He couldn't blame her, and he couldn't explain what had happened, either.

Regan had called just before Kylie'd gotten home to warn him about the transfer. She was at school, so the conversation was, of necessity, short, but it wasn't hard to deduce that their mutual "going with the moment" the night before was producing consequences neither of them had foreseen. With his daughter bearing the brunt of them.

It made him angry. And now it looked as though he was going to have to do something about Skitters.

If the horse stayed, Kylie would insist on riding her. She was convinced that she could break through the animal's fear. And Will was afraid of what might happen if she kept trying. He was going to have to help Kylie face reality, and that was going to hurt, too.

Will was beginning to feel like a damned failure as a father and protector.

As soon as Regan got home, she went to her closet and pulled out her interview suit, checking it over to see if it was ready for action or if it needed a quick trip to the dry cleaners. She had not grown up with Arlene Flynn Duncan Bernoulli at the helm without learning a thing or two.

First, cover yourself—have a safety net in place before you act. And that meant being prepared in case the worst happened and she had to leave Wesley. She loved her job, but she was not going to stay in a position where she had to answer to a bullying principal. Life was too short.

With that in mind, she'd spent her prep period that day contacting the central district office in Las Vegas, Learning Tech and even her old school. She'd signed off to let her personnel file, complete with Pete's less-than-complimentary evaluation, go south if a prospective employer wanted it. And they would. As Pete had said, they needed warm bodies in the classrooms in Las Vegas, so she knew she'd be offered a position—whether she wanted to go back or not. Unfortunately, Las Vegas was the only place with jobs available midyear. She feared that Pete might be able to do her so much harm if she stayed until the end of the school year that she would have a hard time getting a job anywhere. If she was going to take a stand, she had to be ready to retreat.

And she was honest enough to admit to herself that maybe she was looking for a reason to retreat. An easy way out that allowed her to leave before she had to face the fact that she and Will were not going to be able to live in the same place and ignore one another. Will had a daughter to protect and the level of relationship he needed was far beyond what she thought she wanted or was even capable of. She needed to get out, before she hurt any of them more than she already had.

As part of her campaign to make Pete accountable, Regan had submitted a written request for a meeting with Pete and their immediate supervisor, which in this case happened to be the superintendent of schools. She knew exactly when Pete had learned of her request. He'd stalked into her classroom and stood at the rear, glowering at her under the guise of informal observation. Regan kept her cool and added to the documentation she'd spent the previous weekend compiling. It was probably too little, too late, but she was determined to take a stand. She knew enough about bullies to know that Pete was never going to let up on her, but at the very least, she'd go down swinging.

She received word late the next afternoon that the meeting would take place in three days. She was encouraged to have representation, if she so desired. Regan did not "so desire," even though she knew Arlene would think she was making a rookie move. She wanted to keep things as private as possible.

She contacted her friend Cheryl, at Learning Tech, as she drove home, to explain the so-so evaluation that Mrs. Serrano had already faxed her. Cheryl assured her it was only a small part of the overall selection process and that, frankly, Regan was exactly what they were looking for.

Regan hung up, knowing she should feel elated, but instead she felt depressed.

When she got home that afternoon, she fed her horses and decided it was time to have a chat with her neighbor. The old guy now waved at her when he pushed his wheelbarrow down the drive, but he didn't seem to have a lot to say. It was possible, though, that he was more vigilant than verbal.

Regan headed across her property line, being careful to stay on the path and out of his garden beds, and quickly discovered that her neighbor, whom she was to call Chet from now on, was more than happy to respond when asked direct questions.

Yes, Pete Domingo had stopped by once, but Chet had no idea that Pete was anything other than curious when he'd asked a few questions about Regan. He didn't even know Pete was her boss. He thought he was the football coach and Will's friend. In fact, his excuse for stopping was that he was looking for Will.

Regan knew that Will would love that. He and Pete. Friends.

And it turned out Chet did remember the night Pete's car had pulled in so late. He also remembered the other night when Will's truck came late, too. And stayed. Chet was a very vigilant neighbor.

Regan thanked him and promised him full access to all the fertilizer her horses could produce. She added to her documentation as soon as she got home, then wondered if Chet was watching when Will knocked on her door later that night.

No matter. She pulled the door open, but she was unprepared for the powerful emotions that swept over her when she came face-to-face with the man she had to admit she'd been avoiding.

CHAPTER FOURTEEN

"I HAVEN'T SEEN you in a while, so I thought I'd stop by. You know… So we could talk in person." Will knew they were both remembering the last time he'd "stopped by." With some difficulty, he shifted his attention back to business. "I want to know why Pete took Kylie out of your class." He had a pretty good idea, but he wanted confirmation.

Regan stepped back, politely allowing him to enter the house before she answered. It was hard to believe they'd made love, passionately, not that long ago.

"Someone saw your truck here the other night," she said after closing the door. "And Pete's making the most of it."

"Regan," Will reached out, but she took an automatic step back. He let his hand fall to his side and felt something close up inside of him at the distance she put between them. "I would never have stayed if…"

"Hey, I knew what I was risking, and I'd do it again." But she spoke so calmly, he wondered if she meant it.

"What's going on with the job?"

Regan's mouth tightened. "It's becoming clear that I can't work for Pete and it's possible I'll be taking a job elsewhere at the end of this semester."

She was leaving? He hadn't been ready for that. "Kind of drastic, don't you think?"

She moved to the sofa, idly running a hand over the fleece blanket lying along the back. "It's pretty certain, according to those in the know, that Pete will become principal—the school board is paving the way. He'll be looking for ways to get rid of me and I don't want to work under those conditions."

He hated the cool, straightforward way Regan was presenting the facts, although he knew it was her defense. "Is leaving your only option?"

"I have a meeting with the superintendent, but I don't think it's going to do a lot of good. Pete has the home-field advantage." She folded her arms. "It's probably for the best, considering everything involved."

"Meaning me?"

"Yes."

He took a couple of steps forward. "Look, Regan, I know you've had some bad experiences with relationships." She smiled tightly, but said nothing. "And I have Kylie to think of. But maybe if we take things slow, stay sane about it."

Regan shook her head. "We've complicated things enough being just friends. Let's not complicate them more."

He studied her for a moment. Her defenses were a mile high. She was running on instinct and he knew there was no sense in trying to communicate with her now. He'd have to wait until she quit running. Then maybe he could help her move past the fear.

Damn, he hoped so, because this was ripping him apart.

"Then there's not a hell of a lot more to say, is there?"

"No, Will, there's not."

THIS TIME IT HURT. Every other time Regan had eased her way out of a situation that had been getting too close, it had felt uncomfortable yet inevitable—something that had to be done.

Not this time.

And the bizarre thing was that she and Will had barely even started a relationship. One night couldn't even be called a relationship, which only drove home the point of how important it was to end things now before they got crazy.

She spent the rest of the evening trying not to think about Will and instead concentrating on her upcoming meeting with Superintendent Zeiger and Pete. She didn't have much luck.

The next school day passed all too fast and Regan's stomach was in a knot, but she was as ready for her meeting as she was ever going to be. Pete might end up with a Regan Flynn–free district, but he was going to have to work for it. Regan was not going down without getting in at least a few pokes at him.

"We're going to keep this informal," Superintendent Zeiger said, pointing Pete and Regan toward their chairs.

Like her, Pete had dressed in his administrative best and he did look rather impressive in a bullfroggish way as he lowered his well-tailored bulk into a chair. "Neither of you have opted for representation, so let's see what we can do about this situation." He put his hand on Regan's sheaf of papers. "Miss Flynn has some concerns that she has documented here. Apparently some friction has developed between you two, starting with a student prank involving lab materials, followed by some question of athletic eligibility?"

"I'm not certain what Miss Flynn has *documented,* but I assure you, I've done everything by the book." Pete straightened his striped tie importantly as he spoke.

Regan barely kept her mouth shut.

Zeiger leveled a questioning look at Pete. "A home visit at ten o'clock at night? Apparently witnessed by Miss Flynn's neighbor?"

Pete's mouth popped opened, but he immediately clamped it shut again. "I had reason to believe Miss Flynn was looking for a new position. I stopped to tell her about one I had heard of."

Of all the flipping flat-out lies. Regan's jaw muscles tightened as she struggled to maintain her composure. She could almost hear her mother whisper: *Don't show weakness.* It helped.

"It didn't seem professional to mention it at school," Pete continued. "I thought it would be more appropriate in a private setting. I didn't realize she'd try to twist a perfectly innocent incident, one in which I was trying to help her."

Pete began folding and creasing one corner of the manila folder in front of him, then caught himself. His fidgeting subsided as he raised his double chin and announced, "Miss Flynn opposes me whenever possible. In fact, I'd say whatever complaints you've had are in retaliation for me simply doing my job."

"So, you're saying there is some friction, Pete?"

Regan held her breath as she watched him search for an answer. Finally, he settled for a succinct yes. He couldn't very well say anything else, with her sitting across from him, ready to contradict him. "But it's her fault."

Zeiger nodded. "Would you be willing to undergo peer counseling to work it out?"

Pete's eyes widened. "I don't think that would be necessary."

"I do," Regan said. Pete sent her a killer look.

"Pete?"

"Mr. Zeiger, she is doing this just to make me look bad at a sensitive time in my career."

"If that's the case, we need to deal with it. Whether you're principal or not, Pete, you and Miss Flynn will be working together."

Regan could tell from the way Pete was staring at her that as far as he was concerned there was no way they'd be working together in the future. He'd get her for this.

"You know I'll do whatever it takes to help in the smooth running of my school," Pete said.

"Good. We'll set something up."

The meeting ended shortly thereafter. Pete stalked out through the main office. Regan was almost to the door when Zeiger called her back.

"May I take another moment?"

"Sure."

"I called your former principal this afternoon."

Regan's heart skipped a beat as she once again took a seat. She'd had her share of head-to-heads with her former boss. He'd been a weak administrator, but she'd no longer call him a poor one. Working under Pete had put an entirely different spin on the definition of a poor administrator.

"We had a chat. I asked him if he would hire you again. He said he'd hire you in a heartbeat."

Regan let out a silent sigh of relief, glad to have at least one point on her side.

Mr. Zeiger carefully put back his pen in its ornate holder. "I'd hate to lose you as a teacher. I've talked to parents and students over the past few days. They like what you're doing. They think you're excellent, in fact."

"That's gratifying."

"So, that's why I hope you'll take the peer counseling seriously. Pete has some areas to work on, granted, but he's a good man and I think he'll be an excellent administrator with time."

Regan nodded. "Maybe so, but… You also might want to take an informal survey among those who are currently working for him."

"Change is never easy, Miss Flynn. Pete runs a tighter ship than Mr. Bernardi, but frankly, the school needs strong leadership, strong discipline. Things will settle."

"If Pete gets the job."

"If Pete gets the job," Zeiger agreed, but the way he spoke made Regan believe it was a done deal.

WHEN A VEHICLE pulled into her driveway after dark, Regan's heart began to race. She hoped it was Will. She hoped it wasn't. Damn. She crossed to the door and pulled it open. It wasn't Will.

"Do I want to know?"

"I'm giving Mom a time-out." Claire looked around as she stepped inside, suitcase in hand. Regan's eyes widened as she took in the size of the suitcase. "This is cute," her sister said. "A little isolated, but cute."

"Isolated? I have a neighbor close enough to spy on me." Regan closed the door. "How'd you find the place?"

"I just asked at the convenience store. They were very helpful." Claire dropped her bag and walked into the kitchen, taking inventory as she went. She'd had her hair redone since Regan had last seen her and now had a short geometric cut that went well with her retro sweater, clunky jewelry and leggings.

"Well?"

"Not quite the same as your old place," Claire said as she picked up an issue of *Western Horseman* from the kitchen table. She wrinkled her nose before she set it back down.

"Yes, but so much more me."

"Probably so," Claire agreed. She opened the fridge and pulled out a bottle of white wine. "Glasses?"

"I'll get them."

"Actually, I wanted to get out of town and I thought

you might need a little moral support, stuck out here in the wilderness." Claire unerringly opened the drawer that contained the corkscrew and lifted it out with a flourish.

"Thanks."

"I'm serious." Claire plunged the corkscrew into the top of the bottle through the foil and twisted. A few seconds later, she eased the cork free.

"You know there's not much shopping here to clear the head," Regan said, accepting a glass of wine.

"I noticed. This will be kind of like an adventure for me. You know, roughing it? I'm looking forward to meeting your animals."

"How long are you staying?"

"Just a day or two. Then I have to get back for classes."

"So, what happened?" Regan asked after they had settled in the living room with the wine and a bowl of pretzels on the table between their chairs.

"Well, I'm dropping out of engineering."

Regan almost dropped her glass. "Mom will have a cow."

"She already did." Claire smiled before she popped a pretzel into her mouth. "It was a boy." Then her expression sobered. "I don't want to be an engineer yet. Maybe sometime. Right now I want to do something more…people oriented."

"Don't you dare use the phrase *people person*."

"Mom is not happy with my choice." Claire stared down into her wine and gave it a swirl. "I've always wondered why people undervalue teaching as a career choice. I mean, what could be more important than shaping kids?"

Regan smiled. Claire would be a good teacher. She was just crazy enough that her students would never know what was coming. And she was sharp.

"There's nothing more important," she agreed. "But,"

she tilted one corner of her mouth, "you need to know that it isn't like in the books—or the college classes, for that matter. These kids are not empty vessels, waiting to be filled. They fight you tooth and nail sometimes."

"You don't think I'm up to it?"

"Of course, I think you're capable. But engineers make a lot more money, with a lot less yelling."

"That's exactly what Mom said." Claire drank the rest of her wine in one gulp. She put the glass down on the arm of her chair, keeping her fingers wrapped around the stem.

Regan couldn't help her smile. "Heaven forbid I sound like Mom. That's not supposed to happen until I have kids." She leaned over to pour more Riesling into her sister's glass and to top up her own.

Claire looked at her, her expression shrewd. "Are you ever going to have kids, Regan?"

"Well, I'd probably have to find a husband first."

"And you're probably not going to do that, are you?"

Regan stared into her own wine. "Maybe not."

"I didn't think so."

"Why do you say that?"

Claire looked at her like she was kidding. "Oh, come on, Reg. You only date walk aways.'

"Walk aways?" Regan frowned at her sister.

"You only date men that you can walk away from, when the time comes."

Regan shook her head. "Not true." She didn't think... She'd really liked all of the men she'd dated seriously. In the beginning, anyway.

Claire gave her a superior look in response.

"Let's take a look at your most recent beaus. We'll start with Jeff. He was a nice guy. Fun, good-natured, but just needy enough that he wasn't husband material—unless you wanted to help him with every decision of his day, from choosing his shirt to what time to go to bed. You probably liked the fact that he didn't try to control anything, but you couldn't really respect him, could you? So you had to…walk away."

Regan's expression grew somber. "Go on."

"Tyson. *Very* good-looking. Intelligent, fun to argue with…" Claire smiled reminiscently. "But his needs always superseded yours. I knew you wouldn't put up with that for long. The control thing again, you know."

"And Daniel?"

"Ah, Daniel. Perhaps the best of the bunch. Also good-looking, personable. Supportive. And a liar and a cheat."

"But I didn't know he was a liar and a cheat. He appeared to be almost perfect."

"Why did you date him?"

"He appeared to be almost perfect. He gave me space when I needed it."

"Did you have any intention of growing old with him?"

"No."

"Which was why he was perfect. You could eventually walk away." And she smiled in that maddening way she had.

"I don't…" Regan broke off abruptly, compressed her lips.

Claire rolled her eyes. "Regan, did you ever notice that whenever a guy got to a point where he could have a say in your life, you'd end it? I'm talking about before Jeff. Back when you were in college and maybe still believed in true love?"

Regan didn't answer, but she knew exactly what her sister was talking about.

"And then I think you just started dating guys who would cause the least amount of pain when you had to end things. Ones you weren't all that attached to." Claire smiled ironically over her empty glass. "Do you think Mom has anything to do with that behavior?"

"Of course Mom has something to do with it," Regan replied with a scowl. "I know I have control issues. So have you." She rallied a defense. "What's wrong with just dating, without having serious intentions?"

"Nothing. You get companionship. Sex."

"Exactly."

"You have a facsimile of closeness, without risking anything."

That wasn't exactly what Regan had been getting at, but it summed up her relationship with Daniel perfectly.

Claire continued her assessment without noticing Regan's expression. "You get to do what you want. Be what you want. No one has much say in your decisions."

Regan nodded, thinking that all sounded just a wee bit selfish and empty.

"But you lose something, too, Reg."

And that was where the *facsimile* came in. The relationship looked real, but it wasn't.

Regan stared into her wine for a moment. "Have you been reading self-help books?" she finally asked.

"Campus counseling center. I've been a regular since you moved. It helped me put my relationship with Mom in perspective and it's also why I haven't been calling so much." She ran a finger around the top of her glass, making the crystal sing. "I suppose you could send them a tax-deductible donation as a thank you for your quiet evenings."

"So why are you hiding out here?"

"Hey, even counseling has its limits." She smiled. "I miss you and I wish you'd come home."

"You may just get your wish."

Claire leaned forward. "What happened?" she asked.

"Job troubles."

"Tell me about it."

"I have a boss who wants to get rid of me," Regan said wearily. "He is not a person of reason."

"What man is?"

Regan smiled, then told her sister the entire story.

"That doesn't sound good," Claire said, once Regan had finished. "But tell me about the guy. Will."

"I don't really want to discuss it."

"That doesn't sound good, either."

No, it didn't, because there had never been much that Regan wasn't willing to discuss with her sister. But the situation with Will…it was going to remain private. This was something she had to figure out alone and she knew she had some thinking to do. That *facsimile of closeness* comment bothered her. A lot.

The phone rang. The sisters exchanged glances.

"If it's Mom," Claire said adamantly, "you haven't seen me."

Regan sucked in a breath and picked up the phone. There was no one she wanted to talk to right now.

"Cheryl?" Regan had spoken to her only hours ago. "Do you need any other information?

"Yes," her friend said in a sardonic voice, "if this is a bad evaluation, what do you consider a good evaluation?"

WILL SETTLED THE saddle on Skitters's back, trying not to think about the tense evening he'd just spent with his daughter, telling her how things had to be. Maybe he should have waited until the spring or just sent the mare on her way without telling Kylie. But he couldn't bring himself to lie to her and every day he kept the mare was just going to make it harder for Kylie to let go. Ultimately, he decided it was best to get it over with, so his kid could start healing on this front, too. The sale-yard truck was coming tomorrow and Skitters was slated to be on it when it left.

The mare stood stock-still, as she always did when he tightened the cinch, but Will could feel the energy vibrating through her body. A coiled spring, ready to go off at any moment.

One last ride, he told himself, even though he was not a sentimental man. He was almost hoping she'd explode again, to validate the decision he'd made.

Damn it, it was the right decision. He rubbed the mare's neck, felt the muscles start to give a little and then they pulled tight again.

Some horses could take a lot and forgive. Others learned their lessons quickly and they stuck. Skitters was certain that pain was never far away from the human touch. No matter what, that lesson was lodged in her brain. No amount of TLC was going to make her trustworthy with his daughter. Or anyone else for that matter.

The mare moved out as they headed across the river meadows. Will kept his attention on the ride, even though part of his mind kept edging toward thoughts of Regan.

Skitters went willingly, ears forward, moving out, almost as if she sensed these would be her last moments of total freedom. They crossed one low pass over the hills behind the house and then another. Will felt himself relax, his mind again began to wander, but he caught himself.

Maybe he should keep the mare.

For Kylie, as a pet.

Couldn't do it. He had trouble making ends meet, as it was. Adding five more tons of hay a year for an animal that Kylie would almost certainly insist on riding was not going to help either his budget or his peace of mind.

The mare suddenly put her head up. Will pulled her to a stop.

In the distance was the mustang herd, heading for the water hole. Skitters blew through her nose. Will gathered the reins, but she didn't move. She watched.

Will watched, too, as the distant animals walked single file to the spring. Skitters put her nose higher in the air and whinnied, the shrill sound cutting the air.

He could feel the energy again and so he did the sane thing. He stepped off the mare and stood beside her holding the reins, studying her perfect head, her deep brown eyes, which should have been soft, but weren't—except when she was around Kylie. She quivered and whinnied again.

Will flipped one stirrup over the seat of the saddle and undid the cinch tie. Then he pulled the saddle off, dumping it on the ground.

Think, Will.

He unbuckled the throatlatch; the mare didn't seem to notice. One quick move and the bridle slipped off. Will caught the bit automatically, so it wouldn't clack against her teeth. She stood for a split second, then tossed her head and took off for the herd, kicking up divots of sod with her hind feet as she galloped.

Will watched her go, a golden blur, thinking that it was too bad he hadn't had the tools with him to pull her shoes.

But they'd come off with time. They always did.

He pulled the sweaty blanket out from under the saddle and shook off the debris. He folded it and laid it over the back of the saddle. And then he looped the bridle, hung it over the horn, gathered the cinches and secured them over the blanket, finally hefting the saddle to his hip with one hand. He started walking back.

It HAD BEEN a long time since Will had walked so far in cowboy boots. He'd topped the second-to-last rise before he could see the house when the rider appeared. He'd seen his brother in the saddle often enough to recognize him at a distance.

"Taking your saddle out for some air?" Brett asked when he was finally within speaking range. The first time they'd spoken face-to-face in years and Brett was his old flippant self. Which meant he was hiding emotions.

Will cocked a hip to support the weight as he looked up at his brother, who was riding Kylie's old gelding. "Helping yourself to my stuff?" Probably not the best thing to say, considering their past, but Brett didn't flinch.

"I wanted to find you." He nodded at Stubby. "This little pup knew exactly where you were. I'd almost say he's more tracker than cow dog."

"Are you healed?"

"For the most part." Which was something of a lie, because he still had bruises on his face. Brett placed both gloved hands on the saddle horn, one on top of the other. "I wanted to tell you that I'm pushing on."

"What about Kylie?"

Brett pushed his hat back. "You've done a good job with her. I like her."

"She's my world."

"I know. And I wouldn't interfere with that."

Will swallowed before he spoke. "Thank you." His voice was slightly uneven, but Brett pretended not to notice.

"You want to tell me where your horse went?"

Will smiled a little. "Yeah, I'll tell you. I'm breaking the law for Kylie." He gave his brother the story.

Brett shook his head when Will was done, then dismounted stiffly and pulled the reins over the horse's head. "Why don't you load your saddle on?"

Will swung his saddle up on top of Brett's and tied the strings of the two saddles together, securing them.

"You'll get blisters walking in those new boots," Will pointed out. "At least mine are broken in."

Brett smiled. "Maybe I should take them off. Remember when you convinced me to do that?"

"You always were easily led."

"At least I wasn't all pushy. Is Kylie much like Des?"

Will was not surprised by the rapid-fire change of topics. He started to walk and Brett fell into step, leading the horse.

"She has the fire, but I think you've seen that. She isn't so desperate for the attention." He walked a few more paces, then said the bravest words of his life. "You could get to know her better, you know. Be part of her life."

Brett immediately shook his head. "Wouldn't be good for anybody." He raised his chin, his eyes fixed on the horizon. "Nope. I've got a job waiting in Idaho and that's where I'm going. I'll be back to testify, if I remember anything. Which brings me to saying thanks for going after the guys who beat me up. I guess you fight a little better than I do."

Will didn't answer. It didn't seem like there was much he could say.

"Kylie called me."

Will's heart gave an extra thump. "Yeah?"

"She's worried about you. Says you're lonely."

Will swore under his breath. He hated that his kid noticed, hated that she'd tried to do something about it. But he had to admit, she succeeded where he hadn't. Brett had at least taken her calls.

They walked the miles home in silence, which seemed to amplify the sound of their boots clunking over the rocks, the saddles creaking as they swayed in tandem on the horse's back.

"You're crazy if you let that woman go," Brett said after they'd unsaddled the horse.

"You don't understand the situation."

Brett simply lifted his eyebrows. "One of us doesn't," he agreed. He hesitated, then took a step forward and gave his brother a quick embrace. "Don't know when I'll see you again."

Will nodded and watched as his brother walked alone back to his truck.

REGAN STOPPED AT the district office at 4:30 p.m., as per the superintendent's email request. She was ushered directly into his office when she arrived.

Zeiger gave her an ironic smile as he waved her to a seat.

"I received an interesting fax this morning."

Regan nodded.

"You are aware of it, aren't you?"

"Only that the evaluation Learning Tech received was glowing and I know the one in my file was not."

"There's no proof that Pete substituted the evaluation, you know. The signature pages have not been tampered with, so anyone could have inserted the middle pages."

The message was clear. "Pete's going to be principal, isn't he?"

Zeiger gave a slow nod. "All I can give you is an opinion, but, yes, I'd say it's almost a given."

"Then I'd like to transfer to Barlow Ridge."

Zeiger couldn't hide his surprise at her blunt statement. "Have you ever been to Barlow Ridge?" he asked flatly.

"No." But it seemed like a solution.

She'd come up with the idea just that morning. Barlow Ridge was seventy miles away—a rugged seventy miles, from what she'd heard—but it wasn't Las Vegas. She wouldn't be within Pete's sphere of influence and she could keep her horses. Plus, she'd be fairly close to Will while she tried to figure things out and she'd still have her own space.

And damn, but she had a lot to figure out. She was entering unknown territory here and she was scared. But she also sensed that she and Will had the beginning of something that shouldn't be abandoned simply because of a knee-jerk fear.

"You need to take a visit, first," Mr. Zeiger was saying. "Find out what you'd be getting into. Do you have a truck or an SUV?"

"I have a car."

Zeiger winced. "You'd better go soon, before the weather changes." He put his pen back in its holder. "Do you mind if I ask why you want to transfer to Barlow, rather than just go home to Las Vegas?"

"I'm going to face my fears," she said matter-of-factly.

"Miss Flynn, I don't know what you're talking about, but if you end up taking the Barlow Ridge transfer, I wish you all the luck in the world."

CHAPTER FIFTEEN

THE BUS PULLED to a stop and Kylie tumbled down the steps, barely staying on her feet. She raced toward Will, skidding to a stop in front of him. He'd known that she would see Skitters' empty pen from her bus window and assume the worst.

"It's okay, Kylie. You don't need to worry about Skitters."

"It's not Skitters's," she said imperatively, barely sparing a glance for the empty pen. "It's Regan."

"Regan?"

"She's leaving. I was in the office—I wasn't in trouble—and I heard Mrs. Serrano talking to Miss Prescott. She's leaving!"

Will didn't say anything and Kylie stared at him in thunderstruck silence. "You know!" she finally blurted out. Her mouth worked for a moment, then she said, "Well, you need to do something about this."

"Like what?"

"Like...like marry her or something."

Will barely kept his jaw from hitting his boots. "Marry her?"

"Yes. If you guys got married, then she would stay. Marry her." Will frowned at his daughter, started to shake his head. "Oh, come on," she said impatiently. "You guys *like* each other. It's only obvious."

"Kylie. Kid. Even if we do like each other, neither of

us is going to jump into marriage. Regan doesn't want to get married."

"Get engaged, then. That'll give you some time."

Will rubbed his forehead with the tips of his fingers. How to explain this one? The fact that Regan was afraid of committed relationships. "Even if we got together, it would be a long time before we got engaged or married. And," he settled a hand on his daughter's shoulder, "even if we did get together, there is no guarantee it would work out."

"But it might."

"Yeah. It might. But it might not."

"I'd be willing to take a chance. Why aren't you?"

"Regan has plans, Kylie." Will swallowed. "And it hurts when things fall apart. It'd hurt me and, more than that— since you like Regan so much—it'd hurt you."

"It hurts right now, Dad."

"It'd hurt more later."

"Well, you know what?" Kylie blurted, her eyes filling with tears. "I don't care. *I'd* take the chance."

The tears started to roll down her cheeks and she lifted her chin. "If you don't do something, I will."

"Kylie."

"What?"

Will knew he had to prepare them both, just in case he wasn't able to break through Regan's defenses. "Sometimes it's better not to have something than to lose it."

Kylie gave him a pitying look through her tears. "No offense, Dad, but that's just plain dumb."

PEANUT BUTTER WAS grazing peacefully on the lawn when Will drove up. He automatically caught the pony and led him back to the corral.

"Stay put," he said sternly, as he latched the gate.

"Like that's going to help."

The woman standing on the porch was not Regan, but the resemblance was unmistakable. And now he knew what Regan would look like if she dyed her hair blond and cut it into a short choppy do.

"I'm looking for Regan."

"She isn't here."

"Do you know when she'll be back?"

"No."

Will put his hands on his hips, took a moment to re-group. "It's important."

The woman wrapped her hand around the newel post. "You're Will, aren't you?"

"Yes. And you are…?"

"Claire."

"Nice to meet you, Claire." Will faked a smile. It dis-appeared instantly. "Where is she?"

"She's on an interview."

Damn. "Where?"

Claire gave him a long, hard look. "You're just going to hurt her if you chase after her, you know. She isn't in-terested in happily-ever-after."

His mouth tightened. "Right now Regan isn't the one in danger of being hurt."

To his surprise, Claire suddenly smiled. "Tell me, cow-boy. How are you going to handle a woman who's afraid of commitment?"

"I'll start by telling her how I feel."

"Like that's not going to turn her inside out." Claire took a moment to study Peanut Butter, who was idly mouth-ing the gate latch. "What do you know about my sister?"

"That she cuts and runs when she's scared and that I want to talk to her about it."

Claire looked impressed. "She went to visit a school."

"What school?"

"Some Ridge place."

"Barlow Ridge?"

"Possibly."

REGAN SAW THE truck coming for miles across the wide valley. She'd crossed two mountain passes to get to Barlow Ridge, separated by wide expanses of…nothing. The country was beautiful, wild. The kind of place where you didn't want your car to break down, because it would be quite a while before another vehicle passed by.

And she was suffering from a slight case of culture shock.

There was no shopping here, except for one tiny mercantile. No place to eat, except for the local bar. The main street was six blocks long. But Toffee and Peanut Butter would probably like it. She'd never been to a place where the ranches literally butted up onto the town streets, and the term *street* was loosely used.

The truck neared and Regan suddenly recognized both the vehicle and the silhouette of the man at the wheel. She automatically slowed, pulling off the side of the road as far as she dared.

Will was out of his vehicle by the time she opened her door.

But they stayed on opposite sides of the road, regarding one another across the expanse of frozen rutted gravel.

Neither spoke. Regan breathed in the frosty air, wondering who'd be the first to break the silence. It was Will.

"What are you doing out here?"

"Exploring my options." Somehow she managed to put a wry spin on the words.

"At Barlow Ridge?"

"Are you familiar?" she asked, buying time.

"My great-grandfather homesteaded there before he

moved to Wesley. You have to be dedicated to live in Barlow Ridge."

"I don't want to go back to Vegas. I can't afford to keep my horses there."

"Quite a sacrifice, for horses."

"It isn't all for the horses." Regan edged closer to the truth. "What are you doing out here?"

"Coming to find you."

Regan's heart thudded against her chest wall.

"Here I am," she said softly.

"And don't I know it," he replied. He took a slow pacing step forward. "I met your sister."

"What'd you think?"

"That she must be exhausting to live with."

Regan smiled.

A breeze swirled past, blowing frost crystals in a small cyclone. Regan waited for it to pass, thinking this was about as far from the Vegas heat as she could get and still remain in Nevada. And yet she preferred it.

"Why are you doing this, Regan?"

She swallowed before she said matter-of-factly, "I realized that I've never before been afraid of ending a relationship before it started." She focused on the gravel instead of looking at him. It was hard to think, with those blue-gray eyes looking directly into her soul. "Which makes me believe this one is different. It scares me."

There was a beat of silence.

"So your solution is to move to Barlow Ridge?"

"I have two options, because of Pete. Barlow Ridge or Vegas. Barlow Ridge is seventy miles away. Las Vegas is four hundred miles away."

And four hundred miles was a lot farther away from Will than she wanted to be. She pushed her hair behind her ear. "I figured that this way I can keep a job with the district and still be within fairly easy driving distance." She shook her head as she regarded the potholed, washboarded road. "Obviously, I'll have to rethink the 'easy' part."

"Obviously."

"At least it'll give me some thinking time."

"Yeah." Will agreed. He turned to look down the miles of road she had just traveled. "How much time are you going to need?"

She didn't understand what he was getting at, so she slowly shook her head.

"This road. It's hard on tires. I'll need to calculate it into my budget."

Regan almost smiled. Somehow, now that he was here, it was easier to believe that everything would turn out all right.

But in reality, she knew there was more involved than the two of them simply taking a risk on each other. "I don't want to make a mistake, with Kylie involved. I wouldn't hurt her for the world."

"And I think I'm finally beginning to understand that protecting Kylie from situations where people might leave doesn't guarantee she won't be hurt." He took another step toward her, his hands still in his pockets. "And I want to give Kylie a chance to see what it's like to love and be loved. I didn't realize it, but I'd been shielding her from that, too."

Regan drew in a breath and went for full disclosure. "I can't guarantee anything, Will. One of us—all of us—may end up getting hurt."

He looked surprised. "I'm not asking for a guarantee. I'm asking for communication and trust." He took another slow step toward her. "We can deal with just about anything else if we've got those. And as to getting hurt, it's no fun, but a person heals. I know."

Regan's heart started beating even harder as he neared. This was for real. Not a walk away.

"So what do you say?" he asked, his expression intent. "Will you consider the possibility of trying to make a life with me and Kylie?"

She cleared her throat and went with her heart. "I'd kind of like to try."

And the next thing she knew she was in his arms. He swung her around, and when he finished, her feet still weren't on the ground. But her lips were on his mouth.

He slowly lowered her toes to the ground as the kiss deepened. And then he brought his forehead down to touch hers, their frosty breath mingling. It was so cold, the air was starting to burn her cheeks, but she didn't care. She pulled back a little, her expression serious.

"I have to take the job in Barlow Ridge, Will. I can't stay where I am. Maybe I can transfer back to Wesley later."

"I can live with that," he said in a low voice. "It'll be hard on my truck," his expression softened, "but I can live with it."

Regan laughed as she took his face in her hands. "You're a good guy, Will."

"I can get even better," he murmured near her ear. "Come on. It's a long way back to town. We'd better get going." He pressed a kiss to her temple and Regan shivered, but it wasn't from the cold.

"I love you, Will." And she was surprised at how free she felt, saying the words.

"I love you, too. And the way I see things, that's a pretty good start."

* * * * *

THE BROTHER RETURNS

To Gary, with love.

CHAPTER ONE

NO ONE EXPECTED Claire Flynn to last long in Barlow Ridge. Even Claire had her doubts about making the transition to life in the tiny Nevada community, but she had sworn to herself that no matter how great the emergency or how dire the circumstances, she would not ask for help. It was a matter of pride.

And now here she was, going in search of help.

Drat.

She trudged up the rickety wooden steps leading to Brett Bishop's front door. Technically he was her landlord and therefore the logical person to help her with domestic emergencies. But he was also her sister's new brother-in-law, and a bit of an enigma. *An interesting combination,* Claire mused as she raised her hand to knock on his weathered kitchen door. It opened before her knuckles touched wood.

Brett did not look pleased to see her, but then he never looked too pleased about anything. That enigma thing. Claire enjoyed enigmas.

"There's a snake in my house."

His brown eyes became even more guarded than usual. "What kind of snake?"

"Grayish, no markings, maybe twelve to eighteen inches long. Very fast and uncooperative."

It had scared the daylights out of her when she'd moved a box and found it curled up in a corner. The feeling had apparently been mutual, since the creature had shot off toward the washing machine before Claire's feet were back on the ground. It was then that she'd decided to go for reinforcements. If her computer had been connected to the internet, she might have done some quick research on snake removal, but it wasn't, so she took the coward's way out. When she'd made her vow of independence, she hadn't factored in reptiles.

Brett regarded her for a moment, his mouth flattening exactly the way it had when she'd made the mistake of flirting with him during their wedding-duty dance just over a year ago. And then he gave his dark head a fatalistic shake.

"Let's go see what you've got," he said.

WHEN CLAIRE FLYNN SMILED, she looked like she knew a secret, and if you treated her right she might just tell you what it was. Brett did not want to know Claire's secrets. He'd had enough secrets for one lifetime.

He stepped out onto the porch, preparing himself for the inevitable. His brother, Will, had asked him to give Claire a hand when necessary, and Brett had agreed, but he hadn't anticipated snake removal as one of the services required.

"I appreciate this," Claire said as he pulled the door shut behind him.

"No problem." But he did wonder how much more help she was going to need before her year of teaching was over. And he also wondered just how well she was going to fit into this small community, with her choppy blond hair and trendy clothing. Not many women in Barlow Ridge wore skirts that clung and swirled, strappy tops or flimsy sandals. In fact, none of them did. He imagined the locals were going to have a fine old time discussing her.

Claire walked briskly beside Brett as they left the homestead house and headed across the field toward the single-wide trailer she was now calling home. The field had just been mowed and baled with third-cutting alfalfa, so although the walking was easy, he expected the hay stubble was probably scratching up Claire's bare ankles pretty good. She didn't say a word, though, which kind of surprised him.

And she hadn't whined about the condition of the trailer—the only place to rent in Barlow Ridge—which happened to sit on the edge of his hay field. Another surprise. The previous teacher to rent it, a guy named Nelson, had registered at least a complaint a day.

"Where'd you last see the snake?" Brett asked when they were a few yards from the house. Dark clouds were moving in from the south. The evening thunderstorm was brewing early today and Brett hoped he'd be able to get rid of the snake and return home before lightning began to strike.

"It went behind the washer."

Brett grimaced. Nothing like moving a heavy major appliance with his worst nightmare lurking behind it.

Claire opened the trailer door and stood back. The interior smelled of industrial-strength cleanser. Brett wheezed as the stringent odor hit his nostrils.

"You know," he said, "if you just close the door and give the snake a little time, it'll probably pass out from the fumes."

"Very funny."

He sucked in a breath of fresh air, then stepped inside and headed down the hall to a narrow alcove where the washer was installed. Claire was close behind him. He grabbed a broom propped against the wall and handed it to her before taking hold of the washer, keeping his feet as far away as possible.

"What am I supposed to do with this?" she asked, lifting the broom, a clunky wooden bracelet sliding down her arm in the process. Who cleaned house wearing a bracelet?

"Defend us."

Brett took a firm hold and started rocking the appliance toward him, fully expecting the snake to shoot straight up his pant leg at any moment. Damn, he hated snakes.

He finally got the heavy machine pulled out far enough so that he could see the snake coiled in the corner, looking as threatened as Brett felt. A blue racer. Fast but not dangerous. Unless it went up your pant leg.

He reached his hand out for the broom. "Better stand back."

Brett gently nudged the snake into the hall, trying not to dance too much as he blocked the reptile's repeated escape attempts with the broom, before finally managing to send it sailing through the front door. For several seconds it remained motionless, but then it came back to life and slithered off into the grass.

From behind him, Brett heard Claire sigh with relief. He turned to give her an incredulous look.

"Just because I don't want it living with me doesn't mean I want it to get hurt."

Brett closed the door. Sweat beaded his forehead, and it wasn't entirely due to the hellishly hot interior of the trailer. He set the broom back against the wall, noticing that it was damp. He touched the surface again, experimentally, with the palm of his hand. She'd washed the walls.

"Are you some kind of germaphobe?" he asked as he pushed the door wide to let out both the heat and the cleaning fumes. She had the windows open, but the air was still in the heavy pre-thunderstorm atmosphere.

"I prefer it to ophidiophobia."

"Ophidio…"

"Fear of—"

"I know what it is," he snapped. Or at least he could make a good guess. He hadn't realized it was that obvious. "I'm not afraid of snakes. I'm just cautious." Like all sensible Nevadans. He wiped his sleeve over his damp forehead. "Why don't you turn the cooler on?"

"It made a funny noise, like it was losing a bearing." Her green eyes were steady on his. "I didn't want to bother you. I thought I'd find out who the local handyman was."

Brett walked over to the cooler panel and flipped the pump switch, followed by the blower switch. A low screech became progressively louder as the blower wheel began to turn. He quickly snapped both switches off. Yes, it did sound like a bearing was going, and for some reason he hated the fact she had figured that out.

"I'll have a look at it." He could not leave her in a hotbox until Manny Fernandez had time to come round and fix the cooler. She'd likely be using the furnace by that time—which was also probably in need of repair.

"I don't suppose you have any tools?"

She walked into the kitchen and returned a few seconds later with a zebra-striped tool kit.

"It was a gift," she said before he had time to comment. "From the class I student-taught last year."

Brett felt an unexpected desire to smile at the defensiveness in her voice. So Claire's fashion sense had its limits. "They must have liked you."

"We…developed a rapport," she said cryptically, as she followed him outside.

There was an old wooden ladder lying beside the trailer, and Brett propped it up against the siding. A sudden gust of wind almost knocked it over again. He waited a moment until the wind settled down, making the air seem heavier than before, and then he began to climb.

Swamp coolers were not complex machines, and it wasn't too difficult to tell that this one was on its last legs. Claire was in for a warmish time in her trailer. He'd have to see about ordering parts, if they still made them for this dinosaur.

The ladder shifted, and a moment later Claire climbed up onto the roof herself. Somehow he wasn't surprised.

"Another snake?" he asked wryly.

"Just curious. Someday I may have to fix this thing myself."

"You going to be here that long?"

"Ten months, and then back to grad school. What's the prognosis?" she asked.

"Terminal." The wind gusted again and the first faint rumblings of thunder sounded in the distance. The storm was moving in fast. "We'd better get down to the ground." He closed the cooler's heavy hinged cover.

Once they were back on solid earth, Brett put the ladder beside the trailer and handed Claire her tools. "I'm going to Wesley tomorrow. I'll see about getting some parts, if they still make them. If not, I'll see about a new cooler." He felt bad leaving her in an oven. "It's going to be kind of hot without it."

"That's the beauty of being a Vegas native. I'm used to it." She pushed her choppy bangs away from her forehead. They stuck up, giving her a punk rock look. She smiled. "So… You want to go down to the bar and grab a bite or have a drink? As a thank-you?"

He hesitated just a little too long.

"I take it that's a no."

He wasn't sure how to say what he needed to without being insulting and possibly pissing off his brother for not being nice to Claire. "Look," Brett said in what he hoped was a reasonable tone, "I'll help you out whenever you need it, but I'm not much of a socializer."

"What does that mean?"

That I'm not going to risk screwing up again with someone so closely tied to my brother?

"It just means I'm not much on socializing," he said with a touch of impatience. "It's nothing personal." Not the total truth, but close enough.

"All right." She didn't look particularly offended, but the smile was gone from her eyes. "I guess I'll get back to work. Thanks for the help. I'll call you if I need anything." She started for the trailer door.

"There's something you should know, Claire."

She looked back. "What's that?"

"I don't think it was an accident that there was a snake in your house. There was a bunch of kids hanging around, just before you got here. I went to see what they were doing, and they took off running."

"You think they were my students?"

"I'd say it's a real possibility."

Claire considered his words for a moment. "Should make for an interesting year, don't you think?"

"Uh, yeah." That was one way of putting it.

"I think I can probably handle anything they might dish out." She sounded confident.

Brett nodded, wondering if she knew what she was up against. Apparently not. There was a flash of lightning, followed by thunder. "I think I'll head back before it rains."

So HER STUDENTS had put a snake in her house and Brett didn't want to socialize with her. Claire shook her head as she went through the door. Not exactly a welcoming beginning to her new life in Barlow Ridge. She was surprised about her students, and not so surprised about Brett.

She'd only met him three times before deciding to take the teaching job here, but every time they'd been together she'd been struck by his standoffish attitude. With her and with his family.

Well, Claire didn't do standoffish. With the exception of her mother, Arlene, who could still make her quake in her boots, she'd never met anyone who intimidated her. Maybe she should thank her mother for that.

The trailer was starting to cool off as the wind grew stronger, blowing in through the open windows. Another flash of lightning lit the sky, and Claire wondered how safe it was being in a metal can during a thunderstorm. It had to be safe, though. There were lots of trailers in the world and she'd never heard of one being struck by lightning. But leave it to her to be the first.

She sank down in the reclining chair, pulling her knees up to her chest as the sky flashed and a blast of thunder shook the trailer almost simultaneously. This was not only her first night alone in her new home, it was one of her first nights really alone anywhere. As in, no family down the hall, no neighbor on the other side of the wall. No neighbors within a quarter of a mile, for that matter.

It felt…strange.

But she could handle it.

In fact, she had a feeling that she might even grow to like it. If not, she only had ten months to get through before she moved back to Vegas.

Her cell phone buzzed. Claire glanced at the number, debated, and then gave in to the inevitable.

"Hi, Mom." She forced a note of cheerful optimism into her voice. Nothing set her mother off like Claire doing what she pleased and enjoying it. Arlene had wanted her to be an engineer. Claire was talented in math, but hated the cut-and-dried engineering way of thinking. She was more free-form—*way* more free-form—and didn't understand why Arlene couldn't see that a free-form engineer who hated to double-check her equations was probably going to be a dangerous engineer. Arlene resented the fact that neither of her daughters had gone into the high-profile, high-paying professions she had chosen for them before they'd entered preschool. And she still hadn't given up on turning their lives around.

"I called to see how you're settling in."

"Just fine," Claire said breezily, deciding not to share her snake adventure just yet. "I'll be going to school tomorrow to see my new room and do some decorating."

"Any regrets?" her mother asked hopefully.

"Not yet, but there's still time." Claire knew that Arlene wanted her to at least entertain the possibility that she'd be sorry for putting off grad school for a year.

"Well, there's a reason they can't keep a teacher at that school."

"Any idea what it is?" Claire asked innocently.

Arlene did not deign to answer, and Claire decided to change the subject while they were still on polite terms. She sifted through several topics and dismissed them all. Her stepfather, Stephen, was off-limits, since he had moved out of the house, informing Arlene that he would not come back unless she decided being a companion was as important as running her business. Claire wasn't all that sure that Stephen would ever be coming back.

She couldn't ask her for career advice—or decorating advice, since she was living in a run-down rented trailer on the edge of a hay field. But she could try cooking, their only common ground.

"Hey, Mom…" A boom of thunder nearly drowned out her words.

"What on earth?"

"Thunderstorm."

"You shouldn't be on the phone."

"It's a cell phone." Claire decided not to argue. "You're right." She smiled slightly. "Thanks for calling, Mom. I was lonely."

"Goodbye, Claire. It was good talking to you."

Claire pushed the end button. It really hadn't been too bad a conversation. They'd both behaved fairly well. She held the phone in her hand for a moment, then punched in her sister's number. Regan answered on the first ring.

"I've been waiting," she said.

"Why?" Claire knew why. For about nine-tenths of her life, she'd run every decision past Regan, even if she rarely followed her sister's advice. It was a habit that had started when they were young, and continued well into college. It wasn't until Regan had moved away from Las Vegas that Claire realized maybe life wasn't always a joint venture.

"Because you've never lived alone before."

"Well, I've *been* alone," Claire said, "and this isn't all that different."

"So how are you settling in?"

"Fine, now that Brett got the snake out of the house…"

"The snake?"

"My students hid a snake in my house before I got here. It scared the daylights out of me when I found it, and since I don't know anything about snakes, I had Brett come and remove it. Then I asked him out for a beer as a thank-you and he told me he doesn't socialize."

There was silence on the other end of the line, and then Regan murmured, "Don't take it personally."

"That's what he said," Claire replied, swinging her legs over the one arm of the chair and leaning back against the other. "And I'm not. I just thought it was odd, which makes me wonder, why are the gorgeous ones always tweaked in some weird way?"

Regan laughed.

"What?"

"Oh, I was just thinking that you could take a long look in the mirror and ask yourself that same question."

"Ha, ha, ha." They talked for a few more minutes, making plans to meet when Claire made her next trip to Wesley for supplies.

"Speaking of shopping," Regan said, "Kylie is planning an Elko trip and she wants to know when you can come. She says your taste is better than mine, which, I have to tell you, worries her father a bit."

"Tell her to name the day," Claire said with a laugh. Elko shopping was nothing like Vegas shopping, but it was a heck of a lot better than Barlow Ridge shopping or Wesley shopping. And Kylie, Regan's stepdaughter, was a girl after Claire's own heart. A true renegade.

Claire finally hung up and set the phone back on the side table. The thunderstorm had passed without dropping any rain, but the air in the trailer felt fresher, cooler. She got to her feet and headed down the narrow hallway to her bedroom, walking a little faster as she passed the washing machine. Logic told her there were no more snakes lying in wait for her, but her instincts told her to take no chances. She'd yet to have much experience with animals, but when she did, she wanted them to be furry and friendly.

"YOU THE NEW TEACHER?"

Claire smiled at the grouchy-looking woman behind the mercantile counter. "Yes, I am."

"Gonna stay?"

"One year." Claire spoke easily, truthfully.

The woman snorted. "That's the reason the kids are running wild, you know."

"What is?"

"The fact that none of you will stay."

"Yes, well, there's not a lot to do here, is there?"

The woman gave her another sour look, but didn't argue. It would have been hard to. The community had one store, a bar that served food and a community center that looked as if it was well over a hundred years old. Actually, everything in the town looked a hundred years old. Including the proprietress of the store, who was still glaring at Claire as if it were her fault teachers didn't want to settle permanently in a community a zillion miles from civilization.

"I'm Claire Flynn," she said with her best smile.

"Anne McKirk," the woman grudgingly replied.

"You have a nice store." It was definitely an everything-under-the-sun store. Food, hardware, crafts, clothing. One of the soda coolers held veterinary medications. It wasn't a large space, but it was packed to the rafters.

"I try."

Claire unloaded her basket on the counter. She would have liked some fresh fruit, but considering the circumstances, she'd take what she could get.

"Your sister taught here."

"Yes. Three years ago."

"She was good, but she didn't last long."

"She would have had a bit of a commute if she'd stayed," Claire pointed out. Will Bishop, the man Regan had married, lived seventy miles away in Wesley, Nevada, where she now taught.

"Well, it would have been nice if Will had taken over the old homestead, instead of his brother. Then she would have stayed."

"Yes, she would have," Claire agreed. But it hadn't

worked out that way, so now the town was stuck with the wrong brother and the wrong sister.

"You interested in joining the quilting club?"

"I, uh, don't know," Claire hedged. She had never done anything more complicated with a needle than sew on the occasional button. She did it well, but she had a feeling that quilting was more difficult than button attachment.

"I'll have Trini give you a call. Everybody joins quilting club."

"Then I'll join."

Claire said goodbye, then strolled down the five-block-long street to Barlow Ridge Elementary, which was situated at the edge of town. Her trailer was only a half mile away, so she could walk to work on the nice days.

The school, constructed in the 1930s, had a certain vintage charm, but Claire knew from her initial visit that it would have been a lot more charming had it benefited from regular upkeep. It consisted of three classrooms—one used as a lunchroom—a gymnasium with a velvet-curtained stage at one end, two restrooms and a tiny office barely big enough to hold a desk and a copy machine.

Claire unlocked the stubborn front door and went into her room, setting her lunch on the shelving unit just inside. The space was of adequate size, but the equipment it contained was old, tired and makeshift. With the exception of a new computer on the teacher's desk, everything dated from the previous century. There was no tech cart for projecting computer images, only an old overhead projector. No whiteboards or dry-erase markers, but instead a grungy-looking blackboard and a few small pieces of chalk.

She went to run her hand over the board, and found the surface grooved and wavy. Picking up a piece of chalk, she experimentally wrote her name. The chalk made thin, waxy lines, barely legible. Something needed to be done about this.

The desks came in a hodgepodge of sizes and shapes, all of them old-fashioned, with lift-up lids. She'd been thinking about how she would arrange them. Rows…a horseshoe…in groups. The students should probably have a say.

Behind her desk was a door in the wall that opened into a long, narrow closet jammed to the ceiling with junk. Probably seventy years' worth of junk, from the look of things. She'd be doing something about this. Claire hated disorganization and wasted space.

She left her classroom and walked through the silent school. There was another mystery door, at the opposite end of the hall from the restrooms. She pulled the handle, and though the door proved to be a challenge, it eventually screeched open. A set of stone steps led downward.

A school with a dungeon. How nice.

There was no light switch, but a solitary bulb hung from a cord at the bottom of the steps, adding to the torture-chamber ambience.

Claire started down the steps. The smell of dampness and mildew grew stronger as she descended. She pulled the string attached to the light, illuminating most of the basement and casting the rest into spooky shadows. The floor was damp and there were dark patches on the walls that looked like moss. A frog croaked from somewhere in the darkness.

Stacks of rubber storage bins lined the walls, labeled Christmas, Halloween, Thanksgiving, Easter. Others were marked History, English and Extra. Probably some great stuff in that last one, Claire thought as she went to lift the corner of a lid. The bin was filled with old blue-ink ditto papers. There were also several tables, a plastic swimming pool and a net bag of playground balls hanging from an antique metal hook on the wall.

The frog croaked again and Claire decided she'd seen just about all there was to see. She went back upstairs, the air growing warmer and dryer with each step. Once she reached the top she wrestled the door closed and pushed the latch back into place.

"Is that you, Claire?"

The unexpected voice nearly made her jump out of her skin. She pressed her hand to her heart as she turned so see Bertie Gunderson, a small yet sturdy-looking woman with short gray hair, peeking out of the office doorway. Claire had met her the first time two days earlier at the district staff development meeting.

"Darn it, Bertie, you scared me."

The other teacher smiled. "It's refreshing to hear that I'm more frightening than the basement."

Claire followed her back into the office, where she was copying papers on the antique copy machine—a hand-me-down from another school, no doubt. Regan had told her that Barlow Ridge Elementary got all the district's reject equipment. "I was wondering about the blackboards."

"What about them?"

"They're unusable. Is there any chance of talking the district into putting up whiteboards?"

Bertie cackled. "Yeah. Sure."

Claire felt slightly deflated, which, for her, was always the first step toward utter determination.

"You can try," the veteran teacher said.

"I'll do that."

Bertie was still in her classroom working when Claire finally left three hours later. She'd started sorting through her storage closet but gave up after a half hour, concentrating instead on making her first week's lesson plans. She would be teaching five different subjects—some of them at four different grade levels. Regan had already explained that she could combine science and social studies into single units of study for all her grades, but English and math had to be by grade level. The challenge was scheduling— keeping one grade busy while another was being taught.

But Claire loved a challenge, and this would be just that. Plus, she'd have an excellent background for her planned master's thesis on combined classroom education. Old equipment and a wavy blackboard were not going to slow her down.

BRETT'S CELL PHONE rang at seven-thirty, while he was driving the washboard county road that led to Wesley.

Phil Ryker. His boss.

"Hey, pard," Phil drawled, setting Brett's teeth on edge. He had to remind himself to practice tolerance. Phil was an urban boy who wanted to be a cowboy, and being heir to the man who owned most of the land in the Barlow Ridge area, including Brett's family homestead, he was wealthy enough to indulge his dreams. Brett considered himself fortunate to be leasing his homestead with an option to buy, which he was close to exercising, and also to be working for Phil, managing the man's hobby ranch during the three hundred days a year he was not in residence. Those two circumstances were enough to help Brett overlook a fake drawl and words such as *pard*.

"Hi, Phil."

"I won't be able to get to the ranch next week like I planned, but I did buy a couple of horses and a mule, and I'm having them shipped out."

"All right." What now? Brett knew from past experience that the horses could be anything from fully trained Lipizzans to ratty little mustangs.

"One of them is a bit rough. I thought maybe you could tune him up for me."

"Define *'a bit rough.'*" Brett's and Phil's idea of rough were usually quite different.

"Seven years old and green broke, but he's beautiful," Phil said importantly. "You'll see what I mean when he arrives."

"He isn't…"

"He's a stud. I'd like to show him, so I need him fit for polite society." Phil laughed. "I'll get a hold of you closer to the delivery date. Hey, did you figure out that problem with the north well?"

"Yeah. Yesterday. The water level is fine, but the pump needs to be replaced. I sent you an estimate."

"Just take care of it. We can't have that pivot go down."

"Sure can't." Because that would mean that he wouldn't be able to grow hay at a loss. Brett figured Phil knew what he was doing. A hobby ranch that was slowly losing money was a tax write-off and apparently Phil needed write-offs. Brett had tried to interest him in a number of ideas that would make the ranch more economical, perhaps even profitable, but he had his own ideas. Brett gave up after the third set of suggestions was rejected, finally understanding that Phil wasn't particularly concerned about losing money. Must feel good, he mused as he hung up the phone.

Amazingly, Brett found the parts he needed for the swamp cooler at the hardware store in Wesley. Now all he needed to do was go home and get them installed—with luck, while Claire was still at school mucking out her classroom.

He didn't want to spend a lot of time around her. It wouldn't be prudent, since he found her ridiculously attractive, and he was really trying to mind his p's and q's where the family was concerned. He'd spent more than a decade being the missing brother, and before that, he'd been the rebellious brother.

Now he owed it to his family to be the *good* brother. And this was one time he was not going to fail.

CHAPTER TWO

CLAIRE SMILED AT her new class—all ten of them—and wondered who'd masterminded the snake incident. They all looked more than capable of it, but at least the younger students, the fifth and sixth graders, were smiling back at her with varying degrees of curiosity and friendliness. By contrast, the five older students, the seventh and eighth graders, stared at her with impassive, just-try-to-engage-us-and-see-how-far-you-get expressions.

"I'm Miss Flynn," Claire said, as she wrote her name on the overhead projector.

"We know who you are," one of the kids muttered snidely. Claire glanced up, startled by the blatant rudeness, but she couldn't tell who'd spoken. "I'm looking forward to a productive year, and I thought that in order to—"

One of the eighth-grade boys raised his hand.

"Yes?"

"Do you think you'll be here for the whole year?"

"It's one of my goals," Claire said dryly. She knew that her class had had three teachers in two years, each less effective than the previous one. "As I was saying, in order to get to know each other better, I thought we could all introduce ourselves and tell one thing we did this summer. How about starting on this side of the room?" She nodded at the boy in eighth grade, Dylan, who sat farthest to her right.

"I think everyone knows who I am. This summer I slept." He fixed her with a steely look.

Claire quelled an instant urge to jump into battle, as her instincts were telling her to do, deciding it would be wiser to bide her time and get a read on her opponent.

"How nice," she said. She nodded at the girl sitting next to him.

"I'm Toni."

"Did you accomplish anything this summer?"

"No." But then Toni suddenly made an O with her mouth. "Yes," she amended, with a satisfied expression. "I *almost* talked my mom into getting rid of her bum of a boyfriend."

Claire gave the girl a tight smile and moved on.

"My name is Ashley," the redheaded girl sitting next to Toni chirped. "This summer I totally revamped my wardrobe." She jangled the bracelets on her wrist as if to prove the point.

Claire was saved from the remaining introductions by the sudden appearance of a first grader.

"Mrs. Gunderson said to tell you we have sheep!" he squeaked, his eyes wide with excitement.

"Sheep?"

"On the play field."

"And…?" Claire asked with a frown, but her students were already out of their seats and heading for the door. She followed them, wondering if this was an elaborate ruse and if she should order them back into the classroom, but then Bertie emerged from the office.

"Sorry about this. The older kids herd sheep better than the younger ones. It should only take a few minutes. I've just called Echetto and told him to get his buns over here and take care of his flock. The man really should leave his dog when he goes somewhere. The dog works a lot faster than the kids."

A thundering herd of woolly bodies circled past the

front of the school and disappeared around the side. Bertie's class was crowded onto the steps. Trini, the school aid, had the four kindergarten kids perched on the windowsills in Bertie's room, where they laughed and giggled as the sheep ran by again, the older students in hot pursuit.

"They like to watch," Bertie explained, before cupping her hand to her mouth and yelling at Claire's students, "Just get them into Echetto's front yard. He can put them away when he gets back."

Claire was impressed by the way the kids worked in unison to gather the sheep and herd them off the play field, onto the road and then halfway down the block to the house that apparently belonged to Echetto, whoever he was. Ashley and Toni hung toward the rear, but when a couple of ewes made a break for it, they expertly chased them back into the flock. A few minutes later all the kids returned, filed past Claire into the school and took their seats. They'd been smiling while they were outside, but the older ones were once again stony faced—except when they looked at each other.

"Well, this is a first," Claire said. "We don't have many sheep emergencies in Las Vegas."

No one smiled back. In fact, they were making a real effort to make her feel stupid for trying to talk to them like people. "Are you always this rude?" she asked softly.

The younger kids glanced down. The older ones continued to stare at her.

"We can work on manners," she added.

No response, although she noticed the younger kids were now watching the older students, looking for cues.

"This morning I'm going to have you take placement tests, so I can plan the English and math curriculums. Then, after break, we'll do a writing activity. I need you to clear your desks and we'll get going on the tests right now, while you're fresh."

The older kids grudgingly shoved notebooks into their desks, a couple of them muttering under their breath.

The rest of the day passed so slowly and dismally that Claire was beginning to wish the sheep would escape again. She knew the younger ones were not on board with the older ones—yet. But they were watching and learning.

She had to do something. Fast. The headache that had begun shortly after the sheep roundup was approaching migraine status by now.

"I have a list of supplies I'd like you to have within the next week," she announced just before afternoon recess.

Ashley raised her hand and Claire nodded at her. "What about the kids who can't afford supplies?"

A reasonable question, and one that might have denoted concern for those with financial limitations—if it hadn't been for the girl's condescending tone. Ashley, with her salon-streaked hair, Abercrombie T-shirt and Guess jeans, was obviously not going to have difficulty buying five dollars' worth of supplies. And then, as if to make it perfectly clear that she was establishing her own status, she glanced pointedly over at one of the fifth graders, a rather shabbily dressed boy named Jesse.

Claire looked Ashley straight in the eye. "If you have trouble affording supplies, please see me in private."

The girl flushed. "I wasn't talking about myself," she snapped.

"Well, it is kind of you to be concerned about others," Claire interjected, before the girl could name names. "If any of you do not have the opportunity to buy supplies, we'll work something out. Please see me." She smiled at Ashley. "Does that answer your question?"

The girl did not bother to reply. Claire decided to fight

the politeness battle later. She noticed a couple of the younger kids trying not to smile. Apparently they appreciated Ashley getting hers, and Claire made a mental note to find out more about the girl and her family.

The last two hours of the day passed without incident, although it became apparent by then that Ashley held a grudge and owned a cell phone. Ashley's mother arrived just before school ended. She waited in the hall outside the classroom, marching up to Claire as soon as the room had emptied of students.

"Miss Flynn. I'm Ashley's mother. Deirdre Landau."

Claire could see the resemblance in both features and clothes. In fact, the mother was dressed almost exactly like the daughter, in pricey jeans and T-shirt, with expensive hair in a make-believe color. Claire was in no position to comment on make-believe hair colors, since she was a little blonder than nature had ever intended, so she overlooked that detail.

"You embarrassed Ashley today."

"I apologize for that," Claire said honestly. And she was sorry. She wished the incident had never happened, but she wasn't going to let Ashley humiliate a defenseless fifth grader, either.

There was a silence.

"That's it?" Deirdre finally asked.

"What more would you like?" Claire asked reasonably.

The woman's mouth worked as she fought for words. She'd received an apology. Readily and sincerely. And that was the problem. She'd wanted Claire to grovel. Or protest. Or, at the very least, put up a struggle. She tried again.

"A promise not to do it again."

"Fine. As long as Ashley understands that I will not tolerate an intentional attempt to hurt another student's feelings."

Deirdre looked shocked. "Ashley would do no such thing."

"Then perhaps I misread the situation," Claire said in an agreeable tone. "So the next time it happens, I'll just give you a call and you can come to the school and we'll discuss it while it's fresh in everyone's mind."

"I would welcome that."

"Great, because I believe that communication among parents, students and teachers is imperative in an educational situation."

Deirdre blinked. "And I want you to apologize to Ashley in front of the class. After all, she was embarrassed in front of the class."

"Sure." Again, Claire did not hesitate in her response, and it seemed to confuse Deirdre. She frowned suspiciously.

"Tomorrow."

"First thing."

"All right." It was obvious the woman didn't trust Claire's easy acquiescence. "Ashley's waiting. I need to be going."

Claire refrained from saying "See you soon," even though she had a feeling it wouldn't be long before she and Ashley's mom were face-to-face again.

Claire called Regan that night. "What do you do when you're teaching the undead?" she asked as soon as her sister answered the phone.

"Excuse me?"

"Zombies. My older kids behave like zombies, except for when they're herding sheep or sniping at me."

"Echetto's sheep got out again?"

"This is common?"

"Couple times a year."

"Sheep I can live with, but these older kids are mean,

Reg. I thought I'd have a group of sweet rural kids who'd been left to their own devices for too long. And instead I have three snotty ringleaders trying to get the best of me, and a bunch of younger kids learning to follow their lead. Can you tell me anything about Toni Green, Ashley Landau and Dylan Masterson that might help me?"

"Not a lot," Regan confessed. "The only one I know is Dylan, and he wasn't bad as a fourth grader. He just needed a strong hand."

"Well, he didn't get it."

"As to the zombie issue, you're going to have to live with it."

"Meaning?"

"It's a control thing, and you can't force them to be enthusiastic learners. But you can do what Will does when he trains a horse. If they show an appropriate response, reward them. If they act like zombies, ignore it and do your job."

"Kind of like the extinction theory?"

"Pretty much." Regan's voice softened. "You do know you may have a power struggle for a while?"

"I'm getting that idea."

"Stay consistent. Stay strong."

"I'll be Hercules."

"You may have to be," Regan said with a laugh. "Call any time you need moral support, all right?"

"Are you sure you mean that?" Claire asked ironically. There was a time when she'd automatically called Regan before even thinking about a problem.

"I mean it. Anytime." A muffled voice sounded in the background. Regan laughed, then said, "Kylie wants you to promise to come watch her ride at the regional horse show and to wear something to impress her friends."

"Tell her I'll get right on it."

Claire felt better for having called. She had no intention of crying on Regan's shoulder every time something went wrong, but it was good to know she had backup if she needed it.

"BEFORE WE START CLASS, there's something I need to attend to," Claire said as soon as the students were seated following the Pledge of Allegiance. Ashley was already smirking.

"Yesterday I embarrassed Ashley, and I want to apologize for that."

The girl nodded, like a queen granting pardon to an offending subject.

Claire hitched a hip onto the edge of her desk and swung her foot. "In order to avoid this happening in the future, I think I should explain some things to you as a class. I don't want *anyone* to be embarrassed, but if I see you trying to hurt someone else, I will call you on it. It may embarrass you. It's called a consequence. I don't know how many of you have been following the latest developments in self-esteem studies…" The class stared at her blankly. "But the pendulum is swinging from the stroking of egos back to consequences for actions."

Rudy tentatively raised his hand.

"Yes?"

"Would you please translate that?"

"If you do the crime, you'll do the time."

A look of dawning awareness crossed ten faces. Ashley's mouth flattened so much that Claire wondered if it would stay that way forever.

"I'm not exactly stupid," Claire continued. "I can tell when someone is trying to hurt someone else, and I will not put up with it. Any questions?" Several kids shook their heads. "Great. Please get out your math homework."

The fifth and sixth graders had their homework ready.

One of the seventh graders had half of the assignment done. The remaining four older students had nothing.

"Where's your homework?" Claire asked.

"I didn't do it," Dylan answered nonchalantly.

"Any particular reason?"

He shrugged. "Mr. Nelson never made us. Homework was just practice. It was the tests that counted."

"If we could pass the tests, he said we really didn't have to do the homework," Lexi chimed in.

"And did you pass the tests?"

"Yes," the older kids said in unison.

Which made Claire wonder if Mr. Nelson had even bothered to grade the tests. Because after looking at the math placement results from the day before, she was thinking these kids had either gotten a case of collective amnesia over the summer or they hadn't learned the concepts in the first place.

"Well, things have changed," Claire said. "Homework is no longer optional. It is very much required. If you don't do your homework and show me your work, you will not pass math."

The kids looked as if she'd just told them that lunch was canceled for the year.

"But if we can pass the tests…"

"I'm sorry," Claire said pleasantly, "but this is not a negotiable issue."

"That's not fair."

She simply smiled. "In order to be fair, I'll let you do last night's homework tonight. We'll review today. Then, starting tomorrow, homework counts. Now, let's see what you remember from yesterday."

It was another long day. With each lesson she taught, it became more and more apparent that these kids had some serious holes in their education.

After school, Claire was sitting with her elbows planted on her desk, her forehead resting on her fingertips, pondering the situation, when she heard the door open. She shifted her hands to see Elena standing there, biting her lower lip.

"Hi, Elena. What can I do for you?"

"I forgot my math book." The girl went to her desk and took out the book. She hesitated, then asked, "Are you feeling all right?"

Claire smiled. "I'm fine. Just a little tired." *And discouraged.*

"We've never had a teacher that looked like you before," the girl said shyly. "I like your shoes."

Claire smiled again. She liked her shoes, too. It had taken her most of the summer to find the shade of green that perfectly matched her skirt. "Thanks. Hey, can I ask you a question?"

Elena nodded.

"Do you understand the math?"

"I do now."

"Did you yesterday?"

She shook her head, her dark braids moving on her shoulders. "Today you went slower, and I think I got it."

"Thanks, Elena. I'll see you tomorrow."

"See you, Miss Flynn."

So she needed to slow down. All right. She could do that. But it killed her to be reviewing multiplication facts and long division, when she was supposed to be moving on into other aspects of math.

And as far as English went… She glanced down at the stack of poorly punctuated drills in front of her. *Yowza.* She hadn't created this monster, but she was supposed to tame it.

Welcome to the real world of education.

Brett sat down at his computer and took a deep breath. The chores were done, and there was nothing pressing at the Ryker place. It was time. In fact, it was well past time.

Brett was going to college. Online. He just hoped no one found out—in case he failed.

During junior and senior high he'd been a poor student—not because he couldn't do the work, but because he wouldn't. His dad had made a career of comparing Brett's achievements to Will's, and Brett had invariably failed to measure up. Finally, he'd accepted the fact that in his dad's eyes he was never going to be as good at anything as Will was, so he quit trying, telling himself he wasn't really a loser, since he wasn't playing the game.

But still, he had silently resented Will for being so damn good at everything, and resented their dad for constantly reminding him of it.

Brett had eventually gotten his petty revenge, though, and had done a pretty fair job of messing up a number of lives in the process. Not bad for an underachiever.

Okay. First lesson. Concentrate.

Brett started by reading the introduction. Then he reread the introduction, and wondered if maybe he should start with his humanities class instead of algebra.

There was a knock on the door and he literally jumped at the chance to put his education on hold again.

And then he looked out and saw who it was. Claire. With a bottle of wine, no less.

This could not be good.

He opened the door, but only because he had no other option.

"Yes, I know," she said, as she walked in without waiting for an invitation. "We're holding on to our personal space, but I need some help, and damn it, Bishop, you're the only one who can give it to me." She handed him the bottle and walked to the cupboards. "Where do you keep your glasses?"

"Has anyone ever told you that you're pushy?"

Claire smiled at him over her shoulder as she opened a cupboard. "All the time."

"And it doesn't slow you down?"

"Not in the least."

Brett gave up. "Next to the fridge."

Claire opened the cupboard he indicated, then frowned as she pulled out a smallish glass. "What's this?"

"It's a wineglass."

"No. This is an overgrown shot glass. And where's the stem?"

"It's a poor man's wineglass. I can't afford stems. You're lucky it's not a jelly glass."

She smiled again as she took out a second one. "All right. But it's small, so we'll have to fill them more often."

"How long do you plan on staying?"

"Has anyone ever told you you're tactless?" she asked.

He smiled instead of answering.

"And *that* doesn't slow you down?"

"Not in the least."

Brett pulled a corkscrew out of the utensil drawer before Claire had a chance to tear the kitchen apart looking for it. He plunged it into the cork with a little more force than necessary.

"White wine?" he asked.

"Is that a problem?"

"I prefer red wine when I solve problems."

"I'll make a note of that."

"Actually, I can't see us doing a lot of joint problem solving," he said pointedly.

Claire settled herself on one of the mismatched kitchen chairs. "I know that Will asked you to help me when you could. And I may need a lot of help before this year is over."

She accepted the glass he offered, took a bracing drink, then reached up with her free hand to ruffle the top of her hair in a gesture that clearly suggested exhaustion, or possibly frustration. "Are you renovating?" She looked down the hall to the living room, where he was in the process of tearing up the old floor so he could lay a new one.

"The place needs work, so I try to do a little every month. Now, what can I do for you?"

"I'd like some information."

"On...?"

"My kids. My students. I've survived day two, and I'm not ashamed to admit that these kids are close to getting the best of me. That means I have to plan a strategy."

Brett was impressed, in spite of himself. He'd always admired proactive people, as long as they weren't running roughshod over him—or trying to.

"I'll tell you what I know, but you gotta realize I haven't lived here that long."

"But you're a native of the area."

"My grandfather and great-grandfather were natives. Granddad sold."

"Well, you've got to know more than I do." Claire reached down for her purse and pulled out a small spiral notebook. "I'm thinking that if I can just understand the lay of the land, who's related to whom and who does what, maybe I can connect better with the kids. I don't want any dirt or gossip. Just information that's in the public domain."

Brett lifted the wine to his lips, sipped. It really wasn't that bad for white wine. "Don't you have school records with that kind of information?"

"Allegedly, but they're in pretty bad shape. The district

is sending me copies of missing documents, but I want to know about families. Where they live. What they do."

Brett shrugged. "I'll tell you what I can."

"Okay, first off, tell me about the Landaus."

"They're rich." Claire waited, and he expanded. "They're one of the few families here that are not land rich and cash poor. Landau's a nice guy. Ashley is his step-daughter. Only child. He married the mother about three years ago, I think."

"How about Jesse Lane?"

Brett shook his head. "Don't know any Lanes. They aren't locals. It might be that new guy who has the trailer north of town."

"Elena and Lexi Moreno."

"They're related to the Hernandezes."

"Ramon and Lily?"

"Hardworking families. The Hernandezes work for the Landaus. The Morenos have their own place."

"So I have cousins in the classroom, as well as brothers and sisters," Claire said musingly. "Okay. Rudy Liscano."

Brett smiled slightly. Everyone knew Rudy. Everybody liked Rudy. "Rudy's another cousin to the Hernandezes and the Morenos. His dad works for the county-road department. He's the one you yell at when you blow a tire."

"I see. How about Rachel Tyler?"

"Her family has the oldest ranch in the area. They raise nice horses."

"Dylan Masterson?"

"I'm not certain. The Mastersons aren't local. I think they own some businesses somewhere and are out here escaping. I know they built a hell of a place on the other side of town."

"You mean, that A-frame?"

"That's it." Brett drained his glass. "I think she's an artist or something."

"And Toni Green."

"Her mom works at the bar. They live in the rooms over the bar." Brett had been invited to see those rooms before the latest boyfriend had taken up residence, but he'd declined the invitation. "I think she's escaping, too, but for a different reason."

Claire flipped her notebook shut. "Thanks."

"I didn't give you all that much information."

"I just want enough to understand where my kids are coming from, and I didn't want to ask Bertie. I think the ones who are ranch kids for real probably have different references and values than the imports." She refilled their glasses without asking. "In one of my college classes, the prof said that home visits were a must in order to understand your students, but…I think in a community like this, visits might be seen as nosiness unless the families invited me."

"You're right," Brett agreed.

"So, I decided to rely on hearsay."

"Then you should hit the post office and the mercantile."

"You gave me what I need." She leaned back in her chair, studying him in that steady way of hers. Her lips curved slightly. She had a really nice mouth. "So, tell me again, Brett. Why is it that we can't socialize?"

Brett felt his own mouth tighten.

Claire shrugged. "Hey. You're the one who laid down the rules. I was just wondering why."

And then he saw that he'd probably made a major tactical error. He'd already figured out from their first few encounters—and from the fact that she'd taken a teaching assignment in Barlow Ridge—that Claire was a woman who loved a challenge. And that was exactly what he'd given her. Stupid move.

"I didn't say we couldn't socialize. I said I wasn't *much* on socializing."

"You seemed to do okay at the wedding, except with me."

"Claire."

She raised her eyebrows, making her green eyes even wider beneath her pearly lavender eye shadow. He frowned, annoyed at the way she shook his concentration.

"We can socialize, but it has to be on a certain…level." She tilted her head inquiringly, but Brett had a suspicion that she knew exactly what he was referring to. "You were coming on to me at the wedding."

"A little," she agreed, totally missing his point.

"We can't…I mean, we're practically related, and I don't want to create a situation."

"Wow." Claire took a careful sip of wine, her expression maddeningly calm. "You certainly extrapolate things out, don't you? That's almost like jumping from a simple hello into marriage."

"No. It's not." He didn't like the way she made him feel foolish for a perfectly logical statement of fact.

"Well, I think you're dodging stones that haven't even been thrown."

"I like to err on the side of caution."

"That's not what I hear," she said softly. "Rumor has it you were a wild guy back in the day."

"Where'd you hear that?" he asked in an equally quiet tone.

"Around."

"Regan?" Damn, he hoped not. He didn't want Claire to know his story. But she and Regan were sisters.

"No. Actually, a couple of women were discussing you

in the bar when I went in for a sandwich yesterday. You were a rodeo star, according to them."

"Yeah. I was."

Too close for comfort. Those rodeo days had ended up being the dark point of his life, and he wasn't going to discuss them. Period.

Brett slid the cork back into the bottle. Rudeness and tactlessness seemed to be his best strategies. He pushed the bottle across the table toward her. "I was kind of in the middle of something when you came."

She nudged it back toward him before she stood. "You keep it."

"You'll probably need it more than me." He picked up the wine and pressed it into her hands.

"Thanks for the help, Brett. See you around." A few seconds later, the screen door banged shut behind her. Brett watched her walk down the path for a moment, admiring the subtle swing of her hips beneath the swirly skirt in spite of himself.

Claire Flynn was not going to be good for his peace of mind.

CHAPTER THREE

CLAIRE GAVE HERSELF a good talking to as she walked home across the bristly hay field. Once upon a time she'd berated Regan for dating the wrong kind of man—which was truly a case of the pot calling the kettle black, since Claire also tended to pursue guys for the wrong reasons.

She liked to attain the unattainable.

It was a bad habit, and one she was trying to break herself of. Being attracted to Brett Bishop was not a step in the right direction, since she suspected her interest in him was sparked solely by his corresponding lack of interest in her.

But she couldn't get around the fact that there was something about him that made her want to know more. Like, why the barriers? With her, with his brother, and with his niece, Kylie.

There was probably a simple explanation.

Claire wondered how long it was going to take her to figure it out.

ON MONDAY MORNING Claire started her school day by handing out progress reports listing the students' grades in each subject.

"What are these?" Dylan asked with a sneer. Claire was going to start working on his attitude just as soon as she'd made some headway with Ashley.

"Those are your grades for your first week of school. I'd like you to show them to your parents, have them sign the bottom and then bring them back by Wednesday at the latest." The grades were, for the most part, dismal in math and English. Primarily because few of the students were doing their homework.

Dylan frowned. Elena Moreno's mouth was actually hanging open. Only Rudy and Jesse seemed satisfied with what was on the paper. Rudy had all A's. Jesse had straight C's, and apparently that was good enough for him. He was an earnest kid who tried hard, but it was especially obvious he had some holes in his education. His records had yet to arrive from his previous school, and Claire had no idea what his background was.

"Are you going to do this every week?" Ashley asked with disbelief.

"Every Monday. This way there will be no nasty surprises at the end of the quarter. Everyone will know their grades, and your parents will be aware of your progress."

"But making us bring them back signed shows you don't trust us."

"You do know that trust is earned, don't you? I doubt we'll do the parent signatures all year, but I want to start out that way, until everyone is aware of what to expect."

"What're you going to do if we don't bring them back by Wednesday?" Dylan asked in his most obnoxious tone.

"I'll phone or email your parents. Now, please get out your math homework."

Dylan blew out a disgusted breath and made a show of shoving the grade paper into his pocket in a big wad. The other kids tucked their slips away less dramatically, some in notebooks, some in pockets, and started digging for their math books.

"My mom is going to kill me," Toni murmured to Ashley later, as the class left for morning break.

"Mine won't," Ashley responded with a smug lift of

her chin. She spoke loudly enough to make certain Claire heard her. Claire smiled, but it was an effort. She didn't even have the pleasure of knowing that real life would teach Ashley a lesson or two. Ashley's family probably had enough money to cushion her from reality.

Pity.

Ashley didn't have to grow up to be a shallow, arrogant person, but there didn't appear to be much to keep it from happening. And then, as if to solidify Claire's opinion, she heard Ashley through her open window after school, making fun of Jesse.

"Do you live here or something?" Ashley asked in a snooty voice.

"No. My dad works late." The poor kid was often sitting on the swings, waiting for his father to come pick him up, when Claire went home, and she left late most nights.

"Well, I hope he works overtime, so he can buy you some decent clothes."

Claire barely stayed in her seat. But she knew Jesse wouldn't appreciate his teacher coming to the rescue. He probably wouldn't appreciate knowing that she'd overheard the conversation, either.

"Hey, at least people like me," Jesse said.

"That's what you think," Ashley retorted smugly. "Come on, Toni. Let's go."

Claire drew in a breath, let it out slowly, and after a quick look out the window, forced herself to continue her grading. Jesse was still sitting on a swing, and he seemed to be okay. And Claire was going to see to it that he remained okay, at least while he was at school.

THE FIRST MEETING of the school parent-teacher organization was called to order that evening by Ashley's mother, who'd once again raided her daughter's wardrobe. There were at least twenty parents in attendance, in addition to Trini and Bertie. Claire was impressed. The parent-teacher organization of her old school had been comprised of approximately twenty percent of the parents. The Barlow Ridge PTO attendance seemed to be hovering around the one hundred percent mark. Claire was even more impressed with the treasurer's report. These people were either prolific savers, or they were talented at fund-raising. It turned out to be a combination of the two.

They discussed the year's fund-raisers—a Christmas craft show, a chili feed and a quilt auction. Claire knew of the quilt auction via Regan, who now owned two heirloom-quality hand-pieced quilts.

Almost twenty minutes were spent debating whether the PTO's Santa suit would last another season, or if they'd need to buy another before the Christmas pageant. And then they went on to folding chairs. Were there enough? Should the broken ones be fixed or replaced? And when had the piano last been tuned?

The meeting was almost over when Deirdre focused on Bertie and Claire, who were seated at the back of the room. "Have we covered everything?"

"I, um, have a request," Claire said.

Everyone half turned in their chairs to look at her. Claire decided it was a good thing that she enjoyed public speaking, because all eyes—some of them not that friendly—were on her.

"First of all, I'm enjoying working with your kids. We have some ground to make up because of teacher turnover during the past few years, and I was wondering if the PTO would purchase math manipulatives and four novel sets, one for each quarter."

Claire could tell by the way expressions shifted and glances were exchanged that she'd accidentally hit on a sore spot. She wondered what it could be. It certainly wasn't finances, from the sound of the treasurer's report. She tried again.

"The novels in the storeroom are not only old and not entirely grade appropriate, they're in really bad shape," she explained. "I don't know if they'll survive another reading. And as far as math manipulatives go, there aren't any."

"There's a reason for that," one of the parents said. "We've bought several programs in the past that other teachers packed up and took with them when they left."

"You're kidding!"

"Not at all. And I think our new novel sets and some reference books ended up in Wesley at the elementary school when a teacher transferred there. We also bought a pricey math program that left with another teacher, and she didn't even stay with our district. She moved out of state."

Another parent smiled condescendingly at Claire. "How long are *you* planning on being here?"

"I'm going to graduate school next fall. I made that clear when I interviewed here." *And I was hired because no one else would take the job.* Under normal circumstances Claire wouldn't have held her tongue, but she had enough of a fight on her hands bringing her students under control. She needed parental support, or her battle was going to be twice as hard.

"Couldn't you borrow what you need from one of the schools in Wesley?"

"I'll ask."

"It's nothing personal, Miss Flynn." Claire was getting very tired of hearing how nothing was personal in Barlow Ridge. "It's just that we've been burned in the past."

"And I don't think our kids need fancy programs and gimmicks." An older woman near the front spoke up. "They need a good teacher."

Claire was beginning to see that isolation might not be the only problem with teaching in Barlow Ridge. She composed herself before going on the offensive.

"Your children also need discipline and development of a work ethic, if they are going to achieve grade level."

Her statement caused a ripple. "What do you mean by '*achieve* grade level'?" Deirdre demanded in a shocked tone.

Claire frowned. "I mean, that many of my seventh and eighth grade students are behind in at least one subject area—primarily math. They need to catch up. Didn't you get standardized test scores last year?"

There was another ripple as the parents exchanged puzzled looks.

"No."

"None of you received scores?" Bertie asked. The group shook their heads in unison. "I gave them to Mr. Nelson. He was supposed to staple them to the year-end report cards."

"And when did Mr. Nelson do anything he was supposed to do?" Trini muttered.

"Didn't you wonder why the younger kids had scores and the older ones didn't?" Bertie asked the group.

"I just assumed that the upper grades weren't tested. You know how they've messed with the tests lately, changing dates and grade levels…" Deirdre said.

"We have copies in your children's files," Bertie said, with a frustrated sigh. "We'll need some time to locate and duplicate them, but you'll get the scores before Friday."

The meeting was adjourned shortly thereafter, and Claire went into her room to collect her jacket and purse. She had no new novel sets, no math manipulatives—just parents who didn't think she was up to the job of teaching their children. Parents who hadn't been aware of how far behind their kids were.

And even though she didn't need the point hammered home that the parents weren't supporting her, it *had* been hammered home.

"What really fries me," one parent said as she passed by Clare's open door on the way to the exit, "is that the school district must know we have low scores, but they send out the most inexperienced teacher they can find."

"Well, she certainly isn't engaging Lexi," her companion responded. "It looks like all she's doing is drawing lines in the sand and daring the kids to step across. That's not teaching."

Claire swallowed hard and turned off the lights. She and Bertie stepped out of their rooms and into the hall at the same moment. Bertie signaled for her to wait a minute as the two parents made their way to the exit.

As soon as the door swung shut, Bertie said, "Try not to—"

"Take it personally?" Claire shook her head. "It's kind of hard not to."

"These kids haven't had a real teacher since Regan left, and the parents are getting frustrated."

"Well, I can't blame them, but I hate being prejudged."

"That's a tendency here," Bertie said. "You're newly graduated, which is a strike against you. And the kids are complaining, which is another strike. Plus..." She hesitated, then said, "You dress kind of...fancy. Which might put some parents off."

"They don't like the way I dress?" Claire was wearing a knee-length chiffon skirt in a bright floral pattern, a silky peach T-shirt and a chunky necklace. Normal fare for her. But she remembered Elena saying they'd never had a teacher that looked like her.

"Well…" Bertie looked down at her own clothing, which consisted of brown corduroy pants, a white cotton T-shirt and well-worn athletic shoes. "I think it's been awhile since they've seen anyone wear hosiery to school."

"I'm not buying a new wardrobe to fit in," Claire muttered. "I like my clothes." She and Bertie walked down the hall together, exiting the school into the inky darkness of a cloudy night.

"I like your clothes, too. I wish I had the energy to dress better, but I don't." Bertie stuck her key in the lock and abruptly changed the subject as she twisted her hand. "This test thing really annoys me. It's good that Nelson got out of teaching, because I think the parents have cause for legal action."

"Would they do that?"

"Barlow Ridge parents are not passive parents." She smiled grimly before asking Claire, "Where's your car?"

"I walked."

"It's going to storm. Do you want a ride home?"

She shook her head. "Thanks, anyway."

"Coming to quilting club on Wednesday?"

"Will it be friendlier than the PTO?"

Bertie smiled ruefully. "There's some crossover—Deirdre, Willa, Mary Ann. I think they're already betting you won't show."

Claire smiled humorlessly. "In that case, I'll show." She couldn't sew a stitch, but she figured she could either be there, trying to do her part for the quilt auction, or sitting home alone with her ears ringing as the other women discussed her.

PHIL'S HORSES AND MULES arrived while Brett was in the middle of his online class. Horses he understood. Reacquainting himself with math was going to take some time.

He was making headway, but he was glad to give himself a break in order to drive over to the ranch, less than a mile away, and take delivery.

He went to meet the shipper, who opened the door of a trailer to reveal a handsome black mule. Beyond that Brett could see two broad chestnut-colored backs, but the dividers kept him from seeing the horses' heads.

"They're tall," he commented to the driver.

"Yeah. And Numb Nuts, up front, doesn't have any manners."

"Good to hear."

Brett stepped in and ran a hand over the mule's neck. The big animal gave him a get-me-out-of-here look. Brett complied, leading the big guy out of the trailer and over to one of the many individual corrals adjacent to the barn. When he released it, the mule circled the pen once and then went to the water trough for a long drink.

"Where're you from?" Brett asked, suddenly realizing that he had no idea where these animals were being shipped from.

"San Diego. I left them in the trailer last night, because I didn't know if I could get the stud back in."

Phil wouldn't like that, Brett thought. Phil couldn't tell a good animal from a bad one without help, but he insisted that all of his animals be treated right. It was the one thing that helped Brett overlook his boss's other foibles, which included a healthy dose of arrogance coupled with ignorance about matters he wanted to look like an expert in. Such as horses.

Brett stepped back into the trailer to unload a very nice quarter horse. The mare followed him placidly to her pen, and then she, too, went straight for the water.

And now for Numb Nuts.

He had a feeling from the way the trailer was rocking, now that the stallion was alone and wondering where his mare had gone, that his nuts were actually not all that numb.

Brett opened the divider and the horse rolled an eye at him, showing white. And then the animal screamed. Brett untied him, taking a firm hold on the rope close to the snap, and started to lead him to his pen. The stud danced and rolled his eyes again, but he respected the lead rope, and Brett got him shifted safely. As soon as the stallion had drank his fill, however, he started pacing the fence, back and forth, back forth, punctuating every turn with a fierce whinny.

The driver smiled and headed for his truck, obviously glad to be on his way.

Brett decided to let the horse settle in for a day or two before he attempted to tune him up. And as soon as he could, he was going to suggest to Phil that unless he wanted to make a complete spectacle of himself, perhaps he might want to find a calmer animal to show.

When Brett pulled into his driveway, he saw Claire walking across the field toward his house. What now? She met him at his truck.

"I need a favor."

"So do I," Brett said wearily, pushing his hat back.

"What do you need?"

"I need someone to tactfully tell my boss that he's in over his head."

Claire frowned. "Who's your boss?"

"See that ranch over there?"

She nodded.

"It's one of many around here owned by the Ryker family. They have a land company and they lease ranches—including the one that I'm living on. Phil Ryker decided to become a cowboy a few years back, and took over that ranch as his personal hobby. I take care of it for him while he's away."

"I see."

"And he likes to buy horses. And cows. And mules. He even bought some llamas, once."

"And he's just bought something you don't think he can handle?"

Brett smiled wryly, wondering why he was unloading on Claire. She didn't seem to mind, though. "He bought something I *know* he can't handle, and now he has to be convinced of it before he hurts himself."

"Good luck," she said with a smile. Damn, but she had a nice smile.

"Yeah," he said, sobering up. "What favor do you need? Snake removal? Cooler renovation?"

"I'm joining the quilting club and Regan has a bag of stuff for me at her place. If you're going to Wesley this week, could you pick it up?"

"Yeah. I can do that."

"Thanks." She smiled again. "Well, I have a ton of planning to do, so I'll see you later." She took a few backward steps before turning around. "Good luck with your boss."

"Thanks," he muttered. He was probably going to need it.

The next morning Brett made his weekly trip to Wesley, picking up groceries, animal feed, hardware, and vaccines for the new horses. He put off stopping at his brother's place until last.

It was close to four when he knocked on the door. It swung open almost immediately, Kylie's wide smile fading when she saw him. She forced the corners of her mouth back up again.

"Hi. I thought you were someone else."

Obviously. Kylie had grown into a beautiful girl—almost a carbon copy of her mother—which added to Brett's awkwardness whenever he had to face her alone. Kylie always picked up on the vibe and reflected it back, making their one-on-ones a tad uncomfortable.

"Regan has a bag of quilt supplies for Claire that I'm supposed to pick up."

"Oh. Right. I was wondering what this was." Kylie stepped back to retrieve a large plastic bag, which she handed to him. For a moment they stared at each other, neither certain of what to say. As usual.

"Are you coming to watch me ride?" There was a regional 4-H horse show in Elko in two weeks, and Kylie had qualified in several events.

"Yes, I am." He made it a point to watch her ride or play basketball whenever he could. It hurt in some ways, but it was a price he was willing to pay.

"Do you know about the barbecue afterward?"

"What barbecue?"

"Regan wanted to have a get-together since Claire is here, so that she can introduce her around."

Brett automatically shook his head. "No. I probably won't be coming."

"All right." Kylie seemed fine with it. Relieved, in fact. Brett felt the usual twinge of regret.

A truck pulled into the drive behind his, and a kid who looked too young to be driving jumped out. Kylie's face lit up and Brett felt a stirring of protectiveness. Surely Will wasn't letting her date already? She was only fifteen.

"Hi, Kylie. Hi…" The boy's face contorted in confusion for a second and then he said, "I thought you were Mr. Bishop."

"He is," Kylie said. "This is my uncle."

"Oh. Hi. I'm Shane." The boy extended his hand, and Brett gave him points for manners.

"Nice to meet you." He glanced over at Kylie, encountering eyes exactly like his own. "I gotta get going. Nice meeting you, Shane. Bye, Kylie."

"See ya."

CLAIRE PERCHED ON the edge of her desk, an expectant look on her face. After a few seconds of staring silently, she asked, "Is there a problem with the topic?"

The students shook their heads, then began writing in their journals.

Claire waited the full fifteen minutes before asking, "Does anyone want to share?"

As usual, the students sat staring straight ahead. Even the young ones. They were learning fast. Claire sighed and told the kids to get out their social-studies texts. When she'd informed Brett that she could take whatever these students could dish out, she'd meant challenges such as snakes—not things like a stupefying lack of response. And she was fairly certain it wasn't too late for the younger kids, that they *would* respond if it weren't for fear of being laughed at by the older students.

What to do?

Claire drummed her fingers on her desk, then stopped when a few kids looked up at her. She opened her grade book and pretended to study the columns of numbers. The obvious answer was to separate the younger students from the older ones, but she couldn't do that in the space she had available.

She thought back to her professors, with all their pie-in-the-sky educational theories. Never once had it been mentioned that she might be faced with kids who simply refused to engage themselves. Kids who did not want to learn.

Regan had advised her to ignore the stony stares and

reward the behavior that met her expectations, but hadn't mentioned what to do if the behavior of the older kids was tainting the younger ones.

Claire headed for the office phone. Something had to be done before it was too late.

Back in the classroom, she told the fifth and sixth graders to go outside for recess. When the older kids also rose to their feet, she asked them to remain. She spoke quietly, but there was no doubt that she meant what she said. The seventh and eighth graders sat back down.

"We need to talk. You guys are role models for the younger kids. I want to know if you think you're setting them a good example?"

They did not even have the grace to appear ashamed. If anything, they looked smug, and Claire felt her anger growing.

"You guys are acting like a bunch of jerks, and it has to stop. I will not have you ruining the education of the other students. I've phoned Principal Rupert, and if this behavior continues, he will be driving out to have a talk with each one of you on an individual basis."

Dylan and Ashley both smirked. Toni gave Claire a stony stare.

"He's also calling your parents today."

Ashley looked unconcerned, but Dylan and Toni paled slightly. So there was *some* fear. That was good. Maybe there was hope.

"I don't hold grudges," Claire continued. "I'm willing to let bygones be bygones, if you start acting the way you know you're supposed to act." She drew in a breath, wondering if the kids knew how much she was winging it. "Instead of recess, I would like you to write about how your behavior is affecting the other kids. Ashley, I want to talk to you privately."

"Sure," the girl said with a toss of her head. She followed Claire out into the hallway.

"I know you feel safe, Ashley—like no consequence can touch you."

The girl smiled.

"And I want a straight answer. Are you going to set a better example with your behavior? Or are you going to continue as you've been doing?"

"I don't see anything wrong with my behavior, and neither does my mother."

"You don't see how the younger kids are learning from watching you?"

She shook her head.

"Then my only option is to put you where they can't watch you. Your desk will be in the hall for the remainder of the day and tomorrow, until we talk to the principal. We'll reevaluate then."

"I'm going to sit in the hall?"

"Yes."

"How will I hear what you're saying?"

"What would that matter, Ashley? You seem to think you already know everything. Stay here. I'll go get your desk."

Claire took a few steps toward the room, angry with herself for sniping at the girl. She turned back, wanting to give it one last stab. "This is your choice, Ashley. I don't want you out here. If you'll participate in class in a respectful way, I want you in the room with everyone else. You're a bright girl, and you can help the younger students learn."

She raised her chin and narrowed her eyes. But she did not respond.

A steaming Ashley was sitting at her desk in the hall when the younger kids came traipsing in again. Claire stood next to her door and watched the procession. The kids looked first at Ashley, then at Claire. No one said anything.

There was a definite change in attitude, now that Ashley was no longer in residence. Claire took her the work for the afternoon, then closed the classroom door. There would, no doubt, be a hot phone call from Deirdre Landau later. Maybe even a personal visit. But it was worthwhile, if Claire could save her younger students from going over to the dark side.

Surprisingly, Ashley left school that afternoon without summoning her mother. She walked away, her chin held high and her books pressed close to her chest. Toni walked with her, but their heads were not together as usual. Claire felt a little bad, but knew she had to draw the line somewhere.

She graded papers until three-thirty and then went into her storage closet, prior to her usual trip to the basement before going home. Every evening she sorted and carted one shelf of stuff off to the nether regions. She almost had space in her closet now to store the textbooks that were shoved into boxes under her counters. And in the process she had uncovered some useful supplies, as well as some hilarious artifacts of days gone by. She figured that with her box-a-day strategy, she'd have decades worth of haphazardly stored items properly sorted and put away by the end of the semester. If nothing else, she would leave the school better organized than she'd found it—and the students better educated. Even if it killed her. And them.

Claire pulled open the stubborn basement door and started down the stairs, descending into the earthy coolness, which felt good after the heat of the classroom. She had just heaved the box up on top of the lowest stack of rubber bins when she heard a heavy scraping noise, followed by a dull thud.

The door. Someone had closed the basement door.

Bertie must have come back, seen it open…

Claire trudged up the stairs and pushed. The door didn't budge. She controlled a twinge of panic, twisted the handle and pushed again. Nothing. Someone had thrown the dead bolt. She began to pound with the heel of her hand.

"Bertie!"

No answer. Claire pounded until her hand was bruised, more in frustration than from any hope of being heard. It was pretty obvious she'd been locked in on purpose. Three guesses as to who had done it.

She sank down onto the top step and stared at the dangling light. About time for the bulb to burn out, the way things were going. She had a flash of inspiration and shot a glance over her shoulder at the door.

But the hinges were on the outer side. Drat.

The frog croaked and Claire's shoulders slumped.

Could it be she was going to spend a night in the basement? Not if she could help it.

She rose to her feet and tromped down the stairs. The ventilation windows were covered with screens, and they were quite small. And high—probably seven feet off the floor. Claire glanced down at her hips, then back up at the window. What would be worse? Spending the night in the basement or spending the night stuck in a window?

It was a no-brainer. She was going for stuck-in-the-window.

Claire searched for some moderately safe way to get herself up there. With all the stored files and equipment, would it have been too much to ask that a ladder be among them? Apparently so. The only bits of furniture were rickety or broken. An old file cabinet wobbled when she tried to move it, so she started stacking rubber bins. The ones that were full enough to support her weight were also quite heavy. She managed to pile them three high and then climbed on top, grimacing as her hands pushed the damp, mossy wall when she steadied herself.

The window was now at shoulder level, and it wouldn't open. It had no latch.

Claire said a word that was normally frowned upon in a school setting, then climbed off the stack of boxes to find something she could use to break the glass.

THE PHONE RANG just as Brett started working on his algebra assignment. He'd already done all the damage he could to his humanities lesson, and it was time to move on.

"Hi, Brett," Regan said. "Have you seen Claire?"

"Uh, no. I left the bag of supplies inside her door. She wasn't home."

"She's not answering her phone, and I'm getting concerned."

"Maybe she's in the shower."

"For two hours?"

Actually, he could imagine that. Brett glanced out the window and saw the lights weren't on in the trailer, shooting that theory to hell. "I'll walk over to her house."

"Thanks, Brett. I appreciate it."

"No problem."

Maybe it was quilting night, Brett reasoned as he headed across the dark field, flashlight in hand. Or maybe she had a date. On a Thursday? Probably not. Maybe she was still working. That seemed the most reasonable answer, even if it was going on seven o'clock.

Claire pulled into her driveway just as Brett rounded the rear of her trailer. He turned off the flashlight and thought about disappearing when she got out of her car, but then noticed that she was looking...rough. Her white blouse and her face were smeared with a dark substance, which he hoped wasn't blood. It was hard to tell in the fluorescent glow of the yard light. And her skirt was ripped up the side.

Alarmed, he stepped out of the darkness, his movement obviously startling her, and then he saw to his relief that the stains were not blood.

"What are you doing here?" she asked with a remarkable amount of dignity, considering the fact that she was green.

"Regan called. She was worried about you."

"Oh, that's right. I was supposed to—" She broke off and frowned at Brett. "Well, thanks for checking on me. I'll give her a call."

"You want to tell me what happened?"

She shook her head. "No. I think I'll employ that we-need-to-keep-our-own-space rule you invented."

"Suit yourself." His mouth tightened as he fought with himself. She was vertical, obviously not hurt—physically, anyway. He'd love to know how she'd gotten smeared with green gunk, but it was none of his business. Still… "Are you sure?"

"Positive," she said. "Now, if you'll excuse me?" She walked past him into her house, the tear in her skirt exposing a lot of leg as she disappeared. The door closed with a thump.

Brett stared at it for a moment, then turned his flashlight on again and started back across the field.

This was not going to be a restful school year.

CHAPTER FOUR

A GROAN ESCAPED Claire's lips as she saw her reflection in the living-room mirror. She was green.

How had Brett kept from laughing? Or asking more questions?

She blew out a breath that lifted her short bangs, and headed toward the bathroom, where she cranked on the hot water and stripped off her ruined clothing.

Claire had made a career out of trying not to let problems bother her—instead, she let them bother Regan. Regan was a caretaker by nature, and Claire was more than happy to let her sister smooth out the wrinkles in her life. At least until that unhappy day when Regan had moved from Las Vegas to Wesley, and suddenly Claire had found herself dealing with her issues on her own. But to her amazement, after a few false starts and many long phone calls, she had done all right.

She wasn't going to tell Regan about this escapade. Not just yet, anyway. She braced her hands on the sink and let her head droop as she waited for the water to warm up.

Reaction was setting in. Anger. Bewilderment. And a grudging appreciation for Ashley's style of revenge. The kid was good. Now, Claire would have to be even better.

BRETT PACED THROUGH his house. He was supposed to be finishing his math, since it was due the next day, but he also had some work to do in his living room. He'd torn out the existing floor and was down to subfloor. There were bundles of interlocking hardwood flooring sitting there, and they weren't going to lay themselves.

Algebra or flooring? He headed for his computer. When a guy felt like doing flooring, it probably meant he was avoiding something that needed his attention more.

Brett had figured it was going to take some work to bring himself up to speed in his studies, but he hadn't realized just how much he'd forgotten, or at the very least, misplaced in his brain. And it wasn't as if he hadn't used math throughout his adult life, calculating animal dosages, fencing footage, acreage, amounts of feed. But somehow, that came easier than solving for X.

He pulled his yellow legal tablet closer and copied a problem. And then, as he launched into step one, he found himself wondering again just how Claire Flynn had ended up the color of slime.

CLAIRE SPENT MOST of the night staring at her dark bedroom ceiling and debating about how to deal with the situation. Ashley had gotten her revenge, but there was no way for Claire to prove it. So what to do? Confront her and listen to the denial? Contact the principal with nothing but a hypothesis?

Ignore the incident?

Ask Bertie for advice?

She hated to do that, and hated to admit what had happened, but she was going to have to explain the situation to Bertie. The work order to fix the basement window would have to go through her as lead teacher.

Drat.

Claire took extra care with her hair and makeup the next morning. She even wore her favorite dress, hoping she wouldn't be squeezing through any small spaces in it, and she drove, instead of walking, arriving early.

The basement door was still latched from the outside.

Bertie came in just after Claire, and found her standing there.

"Working up courage to go downstairs?" she asked as she went into the office and dumped a cardboard box on the floor.

"No. Surveying the scene of the crime."

Bertie reappeared. "What does that mean?"

Claire shrugged. "Someone locked me in the basement last night."

"No." But even as she spoke, it was obvious from the older woman's expression that she believed her. "Ashley?"

"That's who my money's on. No proving it, though." Claire sighed again. "Any ideas on how to handle this?"

Bertie leaned back against the copy machine and studied the floor tiles for a moment, a deep frown pulling her gray eyebrows together.

"Not an easy one."

"One of the basement windows needs to be repaired." Bertie's eyes snapped up and Claire told her the entire story.

"You know, Wanda would have been here at ten o'clock."

"I hadn't thought of that." Wanda, whom Claire had yet to meet, was supposed to clean the school between the hours of three and five, but she preferred to work between ten and twelve, after her kids were in bed. The district office was unaware, and Bertie saw no reason to enlighten them.

"I wasn't thinking all that clearly, to tell you the truth. I just knew I didn't want to spend the night in the basement."

"I don't blame you. Not with Jim Shannon down there."

"The frog has a name?"

Bertie slowly shook her head. "No. Jim is a ghost."

Somehow Claire wasn't surprised. "Ghost?"

"Yes. It's a long story that has been embellished for years, but to sum it up, someone called Jim Shannon fell down the stairs about eighty years ago, shortly after the school was built. Apparently, they hadn't installed a hand railing and he slipped."

"And he died?" If so, Claire was glad she'd been happily unaware last night, when it had been just her and Jim and the frog.

"The story gets a little hazy there. The consensus is that he lived another ten years after his tumble, but had a permanent limp and held a grudge because of it." Bertie started pulling reams of colored paper out of the storage cupboard. "He's buried on the other side of the fence, and the kids swear that they can hear him moaning in the basement."

"How can someone be buried on the other side of the fence?"

"Family plot. They don't allow it anymore, but sixty or seventy years ago they weren't so particular."

"Well, I wasn't feeling any vibes from Jim. But I was mad enough that he may have been afraid of me."

Bertie smiled and lifted another stack of paper onto the counter.

"What should I do?"

"We have two choices here. We can call Rupert and see what he wants to do about it, which will be nothing, because he won't want to get off his lazy keister and drive out here unless we have the suspect in custody."

"And choice number two?"

"We report the broken window, have the district repair it, pretend nothing has happened and listen for information." Claire cocked her head and Bertie explained. "My little guys are a fountain of information. They hear things from the older kids and share among themselves. All I have to do is keep very busy at my computer. For some reason they think that if my back is turned, my ears don't work."

Claire laughed. "I like plan number two. And now I guess I'd better go and decide how to wage my counter-attack."

"Good luck," Bertie called as Claire left the office.

Claire was afraid she was going to need it.

CLAIRE WAS TALKING to Mr. Rupert on the phone when the students came in at the morning bell, so she didn't see Ashley's expression as she entered the classroom. Claire ended the call a few seconds later and went over to Ashley's desk.

"Would you like to stay in here today?" she asked.

The girl's eyes narrowed as she considered Claire. Their gazes held for a moment as they sized each other up, each of them a little more impressed with the other's abilities than she'd been the day before. "Yes," Ashley said.

"I've spoken to Mr. Rupert. First sign of rudeness and you're back in the hall and he's on his way out for a meeting."

"I understand," Ashley said.

"Good. Maybe we can start over."

But Ashley wasn't interested in starting over. In spite of her promise to avoid being rude, she shot daggers at Claire when she didn't think she was looking, and Claire noticed the kids forming a tight knot around her during recess, probably being filled in on what had happened to Claire the day before.

And even though she didn't need confirmation that the story had been told, she got it shortly after school, when Elena Moreno came in for the coat she'd left behind.

"Did something happen to you, Miss Flynn?"

Claire managed a perplexed expression. "No, why do you ask?"

"No reason."

Mmm, hmm. Well, at least the girl looked concerned.

"Some of the kids kind of noticed a window got broken," Elena added, as she bunched her coat into a wad and stuffed it into her backpack, apparently hoping to jog Claire's memory.

"Mrs. Gunderson has already phoned it in to the maintenance department. But thanks for reporting it." Claire gave her most serene smile. "I'll see you tomorrow."

Elena smiled back, obviously confused. "Well, see ya."

"See ya."

She headed for the door, glancing at Claire over her shoulder before disappearing from view.

Claire let out a small sigh as she heard the outer door bang shut. She hadn't lied to the girl so much as sidestepped her question. And she was going to keep sidestepping until she had this situation under control.

THE QUILTING CLUB met on Wednesdays at seven o'clock, and Claire was determined to attend every meeting—at least until she'd made some inroads into the community. She wasn't going to impress anyone with her sewing ability, but she figured the more she was around them, the more the townspeople would get used to her, and the more parent support she'd have.

Claire had spent her time after school that day catching up on her grading rather than organizing the storage closet. No more trips to the basement for her unless Bertie was in the building and aware of where she was going. The basement buddy system. At exactly 5:00 p.m., she gathered up her tote bag of quilting supplies and locked the school.

Jesse was still waiting by the swings. Ramon had been

with him up until 4:30 p.m., but now the boy sat alone, making patterns in the dirt with his tennis shoe.

"Waiting for your dad?" Claire asked as she walked by on the way to the gate.

"Yeah." Jesse twisted the swing sideways. "He's usually here by now, but he had a longer trip today."

"Trip?"

"He's a salesman. He has a route and today's his long day."

"I see." Claire smiled, wondering why a salesman was living in such a remote area. Maybe the guy just wanted to get out of the rat race. Claire had yet to meet Jesse's dad, but parent-teacher conferences would be coming up, and she'd meet him then.

"You know, if you ever need a ride home, I can give you one."

Jesse shook his blond head. "No. Dad doesn't want me home when he's not there."

So instead, he wanted the poor kid sitting in a deserted school yard? Alone. That made tons of sense.

"I was wondering…"

"Yes?" Claire asked when the boy's voice trailed off.

"Do you have any chores or anything that need doing around your place?"

"Are you hiring out?" Claire asked.

Jesse glanced down at his pants, which had a hole in the knee, and it wasn't too hard to follow his train of thought. "Yeah," he said matter-of-factly. "I was thinking that I could, you know, buy a few clothes."

"It's always fun to buy clothes." Claire gave no indication that she didn't think a ten-year-old should be buying his own clothing. "Yes, I can come up with one or two things."

"Is Saturday morning all right?"

"Can you come on Sunday, instead?" Kylie had a horse show on Saturday, and Claire wasn't going to miss it.

"I can come Sunday."

"Other people might need work done on Saturday, you know."

"Yeah," he said with a bright smile. "I'll check around."

An older model Ford Explorer pulled up in front of the school then and Jesse jumped to his feet. "That's Dad. See ya." He grabbed his backpack and trotted off. "Thanks," he called as he closed the school-yard gate.

Claire stood near the swing for a few minutes after the boy had climbed in and the vehicle had driven away. She'd lifted a hand in greeting to the driver and had gotten a quick, rather distracted wave in return.

She wasn't quite sure what to make of Mr. Lane.

"Is it true the kids locked you in the school basement?"

Claire had barely taken her seat at the quilting meeting when Anne McKirk, the mercantile owner, growled her question. Fortunately, she was sitting next to Claire and hadn't growled all that loudly. None of the other women seemed to have heard.

"Where on earth did you hear that?" Claire asked.

"From pretty much everyone."

"Did you hear who did it?" Claire asked, without really expecting an answer.

"That Landau girl," Anne said promptly. She opened the large plastic bag sitting at her feet and pulled out a quilt hoop with a red-and-blue square stretched across it. "What are you going to do about it?"

"Make her learn something, whether she likes it or not."

Anne didn't say anything more, but she was smiling as she placed her hoop on the long table at which they were seated.

Trini pulled out the chair directly across the table from Claire. "So you came," she said with a smile. "Do you have your stuff?"

Claire plopped her own plastic bag on the table. "Yes. I just don't know what to do with it." Regan had bought the things on the list that Trini had supplied, sending them along with Brett, and Claire had examined them. But she was still unclear on how it all became a quilt.

"Great. Come on over to the cutting table and I'll show you how to make the pieces. We're each making a square for this Fourth of July quilt, so you can learn the ropes and contribute."

Ten minutes later, Claire was back at the long table with a stack of precision-cut red and blue triangles, parallelograms and squares.

"Thread your needle," Anne instructed, without looking at her. She said it in a voice that made Claire believe the older woman thought her incapable of the single act. Well, she happened to be a fine needle threader. It was the sewing part she'd have to fake.

Claire quickly got the hang of the running stitch used to sew the pieces together, and she concentrated on the task, while conversation floated around her, providing a pleasant background. She soon abandoned the flat surface of the table and held the fabric pieces on her lap, frowning as she bobbed the needle up and down, attaching bits of fabric. She'd felt awkward at first, but sewing was becoming more natural to her.

She picked up the two pieces she had just joined, pressed the seam to one side with her fingers, as Trini had shown her, and then pinned a long parallelogram to it and put it back on her lap to stitch.

The other women seemed to have forgotten she was there. She didn't really have anything to say, so she remained quiet and sewed, feeling a sense of satisfaction to be doing something so useful. Maybe she could actually make a quilt.

"What do I do once I get the square sewn together?" Claire asked no one in particular.

"Lap quilt," Anne murmured, her glasses slipping down her nose as she concentrated on her hoop. "Each square is individually quilted to a square of batting and backing of the same size. Then we join *those* quilted squares together and—"

"Instant quilt," Trini finished. "We don't have to use big frames this way, and we can quilt anywhere."

"How many quilts do you need for the spring auction?"

"As many as we get done. We try to finish one for each member, so that would be twelve, including you."

"If you stay that long," Anne said.

Claire pursed her lips and focused on her stitches. Just a few more and the square would be done. She ended the longest seam she'd yet attempted, knotted it off the way Trini had shown her and clipped the thread. Done.

She lifted the square off her lap and felt a breeze as her skirt came with it.

She frowned and gave a small tug. Her skirt refused to let go of the square, and vice versa, and then one of the older women across the table started laughing.

"You…" she pressed her lips together, but couldn't contain her mirth "…you sewed it to your skirt."

Claire gave another experimental tug. "Yes, I did," she agreed. She looked up, her expression serious. "Surely this isn't the first time this has happened?"

Lips quivered and then several of the smiles turned into giggles.

"I can see that the club is going to be a more active place

with you here," Anne said, passing Claire a small pair of scissors. "Just clip the knot and pull the thread."

"And this was my best seam, too," Claire said as she followed directions. The square lifted free a few seconds later.

"Why don't you sew up on the table?" Lexi's mom, who had ignored Claire up to this point, suggested.

"Good idea," she agreed. It felt more awkward sewing on the table rather than on her lap, but she could see she'd have fewer mishaps that way.

"Is this the first time you've quilted?" someone asked.

"Is it that obvious?" Claire replied.

The woman shook her head. "Not at all," she said wryly. "By the way, I'm Elena's grandmother, Gloria."

"Nice to meet you," Claire stated. She rethreaded her needle and started sewing. "Elena's a very nice girl."

"Who wants green shoes just like yours."

"Really? They're quite practical, you know. Green goes with almost everything."

"But do you have any idea how hard they are to find?"

Claire grinned. "As a matter of fact, I do."

The rest of the meeting went better than she had expected. She couldn't say she was a fully accepted member of the group by the time she left, but she had the feeling the others weren't going to mind having her there. Not all of the PTO moms had warmed up to her, but she'd made some headway, and she understood their cautiousness. Even though Claire was by nature an all-or-nothing girl, she'd take what she could get in this case.

BRETT SHOWED UP at the horse show just as it was beginning, and settled in the middle of the stands, using two large family groups as cover. He wanted to watch alone, and if Claire saw him he had a feeling that wouldn't be possible.

The morning air was crisp, but by afternoon he knew he'd be glad to be under the canopy. Even in late September, the midday temperatures could become uncomfortably hot.

Kylie was entered in three events, all of which were scheduled for that day. He'd watch, maybe stop by and give her an "atta girl," then head back to the ranch to put some time in on Phil's killer stud. He knew Regan wanted him to go to the family picnic, play nice and act like he belonged, but the truth was that he *didn't* belong.

The stands were almost full when the show started. He could see all of the fairgrounds from his vantage point—Will's trailer, Kylie cantering her horse in the warm-up arena prior to her first event and Will and Regan sitting side by side on the running boards of the trailer. Claire was standing next to Regan, watching Kylie. She was wearing jeans, something he'd never seen her in before, with a formfitting shirt and white sunglasses.

Brett pulled his attention back to the arena, where the halter classes were taking place. He was here to watch a horse show, not Will's sister-in-law.

CLAIRE HAD SPENT surprisingly little time at horse shows, considering the fact that Regan had once been a show jumper. This show was her third.

"See? It's not all dust and horse manure," Regan commented as they made their way back to the trailer from the arena where Kylie had just taken the reserve champion ribbon in a class called reining. Claire had no idea how the horse or rider were judged, but she could tell from Will and Regan's reactions that Kylie had done a bang-up job. Even Kylie, who had a tendency to be overly critical of her own performance, was grinning widely.

Claire skirted a pile of the stuff that horse shows weren't

made of. "I have to admit, it's nice being out in the sun, watching the kids. What's Kylie's next class?"

"Barrels. It won't be until after lunch."

"Cool. I'm starving."

"We're eating light, because of the barbecue later."

"Fine with me. I just need something to take the edge off."

Kylie and Will were already at the trailer, unsaddling the horse.

"My stop could have been better," Kylie told her father. "He was slow. I think that's why I got second."

"We'll work on it," Will agreed.

Claire wandered to the front of the truck and leaned against the sun-warmed hood, facing the stands. Brett was there, near the top. She'd spent a good deal of time that morning surreptitiously searching the crowd until she'd finally zeroed in on him. Now she found herself checking periodically to see if he was still around.

He was. He hadn't moved, even now when the lunch break had been announced.

Regan came to lean beside her, following her sister's gaze.

"Why is he up there?" Claire asked.

"Better view."

"Will he be coming to the barbecue?"

"I'd be surprised," Regan said softly.

And for reasons she couldn't quite figure out, Claire refrained from asking why.

CLAIRE DIDN'T COME home Saturday night. Must have been a helluva picnic, Brett thought as he propped the ladder next to his house. The place needed a new roof, which he'd be paying for now that he'd successfully negotiated the option to buy, but not for a year or two, the way things looked.

So in the meantime, he'd have to continue climbing onto the roof after each windstorm to replace missing shingles.

He's just finished hammering the last asphalt beauty into place when he noticed a kid walking down the driveway. Brett descended, hitting the ground about the same time the light-haired boy reached the gate.

"Hi," Brett said, wondering if he was there to sell something. Brett had only lived in Barlow for a year, but he knew the school was hell-bent on fund-raising.

"Hi." The kid shuffled his feet. "I'm kinda looking for a job, and I was wondering if you have any chores that need doing. Miss Flynn said—"

"Miss Flynn sent you over?"

"Yeah."

Brett glanced toward the trailer. No car. Claire wasn't there. Maybe she'd told the boy to hit Brett up while they were at school.

"Well…" He really didn't want a kid hanging around.

The boy's face fell. "Thanks, anyway."

Brett groaned inwardly. "Now that I think about it, I have a few things I could use a hand with. Are you any good with a shovel?"

"I guess."

"You guess?"

"Never did a lot of shoveling." He spoke cautiously, obviously wondering if this admission would be a deal breaker.

"Then it's about time you learned. Are you interested in working hourly or for a flat rate by the job?"

"Flat rate."

Brett almost smiled. The kid spoke authoritatively, but Brett had a strong feeling he had no idea what the difference was between the two.

"Flat rate it is. You got a name?"

"I'm Jesse Lane."

"Nice to meet you, Jesse. I'm Brett."

They were almost to the barn when Claire's car pulled into her driveway. Good. He and Claire would be having a discussion about this matter after Jesse went home. Brett didn't appreciate her sending a kid over without so much as a heads-up. *She* might be out to save the world, but that didn't mean Brett Bishop had to help her.

CHAPTER FIVE

CLAIRE WAS PLANTING bulbs in the long-neglected flower bed that ran the length of her trailer when Brett arrived from across the field, determined to set a few things straight. He almost turned back when he saw what she was doing. He'd never had a tenant who'd tried to improve the place before. Most of them just complained a lot and then moved on.

"We need to talk," he said, in what sounded to him like a reasonable voice.

"About what?" Claire used both hands to pat dirt over the top of a bulb.

"Jesse Lane."

"What about him?" She pushed the hair away from her forehead with her wrist.

"I'd appreciate it if you'd talk to me before sending kids over looking for work."

"I didn't send him."

They regarded each other for a moment, and Brett knew they were thinking the same thing. Jesse wasn't a liar. The kid was too earnest.

"You didn't tell him I'd hire him to help with chores?"

Claire stuck the trowel into the dirt. "He's doing some chores for me today, but I told him I'd be gone Saturday and he might want to see if anyone else had chores that day."

"Maybe that was what he meant."

Claire cocked her head. "Did you hire him?"

Brett didn't like the way she was looking at him, as if she'd just decided he might actually be redeemable. "Yeah."

"That was nice of you."

"I can be nice."

"If you say so," she said in a skeptical voice, but he knew she was playing with him. Sometimes he wondered if there was ever a time when she wasn't.

Brett debated for a moment, then asked the question that had been driving him crazy. "How did you get to be green the other night?"

Claire stood up and took her time brushing the dirt from her knees. She didn't seem at all surprised by the abrupt change of topic. "From being in close contact with some rather slimy moss."

"And how did you come into contact with moss?" In Nevada.

"I was in the school basement."

Oh, that made perfect sense. What had she done while she was down there? Rub her face on the wall?

"Run into Jim Shannon?" he asked conversationally.

"Fortunately, I didn't even know about Jim Shannon then."

"What happened?"

"Someone shut the door while I was down there and latched it, so I had to break a window and climb out."

"A kid?"

"Probably."

He tried not to look surprised either by the student's actions or her own. But he was. "That's not a good start to the school year."

"No." She reached down for the trowel, idly wiping

dirt off the metal with a gloved finger. "These kids play hardball."

"Hey. You gotta be tough to survive in Barlow Ridge."

"I guess."

"What are you going to do about it?"

"Nothing. If I get some solid evidence—which is highly unlikely at this point—I may change my mind, but for now it never happened."

"That's probably better than making a big deal over it."

"I guess we'll see. As I figure it, one of two things can happen. Either they give up, or they try harder. And I've got to tell you, I'm really hoping for the former."

WHEN CLAIRE ARRIVED at school the following morning, Jesse was already sitting in his swing, but this time he was not alone. Cuddled in his lap was a fluffy tabby cat.

Claire got out of her car, slung her tote strap over her shoulder and walked to the playground. When Jesse looked up at her, she could see that his eyes were swollen, red rimmed. He had been crying.

"Hi, Jesse. I see you brought a friend to school."

He nodded.

"I don't know if Mrs. Gunderson is going to like that."

"I know." He bit his lip.

"Is there a reason you brought your cat to school?"

"We have dogs and they attack cats."

"How long have you had the cat?"

"Awhile. But Dad is tired of the litter box and he says I have to get rid of her. I can't let her outside to go to the bathroom, because the dogs'll get her."

The boy's voice started to break. Claire lowered herself into the other swing, ignoring the fact that her skirt was now resting in the dust. "Is there someone…"

The boy raised sad eyes and Claire had her answer.

She reached out to stroke the cat, which huddled closer to Jesse. Then she dug a hand into her bag and pulled out her keys.

"You can take her to my house." There was plenty of time for him to walk over there and back before school began.

"Really?" And then his face fell. "She'll need a litter box."

"She'll be all right until lunch, won't she?"

Jesse nodded.

"I'll run to the store during lunch." Surely Anne had kitty litter among her assortment of animal supplies.

"Thanks, Miss Flynn." Jesse stood, hefting the cat up higher on his shoulder. "I'll be back in time for school."

Claire watched him let himself out the gate, and wondered what she'd gotten herself into.

THERE WAS A KID in Claire's trailer. Brett had just finished his morning chores when he glanced across the field and saw a small boy disappear inside.

Brett decided, in spite of his vow to keep his nose out of Claire's business, to investigate. It beat trying to find a snake later on.

It took only a few minutes to cross the field. He was quietly mounting the steps when the door opened and Jesse came backing out. The kid jumped a mile when he saw Brett, and a scarlet flush stained his cheeks.

"Shouldn't you be in school?" Brett asked gruffly.

"I was dropping something off for Miss Flynn."

"Like what?"

"My cat."

"Your cat? Why?"

The boy swallowed and the story poured out. Brett nodded as Jesse talked, thinking that he could see the dad's point of view where the litter box was concerned, but all the same... Making your child get rid of his pet? It seemed a bit harsh. Especially when Jesse was so attached to it.

"And Miss Flynn is going to keep it for you?"

"She just said I could keep it here today. She didn't say anything about how long."

Brett considered the situation, and then he did another nice thing that Claire would probably find hard to believe.

"Well, you know, I don't have any dogs. And I do have a lot of mice in my barn."

Jesse's eyes widened and he started to smile, but fought it, just in case he'd misunderstood. It gave Brett the feeling that he'd already had too many disappointments in his short life.

"I think if she lived in the house for a few days, she'd probably call my place home."

"And I could visit her?"

"Hell..." He caught himself. "Uh, yes. In fact, let's just say I'm boarding her."

"What's that?"

"That's where someone takes care of your animals for you."

"And I pay you?" Jesse asked cautiously.

"You do chores to *help* pay for cat food."

"*Help* pay for it?"

"She'll probably be eating mice and making my barn a better place to be, so we'll go halves. You'd still make some extra money for yourself."

The kid was grinning widely now, and Brett felt an odd sensation spread through his midsection. "Shouldn't you be getting to school?"

"Oh, yeah. Can you catch Sarina if I unlock the door?"

"I imagine I can."

Jesse fitted the key in the lock and turned until the latch popped open.

"Don't forget to lock it," he admonished as he trotted down the steps. "Oh, and Miss Flynn is buying kitty litter at lunch."

"Tell her I'll take care of it," Brett said. "Don't be late for school."

He watched for a moment as Jesse hurried down the drive, his big feet out of proportion with his skinny body, and wondered if the boy was getting enough to eat.

A few minutes later, as Brett hefted the cat, he wondered again. He was no cat expert, but this one seemed bony despite the massive quantities of fluff that enveloped it.

"Hey, kitty." He rubbed a hand over its ears. "Looks like we're roommates for a while." And what a strange turn of events. This morning he'd woken up cat-free, and now here he was, about to bunk with a feline.

He held the cat against his chest, taking a quick survey of the trailer before he started for the door. It was homier than the last time he'd been here, on snake disposal duty. And it smelled good. A subtle odor of spices and perfume teased his senses and his imagination. A couple of camisoles lay draped over the back of the sofa, spread out on a towel to dry. He remembered the lavender one. She'd been wearing it when she'd come to his place, toting her bottle of wine. And though there were now candles and pillows and bric-a-brac on display, the place was surprisingly neat and organized. Somehow he'd had a feeling that Claire would live in a more cluttered environment. With the exception of the camisoles, it looked like a place where an engineer might live—which was exactly what she'd been training to be before the education bug bit her. He remembered her explaining that to him when they'd danced at the wedding, just before she'd started to nuzzle his neck.

Brett let out a breath and headed outside. His cell phone rang as he exited the trailer, startling the cat.

"Easy, kitty," he muttered, juggling the phone up to his ear.

"Hi, Brett," Phil said. "I thought I'd give you a heads-up. I'll be arriving this Friday. You need to contact Marie and tell her to give the house a once-over."

"Sure." Brett held the cat with one hand and the phone with the other as he walked.

"Have you had time to get the stud tuned up for me?"

"It's going to take more than a tune-up." Which was something he planned to discuss with his boss once they were face-to-face.

"Really." The word was delivered flatly. Phil was a wanna-be cowboy, and he genuinely loved animals—even if he didn't totally understand them. But he hated to hear the word *no* in any context. Brett hadn't had to say it too often, but this was going to be one of those occasions when no other word would do. He'd just try to say it in a way that Phil could accept.

"Really," Brett said firmly. "This boy needs serious work."

"I bought a new saddle for him."

"It'll fit other horses."

"I'll make an evaluation when I get there," Phil said curtly. "I'll see you Friday."

Make an evaluation... Brett shook his head. Funny how the CEO replaced the cowboy whenever Phil encountered a roadblock. Well, Phil could evaluate that stud until the cows came home. It wasn't going to change the fact that the animal was too much horse for him.

Jesse showed up at Brett's home at 3:05 p.m. in the afternoon. He must have run the half mile from school.

"Is she doing all right?" he asked as soon as Brett opened the door.

"She's doing fine." He had just got back from the Ryker ranch a few minutes before Jesse's arrival, but the cat was still there, sitting on the back of the sofa, right where he'd left her. "I bought some food and litter at the mercantile. She's all set up."

Jesse dug around in his pocket. "Here," he said, pulling out a small greenish wad of paper. "This'll help until my first payday."

Brett solemnly took the dollar. "Thanks."

The kid smiled. "Where's she at?"

"Living room. Come on in."

"I can only stay for a minute. My dad is coming early tonight, so I have to go back to the school." The cat jumped off the sofa and trotted over as soon as the boy entered the room, throwing herself against his skinny legs.

"Hi, Sarina. Are you being good?" he asked as he lifted her, nuzzling his nose in her fur. Brett could hear her purring from across the room. After a few minutes of mutual affection, Jesse put the cat down. She rubbed her head on his leg. "Can I stop by tomorrow and see her?"

"You bet. We can work up an after-school chore schedule—if your dad doesn't mind."

"He won't care," Jesse said solemnly. "He's glad I have something to do."

Probably glad to have a free babysitter. But Brett didn't know the circumstances, so he decided to give the guy the benefit of the doubt. For now.

There was a quilting session that evening, but thanks to Brett taking custody of Jesse's cat, Claire was able to work late at school without worrying about the animal making confetti out of her laundry or doing whatever bored felines might tend to do.

A smile played on her lips as she stacked her last pile of grading. Brett, who was ticked off because she'd sent Jesse to ask about chores, was now going to board the boy's cat. Brett was obviously more of a softie than he let on, something else for Claire to add to the enigma file.

Most of the quilters were already at the community hall when Claire came in, her tote bag laden with new quilting fabric.

She took a seat across from Deirdre and Trini, then lifted her washed and ironed yardage out of her bag and stacked it on the table in front of her.

"What are you going to do with *that?*" Deirdre asked sharply.

"Make a quilt."

"With those colors?"

Claire was about to explain that she'd matched the colors to the Gauguin print that hung over her bed, but Elena's grandmother, Gloria, interceded before she had a chance.

"I think those are lovely colors," she said, her needle poised in the air. "One of the things I like about quilting is that you can find color combinations to fit any personality." She glanced over her glasses at the beige and white fabric pieces Deirdre was meticulously sewing together. "Everything from exciting brights to ho-hum neutrals." She turned back to Claire just as Deirdre realized she'd been insulted. "So, how are things at school?"

Claire held her breath as Deirdre slowly lowered her eyes to her sewing, her jaw firmly set, then said, "I think things are starting to go more smoothly."

"We're glad you're here," Gloria said, in a tone that dared anyone to disagree with her. "Elena likes your class."

Deirdre looked up, her needle hovering for a second in midair, and even though she didn't say anything, Claire knew what she was thinking.

Not every student liked her class.

BRETT EXPECTED CLAIRE to stop by that night. Jesse had to have explained to her that she was no longer a cat sitter, but to Brett's surprise she didn't show up, and her trailer remained dark. Around nine o'clock, just when he was thinking he should probably check the school basement, he saw headlights pull into her drive. Lights came on in the trailer a few seconds later. No visit tonight. Claire must have faith in his cat-sitting abilities.

The cat had spent most of the evening on the back of the sofa, pretending to be asleep while watching him out of slitted eyes as Brett sat at the computer and tried to beat concepts into his head that he should have understood years ago. He did her a favor and ignored her. She wasn't any trouble, which made Brett wonder again what kind of guy made a kid give away his cat.

Strange situation.

He was going to have to make a point of meeting Jesse's dad. He'd seen him driving through town a few times, but the man never seemed to get out of his vehicle.

The phone rang and Brett answered it, once again expecting Claire. But this time it was Regan.

"Kylie made it!" There was only one "it" his sister-in-law could be referring to, since the horse show season was over and fall rodeo was winding down. Basketball. Kylie's other fixation, which Brett thought might be genetic, since he loved the game and Will hated it.

"Varsity?" He realized he was smiling broadly. Kylie had played junior varsity basketball during her freshman year—much to her disgust. She'd set herself the goal of making the varsity squad the following year, come hell or high water, and now she'd done it.

"I guess that expensive camp paid off," Regan said happily. "The game schedule is on the school website. Will isn't home yet, so he doesn't know, and Kylie made me promise to let her tell him, but I *had* to tell someone and I knew you'd want to know."

"Thanks. I appreciate it."

"Hey, have you heard anything about my sister through the grapevine? She's been very uncommunicative lately."

Brett rarely got close enough to a grapevine to hear anything. "I think she's doing fine," he said, telling Regan what she wanted to hear, and hoping she wouldn't ask him to investigate, since he wasn't going to. He wondered if she knew about the school basement, but then decided it wasn't his place to say anything.

"Just checking," Regan said. "Claire has a tendency to do things the hard way."

"No kidding," he said.

Regan laughed. "Getting to know my sister, are you?"

"Only in the landlord sense," Brett said abruptly. "Thanks for calling, Regan. I'll be at that first game."

CLAIRE SLID LOWER in the tub. The water had finally cooled to the point where she could stretch out and enjoy the flicker of the candles and the heavy scent of lavender. For a few seconds, anyway, before the phone rang.

Drat. She'd meant to turn it off. She splashed water as she got out of the tub and wrapped herself in a thick towel, catching the phone on the third ring.

"Hi, Mom." It was a wild guess, since she hadn't bothered to check the number, but Claire knew it made her mom crazy when she answered that way. Some things were too much fun to give up cold turkey.

"Hello, Claire." Arlene's voice was carefully modulated. "Are you all right?"

"Of course I'm all right. Why would you ask that?"

"You've called twice this week." Claire headed back to the bathroom, eyeing the tub longingly and wondering if she could get back in without dropping the phone in the water and ruining it. Of course she couldn't. "I thought you might be lonely."

"I'm not lonely." Arlene made loneliness sound like a character flaw. "I just want to keep in contact with my daughters. Is that so unusual?"

Yes. Arlene was not a chitchatter.

"No. Not unusual at all," Claire stated, settling on the edge of the tub, her back to the water. "Any word on Stephen?"

"Windsurfing, I believe." There was a pause, and then she said, "I was wondering if you knew when you might be coming down to Las Vegas next?"

"I could come for Thanksgiving."

"I'll be at a conference in San Diego."

"Over Thanksgiving?"

"It butts up against the holiday. Travel is a nightmare, so I thought I'd stay until the following Monday."

And Stephen was windsurfing. Maybe there was a method to Arlene's madness.

"I could pop down some weekend." Four-hundred-mile drive. Slightly more than a pop, but still…

"No. I don't want you to do that."

"What do you want, Mom?"

Arlene let out an audible sigh. "I don't know."

And that was the first time in her life Claire had ever heard a hint of self-doubt from her mother.

"Well, will you let me know when you do know? Or if you want to talk?"

After another heavy silence, Arlene seriously alarmed her daughter by calmly saying, "Yes, Claire. I will."

CLAIRE WAS STILL thinking about her mother's call the following day at school. Arlene had not said one word about Claire's current situation. She hadn't asked about graduate school or demanded reassurance that Claire was indeed going to continue her education. No. She hadn't really talked about anything. She'd just seemed to want to make contact. Which made Claire wonder if she and Regan should strong-arm their mother into getting a medical checkup.

She called Regan right after school. "I think something's wrong with Mom."

"Why?" Regan asked cautiously.

"She's been calling just to chat."

"Sometimes mothers and daughters do that."

"Not our mother and not this daughter. If she wanted to chat, she'd call you."

"Maybe she's changing."

"I prefer the old Mom. At least I knew how to handle her."

"Change is good," Regan said dryly.

"Not when it took me way more than twenty years to figure out how to handle the original."

THERE WAS A new guy in town. Claire couldn't say she knew everyone in Barlow Ridge, but it was a small place and she figured she'd seen almost everyone who lived there. She'd never seen this guy, though. Tall and well-built, blond hair, blue eyes—an Adonis in cowboy boots. Lizard-skin cowboy boots, to be exact.

He nodded at her as he hefted a twelve-pack of beer

from one of the mismatched standing coolers. "Can I get you something?" he asked politely.

"One of those six-packs of grapefruit juice?"

"Sure." He grimaced a little as he handed her the juice.

"Not a fan?" she asked, wondering how many lizards had given their lives for his boots.

"I'm more of an orange-juice man," he said with a crooked smile.

Claire put the grapefruit juice into her basket, debating whether she should allow herself to be charmed. She was leaning toward yes. "It's actually quite good."

"I'll just have to take your word for it." He paused, his eyes never leaving her face. "I'm Phil Ryker."

"Claire Flynn. I think I'm one of your neighbors."

"In this place everyone is your neighbor."

"True, but I'm closer than most. I live in the trailer at the edge of the field."

His smile widened. "You're the new schoolmarm."

Claire regarded him for a moment. "What exactly is a marm?"

"Damned if I know. Are you going to last longer than the other teachers?"

"I think I already have."

He laughed. "I need to get going, but I'll see you around, Claire." It sounded like a promise.

She continued her shopping, picking up some nails to fix a loose board on her porch, a jar of peanut butter, some fairly fresh bread, a box of cereal. She stopped there, since she was walking and didn't want to be toting more than was comfortable.

"So what do you think?" Anne asked as Claire set her purchases on the counter.

"Of him?" Claire guessed, since Phil Ryker had exited the store a few minutes before and there was no one else there.

"Yeah."

"He seemed all right."

"He owns half this valley, you know."

"How nice. Hey, we missed you at quilting the other night."

Anne gave her a nice-try smirk. "Watch him. He thinks if he snaps his fingers he can get anything he wants."

"Thanks for the warning," Claire said as she took her bag. "I'll keep that in mind."

"So, YOU'RE TELLING me the horse needs more work."

"I'm telling you the horse will kill you." An overstatement, but Brett was trying to make a point.

Phil laughed. Brett bit the edge of his lip as he studied the horse that was standing with his chest pressed against the rails of his pen. His head held high and his body quivering, he sniffed the air for his mares. This was no joke.

"How much more time?" Phil asked patiently.

Brett counted to ten.

"I mean, if I can't make the first show in the spring, I understand."

"If you plan on riding this horse in a show, you'll need to find a different trainer."

That got his attention. Finally.

"Like your brother?" Phil asked pointedly.

"Will wouldn't take on this horse for the purposes you intend." Brett glanced over at his boss. He didn't like what he saw. The man's face was set in stubborn lines. "*I* wouldn't ride this stud in a show, and I used to ride bronc. If you lose control of him, he may hurt someone else in the ring. He's an unpredictable horse. Use him for breeding."

That was all the horse had been used for thus far. Had

the animal been of a gentler nature, or if Phil had about a decade more experience, Brett could see trying to show the stud. But the way things stood now, it was a wreck waiting to happen.

"I'll make some calls," Phil said in a clipped voice. The man was not used to being contradicted—even if it was for his own safety, as well as the safety of anyone else in the arena with him.

Brett moistened his lips and tried to come up with a way to make the guy listen to reason. The problem was not only that Phil had rarely heard the word *no,* but that he also had a pretty damn big ego. Not a good combination.

"And I expect you'll find someone who'll take on the job," Brett agreed. "But be careful. There're a lot of guys out there pretending to be trainers who aren't."

"So it seems."

Brett pushed off from the fence. "I've got some work to do." He hoped. He started walking toward the barn. Phil didn't yell after him that he was fired, but he had a feeling it could happen at any time—which meant that his ability to make the payments on the homestead would be jeopardized. But on the other hand, he wouldn't have a dead urban cowboy on his conscience, either.

CHAPTER SIX

"WHAT'S THE PROBLEM, Ashley?"

The girl had been muttering under her breath all afternoon, and when Claire finally called her on it, Ashley had requested an after-school meeting.

"This," she said, showing Claire her social-studies paper. "I answered all the questions right and you gave me a C."

"You were supposed to use the format given in the directions. That was a big part of the grade." And she'd stressed that point when handing out the assignment.

"But a C? That's stupid."

"That's following directions. A life skill."

"My mom says that you don't know what you're doing." Ashley shoved the paper into her notebook.

"Is your mom trained in the field of education?"

"What?"

Claire leaned back against her desk and folded her arms over her chest. "Does she have training that enables her to judge whether or not I know what I'm doing?"

"You don't need special training to see when someone is doing something wrong."

"So what am I doing wrong, Ashley? Maybe you could tell me so I can work on things."

"You want me to make a list?" the girl asked sarcastically.

"Yes. Consider it homework, instead of today's English

homework. I want you to go home, sit down with your parents and make a list of what I need to work on. I'll even send a copy to Mr. Rupert."

Ashley laughed. "You don't mean it."

That was when Claire's easygoing expression shifted to no-nonsense. "I mean it. How can I improve, if I don't know what is bothering you? And since Mr. Rupert is evaluating me, he'll need the list."

"Fine. I'll make a list. You want me to use complete sentences?" Ashley added snidely.

"No. Just make a list."

Claire had a major headache by the time she left that day. No matter how many times she told herself it didn't matter, the situation with Ashley and her mother bothered her. She was trying to help these kids, yet Deirdre seemed to think Claire had moved out to the middle of nowhere in order to pick on her little girl.

Maybe it was time to cart another bottle of wine over to Brett's. He was good at giving her something to think about besides school. In fact, he gave her a lot to think about, and she rather enjoyed it.

Ultimately, though, she didn't go to Brett's. She stayed home and tallied grades in preparation for the upcoming report cards, losing herself in numbers and analysis. Ashley was passing all her classes, but with B's and C's instead of the A's she thought she deserved simply for being cute.

And the math scores for all the students were still disturbingly low. Toni had a natural aptitude and she was picking things up quickly, but she was also careful not to look as if she was enjoying her success when Ashley was around.

Claire knew that one of the biggest problems was that the students needed immediate feedback on their work, to prevent them from repeating mistakes over and over again. The blackboards were unusable, bumpy and shiny from years of being painted and repainted with blackboard paint, to the point where chalk would no longer adhere. She needed the whiteboards she'd ordered the first day of school. That way she could watch the kids work, and correct errors as they occurred. She was doing what she could with slates, but they were not good enough.

Claire called the district procurement department as soon as she got to school the next morning. "I really need the whiteboards I ordered," she said pleasantly.

"We're doing what we can, Miss Flynn."

"Can you do it faster?"

"Miss Flynn, we have a procedure we have to follow. Let me familiarize you. Again."

Claire hung up the phone after being informed of procedure—again—and was about to dial her sister when Ashley strode into the room.

"My mom said she didn't want to make a list off the top of her head. She wants time to think."

"And you couldn't come up with anything on your own?"

"I want to wait for Mom, so I did my English instead." She popped the paper into the hand-in basket, then pivoted and departed, her chin high in the air.

As soon as the outer door had swung shut, Claire went to the office and punched Regan's number into the phone. Her brother-in-law answered.

"Hi, Will. I need a favor."

THREE SHEETS OF white enameled Masonite, purchased from the Wesley lumberyard, came into Barlow Ridge on an empty hay truck late that afternoon. Will had accomplished in half a day what the school district had failed to achieve in two months. Now all Claire had to do was to get the boards mounted without calling on maintenance.

The broken basement window had gaped open until one of the PTO dads had finally screwed a piece of plywood over it to keep adventuresome kids from daring each other to spend the night with Jim Shannon. The plywood had yet to be replaced with glass. Barlow Ridge school maintenance was obviously not a district priority, so Claire was going to have to handle the whiteboard installation on her own.

Just a matter of a few screws and something to attach them to. No big deal. Or so she hoped.

AFTER EVALUATING THE SITUATION, Claire came to the sad conclusion that there were some things a zebra-striped tool kit couldn't handle. Mounting whiteboard was one of them. She needed a drill—preferably cordless—and an extra set of hands.

"Do any of you have a cordless drill?" she facetiously asked her class right after taking attendance. It was the first time she'd ever seen a glimmer of interest on every single face in the room.

"What are you going to do?" Dylan asked.

"We're putting up whiteboard."

"*We're* putting up whiteboard?" Toni asked. "Why are *we* doing it?"

"Because I'd like to *use* the whiteboards before spring break."

"I can bring a drill," Rudy said.

"Great," Claire said.

"Do you know how to use a drill?" Ramon asked curiously.

"How hard can it be?"

"Have you ever used one?"

Claire pretended to give the matter some thought. Then she shook her head and the kids laughed. Even Ashley smiled before she caught herself.

"Are you going to do your drilling in a dress?"

"Is there some kind of law against that?" Claire asked, leaning back against her desk.

"The law of normal behavior," Dylan said, but his sarcasm didn't have its usual bite.

"I might dress for the occasion."

"Wear jeans," Elena said.

"Teachers shouldn't wear jeans to school," Claire said.

"Why not?"

"Because it's important to show respect for your profession."

"You can show respect, no matter what you wear," Elena said.

"Is that a fact? How?"

Elena started to speak, but Claire held up a hand. "Why don't you write your answers in your journals?"

There was a collective groan, but she put up her hand again. "It'll be like a debate. You read your responses and I'll answer them. If you can convince me you're right, I'll..." she glanced at the clock "...give you ten extra minutes during afternoon recess *and* I'll wear jeans to school. But only if you come up with decent arguments."

For the first time since she'd started teaching at Barlow, all her kids started writing at once.

CLAIRE WORE JEANS to school the next day. And boots and a University of Nevada, Las Vegas sweatshirt. Part of the deal. As promised, Rudy showed up with a drill and Dylan had a box of two-inch wood screws. The kids had already toted the sheets of Masonite into the classroom and leaned them against the bookcase.

"Now what?" Elena asked. She, too, was wearing jeans. And green shoes.

"We'll need to find the studs..."

"The *what?*" Ramon demanded. Toni giggled and Claire gave her a sharp look. In Ramon's world, a stud was an animal used for breeding. Claire could understand his confusion.

"A wooden support beam, usually a two-by-four."

"Oh."

"Everybody knows that," Toni muttered.

"Do you know how to find a stud?" Claire asked the girl.

"You use a stud finder."

Ashley smirked, thinking her friend was being sarcastic, but the smirk disappeared when Claire said, "Right." She handed the girl a small plastic box. "Have at it."

Toni went to the wall and started running the box over the surface. "Here's one."

"How do you know this geeky stuff?" Ashley demanded, and Toni looked embarrassed.

"My mom's last jerky boyfriend was a contractor," she said as she handed the stud finder back to Claire.

"Your mom needs to…" The sentence went unfinished as Claire shot a warning look in Ashley's direction. She noticed that Toni, tough as she was, seemed to automatically assume that Ashley's opinion was more important than her own.

"Here, Ashley. Find a stud on the other side of the board."

Ashley drew in a breath and looked as if she wanted to protest, but by some miracle she didn't. She snatched the stud finder and began tracing it over the wall as Toni had done. After a few seconds, she said, "There isn't one over here."

"Give it to me," Dylan said with impatience. He took the device and quickly located another stud.

"How did you…?"

"I have skills," he said. He tossed the little box in the air, then handed it off to Jesse.

"Okay, now, let's measure the distance and calculate where we need to drill holes in the whiteboard. Elena, you and Lexi can do that, and then Jesse and Ramon will measure it out on the board."

"IT WAS SO MUCH FUN. We figured out how to put the whiteboard over the chalkboards, and we measured so that we hit the studs just right with the screws. Miss Flynn let all of us use the drill. Then when we were done, she had Oreos for us and we got to draw on the boards. She has tons of dry-erase markers."

Brett smiled tolerantly as Jesse bounced along next to him on the way to check the electric fence that surrounded his back pasture.

"So nobody gave her trouble today?"

Jesse thought for a moment. "Nope." He watched with interest as Brett disconnected the hot wire from the fence. "What are we doing?"

"Looking for places where dried grass or weeds are touching the wire. It grounds the fence and then it doesn't work."

"Why do you use an electric fence?"

"It keeps the cows where they belong."

"Oh." The kid nodded. "Does it hurt a lot if you touch it?"

"Some."

Brett thought about teaching Jesse how to lay a piece of grass on the wire in order to see if electricity was flowing, but then decided against it. If the weed was wet, the kid would get shocked instead of just feeling a mild vibration. Better that he thought all electric fences were hot.

"If you see these insulators on the fence posts, you need to stay away, okay?"

"Okay."

They continued around the perimeter of the fence. Every now and then Brett stopped to whack some high weeds down or pull a tumbleweed free. When they got back to the gate, he put the hot wire back into place.

"Is it on now?"

"It's on. I can put the cows out here tomorrow." They started for the house. "Where's your dad meeting you tonight?"

"The school."

"He can pick you up here, you know." Brett would really like to have a chat with the guy. He wanted to figure out what Jesse's situation was because, frankly, the kid was kind of growing on him. He wanted to make sure he was being taken care of.

"I'll tell him." Jesse jumped over a big rut, then glanced at Brett. "What were you doing when I came today?"

He'd been sweating over his math lesson. He'd had to redo the previous one because he'd failed the quiz, which made him feel like the king of all losers.

"I have an online class and I wanted to submit the lesson before I forgot."

"What kind of class?"

"Math."

"You're taking math?"

"No big deal."

"Yeah, but you're old."

"So?"

"Well, didn't you learn all this stuff a long time ago?"

"I was supposed to, but…" He hesitated, not wanting to confess to this kid that he'd made some stupid choices for some stupid reasons. "Long story."

"I've got time," Jesse said in a grown-up way.

Brett reached out and ruffled the kid's hair. "No you don't."

"What kind of math are you learning?" Jesse asked as they approached the house.

"Algebra."

"Is it easy?"

"I wish," Brett muttered.

"Not easy?"

"I've done easier stuff."

"You need help?"

Brett shook his head.

"Because Miss Flynn is *really* good in math. I didn't understand a lot of stuff when school started, and she made it easy to understand. And she says that if we fifth graders work hard, she'll have us ready to take pre-algebra in seventh grade and algebra in eighth grade!"

"That sounds good. You'd better work hard."

"But…"

"I'm doing all right. I only meant I wish it was easier. I didn't mean I couldn't do it." *Yes, you did.*

"Oh." Jesse was quiet for a few minutes, then said, "Miss Flynn said that if we do pre-algebra before we go to high school, then we'll be able to get all the way through calculus before we graduate." He frowned. "What is calculus?"

"It's…" Brett almost said "hard math," but he caught himself. No sense giving the kid ideas. "It's upper-level math. And it's important to take it, if you plan to go to college. You are planning to go to college, aren't you?"

"Yep. Did you go?"

Brett opened his mouth to sidestep yet again, when Jesse said, "No, I guess you didn't, if you're taking algebra now."

"I wanted to go."

"Really? What'd you want to be?"

"I don't know. I just thought it was important to go. To use the brain God gave me." Which he'd failed to do, time after time. "Since I didn't go right after high school, I decided to go now. Online."

Jesse nodded approvingly.

"What does your dad do, Jesse?"

"Sales. He has a route and he travels."

"What does he sell?"

"Different stuff. It changes."

"Why'd you move here?" Barlow Ridge wasn't exactly a hub of sales activity.

"Dad said it was quiet and he wanted a quiet place. We used to live in Reno. We lived in a trailer park, but Dad couldn't leave me home alone while he did his route, because it wasn't a good part of town."

"So you like it here?"

"I liked living with my grandma in Carson City the best, but this is all right. I like coming here and working for you."

"You used to live with your grandmother?"

"My *great*-grandma. Then she got sick and had to be put in the rest home, so Dad came and got me. I talk to her on the phone sometimes when she's feeling better."

Brett wanted to ask Jesse where his mom was, but he was afraid of the answer. No sense grilling the poor kid.

"Dad didn't know a lot about being a dad, because Grandma always took care of me, but he's learning."

Brett forced the corners of his mouth up. "That's good."

"Yeah." Jesse suddenly ran ahead and grabbed a rope hanging from the apple tree. He kicked off from the ground and lifted his feet, swinging out in a big arc.

"There used to be a tire on this rope. Maybe I can find another."

"That'd be cool," Jesse said, kicking up a cloud of dust as he skidded to a stop.

"Easier on the hands, too. I'll see what I can do."

ASHLEY'S ATTITUDE WAS just a bit too self-satisfied for Claire's comfort the next day. She exchanged so many secret glances with Dylan and Toni that Claire made it a point to check for tacks on her chair.

For journal that day, Jesse wrote about his cat, Sarina, and how fat she was getting living at Brett's house. He ended with the observation, "I'm glad she's there, so the dogs don't get her and she gets lots to eat. Sometimes I'd cook her eggs when Dad forgot to buy cat food."

Claire stamped the page with a shamrock twice—once to indicate she'd read it, and a second time for good measure. Jesse had written a lot more than usual. At the beginning of the school year, she'd had to struggle to get two sentences out of him. Here, he'd written over half a page about his cat. Progress like that was worth getting choked up about. The lump in her throat had nothing to do with a young boy trying to feed a pet on his own.

THE STALLION JERKED his head again, out of reach. Brett calmly put his hand on the horse's poll and applied light pressure. The horse dropped his head slightly and Brett immediately released. He continued until the animal was once again dropping his head as Brett had taught him, but as soon as the bit came close to his mouth the head snapped back up.

Brett continued the exercise until he was able to slip a finger in the horse's mouth, in the gap between the front and back teeth, and massage the gum without the horse going bonkers. He rubbed the bit over the animal's mouth. Opened the mouth and slipped it in and out. Small steps.

It took an hour before he could put the bit in the horse's mouth and slip the bridle over his head without provoking a reaction. Brett had just finished the lesson and released the horse when Phil came ambling out with a gangly black-and-white pup on a leather leash.

Phil frowned when he saw that the stud wasn't bridled. "I thought you were working with him."

Brett looped the reins over the bridle. "Have *you* been working with him?"

"A little here and there." Phil leaned down to scoop up the pup, who'd settled his behind on his boot.

"If you want me to train the animal, then you have to stop working with him."

Phil opened his mouth, probably to say that it was his horse and he'd do what he damn well wanted to, but Brett cut him off. "It confuses the horse. We use two different methods." *And your method sucks.*

Phil-the-Boss struggled with Phil-the-Cowboy. "I guess I can see that."

The pup squirmed, trying to get out of Phil's arms so he could investigate the interesting smells in the corral.

"Where'd you get him?" Brett asked.

"The pound in Wesley. He needed a home."

And that summed up Phil. He was a guy who didn't know jack about the expensive horses he bought, but rescued pound puppies. His heart was in the right place; it was his refusal to listen and his lack of animal sense that did him in.

"After I get the stud settled, I can work with the two of you together," Brett suggested. "My way's not the only way, but consistency will speed the training process." And it'd keep the horse from being ruined, and Phil from getting injured.

"Sounds reasonable," he agreed. "Let me know when

you're ready." He glanced over at the pens on the other side of the barn. "Maybe I'll take Bella out for a ride."

"That would be a great idea," Brett agreed. Because Bella was bombproof.

Phil put the pup back on the ground. "That new teacher. She's related to you, right?"

He felt instantly wary. "By marriage. Her sister is married to my brother."

Phil smiled as if he'd just discovered an important clue in a treasure hunt. "What can you tell me about her?"

"Not a lot."

The other man regarded him for a moment. "Am I stepping on your toes here?"

"No." The abrupt answer sounded like a lie.

"You sure?"

"Positive."

"All right." Phil started toward the barn. "You don't know her favorite wine or flower or anything?"

"Nope." Brett tried to make the word sound light as he handed Phil the bridle. "Wish I could help you, but I don't know her all that well myself. I gotta get back to my place and feed."

CLAIRE HAD BARELY started her morning grading when Bertie came into her classroom holding the wireless phone.

"Mr. Rupert." It was obvious from her expression that this was not a happy call.

"Good morning, Mr. Rupert," Claire said as she put the phone to her ear.

"Good morning. We have a parent problem."

Claire quickly flashed through all the possible problem scenarios. As far as she knew she hadn't ruffled any feathers over the past few days, but she took a guess anyway. "The Landaus?"

"Yes. Apparently you had their daughter involved in some kind of school maintenance?"

"What?"

"That's what I said," Rupert said. "I thought you had her mopping floors for detention, but apparently you had her using power equipment without proper safety gear."

Claire closed her eyes. "You mean, the cordless drill."

"Yes."

"Guilty," Claire said. "I had the class putting up the whiteboards."

"What whiteboards?"

"The ones I use on a daily basis to improve their math skills." She told him the story, procurement procedure and all, ending with how the math homework scores had already improved—now that she could send the students to the board to work, and correct errors as they happened. The whole class was getting involved. Finally.

"I see."

"So what happens now?"

"What happens now is that I scramble. The Landaus wrote a letter to the board. They wrote a letter to me. For all I know they wrote a letter to the governor. I don't think the Landaus realize how hard it is to get a teacher to move to Barlow," Rupert finished with a growl.

"So…"

"So I'll do what I can to fix things. You may end up with a reprimand in your file."

"That probably won't be good for future employment."

"I'll word it as nicely as I can. It only stays for two years. If there's no more trouble during that time, the letter gets trashed."

"But *I'm* not staying for two years."

"Hey, maybe that's something for you to consider."

"I don't think so. But thank you for helping."

"I'll keep you posted."

CLAIRE EXITED the mercantile a half hour later, a bit winded after her usual skirmish with Anne, just as Phil pulled to a stop in front of the store. He got out of his truck, and a young black-and-white dog jumped out after him, making an eager beeline for Claire.

"What's his name?" She knelt to ruffle the animal's fuzzy coat and was bombarded with enthusiastic doggy kisses. She laughed as she fended him off. He was obviously a dog of dubious ancestry, which surprised her. She would have pegged Phil as a purebred kind of guy.

"Toby."

"Toby," Claire repeated, and the pup's ears perked up. "Oh, you know your name?"

"He should. He hears it enough. *Toby, no. Toby, down. Toby, off the couch.*" Phil grinned as the pup cocked his head and stared at him, obviously trying to figure out what his dad wanted. Claire gave the pup a final pat before straightening up again.

Phil reached down to snap a leash onto Toby's collar. "Hey, I know it's a ways off, but would you like to hear the folksinger who's coming to town over Thanksgiving? She's a Wesley girl and she's supposed to be good."

"You mean, spend an evening not grading or planning or doing teacher stuff? I don't know...."

"I've heard that I'm slightly better company than a red pen," Phil said with his confident, crooked smile.

"All right, you've convinced me. I'll mark my calendar. It's the Wednesday before Turkey Day, right?"

The pup squirmed as a car drove by, and Phil lifted a hand in greeting. "Right."

"I should be going," Claire said, recognizing two of her fifth graders in the car. "I'll see you then."

"Can I pick you up?"

Claire shook her head. "I'll meet you there." That way if things didn't go well, she had an easy means of escape.

THERE WEREN'T AS many women at the quilting session as usual, but other than that, everything was the same. Anne was crotchety and Deirdre was cold, giving no outward indication that she had lodged an official complaint against Claire. And everyone else, including the other PTO moms, was friendly enough. Claire wondered how they were going to feel after the report card meeting the following week.

"Those squares are pretty," Trini commented as Claire pulled out her two completed quilt blocks and smoothed them on the table. She'd worked an abstract design of oddly shaped pieces she could cut with the rotary cutter, and the wild colors suited the pattern well.

"Thank you. I'm working on developing my free-form side," she added facetiously.

Anne gave a snort. "Maybe you should work on your seam allowances instead." She had a point. Claire's seam allowances tended to narrow or swell from the prescribed quarter inch. Even so, with some tugging and creative pressing, her squares came out...well, almost square.

She raised her eyes to see several of the other women watching her, and Trini seemed to be holding her breath as she waited for her response. Claire gave a small conspiratorial smile and then refocused her attention on her sewing. Anne went right back on the offensive.

"Saw Brett Bishop hanging around your place the other day."

"He's working on my furnace."

"Oh." Anne seemed disappointed.

"If you watch, you might see Phil Ryker hanging

around, too," Claire added helpfully. "He asked me to go hear the folksinger with him."

Claire heard a rapidly suppressed chuckle.

"You're going out with him?" Anne sounded disgusted.

"Hey. I like Phil," Gloria interjected. "Money and good looks. What's not to like?"

"He lacks substance," Anne said.

"How do you know?" Gloria demanded. "He looks like he has substance to me."

"Well, what he's lacking in substance, he makes up for in the way he wears his jeans," Trini added. "Have you seen how they…" She shut her mouth suddenly, as laughter erupted. "Hey. It's just an observation."

The rest of the meeting was devoted to an analysis of various men—celebrities and community members. No one was safe, and Claire's stomach ached from laughing by the time she packed her tote bag. A breakthrough with the quilting club.

"Nothing gets to you, does it?" Trini asked her, as she and Claire were leaving the meeting.

"What do you mean?" Claire was still focused on their candid dissection of men.

"Anne keeps jabbing at you every meeting, and you never flinch. I'd be in tears if she was doing that to me."

"But she's not, which just proves she has a heart. She only jabs people who can take it."

"You're nuts," Trini said with a laugh.

"That goes without saying. I'm teaching in Barlow Ridge."

And liking it.

CHAPTER SEVEN

DEIRDRE LANDAU HAD signed up for the very first report-card conference, and as soon as the kids cleared out of the classroom at three o'clock, she sailed in with the air of an overly busy woman who wanted to get a mere technicality out of the way. Just give her daughter a few compliments, hand over the report card and she'd be off.

Claire bit her lip as she gathered her grade book and seated herself across the table. Something seemed odd here.

After exchanging a few pleasantries, Claire showed Deirdre her daughter's report card, making the point that Ashley should be making better grades than C's and that perhaps together they could work out some kind of a strategy.

Deirdre frowned, checked the name at the top of the card and then traced a manicured fingernail down the column of C's, making Claire wonder just who had been signing Ashley's weekly progress reports. She was about to ask, when Deirdre's eyes locked on hers.

"Ashley had straight A's until this year."

"She's not doing A work now."

"Because you're not doing A-level teaching."

Claire drew back. She knew from years of sparring with Arlene that meeting an assault with an assault was not always the best strategy. Quickly debating tactics, she decided that data collection was the safest track.

"Ashley's been at this school for…"

"This is her third year."

"And before that…"

"She attended school in Boise. Where she was also a straight-A student." Deirdre's chin rose self-righteously.

"She *is* capable of straight A's," Claire agreed.

"Then she should have straight A's, shouldn't she?"

"Yes."

Deirdre's expression hardened as she leaned toward Claire. "Then why doesn't she have the grades she should have?"

"Because she's not doing the work she should do."

Her mother straightened. "She knows the material."

"Yes." Most of it anyway, though her understanding was slipping in a few areas. But Ashley was bright, and much of the time, she could keep up by simply listening in class.

"Then…?"

"Part of the grade is for participation, which includes homework and class discussions. Ashley doesn't do homework and she's not a…helpful participant in class discussions."

"You should grade her on what she knows."

"I'm trying, Mrs. Landau. But Ashley doesn't know how to fulfill obligations. Homework is an obligation, and so is class participation."

"I don't think *obligations* should carry so much weight." Deirdre ground out the word. "The grade should be based on what the student *knows*."

"Mrs. Landau," Claire said gently, "the world is not going to change for Ashley, depending on what she does or doesn't want to do. If she grows up and doesn't feel like doing her taxes, the IRS isn't going to let her off the hook because she knows how to do them but chooses not to."

"That's a ridiculous comparison."

"Work ethic and self-discipline are important." Claire knew from firsthand experience. "I'm trying to help Ashley become a better student."

"By giving her C's."

"It's what she earned. She knew the parameters going in. I explained to the students—"

Deirdre raised a hand, cutting Claire off as she suddenly rose. "I've heard enough for now. I'm bringing my husband the next time we meet. And I think Mr. Rupert will be here, too, and then we'll see about your grading practices." She turned and marched out of the room, leaving the report card sitting on the table.

"Mrs. Landau—"

But the outer door clanged shut. Claire let out a breath. Short of chasing the woman and tackling her in the parking lot, there wasn't much she could do.

She straightened the chair that Deirdre had pushed aside, then went to the door. Mrs. Hernandez, who spoke very little English, was waiting, her eyes wide as she stared at the door Deirdre had just slammed behind her.

"Buenas tardes," Claire said pleasantly.

Mrs. Hernandez nodded, her expression cautious. Claire smiled, searched for the proper Spanish to explain what had just occurred. *"Una equivocación pequeña."* She held her thumb and forefinger millimeters apart, to emphasize how small the misunderstanding had been. "It's nice to see you. Come in." When the woman hesitated, Claire added, *"Venir, por favor, adentro,"* and gestured to her classroom.

Mrs. Hernandez followed Claire inside and perched on the edge of her chair, obviously wondering if she, too, was about to be involved in a loud and unpleasant misunderstanding. Fortunately, the meeting went well and Claire's Spanish, though rusty after a few years on the shelf, came back fast. The Hernandez kids were working hard, their grades were improving and they were making up for lost time. Mrs. Hernandez was beaming by the end of meeting.

Toni's mom, Marla, was waiting in the hall, glancing at her watch, when Claire ushered Mrs. Hernandez out. Claire was actually running ahead of schedule, thanks to Deirdre Landau's abbreviated meeting, and that seemed to be a good thing, since Marla was obviously in a hurry.

"Deke is expecting me home pretty soon," she said in a husky voice that came from breathing too much cigarette smoke in her working environment.

"This shouldn't take long," Claire said, pushing Toni's report card across the table. "As you can see, there is room for improvement, but Toni has made some good progress since that first weekly report I sent home."

"What weekly report?"

"The weekly progress reports?" *You know, the ones you sign...or supposedly sign?*

The woman frowned. "Toni's in charge of her own grades. I've got enough on my hands with Deke and the bar."

"Do you sign the reports she brings home?"

"Toni's better at my signature than I am."

Claire leaned forward, intrigued. "Doesn't that bother you?"

Marla shook her head. "I trust Toni. I have to. My only concern is that she behaves. You called that one time and I'm guessing there wasn't any more trouble after that?"

"No trouble."

"Great. Well, thanks a lot. Toni seems to like you okay, so you must be doing something right."

"Thank you," Claire said. She rose from her chair, feeling amazingly gratified. *Toni liked her? Wow.*

So much for being good at reading the kids.

And so much for signed weekly progress reports, she

thought after escorting Marla to the door. Apparently it wasn't the parents who were doing the signing.

Her final meeting of the evening was with Tom Lane, Jesse's dad, and she was slightly surprised that the guy showed up. Jesse waited in the hall.

Tom was a quiet man who didn't meet Claire's eyes very often, but he seemed concerned about his son, and pleased with the straight B's and C's Jesse had earned. Claire told him how much she enjoyed Jesse, and tentatively offered to drive the boy home after school if he ever needed a ride. The father hesitated, then declined, telling her his dogs were unpredictable with strangers and he didn't want his son home alone. The fact that Jesse was sitting out in the hall at that moment underscored the point.

Claire thanked Tom Lane for coming and saw him out, waving at Jesse before disappearing back into her room. The meetings were over. She'd survived. All she had to do now was get her quilting supplies, which Brett had once again picked up from Regan in Wesley, and then she could settle into a hot bath.

BRETT HAD A FEELING he wasn't going to be a college graduate—at least not in the foreseeable future.

Algebra was kicking his butt.

He should have learned this stuff back when he was younger and his brain worked better. He hit the X at the top corner of the computer screen and brought his world back to normal. A half hour later he was laying floor when he heard a knock on the kitchen door.

It was Claire, there to pick up the stuff Regan had sent back with him on his last trip to Wesley. He'd meant to drop the things off while she was at school, but he hadn't gotten around to it.

"Hi," he said. "The box is right here. It's light."

"It should be. All it has is quilt batting and thread in it." She patted the top, then nodded at the carpenter knee pads he was wearing. "Home repairs?"

"Yeah. It's time." It was past time, in fact. The old flooring was worn-through linoleum, circa 1970.

"I thought you leased this place," Claire said as she walked past him to peek into the living room, where he had about half the new floor down.

"I've optioned to buy, so my lease payments will turn into mortgage payments."

"I was wondering why you were my landlord instead of Phil."

"All pastures and rentals go with the lease, so I'd be your landlord regardless."

Sarina chose that moment to saunter out of Brett's bedroom and pick her way across the new flooring. She stopped at Claire's feet, her yellow eyes inquisitive.

"How's the roommate?" Claire asked, leaning down to stroke the cat.

"She's working out."

Sarina suddenly rolled over onto her back and stretched, showing off her white belly. Claire tickled the animal, who gave a playful kick with her hind legs, then jumped to her feet and strutted away.

"Jesse writes about her in his journal, and I can see why. She's a character." Claire shifted her attention back to Brett. "He also writes about you, you know."

No, Brett didn't know, and it kind of embarrassed him to have Jesse writing about him. "Maybe I'm a character, too."

Claire nodded, humoring him. "He likes coming here."

"I like having him around," Brett admitted.

"It must get lonely here sometimes," she said, tilting her head inquisitively.

"Not really."

"But you spend so much time alone. You live alone. You work alone."

"I'm used to it."

"I'm not." Claire blew out a sigh. "I don't mind living alone, but when I hit a rough spot in life I like companionship. You're not like that, are you?"

No. The last thing Brett wanted, when times got rough, was companionship. Every tough spot in his life he'd gotten through alone—except for the time he'd gotten the shit beat out of him trying to stop the theft of some livestock. Then, Will had camped in the hospital until Brett had come around. He'd refused to see his older brother, so technically, he'd gotten through that spot on his own, too, but it had helped knowing that Will was there.

"No. I'm not like that," he said, getting back to her question. And that was when he realized Claire wasn't as animated as usual. He'd been so focused on protecting himself, he hadn't noticed. "Are you having a rough spot?"

"No. Just exhausted from parent meetings."

She lifted the box into her arms, gesturing toward the door with her head. "I should get going. I can't believe how much paperwork ten students can generate, and I didn't get anything done at school tonight because of parent report-card meetings."

Brett walked with her, opened the door.

"How did they go?" he asked.

"Some were great. Some were…not so great."

"How so?" He leaned a forearm on the door frame.

"I can't really talk about parent meetings," she said.

He cocked his head. "How many good meetings and how many bad?"

"Do you ever get tired of asking personal questions?"

she asked, mimicking the same words he had once said to her.

"No. But I respect your right not to answer."

"Thank heaven for small favors." She smiled, and he couldn't help smiling back.

"Do you want some company, Claire?" he asked softly. It was almost nine o'clock. He'd done enough work for the night. He could listen if she wanted to talk. He just didn't want to answer questions about himself.

She shook her head. "No. I think I need a glass of wine and a bath."

He had a feeling she was lying. "All right. Just don't pass out in the tub."

She smiled again. "I'll try, but no promises."

"I'll see you, Claire."

He did want to see her, which was something that surprised him, and he didn't want her to be lonely. He knew how painful a bad case of loneliness could be.

BRETT HAD TO make a trip to Elko the next morning, and he spent most of the next day running errands and buying supplies—feed, flooring, food—he couldn't get in Wesley. He ate dinner alone before starting home, only to put a nail through one of his new tires about twenty miles out of Wesley, in an area with no phone service. He spent a ridiculous amount of time trying to loosen overly tight lug nuts before he finally managed to free them and replace the ruined tire with his spare.

It was almost eleven o'clock, a half hour before closing time, when he pulled into the Wesley grocery-store parking lot to pick up the two things he'd forgotten in Elko, coffee and toilet paper. Both kind of essential to life. A group of kids were hanging out next to the door, laughing and pushing one another.

And he recognized one of them.

"Kylie!"

The laughter faded from Kylie's face as she heard her name called out in an authoritative tone. The guy who'd had his arm around her stepped back a bit. She glanced up at him, then walked over to Brett.

"What are you doing?" he asked, eying the group of kids. They didn't look like criminals, but it was hard to tell these days.

"Hanging around. We're about to play fugitive." She spoke breezily.

He was familiar with fugitive—a game where kids ran around town, usually after curfew, trying to find one another. It was a teenage version of hide-and-seek, often played with cars.

"Are you sure that's a good idea?"

Her expression shifted as she realized that he wasn't making conversation; he was getting parental. "Hey, my dad knows about it."

"He knows you're going to be out running around town after curfew?"

Kylie's eyes narrowed ever so slightly, making him wonder if Will did indeed know all the facts. "Yes," she said stonily. Brett could see that she was very close to telling him to mind his own business. "And he knows I'm staying with Sadie tonight."

"So if I call and ask him, you're all right with that?"

She drew a deep breath through her nose, then bluffed. "You can call him."

"I will." Brett reached in his pocket for his phone.

Fifteen minutes later he was dropping a pissed-off Kylie at her house. She'd been embarassed when he'd ordered her into his truck in front of her friends, so he thought she would probably storm back *out* of the truck without a word as soon as he got her home. He'd been mistaken. Instead she gave him a long, cold look.

"You had no right to do this."

"You were lying to me."

"I don't see why you have the right to interrogate me to begin with," she muttered. "You're barely part of the family." And that was when she got out of the truck and stomped away.

Will stepped onto the porch as Kylie marched up the steps, her back ramrod straight. He raised a hand to Brett, who nodded back before putting the truck in Reverse. Will already had the story. No sense hanging around, getting in the way, and no sense dwelling on something an angry kid had said to just hurt his feelings.

"Miss Flynn..." Mr. Rupert drew in a deep breath, clearly audible over the phone line. "Don't get me wrong. I'm thrilled to have you teaching at Barlow Ridge. But what is going on between you and the Landau family?"

"Another complaint?"

"Mmm, hmm."

"Grades?"

"Mmm, hmm."

Claire rolled her eyes and studied the ceiling. "Do you want me to change them?"

There was a long pause, which told her how tempted the principal was to say yes. "I want you to stick to your standards," he said at last. "But if you can come up with any way to placate this woman, or better yet get her on your side, please do it."

"I will, when the opportunity arises."

"The opportunity is here. We're having a meeting. The three of us."

"When?"

"Tomorrow. Three o'clock."

"I'm sorry about this."

"It isn't your fault," he said with the air of someone used to dealing with such situations. "I'll see you then."

CLAIRE HAD A hard time concentrating on her sewing during the quilting session that afternoon. As usual, Deirdre gave no indication she was actively stirring up professional trouble for Claire.

The quilters were packing up after the meeting when Claire strolled over to Deirdre's end of the table. She waited until the other woman glanced up from her beautifully pieced square.

"I thought you'd like to know that I'm changing all of Ashley's grades to A's," Claire said.

There was a beat of silence before Deirdre said, "You are?" Suspicion hung heavy in her voice.

"Yep." Claire slung her tote over her shoulder and headed for the door. Deirdre caught up with her at her car.

"I don't understand this."

"It's what you wanted, right? A's for Ashley? Well, now she has them."

Deirdre pursed her lips, uncertain as to whether she'd won or not. Claire thought that maybe she wasn't even certain of what she wanted at this point.

"I'll see you tomorrow," Claire said, and then she got into her car, leaving Deirdre staring at her through the windshield before she turned and walked back into the community hall.

Claire honestly didn't know if Deirdre would blink, but she got her answer later that evening when there was a knock on her door.

"You don't seem to have a phone number," Deirdre said by way of greeting.

"I have my cell," Claire said. "I saw no reason to pay two phone bills."

"Yes. Well." The woman drew herself up. "I'd like to talk to you about Ashley's grades."

"Please come in." Claire stepped back, wondering if Deirdre had ever been in an honest-to-goodness trailer before. Indeed, she crossed over the threshold cautiously, then she blinked in surprise. Claire had made the place habitable with overstuffed furniture and afghans in pale blues, greens and purples, plus pillows and candles in the same tones. She was a big believer in the importance of environment.

"Have a seat." Claire waved at the sofa, which she'd wrapped in a huge plum throw in order to disguise what lay beneath.

"Thank you, I'll stand." Deirdre briefly pressed her lips together. "Why did you change Ashley's grades?" she asked quietly.

"Before I answer, may I ask if you honestly believe I don't know what I'm doing?"

"This is your first year teaching."

"After about five years of college plus half a year of student teaching and half a year of long-term substitute work." Claire was almost grateful, now, that she'd changed majors three times.

"Ashley's grades were perfect until this year."

"If a teacher gives all A's and B's, then usually no one takes a closer look at what they're doing...or *not* doing."

Deirdre fixed Claire with a unsmiling gaze. "You were serious about these kids having holes in their education, weren't you?"

She nodded. "I was surprised."

"I do think you are too hard on Ashley. I mean, putting her in the hall and embarrassing her."

"I'm not doing that to embarrass her. I'm trying to do what's best for the entire class and, frankly, Ashley has an attitude. And it spreads to the younger kids. If they think there are no consequences, then…" Claire spread her hands.

Deirdre set her jaw. "You'd honestly leave her grades as A's."

"I can give her an A on everything, whether she turns in homework or not. But I don't think you want me to do that."

"No," Deirdre said softly. "That's not what I want." She paced a few steps. "I want to know what's going on. I want to know what Ashley's doing and where the trouble spots are."

Claire smiled weakly. "That was what the progress reports were supposed to be for."

"I still haven't seen one."

"I hand them out every Monday. Ask for it. Also, you can stop by anytime. And I'll contact you if there's anything you need to know about." Claire paused. "I am on Ashley's side, you know," she added gently.

Deirdre took a step toward the door. "I'll call Mr. Rupert tomorrow and cancel the meeting, but I would like to meet with you and go over Ashley's grades again. Her real grades."

"That would be good. I think Mr. Rupert will appreciate not having to make that drive," Claire said.

"And you and I will talk more often."

Claire kept a straight face as she said, "I look forward to that."

THERE WAS NO getting out of the community Thanksgiving celebration that was held the Friday before the actual holiday. Everyone came to the event—even confirmed hermits.

As soon as Brett walked into the community hall, Jesse

waved him over to where he was sitting with Claire, Trini and her husband and a couple of younger kids.

"Hi, Brett." Jesse stood up. He was smiling widely, expectantly, practically vibrating with excitement. For the life of him, Brett couldn't figure out why.

"Hi, Jess." He offered a tentative smile, buying time. What was he supposed to do?

The kid's expression started to shift toward disappointment when Claire caught Brett's eye and gave the fabric of her blouse a discreet tug. Brett felt a rush of relief.

"That's a nice shirt, Jesse. Hey, new jeans, too." The kid beamed and held up one foot. He was wearing cowboy boots. Quite possibly vinyl, from the look of them. Brett smiled. "Somebody went shopping."

"I told you I was going to spend my payday money wisely."

Brett felt his heart twist. He'd assumed *wisely* meant saving some and spending the rest on a CD or a video game or something. He'd never dreamed the kid was going to buy himself clothes.

But Claire had known. He could see it in her face.

"Can you sit with us?" Jesse asked.

"You bet, if Miss Flynn can make room."

"Oh, I can make room," she said. Then something across the hall caught her eye and she smiled. Brett glanced toward the door and saw that Phil Ryker had just walked in. He headed straight for her.

"Hey, pard."

Brett forced a smile. "Hi, Phil."

To make room for Phil, Claire slid closer to Brett, momentarily bringing her thigh up against his. Brett didn't budge. Phil eased onto the bench on her other side, and she slid away from Brett, who wondered if her thigh was now pressed against Phil's. He scooted a few inches closer to Jesse, giving Claire room that she didn't take advantage of.

Not that it mattered.

"I still have some money left, so I can make my cat-food payment," Jesse was saying.

Phil leaned forward to look at Brett, who was trying hard not to notice his boss staring at him.

"You make this boy pay for cat food?"

"He boards my cat," Jesse stated proudly.

"It's kind of a sideline," Brett said.

"I thought you weren't able to make the celebration," Claire said to Phil, drawing his attention away from Brett, who wondered if she'd done it purposefully. If so, he was grateful.

"I changed my plans," Phil said, in a way that made Brett grit his teeth harder than *"pard"* did.

"Look," Jesse said excitedly. "The line's starting. Wanna get our food now? And there's Ramon. He must have just got here. I'm spending the night with him."

"Let's go," Brett agreed. He was on his feet before Jesse was. He wanted to get away from Phil and Claire.

Much to Jesse's disappointment, Brett steered him to another table after they'd filled their plates, but Ramon plopped down a few minutes later, along with his sister, and Jesse was happy.

The rest of the evening went well. Jesse was pleased that Brett stayed with him, and Brett enjoyed listening to the kids jabbering away on the same topics that he and his friends had talked about at the same age—the fort they wanted to build in the willows, the best kind of four-wheeler, the upcoming basketball season. Claire and Phil were at their original table, and talked throughout the meal. Claire seemed to find Phil quite amusing.

The pastor from Wesley gave a sermon, and everyone in

the room took a moment to count their blessings and give thanks. Jesse was smiling when they raised their heads, and Brett had a feeling the boy was thankful for his new clothes and a place to keep his cat.

People began gathering plates and washing dishes. Brett offered to help, but he was shooed away, so decided to take the hint and go.

"Are you leaving?" Jesse asked with a touch of disappointment.

"Important math lesson," he answered, using an excuse he figured Jesse could understand. "Due tomorrow. I need to get working."

"You shouldn't leave it to the last minute. Hey, have you talked to Miss Flynn yet?"

"About what?" Claire asked. She was gathering plates at the next table, but had been close enough to hear her name. Brett decided to come clean before Jesse made a public announcement.

"I'm taking a math class online."

"What kind of math are you studying?"

"Algebra 1," Jesse declared, beaming with pride.

"Algebra 1?" Claire did not seem impressed. Brett couldn't really blame her. She'd probably had math courses he'd never even heard of, and here he was relearning the stuff they taught in eighth grade.

"Differential Equations was full," he muttered, glad that Phil wasn't close enough to hear the conversation. "I'm saving that for next semester. Now—" he smiled at Jesse "—it's been great, but I've got to go."

"See ya, Brett." Jesse always said his name proudly, as if he was claiming him as his own.

"Bye, Jess. Have fun at Ramon's house."

Brett nodded at Claire and then made his escape.

The icy November air enveloped him as he stepped outside, chilling him and making him realize just how much he'd been sweating. And it wasn't due to the overheated room. It was due to Claire Flynn looking at him as if he was an idiot because he was just now learning algebra.

CHAPTER EIGHT

CLAIRE'S SMALL CAR was gone all day Saturday, and Brett took advantage of the fact to install a new thermocouple on the water heater without her being there, distracting him. He really wished things would stop falling apart in the trailer so that he wouldn't have to keep going in, because while he was there, he thought about her. A lot. They weren't exactly G-rated thoughts, either.

Of course, after the community Thanksgiving, she probably thought he was too stupid to mess around with, so he was safe to fantasize to his heart's content. His theory was shaken that evening, however, when Claire came calling. The teakettle whistled as he answered the door. He couldn't ignore it, so he motioned for her to come inside. "You want a cup of coffee?"

"Sure."

"It's instant," he warned.

"That's fine."

Claire took the cup from him a few minutes later. She was wearing pale pink nail polish and small silver rings that emphasized the daintiness of her hands—hands more suited for delicate china than the heavy mug she'd just been given.

"Was I supposed to bring something back from Wesley yesterday?" he asked.

"Nope," Claire said briskly. "I came to see if you need

help with your algebra class. Rumor has it that you're not doing your homework until the last minute."

Brett took a big swallow of hot coffee. "Been talking to Jesse?"

"He's concerned." Her green eyes held an amused light. "I mean, you *are* old, you know."

"Old doesn't mean stupid."

"It does if you're ten. And he told me you were afraid to ask for help."

Brett's mouth flattened. Jesse was an astute kid, even if he had confused fear with stubbornness. "I don't need help."

"I honestly don't mind. It would give me something to do."

"Oh, you mean, besides grading papers and getting all that stuff ready to teach?" He attempted an offhand smile, but had a feeling it wasn't all that convincing. "I'm doing all right on my own."

Claire took a slow sip, watching him over the top of her cup, and Brett had to force himself not to stare at her mouth. "Does it come back fast? The math, I mean?"

He thought about continuing to fake it, but decided to come clean. It would save time. "Hard for it to come back when it was never there in the first place."

"*Never* there?"

"They didn't have exit proficiency exams when I was in high school," Brett explained. "I pretty much cheated my way through math and got away with it."

He almost laughed at how shocked she looked. So Claire wasn't a total rebel.

"Hey, I'm doing my penance." In fact, penance could be his middle name.

"I guess you are." She picked up a copy of *Moby Dick* lying on the sideboard, and made a face.

"I'm taking humanities, too."

"There is nothing humane about having to read *Moby Dick*." She set down the book. "Did you graduate high school?"

"Barely. I was more interested in roping and riding than in studying government or solving for X."

Claire took the information matter-of-factly. "So you have holes in your education."

"Holes you could drive a Mack truck through." He took another swig of coffee. It was almost gone, and soon he wouldn't have anything to focus on except her.

"You'd never know it," she commented. "Maybe…" She frowned and shook her head.

"Maybe what?"

"Maybe if you're having trouble with algebra, it's because you don't have the necessary base to build on."

"Algebra is eighth-grade math."

"Which you haven't seen in what? Over twenty years?"

"Maybe."

"I could help you out."

He shook his head. That was the last thing he wanted. He couldn't say why, but it was important to him that he conquer this on his own. "You want more coffee?"

"I'm good." Her cup was almost full. She smiled wryly. "Trying to sidetrack me?"

"Why would I want to do that?" He took his time measuring coffee crystals and then adding hot water.

"It's kind of funny," she said as she watched him. "Will's a coffee-brewing fanatic and you make instant."

"Will and I are different in a lot of ways."

"So I gathered." He gave her a quick look, but there didn't seem to be any underlying meaning to her words. She further exonerated herself by saying, "Regan and I are different, too."

"Yes," he agreed. He and Regan had gone out a time or two before she'd hooked up with his brother for good.

"Are you going to Will and Regan's for Thanksgiving dinner?"

Brett shook his head. Claire didn't look surprised.

"Then I guess there's no sense asking if you want to share a ride."

"Sorry."

She looked as if she wanted to ask him what the deal was, why he avoided family get-togethers. But she didn't.

She glanced at the kitchen clock. "I have to get going. I'm meeting Phil at seven."

"Phil?"

"Yes. We're going to the bar to hear that folksinger from Wesley." She must have noticed his expression. "You don't care if I go out with your boss, do you?"

"It's none of my business."

"If you say so," she said as she set her cup aside.

"What does that mean?"

She looked him square in the eye. "It means that I get vibes from you."

"Vibes?" He didn't like the sound of that.

She continued to regard him steadily. "Yes. You know. The kind of vibes you feel when someone is interested in you? Even if he doesn't want to admit it and won't let you help him with his math?"

"Claire…"

"Don't," she said, taking a step closer to lay her palm flat against the front of his shirt. "There's no need to say anything." She patted him lightly and then headed for the door. "I'll see you later. And if you ever do need help with your *math*—" she smiled in a way that made his groin tighten "—you know where to find me."

PHIL RYKER WAS very sure of himself. He was rich, handsome, charming, and he knew it. Claire had a strong suspicion that if they'd been anywhere else, he would have been making some serious moves on her, but Barlow Ridge was a tiny town that didn't see a lot of entertainment, so he was being careful. He had to be, with so many people casting speculative looks their way.

Claire settled back in her chair when the music started, enjoying the performance and ignoring the curious glances, thinking it was a good thing she wasn't self-conscious, because if she were, she'd have her jacket over her head by now. Phil seemed to enjoy the attention.

The singer, a local girl who toured the country with a bluegrass group, was surprisingly good. Many of those in the audience knew her, and after she'd finished her hour-long show she was surrounded by people.

Phil turned his attention to Claire. "I liked her," he said, a note of surprise in his voice.

"Me, too."

"Let me get you another drink." He took her glass and went to the bar without waiting for an answer.

Claire was getting tired of Phil-in-command. She watched as Marla flirted with him a little, stopping when Deke, her boyfriend, ambled through the door scratching his chest.

Phil returned a few seconds later with a Manhattan and a glass of wine. "Where were we before the music started?"

"You were telling me about your horse." And trying to wow Claire with a lot of names she'd never heard before.

"But you weren't really all that interested in my horse, were you?"

Claire gave the wine a slow swirl. It wasn't so much lack of interest as not being impressed by the idea of owning a zillion-dollar horse for the sole purpose of bragging about its pedigree. She was much more impressed by Toby, the mutt, which was why she was giving Phil the benefit of the doubt. A guy who picked a dog out of the pound had to have some redeeming qualities. She just wished he'd get over trying to impress her, so she could discover what those redeeming qualities were.

"I don't know a lot about animals," she confessed over the top of her glass. "My sister is the horse nut."

Phil shifted in his chair, letting one arm drop over the back, affecting a relaxed pose. "How is it that one sister's a horse nut and the other knows nothing about animals?"

"I wanted to be an actress. Regan wanted to ride on the Olympic equestrian team. We both followed our own dreams."

"You don't seem to be acting," he pointed out.

"Are you sure?" Claire asked with a half smile.

It took Phil a moment to catch her meaning. He smiled in turn, but it didn't reach his eyes. Claire could see that he didn't like to be played with. She could also see that she represented a challenge to him. Apparently, women didn't normally toy with Phil Ryker.

"I'm not acting," she said gently, "but I've never been able to let a straight line go by."

"I'll have to be more careful around you." He tried to sound as if he was kidding, but Claire had the feeling he wasn't.

"Always a wise strategy." She toasted him with the glass of wine Marla had drawn her from a box with a plastic spigot. Phil answered her salute and sipped his drink, studying her in a way that made her think he was planning his strategy.

"Where do you live when you're not at your ranch?" she asked.

"I have a place near the home office in California. The

folks own land in Nevada, Oregon and Idaho, but we manage most of it from San Luis."

"So you live here part of the year and in California the rest?"

"I like to get away," he said, with sincerity, and Claire realized she was finally getting a glimpse of the real Phil. "I like the slower pace of life here. I like the animals. Ranch life appeals to me."

"What is it about ranch life, exactly, that you like?"

He grinned. "It's hard to say. Maybe I watched too many westerns as a kid, but I like the independence and I like fighting the elements. I like being my own boss."

"I thought you *were* your own boss," Claire pointed out.

"I'm on Dad's payroll."

"Ah." She traced a finger around the edge of her wine-glass—which was exactly like Brett's oversize shot glasses. "So will you be the big boss of the family company someday?"

"No. I think my sister will be the big boss. Frankly, I'd kind of like to settle on the ranch, try to raise some cows or horses. Just lead the simple life."

"You aren't afraid of getting bored?"

He shook his head. "I'll find things to do. I want to show my horses, and I was thinking of joining the volunteer fire department."

"The fire department?"

"Yeah," he said, the charmingly crooked smile once more making an appearance. "I always wanted to be a fireman."

"This world needs more firemen," Claire agreed.

Phil slid his hand across the table and touched the large square stone in her ring. She arched an eyebrow and he pulled his hand back, letting it settle on the edge of the table.

"You're no pushover, are you, Claire?"

"Did you think I was?"

He shook his head. "No. I think you are a damn intelligent woman."

"But you were hoping I'd also be easy?"

He laughed. "Maybe."

"Well, I'm not."

It was his turn to smile evilly. "Not even after another drink?"

"Not even then," she said, pleased that he could tease.

"You can't blame me for trying."

"I don't blame you one bit. And I have to tell you, I like you better when you're just…Phil." She spoke gently, watching his reaction. He frowned, and she thought he was going to profess ignorance, but instead he said, "I've never had anyone tell me that."

"I prefer honesty to flash. I can't help it."

"Okay. I'll tone down the flash."

Claire finished the last drops of her box wine. "I really should be getting home." Especially now that things were going well between them. "I'm driving to Wesley early tomorrow for Thanksgiving."

He walked her to her car, and when they got there she offered her hand, which was probably not the way he'd intended to end the evening. "It's been fun."

"Yeah." There was a touch of irony in his voice.

Claire laughed and kissed his cheek. "I'll see you, Phil. Thanks for asking me out."

THANKSGIVING DINNER AT the Bishop house was a low-key affair. With only four people, and none of them football fans, it could hardly have been anything else. The home-made rolls turned out well, the pies Claire had baked that morning were much appreciated and the turkey was roasted exactly on time.

After dinner was over Will and an uncharacteristically quiet Kylie headed out to feed, and Claire was able to ask Regan a question that had been bothering her for quite a while.

"What's the deal with Will and Brett?" she asked.

Regan handed her the dish of mashed potatoes. "Deal?"

"You know what I mean. Brothers living less than a hundred miles apart and one of them chooses to spend Thanksgiving alone."

"They were never close," Regan said, carrying the empty turkey platter to the sink and dumping it into the soapy water.

"And that's it?"

"What more do you want?"

"I want to know why," Claire said, stretching plastic wrap over the potatoes. "The whole situation strikes me as odd. I mean, Brett goes to all the public family events, but none of the private ones. Why?"

"Sometimes it's hard to pin down the why," Regan said vaguely, lifting a dish out of the draining rack and wiping it dry.

And sometimes it's not. Regan had information she didn't want to share.

Claire debated as she gathered cutlery off the table and transferred it to the dishwater. Yes, she was curious about Brett, but it was none of her business. She decided to take the high road. If Regan didn't want to tell her the story, fine. Brett was part of Regan's family, not part of Claire's.

But the whole situation was driving her crazy.

"Kylie said that her first basketball game is coming up soon."

"Yes," Regan confirmed more cheerfully. "We have a schedule printed out for you."

"She seemed kind of quiet at dinner."

"Yeah." Regan continued to wipe the already dry plate. "She broke curfew the other night and Brett brought her home. She's not happy with any of us right now. Brett embarrassed her in front of her new boyfriend and then we grounded her."

"Brett brought her home?"

"Total fluke. He happened to see her out late and realized it was a little *too* late. And then, because we grounded her she didn't get to go to the Harvest Dance. Her boyfriend took someone else, and now *those* two are a couple and Kylie's left out in the cold. She's hurt and furious, and guess who's she's blaming?"

"Everyone except herself?" Claire remembered those days well. "Parenthood is hard, isn't it?" And Regan had pretty much been tossed into the deep end when she'd married Will. Will's first wife had left when Kylie was only an infant, so Regan was, in essence, the first mother the girl had ever known.

"Yes. You know what's best for the kid, and you know what it feels like to be a kid." Regan blew out a breath as Claire gently pried the dry dish from her hands and replaced it with a wet one. Regan automatically began to wipe again.

"Speaking of parents, what do you think Mom's doing in San Diego right now?"

"I hope she's having dinner with Stephen."

"Think they'll work it out? I mean, do you think Mom will ever change?"

"I could make all kinds of comments about pigs flying and hell freezing over but…" Regan glanced at her sister conspiratorially "…I don't think there really is a conference in San Diego. I think she's gone there to patch things up."

"And she's covering herself, in case she fails." Claire nodded appreciatively. "Smart woman."

BRETT GOT PAID twice a month, and his payday became Jesse's payday, as well. He made certain that he had enough cash on hand to pay the boy on the fifteenth and the thirtieth. "Are you going to buy more clothes?" he asked on the payday immediately following Thanksgiving—which was in itself a cause for thanksgiving. Phil hadn't mentioned riding the stud again, and he hadn't fired Brett, either.

Jesse nodded.

"Saving money to buy clothes is a mature thing to do," Brett said. "I'm impressed. But don't you think maybe you should spend a little on something more…fun?"

The look of pride faded from Jesse's face. "Dad couldn't afford school clothes this year, and I'm tired of wearing stuff that doesn't fit," he said stiffly.

Brett felt that twisting sensation in his gut again, and he attempted damage control. "Sounds like you know what you're doing. I never was any good at managing my money." He tucked his wallet back in his jeans pocket. "Maybe you could give me some pointers."

Jesse slowly smiled. "I didn't only get clothes, you know. I got a better backpack, and a web belt with a cowboy buckle."

"Sounds cool."

"I'll show you the belt tomorrow."

"Can't wait."

Brett set out a couple of cookies and a soda pop—not exactly health food, but there was a place for indulgence food, too. He leaned against the door frame when Jesse left, watching as the boy happily trotted down the drive, wearing his new finery.

Shit. If he'd known the kid didn't have decent clothes, he would have bought him some.

Brett zipped his coat against the cold November air and went to his truck. It was feeding time at Phil's, and he wanted to get done early so he could work on his math and get another chapter of *Moby Dick* under his belt. He pulled open the door and there, sitting on the driver's seat, was a book. A textbook, to be exact. *Pre-algebra.*

Damn. Claire had left him a present. He pushed the book aside and got into the truck, but while he waited for the glow plugs to heat before turning on the ignition, he picked up the text and flipped through it. Then he stopped. Read a little. He frowned and then turned back a page. He read some more, studied the example, closed the book and put it on the seat beside him.

Okay, maybe Claire was right. Maybe he had to brush up on some basics before proceeding, and maybe this book would help. Even though he'd made it clear he didn't want help, and she'd dropped the damn book off, anyway.

She's a teacher. She probably couldn't help herself.

He turned the key and the engine chugged to life.

Either that or she recognized a guy in trouble who was too stubborn for his own good.

It wasn't until the pep band started playing the national anthem and the crowd rose that Claire managed to spot Brett on the opposite side of the gymnasium at Kylie's first home game. She turned her attention back to the basketball court as the referee prepared for the tip-off.

Wesley's first game of the season was against the town's archrival, the team that had taken the state championship from them the previous season by two points. Emotions were running high on both sides. Thirty seconds into play the whistle blew for the first foul.

"I hope this doesn't set the tone for the game," Regan muttered, as the ref held up fingers to indicate Kylie's number.

It did. By the end of the first half a technical had been called and two players, one on each team, had fouled out. Kylie was close to being the next player benched, with four fouls of her own.

"Play nice," Will said under his breath as the second half began. But Kylie played for only a matter of minutes before the coach took her out, too.

"Good," Regan said. "She needs to settle down and focus on her play."

"Since when did you become a basketball expert?" Claire asked. Claire had been the one who'd played basketball in high school for two years. Regan had been too busy at the stables to participate in high-school athletics.

"Since I became a mom," Regan said, her attention on the game. She flinched as one of the Wesley players missed an easy layup. "She needs some time to regroup. She's taking too many chances, and she's letting that Spartan girl get to her."

Claire knew exactly which girl Regan was talking about. Number 12. She was about Kylie's size, with long blond braids and an aggressive attitude. She had three fouls—all against Kylie. And two of Kylie's fouls were against her.

"Kylie does get her dander up."

Will and Regan nodded in unison, their eyes on the game. Claire glanced across the court at Brett. Even at a distance she could see that he was scowling. Apparently, the entire family took basketball seriously.

Kylie went out on the floor again at the start of the

fourth quarter. And she did seem more focused. Her play was calmer, more methodical. The Spartan girl, on the other hand, was starting to get frustrated. The Wesley team was winning by four points, and number 12 was doing everything she could to turn that around.

She attempted to steal the ball from Kylie again, who neatly sidestepped her. The girl overreached and lost her balance, tumbling onto the floor. Another player tripped over her and the whistle blew. Kylie handed the ball off to the ref and calmly waited for play to resume.

The girl got to her feet and walked by Kylie, muttering something as she passed that made Kylie snap to attention. She said something back and the girl stopped short, turned and made an aggressive move toward her.

The Spartan coach shouted at his player and she grudgingly turned back to the court. Kylie walked to her position and the game resumed. Kylie got the ball almost immediately and headed down the court, maneuvering neatly around several opponents. She had just squeezed through a small gap when number 12 made a diving grab for the ball and crashed sideways into her. The crowd gasped as Kylie went down, her head smacking the floor hard. And then she lay still.

Regan and Will were instantly on their feet and moving, Claire close behind. They made it to the far side of the court just as the crowd surrounding Kylie parted, and she sat up with the help of the trainer, hugging her arm to her body. Brett was kneeling next to her, his expression taut. He stood and moved to the sideline, almost bumping into Will as the trainer helped Kylie to her feet and escorted her off the court.

Will pushed through the players to catch up with them, with Regan, Brett and Claire following behind. He glanced over his shoulder at Regan as they approached the training room.

"You go," she said. "It's a small room," she explained after the door closed. She reached out to touch Brett's arm, drawing his attention. "Are you all right?"

"I'm good." But he didn't look good. "It's just…the sound her head made…" He seemed to be speaking more to himself than Regan, who ran her hand up and down his arm in a gesture of acknowledgment and empathy. Claire stood by, watching, the odd man out. There were undercurrents between Brett and Regan that she didn't understand, undercurrents that made her vaguely uncomfortable.

The door opened several minutes later and Will came out.

"They're icing her arm and the bump on her head," he said, "and I have a list of instructions on how to monitor for a concussion." He smiled weakly at his wife. "I didn't tell them how much experience I had with that in the rodeo."

"What about her arm?" Brett asked.

"We have to wait until Monday and then get it x-rayed."

"Other than that, she's fine?"

"For the most part. She's mad she's missing the end of the game."

A huge cheer from the crowd nearly drowned out his words.

Brett shifted his weight, his body language radiating discomfort. "Well, if she's okay, I'll think I'll get going. I'll call later, to find out the prognosis."

Will nodded, but Regan looked uncertain. "Brett—" she began, but he shook his head.

"I need to go." A few seconds later he was striding down the narrow strip of floor between the basketball court and the bleachers. The crowd was on its feet, screaming as the score was tied, but Brett didn't even seem to notice.

Regan let out a breath. "I'll bet she said something to him."

"You think?" Claire asked.

"I wouldn't be surprised."

BRETT'S TRUCK WAS parked in the supermarket lot when Claire pulled in to do her weekly shopping before heading home. It wasn't uncommon to meet Barlow Ridge residents in the Wesley grocery store, since living in Barlow meant a person had to stock up whenever he managed to get to a store of any size. But somehow Claire didn't think Brett was going to believe this meeting was accidental.

She counted to ten before entering, and then decided to let fate take over. If she ran into him, she did, if she didn't, she didn't.

Fate led her straight to the produce department, where she found him dropping potatoes into a plastic bag. He looked up before she could get her cart turned around.

"So what's the secret of choosing a good potato?" she asked with a half smile as she wheeled her cart closer. Brett did not smile. "Sorry," she said. "And I'm not stalking you. I just need to pick up a few things before heading home."

"Yeah, I figured." He tied a knot in the top of his plastic bag and dropped it in the cart. "I suppose you're wondering why I tore out of the game like that?"

"Of course," she said softly, "but I don't need to know."

"It's no big deal. Kylie and I haven't been getting on so well since the night I found her out late and made her go home. I thought she'd be happier if I wasn't there."

But there was more to the story than that. Claire sensed it, and wondered if Kylie really had said something when Brett was kneeling next to her. Kylie tended to speak her mind.

"Kids can be cruel, Brett. A lot of times they don't realize adults have feelings, too."

"Yeah. Come to think of it, I remember thinking like that myself." His features relaxed some, making Claire even more aware of his attractiveness. Making her want to spend some time with him.

"I didn't get to eat anything at the game," she said. "I don't suppose…" A shift in Brett's expression stopped her from finishing the invitation. "Of course not. We have long drives ahead of us."

Even though she thought they would both benefit from a shared meal. It would help him relax, put things into perspective, and it would save her from having to eat pretzels out of a bag on the drive home.

"Actually…" Brett's quiet voice stopped her. "I wouldn't mind having a bite to eat with you, but I have to make another stop before I go home."

"Well, maybe some other time?"

"Yeah. Maybe." He surprised her by reaching out to brush her cheek briefly with his fingertips. "Thanks, Claire."

And then he wheeled his cart away.

She resisted the urge to touch where his hand had been, but she could still feel the warmth of the simple caress. She automatically started moving toward the organic section, a little amazed that a brief encounter in the produce department could give her so much to think about.

CHAPTER NINE

"LET ME GET this straight. I have to find a guy to wear the Santa suit?"

Fifteen heads nodded in unison. Claire was beginning to dread PTO meetings. "Why me?"

"It's your turn. We've all done it."

"I take it this isn't easy."

"We have a list of everyone who's already been Santa," Trini said helpfully.

"I need a list of the guys who *haven't* done it so far." Claire took the printed list and quickly scanned it. Brett wasn't on it. Well, he would be next year.

"Do you think any of these guys would be up for another Santa stint?"

"Maybe. It's not that bad," Bertie said in the kind of voice a mother might use if she was trying to convince a child that going to the dentist would be fun.

"Oh, all right," Claire said, pretending she had a say in the matter. She had two weeks to find a Santa and, she'd start working on it tonight.

BRETT WONDERED WHAT his life would be like when he no longer had a beautiful blonde showing up on his doorstep whenever she got the whim.

"Hi. I brought you something. A bribe, actually." Claire pushed by him into the kitchen and deposited a wicker basket on the table. It was bread. Fresh out of the oven.

"You cook?"

"Of course I cook. It's just chemistry."

"And I suppose you're good at chemistry."

"Yes, I am."

He lifted the corner of the cloth that covered the bread. "Looks good."

"It is."

"Is there anything you're not good at?"

"No," she said lightly, wondering if he was making a double entendre, or if it was just wishful thinking on her part.

"So why are you bringing bribes?"

"I need someone to dress up as Santa at the Christmas play."

"And you want me to help you find…" His voice suddenly trailed off as realization set in. *"No."*

"Please?"

He shook his head, and then had a flash of brilliance. "Ask Phil."

"He won't be here."

Brett hated that she already knew that and he didn't.

"It's really hard to get someone to do this because practically everyone in Barlow has been Santa at least once already, and since I'm the new teacher they're making me do it, and… Please, Brett?"

"No." He continued to shake his head. "I'm not that kind of guy."

"What kind of guy?"

"A Santa kind of guy," he said gruffly.

"Oh, I don't know." She nodded at Sarina, who was studying them from under one of the kitchen chairs.

"That's different." He paced to the sink and put some

dishes in the water he'd run just before Claire knocked. "Have you asked anyone else?"

She pulled a list out of her jacket pocket and showed it to him. "These are the people who won't do it. Can you think of anyone who isn't on it?"

No one suitable. Deke would probably be drunk. Little Manny Fernandez—he was maybe half a Santa.

"The kids need a Santa, Brett."

Brett wondered briefly if a kid like Jesse still believed in Santa—even a little—and then he had an idea.

"What?" Claire asked softly, sensing his shift in attitude.

"If you can find out what Jesse wants for Christmas, I'll do it."

"That's all?"

"I want to get him something kind of special. And I have to figure out how to give it to him so it doesn't look like charity."

She smiled slowly, watching him fight not to smile in return. "All right, Scrooge, I'll see what I can do."

"Then I'll wear the stupid suit," he said with a scowl.

"And now I'm going to do something I've wanted to do since the wedding." She rose up on her toes and, taking his face between her palms and pressing her body lightly along the length of his, she kissed him. Softly. Warmly. A friendly thank-you kiss that shouldn't have given him an instant hard-on. He worked to keep frowning as she pulled away.

"Oh, come on, Brett, you didn't mind, did you?"

"I think it's obvious that I didn't." His anatomy was sending out all the proper signals.

"No," she said softly, raising her fingers to gently tap his forehead. "I mean, up here."

He caught her hand, held on for a moment. He didn't have a straight answer. No, he didn't mind. Yes, he did mind. They were both the truth. If she were anyone else, related to anyone else, he'd probably already have been actively working toward getting her in the sack.

"Thank you for agreeing to be Santa." She squeezed his fingers and slipped her hand free, taking a backward step to put some space between them.

"Just find out what Jesse wants, okay?"

"I'll do my best."

A few seconds later, he was alone and wondering what he was doing. With Claire. With Jesse.

He didn't know.

Jesse needed someone to take an interest in him, and Brett found himself stepping into that position more and more. And liking it. But the big question was why? Was he helping Jesse, or filling an empty hole in his own life?

Brett was still smarting from what Kylie had said to him at the game, when she'd opened her eyes and seen him hovering over her. *"I want you to leave me alone."* And she'd meant it.

He tried to tell himself Kylie was just angry about being caught in a lie and having to pay the consequences, that she'd get over it. But it bothered him. A lot.

AS PROMISED, CLAIRE discovered what Jesse wanted for Christmas from a writing assignment, and after that she managed to wheedle Brett into going shopping in Elko with her.

Brett pulled into her driveway at 5:00 a.m. one Saturday morning. Claire wrapped her mulberry scarf around her neck, grabbed her purse and let herself out into the frigid predawn air.

Brett was not smiling when she slid into the passenger seat.

"Stop looking like you're not going to enjoy this," she said sternly before burrowing down into her coat. The truck was cold, even though the heater was blowing, and she was beginning to wish she'd brought along a cup of coffee. Brett granted her wish by indicating the extra travel cup in the holder between them.

"You're a good man," she said with a sigh as she picked up the cup closer to her.

"How many kids are we shopping for?"

"Ten."

"Ten?"

Claire looked at him out of the corner of her eye. "It started as six, but since it wouldn't be right for some kids to get a gift and others not to, Bertie approached the PTO for financing. We're going to get something for every kid. I'm responsible for my class. Bertie's responsible for her class."

"Ten presents." Brett took a moment to digest the new plan of action. "What does Jesse want?"

"Well, he wants a bike, but that's kind of pricey, so you might consider a winter coat. His is pathetic. A hooded sweatshirt under a lightweight fall coat. And he did mention a coat in his journals."

"Yeah. I guess that'd be good."

But when they got to Wal-Mart, Brett went straight to the bikes.

"I thought—"

"I'll get him both."

Claire sucked in a breath. "Brett…" He sent her a frowning glance. "That's a lot of money. More than the other kids are getting."

"I know." He ran his hand over the curved handlebars of the floor model. "But I'm thinking, what the hell. I'm entitled to give my best employee a Christmas bonus, aren't I? Santa can give him the coat."

"I still—"

Brett turned toward Claire then and put his hands on her shoulders, stopping her midsentence.

"I want to give Jesse a bike." He squeezed lightly and then let go. Claire turned back to the bikes, still feeling the phantom pressure of his grip.

She had to clear her throat before saying, "Well, which one is the Christmas bonus?"

"None of these. We're going to the bike shop downtown."

"If you say so." Claire perused her list again. "But we're going to need a cart for this other stuff."

Jesse ended up with an awesome bike. Claire had a feeling it was exactly the bike Brett would have bought himself. It had all the necessary extras to allow Jesse to ride to school in style and to also tear up the trails.

Brett was really pleased with the purchase. He made certain, after that, that Claire didn't pick out a geeky coat, nixing a red one in favor of dark blue, and he added a knit hat with a popular insignia and gloves.

"How are you giving out the other presents?" he asked after they'd ordered lunch at a small downtown café.

"Mrs. Presley is going to pretend Santa left some stuff at the post office. She's going to have her husband deliver the gifts on Christmas Eve."

"That's nice."

"I don't know what we're going to do about Jesse's gift, though."

"Why?"

"When I talked to his dad at the parent meeting—"

"The guy actually came to the parent meeting?"

"Yes, he did."

"He came to something that involved his kid?"

"I believe I established that." Brett took the hint and shut up. "He has not been a dad for long, by the way."

"Jesse said something about that."

"Yes. He paid his child support all along, but he had minimal contact with Jesse until his grandmother got too sick to take care him." Claire did not like the stormy expression on Brett's face. "He was only eighteen when Jesse was born," she explained.

"That may seem like an excuse to him, but it isn't."

Brett spoke with a quiet intensity that startled Claire. She leaned back as the waiter delivered their sandwiches, but her eyes stayed locked on his.

"Why do you say that?"

Brett shook his head. "Why do you think it might be hard to deliver Jesse's present?"

"I told Tom—that's the father—that I'd be happy to drive Jesse home on the nights when he was working late, and he was adamant that he didn't want Jesse home alone."

"He prefers him freezing his ass off in a school playground."

"And he also said that his dogs were unpredictable and that it wasn't safe for strangers to come to his place unless he was there."

"Oh, yeah. That's a good environment for a kid." Brett looked a little sick as he pushed his plate away.

"Hey." Claire reached out and placed her fingers over his. "He does seem to care about Jesse. And he said that the dogs love him."

"If he cares about Jesse, then why doesn't he take care of him?"

"Maybe he doesn't know how to?"

"I know how to, and I'm…not a father."

Claire squeezed his fingers, surprised he hadn't pulled them away. "One thing I learned from my stint student teaching is that there are always kids we want to take home with us, to save. But we can't."

Brett held her gaze, the expression in his dark eyes very, very serious. "I don't know if I can play by those rules," he said quietly.

He slipped his hand out from under hers and picked up his sandwich, taking a bite. Finally he said, "I'll do my best, but no promises."

Jesse Lane was a superb actor, or so it seemed to Brett, who spent most of his Christmas pageant audience time smiling as he watched his protégé chew the scenery in the role of a forgetful elf who was delaying Christmas.

Brett sat near the back of the room, sandwiched between the Moreno clan and old Grandpa Meyers, who always traveled out from Wesley to watch his great-grandkids perform. Brett made sure that Jesse saw him, and then, after the first play ended, he slipped out the side exit. Re-entering through the front door, he stepped quietly into the darkened office before anyone noticed him.

Santa. He couldn't believe he was doing this.

He'd missed Kylie's Santa years, and although he was now able to get her something for her birthday and Christmas, in the role of an uncle, it all felt so inadequate. A small part of him acknowledged that his indulgence of Jesse was a compensatory move. A larger part of him knew he cared for Jesse, plain and simple. The boy had weaseled his way into Brett's heart.

And where the hell was Jesse's father? His kid was in

a play and he couldn't take time out of his busy schedule to show up. Jesse had probably bummed a ride from the Hernandezes.

Well, Brett would take him home if he needed a ride, whether his dad had rules about it or not. Brett wasn't concerned about unpredictable dogs. He wanted to make sure the boy wasn't staying alone, that the dad wasn't out on his sales route. Jesse was amazingly reticent about his home life, considering how willingly he poured out everything else.

Brett locked the office door and peeled off his jacket and boots. He pulled on the velvety red pants over his jeans and tied the drawstring. Next the jacket. He buttoned it halfway, then shoved the homemade stuffed belly into the front. He glanced down. He looked more pregnant than fat. Oh, well. Closing the jacket, he buckled on the black belt, slipped his feet into his cowboy boots and tucked the pant legs into the tops. Next, a white wig.

His head was instantly hot.

And now the beard. He grimaced as he held up a mass of silvery curls. How many guys had breathed into this thing? During cold-and-flu season?

It's for the kids.

Fastening the beard in place, he slapped the Santa cap on his head. *Ho, ho, ho.*

He opened the office door, peeking out just as Bertie appeared at the stage door. She held up five fingers, indicating five minutes, then pointed to the door he would use to enter the gym and begin spreading Christmas joy.

He still couldn't believe he was doing this.

THE LINE OF KIDS wound around the gym. Parents snapped pictures and waited for their little ones to confide to Brett what they wanted for Christmas. And damned if he didn't have a real desire to fulfill all their wishes.

Next year, maybe he'd go shopping after the Santa stint. *What on earth was he thinking?* He wasn't doing this twice.

But…it really wasn't that bad. Except for the damn beard. He couldn't wait to get that off.

Even the older kids sat on Santa's lap. It was part of what he appreciated about small towns—that older kids stayed kids for a while and they set an example for the younger ones. For the most part, anyway.

Jesse obviously recognized him. He had a conspiratorial gleam in his eye as he asked for a 4x4 pickup truck. A Dodge diesel crew cab, if Santa could swing it. Brett told him he'd do what he could.

Toni was next and she sat on the edge of his knee, barely making contact. She looked into his eyes, obviously trying to guess his identity. Brett gamely asked what she wanted for Christmas.

"Honest?" she asked with a touch of grim irony.

"Yes," he answered, surprised at her response.

"I want a real place to live. Just me and my mom."

Brett didn't know what to say. He handed her a candy cane and she got up, and then Ashley made a big show of sitting on Santa's lap, giggling as she wrapped her arms around his neck, leaning her cheek against his in a cheesy way and smiling as her stepdad took a picture. Once the photo shoot was over, she jumped up and went to join Toni, without saying a word to Brett.

Nice kid. He had a feeling that if Ashley lived anywhere except for Barlow, she wouldn't have a thing to do with Toni.

Funny. He'd never thought about kid dynamics much until Claire came breezing into his life. And speaking of which, his eyes strayed over to where she was talking to a couple of parents—who were actually listening to what she had to say. She was making inroads. And looking good while she did it, in a long black skirt and a sparkly green top.

She always looked good. And he wasn't the only guy who seemed to be noticing. Several guys, single and otherwise, seemed to be ogling her.

"Santa?"

Elena Moreno got his attention before she took her turn on his rapidly numbing knee. He smiled through the beard and she took her seat.

BRETT HAD JUST finished his duties and was talking to a small boy when the gym door opened and Jesse's dad came in. Claire had to fight to keep her mouth from popping open. One side of the man's face was burned bright scarlet. The wound was obviously fairly new, just starting to scab over. Maybe he'd actually had a legitimate reason for missing Jesse's performance, because he wasn't looking well.

She glanced at Brett, who was now working his way through the crowd with a determined look on his face. Claire went into action. It wouldn't do to have Santa assault a man in front of an audience.

"Santa, may I have a word?"

She spoke firmly, and Brett slowed down. Jesse appeared out of the crowd then and walked over to his father, handing him his goodie bag and costume. The guy took it, laid a hand on his son's shoulder, more as a steering mechanism than out of affection, and pushed the door open. A second later the two Lanes disappeared out into the night.

Claire did not say a word, but took Brett's hand and pressed her classroom key into it. He understood. He couldn't exactly get into his truck and drive away wearing the Santa suit—at least not without disillusioning any small child who might see him. And since his clothing was still locked in the office, he had no choice but to disappear.

He pretended to be heading back to the stage, but instead slipped into Claire's dark room and managed to fumble his way past the student desks to her chair without hurting himself. He pulled off the hat and let out a long breath.

He couldn't shake the image in his mind of Jesse's dad steering him out that door. What in the hell had happened to the guy, and why hadn't Jesse mentioned that his dad had been hurt?

Brett was still mulling the matter over when Claire opened the door and snapped on the lights.

"Are they gone?" he asked, blinking as his eyes adjusted.

"Every one of them."

He yanked off the wig and beard, rubbing a hand over his head and ruffling his hair. "I was afraid to take the damn thing off, in case some kid came in. I should have put my clothes somewhere more accessible."

"Should have," Claire agreed, holding up a big bag that held his jeans and shirt. "You want to come to my place and have a celebratory drink after you change?"

"I just want to go home."

"You are really chipping away at my confidence," she said as she strolled closer, swinging the bag on one finger.

Brett stood. "I don't think anything shakes your confidence."

She stepped even closer, near enough for him to smell her perfume. Something with a spicy cinnamon base that made him want to pull her onto his lap, press his face into her neck and inhale deeply—before he did some even better stuff.

"Just a nightcap. As a thank-you." She ran a finger down the front of the soft red suit. "And you can start the furnace, because it went off just before I left and the reset button isn't working."

"All right." He couldn't exactly leave her without heat. Brett reached out and took the bag. "I'll change in the office."

THE FUEL LINE on the furnace was plugged. Brett blew it clear and pushed the button. The furnace hesitated, then gave a shudder and started to hum. A minute later the blower came on and warm air wafted out through the vents. Claire went to stand over one of the grates, letting the warm air flutter the hem of her silky skirt.

"The tank must have been low when they filled it. Sometimes debris gets into the line."

"I do seem to use a lot of fuel," Claire agreed. "I like to be warm."

"Do you miss the Vegas heat?"

"Not as much as I thought I would. I won't mind going back, but I do like it here. Even if it does get cold."

"I'm surprised."

"I bet you are," she said. "You thought I was a hothouse flower, didn't you?"

"You are more...adaptable than I'd first thought." In fact, she was a hell of a lot tougher than he'd imagined she'd be. Definitely tougher than Mr. Nelson, and a lot less whiny.

The trailer was warming up fast. It had its problems, but poor insulation wasn't one of them. Claire eventually shrugged out of her coat and went into the kitchen. "What do you want? I have wine or wine."

"I'll take wine."

She brought two glasses—with stems. One was filled

with red and one with white. "I remembered that you prefer red." She raised her glass. "To Santa."

"To Santa."

"Sit down," she said, after their first sip. "Relax. You've earned it."

She settled on the plum-colored sofa, stretching out her legs to rest her heels on the coffee table. "What do you think happened to Jesse's dad?" she asked conversationally.

"It looked like a flash burn."

Claire frowned. "Jesse hasn't said a word about it."

"Have you noticed that he doesn't talk about his dad much?"

"Maybe because they haven't been together that long."

Claire crossed her ankles, making the sparkles on her less-than-sensible shoes catch the light. "It's good that you're there for him. Kids need someone to talk to."

"Yeah," Brett agreed, feeling slightly ill at ease. He wasn't used to being the good guy.

A silence followed. Claire seemed totally comfortable with it—more comfortable than Brett was, anyway. He felt aware. Hyperaware.

"What are you doing for Christmas?" he finally asked.

"I think I'll go to Las Vegas and spar with my mother."

"Sounds like fun."

"It's more fun than it used to be, now that she's finally seeing me as an adult."

"She didn't before?"

"It was my own fault. I was blissfully flaky, and then Regan moved and my world came crashing down."

"Why?"

"I was on my own. Decisions that I would have automatically asked Regan for advice on, I had to make myself, since I felt dumb calling her all the time. I had to handle Mom on my own. I had to grow up." Claire reached out to take his half-empty wineglass, and placed it on the end table next to her own, then smiled languidly at him. "It was awful."

He knew exactly what was coming next, and he didn't resist when she curled her hand around his neck and pulled his lips down to hers.

Her mouth was as inviting as he remembered. No, it was better. As was the feel of her body snuggled up against his. He let his hand skim over her. Lightly, while reminding himself that this was just a thank-you kiss, like the one in his kitchen. A mistletoe-type Happy Holiday kiss.

Who was he trying to kid? This was a toe-curling, groin-hardening kiss.

"Are you much of a fighter?" Claire asked, when she finally came up for air.

"What?" he asked huskily. He brushed the hair away from her temples with his fingertips, wanting to go on touching her.

She suddenly rolled on top of him, smiling down into his eyes. "As I continue my assault on your virtue, will be you be putting up a struggle?" He wanted to smile, but managed not to.

"Yes." Or so his mind said. Although his body had different ideas.

And it seemed to be winning.

She cupped his face in her hands and kissed him deeply. His mind was losing. When she came up for air once more, he tried again.

"Clai—" She cut him off with another hot kiss.

"You may as well surrender."

"No." But his hands were at her waist, traveling over her hips, then cupping her butt to press her into his erection.

"You'll have to be more convincing than that," she commented wryly. "I know all the arguments, but..." She brushed her lips over his. "I also know that you shouldn't spend your life alone."

"I can have company, if I choose."

"But you're not choosing."

"So I'm going to have company thrust upon me?"

"It's for your own good."

Now he did laugh. "You're doing this to help me out?"

"I think you're a good man who needs companionship." She raised her eyebrows suggestively.

"You might be surprised about the 'good man' part."

"But I'm not wrong about the companionship part," she said, unfazed, "and I think we could be good together."

"I'm not denying that." But there was more to life than momentary pleasure. There were long-term consequences, and if there was one subject he was familiar with, it was long-term consequences. "I'm tempted," he said truthfully.

"But not quite ready to make the big leap." She eased away from him, and he immediately missed her warmth, her softness. Her scent. "No hard feelings?"

She reached for her glass and drained the last few drops. In spite of her such-is-life attitude, he wondered if he'd hurt her feelings. He reached out to touch her face.

"I like you, Claire, but there are some issues here that..." He paused, trying to figure out how much he wanted to say. How much he could say.

"Hey, it's fine, Brett. Honest. If I wasn't ready for rejection, I wouldn't have come on to you. I *am* tougher than I look."

As he stepped out into the cold night a few minutes later, however, he had a feeling that Claire was not quite as bulletproof as she pretended.

CHAPTER TEN

THE KIDS OF BARLOW RIDGE had a happy Christmas, thanks to Claire. Brett discovered this not from Claire, who'd kept her distance during the week preceding Christmas vacation, but from Anne McKirk, when he stopped by her store the day after a rather lonely Christmas.

"So you stayed here for Christmas, did ya?" she asked.

"I did."

Regan had called and invited him to dinner, as she always did, but he'd told her he'd see them all at Kylie's game a few days later. Claire was in Las Vegas and Phil was in California. Jesse was supposed to be in Carson City visiting his great-grandmother.

Brett was totally alone. It wasn't a new state of affairs, but this year it felt different.

"Do you know anything about this Lane guy?" he asked Anne as he paid for his groceries.

"Hard to know anything about a guy you never see."

"But, Anne, you know everything."

She pretended to be insulted, but she wasn't. "Not this time. The only thing I do know is that he's living in that place rent-free because it belongs to his ex-mother-in-law."

Or perhaps Jesse's grandma. "Is she local?"

"Nope. She and her husband bought the place as an investment years ago, and then the husband passed away."

"I wonder why she hasn't sold."

"Hernandez offered to buy it from her once, but she didn't sell because she's leaving it to her grandson."

So Jesse had a legacy, too. Five acres and a trailer house. Not bad for a ten-year-old who didn't have a decent winter coat. Brett wondered if Jesse was aware of his inheritance.

"That clears some stuff up, Anne. Thanks."

"No problem." She walked him to the door, glancing out at his truck. "Where're you going with that bike?"

"Christmas bonus that I need to deliver."

Anne smiled briefly, in spite of herself.

THERE WERE TWO trailers on the Lane place, one behind the other, and two nasty-looking dogs. No wonder Sarina seemed so happy living with Brett. She could relax.

The dogs charged the truck as Brett drove in. He put the rig in Neutral, and watched as the animals took aggressive stances within easy attack range, teeth bared, the hair on their backs bristling straight up. So these were the dogs that loved Jesse. Damn, Brett hoped so.

He let out a breath and put the truck in Reverse. The dogs took deliberate strides forward in unison, their teeth still bared as he swung the truck around. He would not be leaving the bike as a surprise. Instead, he'd have Anne give him a heads-up when the Lanes returned, and then he'd deliver the bike.

As it turned out, though, Brett didn't have to deliver it. Jesse showed up at his place the next day, wearing his new Christmas coat and hat, worried because he'd missed chores without telling Brett, but thrilled that he'd gotten to spend Christmas with his great-grandmother.

"Dad had friends to go see, so I spent the whole day with her and the other old people until it was their bedtime." He smiled sadly. "Old guys have bedtimes. Isn't that weird?"

"Totally," Brett agreed. "Hey, speaking of chores, I have something to tell you." Instantly, Jesse looked worried. "Something good," Brett amended. "Come on. I'll show you instead of telling you."

He led the way to the enclosed side porch and opened the door. The bike was leaning against a saddle rack. Jesse's eyes grew as big as saucers.

"No way," he said softly.

Brett smiled. "You've worked hard. This is your Christmas bonus."

"A Christmas bonus? For real?"

"For real."

Jesse slowly approached the bike. He ran a hand over the handlebars, just as Brett had done in the store, and then grinned at him over his shoulder.

"Too bad there's so much snow, or you could try it out."

"This is an all-terrain bike. I *can* use it in the snow."

Brett had his doubts, but he was not going to spoil the boy's fun. "Well, let's go see what you can do."

CLAIRE LEANED AGAINST her sink and watched Brett and Jesse playing in the snow. The bike was eventually abandoned for snowballs, and then, after a pelting that must have soaked both of them clear through, Brett lifted the bike and carried it back into the house, Jesse following close behind.

Claire turned away from the window. It was awful being jealous of a kid—especially one she liked—but why couldn't *she* get any kind of response out of Brett other than one that was physical and obviously quite resistible?

And why was it bugging her so much? Rejection was part of the game and had never bothered her before. Was this her contrary nature, wanting what it couldn't have? Or something more?

She knew which one it felt like, and it wasn't the one that would make Brett a happy man.

PHIL RYKER HAD decided to become a full-time rancher. Brett listened numbly in silence as Phil explained over the phone that he was moving the base of operations for his other businesses to the ranch, and since he'd be living there full-time, he'd decided he might as well run the ranch, too. He could hire an hourly worker for about two-thirds of Brett's salary, so as of June 1, there was a good chance he would no longer need Brett's managerial services, except on a consulting basis.

Brett set the phone on the counter when Phil was done explaining, his stomach pulled into a tight knot.

Now what was he going to do? He didn't have a way to make a living in Barlow unless he managed a ranch—the only work he'd ever done besides rodeo riding in his entire life. And he knew that even if he got a regular job somewhere else, he wouldn't be able to swing mortgage payments for the homestead along with rent for a place in his new locale.

He leaned on the counter and stared into space, wondering how the hell this was all going to play out. Phil would run the ranch into the ground in no time, but what did that matter when a guy had tons of money and didn't care if the place paid for itself? Maybe that was the problem. Maybe Brett had been too efficient. The ranch finances had been easing closer toward the black every month. Maybe Brett should have made more of an effort to provide Phil with a nice fat tax write-off.

Brett had hoped he'd have a plan before anyone found out about his predicament, but it didn't work out that way. His brother called early the next day.

"I heard that Phil's taking over the ranch." Will sounded

concerned, which always made Brett feel defensive. Will had no business being concerned about him.

"Word travels fast. I just found out myself yesterday."

"What now?"

"I wait and see if he can handle it. If he can't, I imagine he'll take me back on. If he can, well, I go looking for employment elsewhere. I don't have much of a choice."

"What about the homestead?"

Brett had known the question was coming, but it still irritated him to hear it spoken aloud. "I don't know."

"Maybe I could help with the finances, if things don't work out with Phil, so you don't lose the place."

Yeah. As if Will was swimming in money. "No," Brett said curtly.

"You could at least hear me out. We could form a partnership."

"No."

"You could pay me back."

"No."

"You aren't a stubborn son of a bitch or anything, are you?" Will challenged.

"I don't want help."

"That's not always a positive," his brother said. And then he hung up.

Brett put his own phone down. Way to go. Alienating the rest of his family again. But he wasn't going to take charity in the form of a partnership. Especially from Will. He already owed his brother a bigger debt than he could ever repay. He wasn't going to add to it.

LATER THAT AFTERNOON, Claire came tramping across the field, following the trail Jesse had made with his bike.

Brett didn't know if he was strong enough to handle another outpouring of sympathy. But at least she wasn't carrying a bottle of wine, which made him think that maybe she didn't know. Maybe she had a problem of her own. Snake, cooler, furnace. Yeah. It could be something she needed help with.

That hope was put to rest as soon as he opened the kitchen door.

"I heard about Phil," she said, in place of "hello."

He silently stepped back to allow her entry. He knew better than to try and stop her.

"What are you going to do?"

"I don't know." He was tired of the question. Tired of hearing it, tired of mulling it over. And it had only been a day since Phil had called. Brett was beginning to think maybe he should simply drop his option, throw his bedroll into the back of his truck and hit the road—which was the way he'd handled all difficulties in his life up until now.

But if he did that, who was going to take care of Sarina?

The answer—Claire—was in front of him, watching him with a steady, matter-of-fact gaze.

Okay, then who'd look out for Jesse? And was Brett willing to blow out of Kylie's life again? No. Even if she was angry with him, he still wanted to be there. He didn't know whether he was motivated by paternity or penance—maybe a combination of the two—but he needed to be part of her life.

"Is this a done deal?" Claire asked, boosting herself up on the counter. So much for an outpouring of sympathy.

"Not yet."

"How hard is it to run a ranch? I mean, could Phil do it?"

"Maybe."

Her mouth twisted ironically, and Brett told her the truth.

"With no practical experience. It's hard. It takes more than general business savvy."

"He said he was hiring an hourly guy."

"Who will only be as good as the directions Phil gives him, unless he's a pretty out-of-the-ordinary hourly guy, and those kind of people don't work for what Phil plans on paying."

"So the real problem is how, once he figures out he can't run the ranch, to ease things back to the current situation with his ego intact."

Brett nodded slowly. "Yeah. I guess that is the real problem."

"Do you want to keep working for him?"

"Right now, it's the only way I can buy the homestead. I'm not in a position to work elsewhere and make payments on this place, plus pay rent wherever I'm working." As it was, most of what Phil paid Brett went to living expenses. He was fortunate that his small herd of cows not only paid for themselves but usually gave him a bit of profit— enough to invest in home repairs occasionally, although not enough to live on. If he had to rent another place, he'd have to make nearly double what he was making now. Not likely, in his chosen profession.

"Why are you taking college courses?"

The sudden shift of topic threw him. He shook his head.

"Are you doing it in order to get a degree you can use in some profession? Are you doing it for personal satisfaction?"

"A little of both," he answered cautiously.

"If you got your degree, would it be one that you could use here in Barlow?"

He didn't answer. Claire slid off the counter and crossed to where he stood. "Brett, you can talk to me. I won't tell anyone."

But he'd made a career of not talking, at least about things that mattered.

"What do you think you'll do with a degree?"

"I think…" He looked down into her eyes and promptly lost his train of thought as he remembered the other evening in her trailer.

"You think…?"

"If I can get a degree in business management, or maybe agricultural economics, I could combine it with my practical experience and get a real job. Even if it's with a government agency, I'd make more than I make now. Under those circumstances, I'd probably be able to work elsewhere and still make payments on this place, if I live frugally." A condition for which ranch management had prepared him well. "Eventually, I'd either retire here or turn it into a money-making proposition, depending on the market."

"That's a good plan."

"If I hadn't been thirty-three when I started, it might have been a good plan."

Claire smiled that secret smile of hers, making him wonder what she was thinking. She stepped back, giving him the space he thought he wanted, until he began fighting the urge to close the gap between them again. But if he'd learned nothing else in his screwed-up life, he'd at least learned self-discipline. The hard way, of course.

"I'm curious, Brett. And probably out of line, but why is this homestead so important to you?"

"It's a family thing." Even if he hadn't gotten along so well with his father, he had adored his grandfather, who'd once worked this same land.

"So family is important to you?"

He'd blundered into the trap, probably because he was thinking about how good she looked.

"Because if it is, well, I gotta tell you, I don't understand why you're so standoffish with your own family."

It was a legitimate question. And one he couldn't answer, because there were more people involved in the answer than just him.

"If I told anyone, it would probably be you, but…"

"You've kept it quiet for so long, you can't imagine
sharing."

"Yes." Not the full truth, but close enough. And it
seemed to satisfy her. She really hadn't expected him to
share.

"I'd much rather be told to mind my own business than
be lied to." She went back over to the counter, but this time
simply leaned against it.

"Have you been lied to?" Brett latched on to the change
of topic.

"Who hasn't?"

"By someone you trusted?"

She wrinkled her nose. "One of my college boyfriends
turned out to be a real snake. It was quite the learning experience." Brett was glad to see a wry smile playing on
her lips, telling him she was well over whatever had happened. "I thought he was wonderful—trustworthy, honest
and brave. A veritable Eagle Scout. But then I found out he'd
been lying to me for practically our entire relationship. Not
an easy pill to swallow for someone who fancies herself a
student of human nature."

"Anyone can make a mistake."

"I lent him money."

"Ouch."

"Yes." She looked out the window, feigning interest
in the scenery as she spoke. "As near as I can figure, he

spent it on his other girlfriend. She was more demanding than I was."

"How could anyone be more demanding than you?"

She shifted her attention to him and a slow smile curved her lips. He had a feeling he'd made another mistake. He was further convinced when she raised her forefinger in a beckoning motion.

He held his ground. Her eyebrows went up.

"What good is it being demanding if no one acquiesces?"

"Acquiesces?"

"Gives in. Agrees. Plays ball."

Oh, he'd like to play ball.

He shook his head, but he couldn't keep from smiling at her audacity.

"I like it when you smile," she said. "You don't do it enough."

"Maybe I've never had that much to smile about."

"Maybe you need someone to bring a little joy into your life."

"Claire, you make my life difficult."

"Hey." She spread her hands. "I'm only trying to help."

"And don't think I don't appreciate it. I hope I won't insult you if I shoo you on your way, so I can get some work done."

"No. You've done so before. In fact…" she thought for a moment "…I don't think I've *ever* come over without you shooing me away."

"You're exaggerating."

"No, I'm not," she said sincerely.

He thought about it. Maybe she was on the mark there. "If I don't shoo you away, what are you going to do?"

"Avoid my grading by helping you with your floor."

"My floor's done."

"There's always your math."

"It's coming easier." And it was, thanks to Claire and her pre-algebra textbook with the answers in the back. If he passed the final in a week, he'd pass the course, which had seemed impossible when he'd started the class in September. He cleared his throat. "I never did thank you for the book."

"No need," Claire said lightly. "But we could continue to talk about your future. Over a drink, maybe."

"You really do want to avoid that grading, don't you?"

"Or maybe I just want to spend time with you."

"I don't know that anything will come of that, Claire."

"But it might."

He did not respond, hoping she'd take the hint. If she'd been anyone else, related to anyone else, he would have been pulling glasses out of the cupboard and uncorking the wine.

As it was, he was still tempted. They were both adults, responsible for their own decisions.

Claire sighed, her expression resigned as she sauntered up to him and placed her hands on the planes of his cheeks. Her palms were firm and cool as they gently stroked the rough stubble.

"There are so many things about you that I wish I understood. But…" She leaned toward him, and then, just when he thought she was going to kiss him again, she dropped her hands to her sides and took a half step back. "I'm going to give you a break and leave you in peace."

He reached out and stopped her before she could turn away.

"Claire." He had no idea what he wanted to say. "You…"

Deserve better? Too hokey. Even if he did believe it. "You need to understand that this isn't easy for me."

"Then maybe you should give in to temptation."

"You deserve better." *Shit.* He'd said it. Obvious proof that, thanks to her, his brain was turning to mush. To his surprise, Claire laughed.

"Are you kidding? I drive my mother crazy. I depend far too much on my sister. And I pick on little kids for a living." She arched her brows. "Think about it."

And he did, long after she'd let herself out the kitchen door and started across the field for home. She might do all those things, but she still deserved better.

JESSE WAS UNUSUALLY quiet when he came to do chores on Monday after school. Brett knew that sometimes a guy needed to be left alone when he was like that, and other times he needed to be drawn out. This felt like one of the latter times.

"What's up?" Brett asked, deciding on the direct approach.

Jesse cast him a sidelong look. "Just some stuff."

"Home stuff or school stuff?"

"School."

"Grades?"

"No. It's just some stuff that's been goin' on for a while." He kicked a rock with enough force that Brett knew it had to be something serious—to Jesse, anyway.

"Have you talked to your dad?"

"He's been busy lately."

The boy's voice was defensive enough that Brett decided not to push. After all, whether Brett approved of Tom Lane or not, he was Jesse's dad.

"So what's bugging you?"

"Ashley." Jesse said the name in a low, disgusted voice.

"How so?"

"She makes fun of me."

"She's a bully."

Jesse looked shocked. "She's a girl."

"Hey. Girls can be bullies. I've been pushed around by a woman or two."

"You have?" Jesse asked, sounding dubious.

"Oh, yeah."

Jesse climbed into the tire, now encrusted with frost, that Brett had attached to the rope in the apple tree just after Thanksgiving. "Like who?"

"Nobody you'd know." Brett watched as Jesse spun idly in a slow circle.

"You know, lots of times when people treat you bad, it's because they're insecure or afraid."

"I don't think Ashley is afraid of anything."

Brett shrugged. "Maybe she needs to pick on people to reassure herself that she's the best."

"Or maybe she's just mean."

Brett gave up on psychology. "Maybe she *is* just mean." He leaned against the fence. "What do you do when Ashley makes fun of you?"

"Sometimes I walk away like Grandma taught me. And sometimes I say things back."

"Which one works the best?"

Jesse thought for a moment. "Neither one seems to work too great, 'cause she keeps doing it."

"I guess you're going to have to change tactics."

"How?"

"Well, when you're working with a horse, you make it hard for him to do the thing you don't want him to do, and easy to do the thing you *do* want him to do. You can do the same with people." Sometimes. It didn't seem to work with Claire.

Jesse frowned. "All right," he said uncertainly, obviously at a loss as to how he could do that with Ashley.

"So, how could you make it harder for Ashley to pick on you?"

"Not go to school?"

"That'd work," Brett agreed with a slight smile, "but I don't think Miss Flynn or your dad would approve."

Jesse grinned. "Stay away from her, I guess, but that's kinda hard when we're in the same room."

"Maybe you could be nice to her?"

"Huh?" It was the second time Brett had shocked the kid in the space of five minutes.

"Think about it. If you said something nice to Ashley before she had a chance to say something rotten to you, what would happen?"

"She'd probably say the rotten thing, anyway."

"Yeah, but how's she going to look to other people?"

Jesse considered for a moment. "Like a jerk?"

"Probably."

The boy screwed up his face. "I'm not going to like being nice to her."

"I know."

"But I'll try."

CLAIRE WAS PULLING a cardboard box out of the trunk of her car in front of the community hall when Brett stopped at the post office on his way out of town. She waved at him and he crossed the street, wondering what she'd say if she knew she'd been the subject of his thoughts for most of the day.

"I hear you've been plotting strategy with Jesse concerning Ashley," she said as Brett took the box so she could close her trunk.

"I told him to be nice to her," he said, surprised. "What happened?"

"It worked."

"It did?"

"Yep." Claire reached for the carton, and he handed it to her. "He was nice, Ashley was not, and Toni and Dylan finally came down hard on her for picking on a younger kid for no reason. It startled the heck out of her."

Brett couldn't say he was overly concerned about Ashley, and was about to say so, when two cars pulled in close to Claire's. Claire smiled at Trini, who nodded as she walked by, also carrying a cardboard box. Deirdre was carrying two fancy leather tote bags when she entered the hall a few seconds later, without looking at either Brett or Claire.

"So what happened?"

"We had a life lesson in class about doing unto others, which most of the kids seemed to understand—except Ashley, of course." Claire started toward the community hall. "Jesse told me that you were the one who suggested that he be nice to her instead of fighting back."

"She was making fun of him, so I told him to use reverse psychology to try to get her to stop. You know, make it hard to do the wrong thing and easy to do the right thing."

Claire gave him an odd look. "Will you be using that reverse psychology thing on Phil? You know, make it easy for him to leave, hard to stay?"

"Not a bad idea." And actually, it wasn't, except for the fact that if things got hard, Phil would simply hire someone temporarily to make them easy again.

"Well, I'd better get in there," Claire said.

"Yeah." Brett opened the door, but neither of them moved, until Anne started across the street from her store, toting her own box.

"I think we need to get together and…talk," Claire said in a low voice.

"Probably," Brett conceded. It seemed almost inevitable.

BRETT KNEW HE WAS in trouble when he spent more time thinking about Claire than about his shaky job situation as he drove to Wesley to pick up parts for Phil's flatbed the next day. He wasn't deluding himself into believing Claire wanted a future with him. She wasn't the type to settle on a ranch, he wasn't the type to settle elsewhere, and they were both aware of those facts. No, Claire wanted a challenge, and he was that challenge. And he kind of felt like letting her win.

As long as they were honest. That was the important part. That was the part that had come back to bite him in the ass once before. He never would have hooked up with Des all those years ago if she had been honest with him and told him she was only taking a break from her marriage to Will, not ending it. He might have had issues with Will at the time, but he wouldn't have slept with Des if he'd known she was only using him to get back at her husband.

Claire was different, and now that he knew her, he believed that when things fizzled they'd be capable of maintaining Flynn-Bishop family dynamics in an adult way.

Hell, he was barely part of the family dynamics, anyway.

He was smiling by the time he pulled into Wesley.

CHAPTER ELEVEN

"You'll be done in time for the quilt show."

Claire, who'd been arranging her finished squares on the worktable, looked up in amazement at Gloria's statement. She had just assumed that she'd be excused from the show.

"Oh, I don't think so," she said. The workmanship of her early squares was noticeably amateurish, which was fine with her because it allowed her to see her progress, but that didn't mean she wanted to share it with everyone else in the community.

"You don't have to sell your quilt," Trini pointed out.

"I don't want to display it, either."

"Why not?" Anne demanded.

"I think it's obvious."

"With colors like that, no one will be looking at the craftsmanship, and even if they do, so what?"

Claire took her seat without replying, picked up her work and ran a few stitches onto her needle. She had never in her life publicly displayed anything that was less than her best effort. It was one of the small survival tactics she'd adopted to keep her mother off her back, and by now it was deeply ingrained.

The group fell silent. Claire sewed for a few more minutes, her head down until the silence became overwhelming.

"Oh, all right," she said. "*If* I get done, I'll display." But Arlene would not be getting an invitation.

The session broke up late that evening. As they were approaching the date of the show, these quilting nights were lasting longer. Claire wasn't complaining. She enjoyed her time away from the trailer, which seemed to be getting smaller every day. Still, she had only four more months of trailer life and then she'd be able to walk in more than two directions again.

But although she wouldn't miss her compact home, and she was looking forward to more convenient shopping, she knew she was going to miss her job. Teaching a small class—even one that required a prodigious amount of prep work—was so much more intimate and rewarding than her student teaching had been. And as far as professional freedom went, she was her own boss. She decided how, what, where, when and why. With no one else collecting lesson-plan books, asking for justification, questioning strategy.

On the other hand, she was solely responsible for the achievement scores, so if the kids bombed there was no question about who was to blame. The previous three teachers at Barlow Ridge Elementary hadn't cared. But Claire did. And she hoped with all of her heart that the person who took the job after she left would care, as well.

The school was dark when Claire stopped by on her way home to pick up her grade book so she could work on attendance tallies. They were due the next morning, and she'd completely forgotten, due to the day's impromptu lesson on the Golden Rule. She left her headlights on so she could see to mount the steps, then froze as something moved in the shadows.

"It's just me, Miss Flynn," Toni said as she stepped into the light, her hands shoved deep in her pockets.

"Toni, what are you doing here?"

"I was just out walking. Sometimes I stop and sit on the swings. Like Jesse."

*At nine o'clock in cold weather, when other kids were
curled up with their video games, televisions and iPods.
Yeah.*

"Does your mom know where you are?"

"She doesn't care, as long as I'm back before Deke takes
off for his shift."

"Which is…?"

"Soon. I'd better get going."

"Toni, is everything all right? At home, I mean?"

The girl didn't answer immediately. "Things have been
better."

"Is there anything you need help with?"

"I don't think there's anything that can be helped. I don't
like Deke and my mom does."

"What don't you like about him?" Claire asked carefully, wondering if she had a situation on her hands.

Toni gave her a shrewd look, guessing the exact direction of Claire's thoughts. "He's not being creepy or anything—he's just an ass." Her eyes suddenly widened, as she
realized what she'd just said to a teacher. "What I mean,"
she said quickly, "is that he only thinks about himself. Nobody else. And he wants my mom to do the same thing."

"Which doesn't leave a lot of time for you?"

"I don't need a lot of time."

But she needed some.

"I had a stepfather once who wanted all of my mom's attention," Claire told her. He hadn't lasted long. Arlene was
not a woman who put her husband ahead of her business.

Toni looked interested. "You had a stepfather?"

"Two of them. I really like the one I have now, but the
other…" Claire wrinkled her nose.

"So what did you do?"

"I focused on everything else in my life. Like my

schoolwork," she added with mock sternness. Toni grudgingly smiled. "I closed my bedroom door a lot." She raised her eyebrows before saying gently, "I did *not* go walking around by myself after dark." Even if it was Barlow Ridge, Toni shouldn't be out in the cold alone.

"I should get back," she agreed.

"I'll walk with you."

The girl shook her head. "You don't have to. I'm going straight home. Honest."

Claire believed her. "You can come see me anytime, you know."

"Or I can close my bedroom door and pretend not to hear them fight." Toni smiled slightly, then turned and headed down the empty street.

Kylie reminded Claire a little of Toni and a lot of herself. They thought alike, and had similar tastes, which made it all the more difficult to bypass the purple fabric in favor of black for her quilt border.

"The other quilters said to buy black border fabric."

"I know it'd look cool with black," Kylie said, "but the deep, dark purple is so pretty, and it matches the flowers."

"We'll buy some purple for your quilt."

"You're going to make me a quilt?" Kylie asked happily.

"I'm going to teach you to quilt."

Kylie made a face. "Wouldn't it be easier on both of us if you just *made* me a quilt?"

"Nope."

Kylie huffed dramatically and then pulled the purple bolt from the rack. "How much will I need?"

"I just happen to have the list I followed for my quilt." Claire pulled a sheet of paper from her purse. "And we'll need to pick a few more colors."

"ARE YOU READY for the next game?" Claire asked later, as they piled bolts of fabric on the cutting counter and gave the clerk the list of yardages.

"Very ready," Kylie said. "We play the Spartans again."

"That should be fun," Claire said ironically. Kylie had missed two games after the previous Spartan game because of her injured wrist.

"Yeah. And I have a horse clinic with Dad on the same day, so I'll be busy."

"Kylie, I've got to tell you, horses and basketball are a weird combination."

Kylie tilted her head. "No, they're not. I know lots of kids who do both. Basketball is the only sport we can work into the rodeo schedule."

"Okay, maybe it's not weird here, but everywhere else in the world it is."

"Everywhere else in the world is dumb, then," Kylie said. "So, are you coming to the clinic?"

Claire almost said, *"Yeah, right."* Horses and dust were still not her favorite things. If Kylie wasn't performing, she probably wouldn't be there. "I'll come to the game."

"Phil wanted us to use his stud as a demonstration horse, but Dad won't do it."

"Really. I didn't know your dad knew Phil."

"He's been talking to Dad about training and buying horses and stuff. Dad's hoping Phil'll get smart and sell the stud before it hurts someone."

"I think Brett is hoping the same thing."

Kylie gave Claire a sly look. "Phil's kind of cute, even though he doesn't have a lot of horse sense."

Claire nodded. "Yes. I agree he's on the hunky side." There was no use denying the obvious.

"And Regan thinks he likes you."

"Is that a fact?"

"So, are you…you know."

"What?" Claire asked innocently.

"Are you going to do anything about it?" Kylie asked with a touch of impatience.

"Probably not."

"Why?"

"Because he just doesn't do it for me."

Kylie's mouth dropped open. "Nuh-uh."

"How many cute guys do you know?" Claire asked patiently.

"A lot."

"How many would you date?"

"A lot," Kylie responded with a sassy smile.

"Are there any who are cute but aren't dating material?"

"Yeah."

"Phil's one of those. Cute guy, but I'm not feeling the chemistry."

"But don't you get lonely out there in Barlow?"

"I was when I first moved there, but now…" Claire cocked her head. "It's kind of funny, but I'm not so lonely anymore."

"Regan thought you'd be climbing the walls."

"Is that a direct quote?"

"Mmm, hmm."

"Well, it's different than where I used to live, that's for sure. And I won't mind going back to a city. But I have to admit that there are some things I've found in Barlow that I haven't found elsewhere."

"Like what?"

Like Brett. She couldn't get the guy out of her head, and what's more, she didn't particularly *want* to.

"I've never lived in a place with a strong sense of community before," Claire said, coming up with a truthful answer she could share with her niece.

"Regan says it's like working in a fishbowl. Everyone is watching what you do."

Claire gathered up the neat stack of fabrics the clerk had pushed across the counter toward her. "Am I the topic of many conversations at your house?" she asked her niece mildly.

"A few."

"Good or bad?"

"I plead the fifth."

Claire rolled her eyes, since she'd been the one who'd taught Kylie the phrase during another boyfriend interrogation.

"Do you see Uncle Brett very often?" Kylie asked the question with studied casualness.

"Every now and then. I'll probably see him at your last game."

"I don't think so," Kylie said.

"What makes you think I won't?"

"I, uh, said some things to him when I was angry, and he hasn't been to a game since."

"How bad?" Claire asked flatly, remembering Regan's guess that Kylie had done just that.

"Bad enough, I guess."

"Phil has been keeping him busy," Claire hedged, even though she knew that wasn't exactly true. Phil had been trying to handle things alone. "You might try apologizing."

"Yeah. I've been thinking about that."

They were almost to the car when Kylie said casually, "I got asked to the prom, you know."

"No, I didn't know. Why didn't you tell me sooner?"

Kylie gave her a cheeky grin. "Because it happened about twenty minutes ago, while you were in the fitting room. He called my cell."

"Very classy," Claire said. "Who is it?"

"New guy in school." Kylie swung her shopping bag. "His family comes from Wesley, but he was born in Colorado. Now they've moved back. His dad used to know my dad when they were kids."

"That's cool."

"I thought so." Kylie waited while Claire unlocked the car. "If I apologize to Uncle Brett, will you go prom-dress shopping with me?"

"I promise you, Kylie, there is nothing I like better than prom-dress shopping. But maybe, for safety's sake, we'll bring Regan along this time."

Kylie grinned, clearly remembering her parents' horror at the modestly cut, yet outrageously sequined black dress the two of them had picked out the previous spring. "Yeah. I think that might be good."

ONCE HE'D DECIDED to take up residence in Barlow Ridge, Phil Ryker wasted no time in becoming an active member of the community. He joined the volunteer fire department, having no idea that the local boys didn't particularly want him as a member. He attended the quarterly community board meeting and volunteered for the Chili Feed committee. He showed up at community dinners, ate lunch at the town bar. And in his spare time he ran the ranch—which wasn't all that time-consuming in January—especially since Brett still did all the feeding. Come February, though, when calving started, he'd probably have less free time on his hands, since Brett had every intention of letting Phil share in the responsibilities, all in the name of teaching him what he could expect once he was on his own. The one place Brett didn't want him sharing responsibility was in the round pen.

The headstrong stud was making progress now that Phil had stopped working with him on the sly, but Brett didn't believe a man with Phil's limited abilities had any business bringing such an unpredictable horse into the show ring. Brett was beginning to think that Phil was getting the picture after the stud shied once and slammed him into the arena rails. Phil had been muttering something about the horse being replaceable as he'd limped away.

A few hours later, Brett found out just how serious his boss had been. Phil pulled into the drive with his dog, Toby, sitting in the seat behind him. The dog had a red bandanna tied around his neck. Brett tried not to notice.

"I'm going to be taking off for a few days this Friday," his boss said.

"All right."

"Got a new show prospect."

Brett avoided saying *"It's about time,"* mainly because there was always a chance that this prospect would be worse than the last one had been. "If you want, I'll take a look at him for you," he offered.

Phil flashed his superior smile. "No need. This one's well broke. He's a cutter."

"Are you taking up cutting?" The rich man's arena event.

"I'm considering it. Anyway, I'll be back on Sunday night."

ABOUT THE LAST thing Claire expected after an exhausting day at school was to find Phil Ryker waiting outside, next to her car. His truck was parked across the street, the engine idling. Toby sat in the backseat with a cute bandanna tied around his neck.

"Rough day?" Phil asked as Claire approached.

"Does it show?"

"You're not smiling."

"Not so much rough as exhausting. We're getting ready for achievement tests." And Claire was determined that her kids were going to do themselves proud.

"So what would you think of getting away for a weekend?"

"How so?" she asked cautiously. She and Phil had seen each other a few times after their folksinger date, but to Claire's relief, he'd shown no interest in pursuing anything but a friendship with her. Until now.

"Well, I'm heading over to California to look at a horse." His smile exuded confident charm. "I can offer warm weather, no students, and my parents have a nice guest cottage you could have all to yourself." His expression became more serious. "I know this is last-minute, but I'd like to have company, and you look as if you could use a weekend away. Just friends."

Claire couldn't help but appreciate the offer, even if she had no intention of taking him up on it. "Phil, I can't."

"Are you sure?"

"Yes, I'm sure," she said with a note of apology in her voice, but without an explanation. Explanations led to debate, and Claire wanted to keep her relationship with Phil exactly as it was now. He might be saying "just friends," but weekends away were not usually "just friends" situations. "Thanks for asking, though."

Phil hesitated, as though contemplating tactics, before giving in gracefully. "All right. If you change your mind, I'm not leaving until tomorrow night."

"I'll keep that in mind," Claire said gently. *Now, please...just give it up.* If she spent a weekend with anyone, it was not going to be Phil.

BRETT BOOTED UP the computer Friday morning after tending to Phil's animals. The email he'd been both anticipating and dreading was waiting for him. He pulled in a ragged breath, double clicked the icon and then waited for what seemed like two years for the screen to open.

He'd passed algebra.

A foolish grin spread across his face.

He'd passed algebra with a fairly respectable C. And he'd gotten a B+ in humanities—*Moby Dick, Beowulf* and all.

But he didn't really care about humanities. He'd conquered algebra—and he even understood it. He'd been terrified that it had been a case of too little, too late, and that he'd be ponying up several hundred more dollars in order to take the class again.

Now he could sign up for other classes and torture himself for another semester. He logged on to the site and started perusing the catalog, feeling a hell of a lot more confident than he had the time before.

He signed up for two more classes and logged off, leaning back in his chair and staring at the computer desktop until the screensaver finally popped up.

He owed Claire a thank-you. If she hadn't dropped off the pre-algebra book, hadn't given him a firm push in the right direction, he might still be trying to figure things out. But what kind of thank-you was appropriate?

One from the heart. Claire had had him running scared for most of their short acquaintance, but it was time to admit that, yeah, there was an attraction there and, yeah, maybe he should do something about it. Instead of expecting the worst to happen, as usual, maybe he needed to have some faith in the two of them and their ability to handle things in a civilized way.

Claire liked wine and she liked conversation. He'd start there.

CLAIRE HAD ATTACHED black borders to all her squares and was ready to begin the quilting process, but, regardless of what her fellow quilters said, she knew her masterpiece wouldn't be done in time for the show. And she made the mistake of saying so.

"We're going to get out the frame for you," Anne said grimly.

Claire's head snapped up. "The frame? Is that like a torture device for people who don't get their quilts done in time?"

Trini giggled. "It's a quilting frame. Instead of lap quilting, you'll piece your entire top, then we'll baste it to the batting and backing, put it in the big frame and we'll work together to quilt it."

"But then it won't be all mine."

"No," Gloria said. "It'll be a collaboration of friends."

It was hard to argue with that, so Claire didn't even try. And she liked the warm feeling the simple words brought.

When the women finished for the evening, they decided it was high time for a post-quilting libation, so they locked the community hall, loaded their supplies in their various cars, then walked the two blocks down the street to the saloon.

Marla was alone at the bar. She looked up from a magazine she was reading as the quilters entered the nearly empty establishment and headed, as a group, to the sofas near the propane fire. Claire dropped her coat on a chair and went to order the first round of drinks. It was the least she could do for her fellow quilters, who were going to see to it that her quilt didn't end up as a pile of squares stuffed in a linen closet somewhere. She smiled at Marla and leaned her elbows on the bar.

Marla did not smile back. "You have some nerve coming in here after telling my kid that Deke was no good," the woman hissed.

Claire instinctively recoiled, lifting her elbows back off the bar. Marla had to be talking to someone else, but there *was* no one else. The venomous accusation was aimed at her.

"I never said anything about Deke."

Marla gave her a disbelieving look with narrowed eyes. "Then what did you say?"

"Nothing." Claire was so astounded that she almost stuttered. She could handle confrontation just fine, when she was expecting it, but this was coming out of nowhere.

Marla stepped from behind the bar then, moving to stand directly in front of Claire, her heavily made up eyes fixed on her face. "I don't believe you." She thrust her jaw forward. "Toni wouldn't make up stuff like that, because she knows she'd be in deep shit if she did."

"I don't think Toni made anything up, but I think there's been a misinterpretation." Claire had had enough backpedaling. "Maybe we should talk to Toni?"

"She's doing her homework, and I think you've said enough already. And you'd better damn well watch what you say at school, too, or I'll be filing a harassment claim."

Anne's hand settled firmly on Claire's forearm, startling her, since she hadn't heard the older woman approach. "Come on," she said, her focus on Marla. "We're taking our business elsewhere."

"I want to—" Claire pressed her lips together instead of finishing her sentence. As much as she wanted to straighten out the situation, Marla was not in a mood to listen to reason, and Claire didn't want to get Toni into more trouble. Or give Toni the opportunity to get *her* into more trouble. Claire needed facts before she could proceed. "I think you're right," she said to Anne.

The other quilters had already gathered their purses and coats. Trini handed Claire her belongings, then the other women closed ranks behind her as she and Anne made their way out of the bar into the frigid night air.

"Don't take it personal." Anne muttered the words that Claire had come to think of as the motto of Barlow Ridge as they walked across the street to their cars. "She picks bad boyfriends, then defends them to the death."

"Is he abusive?" Claire asked.

"Deke?" Trini snorted, making Claire feel slightly better. "He's too lazy to be abusive. If Marla kicked him out, he'd starve."

"But he has a job."

"Only because she pushes him out the door at the right time every day, and he doesn't want his pickup repossessed," Deirdre explained. And that was when Claire realized Deirdre had been one of her supporters just now. Either that or she hadn't wanted to be left alone in the bar.

Anne settled a hand on Claire's shoulder. "Marla's a flake, Deke's a lazy bum, and that's just the way things are. There's not a damn thing you can do about it, so don't waste your energy worrying about it."

"What about Toni?"

"Toni will be fine," Trini said. "Honest. She just has to put up with the headache of living with two morons. She's smarter than both of them. Gets it from her real father."

"You're sure?"

"Positive."

But even if Toni was fine, Claire still felt depressed by the confrontation. She didn't know if Toni had lied or Marla had misinterpreted. All she knew was that, once again, she had a situation on her hands—as well as a potential harassment claim and probably a whole lot of rumors.

But at least this time her situation didn't involve the Landaus. It was always good to change things up.

CHAPTER TWELVE

CLAIRE DIDN'T GET home at eight…or nine. Brett was wondering what was taking so long at quilting when he saw headlights turn off Main Street and head down their road. He grabbed the bottle of wine and started across the field to meet her, arriving at the trailer just as she pulled into the drive.

Claire got out of the car. "Brett? Is something wrong?" There was a note of alarm in her voice.

"No. I, uh, just came to see you." Maybe he should have called first. "What happened to you?" Because it was obvious from her distracted demeanor that something had.

"Parent meeting," she said ironically, as she trudged up the stairs.

"Can't get enough of those, can you?" He followed her, planning to deliver his gift and find out what was wrong.

"Apparently not." She concentrated on fitting the key into the lock. "And I think I'm banned from the bar."

Okay.

She tried to turn the key, but it refused to give. She tried again, then rattled the knob in frustration before Brett gently moved her hand, took the key out of the door, turned it over and reinserted it. The lock popped open with one twist.

"Thank goodness for the Y chromosome," she murmured as she pushed the door and preceded him inside. The furnace clicked on as the cold air swirled in after them.

Claire adjusted the thermostat. "It'll warm up fast in here. It's the one great thing about living in a tin can— it's cozy." She hugged her coat around her in a self-protective way.

"Yeah. Cozy." Brett reached out to push wisps of blond hair away from her cheek, feeling protective, wanting to make things better for her. Thinking that he'd like to know what the hell was going on. "You want to tell me what happened tonight?"

"Marla thinks I bad-mouthed Deke to Toni, and she kicked me out of the bar." Claire shrugged out of her coat and draped it over the back of the sofa. "It bothers me, because I wouldn't do something that unprofessional. But word travels fast in a small town, so I'm probably as good as guilty. And Marla also threatened to file a harassment claim. Mr. Rupert is going to love that."

"I don't think she'll file a claim. It takes too much energy."

"You think?" Claire moistened her lips.

"I'm pretty damn certain."

"Then I'm glad you picked tonight to come calling. Otherwise, I probably wouldn't have slept much." And then she noticed he'd not only come calling, he'd come bearing a gift. All that was missing was the wilted bouquet of daisies. "You brought wine."

"Yes."

"*You* brought wine," she repeated.

He couldn't help smiling. "Yes."

"I already feel better," she said dryly. Then she cocked her head. "*Why* have you brought wine?"

"To thank you." The smile was still plastered on his face, albeit a little self-consciously. "I passed the algebra class."

There was a long beat of silence, as if she couldn't quite

grasp what he was saying, and then she smiled for real. A Claire smile. "I knew you would."

"At least one of us did."

"Would you like to open that bottle?" Claire asked, stepping out of her shoes. "I could use a glass. Or two."

"Sure."

She walked into the kitchen in her stocking feet and pulled a fancy contraption out of a drawer. Brett gave it a skeptical look. "Do you need to have a license to run that thing?"

"I'll do it." She reached for the wine, but he stopped her, his hand covering hers as he gently eased the bottle away.

"I can figure it out. That Y chromosome, you know." He proved his point by flipping the corkscrew into working position over the bottle.

Claire edged past him in the tiny kitchen and opened a cupboard. "So what now?" she asked as she stretched up on her toes to pull two wineglasses down from the second shelf.

"I signed up for another math class, before I forget everything, and biology 1. It's going to take about ten years to get a degree this way, but at least I'm chipping away at it."

"Hey," she said softly, "you have a goal. You're working toward it. That's commendable." She set the glasses on the counter as he eased the handles of the corkscrew together, pulling the cork smoothly out of the bottle. He poured a healthy quantity of wine for each of them.

Claire raised her glass to touch his with a musical clink. "I'm glad you're here. On many levels."

"I'm glad I'm here, too." It felt good. Natural.

And it still felt natural when she took him by the hand and led him out of the kitchen to the sofa, pulling him down to sit beside her. "Sorry about the rant," she said as they settled in.

"You're entitled. Marla is kind of a nut, you know."

"Kind of?"

"And the people here like you."

"Most of them," she agreed. She touched her glass to his again, and then they sat in silence, shoulders and thighs touching as they sipped wine and stared at the faded wood paneling on the opposite wall.

"I'm kind of picturing a crackling fireplace over there," Claire murmured after several minutes. "What are you picturing?"

"Waves on the beach." He stretched his arm out along the back of the sofa and she let her head rest against it.

"So what's changed?" she asked softly. "You're here and all of your barriers are down. I barely recognize you."

He didn't feign ignorance. The vibes humming between them were too strong. "I'm ready to admit we're consenting adults."

"You've finally quit worrying about Will beating the snot out of you if you hurt my feelings?"

Brett smiled, not altogether surprised she'd figured that one out. "That, too."

She set her wineglass on the end table and shifted position, pulling one foot up under her. "So you just suddenly came to this realization?"

"I lied before. I do get lonely." He reached for her hand and interlocked his fingers with hers.

"We all get lonely," Claire said, leaning closer, her lips grazing his cheek and then the corner of his mouth. "It's just that some of us do something about it."

"That's what I'm doing now," he said, turning his head

to gently nip her full lower lip. She touched her forehead to his.

"May I say, it's about time?"

CLAIRE BEGAN UNBUTTONING Brett's shirt, half expecting him to come to his senses and stop her, but when her fingers fumbled, he set his wine on the end table and undid the remaining buttons himself.

Okay, this is a good sign.

And he was a beautiful man, lean yet well muscled.

She smoothed her palms over his chest, pushing the fabric of his shirt away from his shoulders. His stomach muscles contracted with the action. They were rock hard, as were other parts of him. She pressed a kiss to his pectorals, circled his nipple with her tongue. His hand buried itself in her hair as she circled the other nipple. He caught his breath, then eased her away from him, kissing her deeply while trying to undo the square pearl buttons on her sweater with one hand. He got the first one undone, awkwardly, and then another, more smoothly this time. Finally, the third and fourth buttons popped open, revealing the swell of her breasts. He traced the tips of his fingers over her exposed flesh as he continued to kiss her.

"You're beautiful."

"So are you," she whispered.

He smiled at her as he pulled back, but then his expression grew serious. "I don't have anything to offer you."

She couldn't repress a small surprised laugh. "Like what?" she asked. No one had ever made a qualifying speech to her before making love. Especially an old-fashioned one about offering things.

"Like anything."

"Maybe I don't want anything." And maybe she did. She wasn't sure, but time would tell. "If you're trying to say this is a no-strings deal that does not involve our siblings and will *never* involve them, trust me, I understand and agree."

She took hold of his belt buckle with both hands, letting her fingers slide between metal and muscle as she whispered, "So please, just shut up and make love to me."

She didn't have to ask twice.

Claire had never been touched so reverently before, had never felt such a shared sense of lust and tenderness.

When he entered her, it hurt a little, because it had been a long time since she'd made love. But he stilled and waited for her to adjust, without asking if she wanted to stop. He could probably read the answer to that question in her eyes.

She wrapped her arms around him, cupping his head with her palm and smoothing the fingers of her other hand over his spine, and then he began to move.

They made love silently, lost in each other. It was over far too soon.

Afterward, Brett lay on his back, his arm around her as she curled against his side. She'd known it would be this good, but she wondered if Brett had been prepared. From the way he was focused on the ceiling tile above them, a frown drawing his brows together, she had the feeling he hadn't been.

She stirred, and his arm tightened protectively, pulling her closer, but she wasn't fooled. He might want to protect her, but he wasn't comfortable to have her so near. He was already shutting down.

Maybe he'd been solitary for too long, or maybe there was some other reason he had trouble letting himself get close to someone else. Whatever it was, she eased away from him, allowing him his retreat, knowing it was the only thing she could do.

A moment later he sat up and swung his legs around

so that he was sitting on the edge of the bed. Claire resisted the urge to reach out and run a hand over the corded muscles of his back. Instead, she tucked an arm under her head and waited for the farewell speech she knew he was working on. But Brett remained silent. He sat, gripping the mattress on either side of his thighs, staring out the darkened window, and Claire decided that she might as well be the one to set the wheels in motion. She knew this was not the time for analysis or a speech. They both needed a little space, a little time to figure out where they wanted this thing to go.

She got out of bed, pulled her kimono off the brass hook on the back of the bedroom door and slipped it on, cinching the waist. Then she picked up Brett's jeans and held them out to him, her finger through a single belt loop.

"It's late," she said, "and we both need some thinking time."

He looked both surprised and relieved.

He took the jeans without a word, dressing quickly, his movements precise. She walked out to the living room with him and waited while he put on his shirt and coat.

He turned toward her, looked as if he wanted to say something, but Claire was having none of that. The less said, the better for now. It was best that things be left unspoken than to say something that would be regretted later. She cupped his face, gave him a quick, soft kiss, then put a hand on his back and propelled him to the door. He went quietly.

"Are you—"

She put her fingertips to his lips, effectively shushing him.

"Don't ruin things, Brett. I'm fine."

And I hope you are, too.

BRETT'S LIVE-FOR-THE-MOMENT evening had not gone as planned.

During the chilly walk home, he told himself repeatedly that this was no different than any other time he'd gone to bed with a willing woman. Except for her connection to his brother.

But everything about it felt different.

Maybe if they hadn't been so good together, maybe if he hadn't realized just how tenderly he felt toward her, he wouldn't feel so damned guilty. But he did. He was lying to her, lying to himself and lying to the world.

His gut told him that if he and Claire continued on this track, things could get serious, and then he would owe her the truth. But how fair would it be to Will to tell yet another person the secret? As it was, only Regan knew the truth. On the other hand, how fair was it to Claire to continue as they were without telling her? Was it not entirely possible that what he was feeling was one-sided? Claire was attracted to him, yes, but that didn't mean she wanted anything serious. In fact, she'd pretty much indicated the opposite.

He stomped the snow from his feet before stepping into his kitchen. Sarina opened her yellow eyes and blinked at him before narrowing them again, feigning sleep as she laid her chin on her front paws.

Brett crossed over to the fridge and pulled out a beer, suddenly glad that Claire had handed him his pants and sent him on his way. He could not remember another time in his life—other than his disastrous experience with Des—when sleeping with a woman had given him so damn much to think about.

And he really hoped he was overreacting.

CLAIRE DROVE TO Wesley on Sunday just to get out of the house, clear her head. Brett had been right about one thing—having her sister married to his brother was a bit of a complication. So she wouldn't be discussing Brett with Regan. But there were a host of other things, like Marla, that she could talk about. And besides that, she just wanted to spend time with her sister. It had been awhile.

"Have you heard from Mom?" Regan asked as soon as she answered Claire's knock.

"Not since last Saturday." Claire stopped just inside the door. "You've been painting." Regan had been slowly refurbishing Will's old ranch house, and the kitchen walls, once a boring off-white, were now a warm apricot.

"I'm making curtains next."

"When the homemaking bug bit you, it bit hard," Claire commented, taking the cup of tea Regan had brewed for her.

"Look who's talking—the queen of quilting."

Claire laughed. "If you could see my quilt, you'd demand my crown back. The colors are good, but some of the squares look like I did my sewing in the dark. The other women helped me put it together yesterday, and we've started quilting it." And it had been fun working around the big frame—almost like an Amish quilting bee, except that the conversation had been a bit on the raunchy side. Another good thing had come out of the quilting session, too. Claire now knew that her fellow quilters believed she hadn't bad-mouthed Deke. If rumors circulated, they'd do their part to set them straight.

"I can't wait to see this quilt." Regan set a plate of shortbread in the middle of the table, then took a seat opposite her sister.

"It'll be on display at the show," Claire said fatalistically.

"But I might miss it. There's a conference in Las Vegas at about that time, and I'm going to go visit Mom. In person. There's something going on."

Claire took a bite of shortbread. "Like…?"

"I tried to call her at work this week, when I couldn't get her at home. Her associate said she wouldn't be in for several days."

"Mom, shirking her duty?"

"I knew we should have insisted on a medical checkup," Regan said, before stirring sugar into her tea.

"Do you think she's working on reconciling with Stephen?"

Regan shook her head and set the spoon on a saucer. "I finally got a hold of her at home. She said she was taking a few days off, but when I asked some questions she said she didn't have to clear her decisions with us."

Claire snorted. "I remember saying the same thing to her once and getting grounded."

"I asked about Stephen, thinking that maybe they were working things out, but she told me he's still in San Diego and has no intention of moving back to Las Vegas."

Claire brushed the crumbs off her fingertips, frowning in concern. "You don't think Mom is home nursing a broken heart, do you?"

Regan debated for a moment. "I didn't get that impression. But she was definitely sidestepping."

"Maybe a health crisis she's not telling us about?"

"She swore she wouldn't keep anything like that secret."

Claire pushed her plate aside and reached for her teacup. "Maybe now that we've been such major disappointments, Mom's gone off the deep end?"

"That's closer to what I was afraid of, but..." Regan's mouth tightened. "I called Stephen. Damned if he isn't being as evasive as she is."

"So, it's over, but he's covering for her?"

"As weird as it sounds, that's what I think."

"Maybe they don't need our help, Reg."

"I just hope they aren't doing anything illegal."

Claire laughed. "Hey, not to change the subject, but I'm supposed to firm up a prom-dress shopping date with Kylie, and I was thinking about the first Saturday in March." She got up to pour more hot water into her cup. She lifted the pot in Regan's direction, but her sister shook her head. "You're coming along, aren't you?"

"After last time, yes."

"There was nothing wrong with that dress," Claire said defensively. "It was practically a turtleneck."

"I think it was the sequins and the way it fit," Regan remarked dryly. "And the first Saturday in March works fine for me. We'll have fun."

"So, does Will approve of *this* boy?" Claire asked, dunking her tea bag. Kylie had yet to have a boyfriend Will wholeheartedly approved of. Even that cute Shane kid hadn't received full marks.

"Will grew up with this one's dad, but I haven't figured out if that's helping or hindering. I guess they dated some of the same girls in high school and competed against each other in rodeo."

"Montagues and Capulets?" Claire asked.

Regan grinned. "Not quite. Honestly, I think the only thing Will has against the kid is that he's another boy interested in his daughter."

"I guess that's a dad's job," Claire said. "Which is why I was so glad that Mom was between husbands while I was in high school."

"Weren't you lucky?" Regan asked sarcastically.

"Very," Claire said with an air of self-satisfaction. "And when I wasn't, I had you to help bail me out." She reached across the table to pat her sister's hand. "Thanks."

JESSE'S DAD WAS sitting alone at a table in the corner of the bar when Brett dropped by to pick up a sandwich on his way home from Wesley. He ordered his lunch, debated for a moment, then ambled over. "Hi," he said to the wary-looking man. "You're Jesse's dad, right?"

"Right."

Brett stayed planted where he was, close to the table, until the seated man took the hint.

"You wanna sit down?"

"Yeah." Brett pulled out a chair.

"I'm Tom," the man said. "But you probably know that."

Brett didn't know how he would have known, since *Tom* had never spoken to him before.

"Brett Bishop."

"I know." Tom studied his hands for a moment. They were beaten up, red and covered in a rash. Not exactly a salesman's hands. "Jesse likes working for you. Thanks for letting him do that."

"I like Jesse."

The man's eyes flashed at Brett's tone, which was more pointed than he'd intended. But now that he thought about it, the guy deserved to be challenged. He had never taken the time to meet or find out anything about the man his son was spending so much time with. For all he knew, Brett could be some kind of a deviant.

"I like him, too," Tom muttered defensively.

"You're his father."

"Yeah." Tom pushed his drink in a small circle, leaving a trail of moisture on the table. "But he's only been with me for about a year. It's a learning curve."

"Divorce?"

"We were never married. Jesse's mom left me while she was pregnant, and moved in with her grandmother. Then she moved on altogether and her grandmother raised Jesse on her own."

"So you didn't have contact?"

"Not much, and I'm not exactly proud of that." Tom frowned as he focused on the drink again. "But I wasn't living a kid-oriented life, either."

Sometimes you change your life when you have a kid....

But Brett hadn't, so he was in no position to cast stones. He'd run away from fatherhood, too.

"I know what you're thinking," Tom continued in a low voice, talking more to the table than to Brett. He looked tired. "Before Jesse was born I was a chemistry major, but then I lost my scholarships and quit school. I had some problems." He twisted his mouth. "I had some problems with depression and I couldn't focus. I kinda gave up."

"You never went back to school?"

He shook his head. "I kicked around from job to job. Didn't really matter, since it was just me. Then Jesse's grandma went into the rest home and suddenly I'm responsible for a kid. And I wasn't exactly rolling in dough."

"So you came here?"

"Free place to live. I have my sales route and I've been working to expand it. I'm kinda piecing a life together."

"That's good," Brett said. He was surprised the man was letting go with so much information—until it dawned on him that maybe Tom still wasn't over his depression. Or maybe he felt another one coming on, which could explain why he looked so tired.

Maybe he was trying to set things up so there'd be someone to look out for Jesse, if that happened.'

"You know," Brett said, "I'd be happy to let Jesse stay with me for a while, if you ever had an extended route or anything."

Tom Lane's jaw shifted sideways as he studied Brett. "Yeah. I'll keep that in mind." He pushed his chair back. "I'd better be going. School's out soon and I'm not usually here this early. Don't want to miss the kid."

Tom went to the bar and paid his tab, counting out the exact amount and not leaving a tip, giving Brett the feeling that he didn't have a lot of money to waste on a drink in the afternoon.

Maybe Brett should have picked up the tab—for Jesse's sake.

IT WAS NEARLY ten o'clock when the phone rang, and Brett caught it on the second ring, hoping it was Claire. He wanted to talk to her, even if he hadn't worked out what to say.

But it wasn't Claire—it was Phil, sounding panicked. "I need some help."

"Calving?" What else, this time of year? But then, with Phil, it could be as minor as a stopped-up drain,

No such luck.

"The cow's having some kind of problem."

"Be right there."

Five minutes later Brett pulled open the barn door. The cow was down, obviously in distress. Phil was staring at her from the wrong side of the pen.

"How long has she been straining like this?" Brett asked, grabbing the disinfectant off the shelf before he climbed over the rails and dropped to the other side. The cow didn't even roll an eye his way.

"I don't know."

Brett started applying the disinfectant to both himself and the business end of the exhausted cow. "What do you mean, you don't know? You put her in the barn when she went into labor." Just as Brett had told him to do with the heifers. "Haven't you been checking on her?"

"I didn't think she'd have any problems. She's in a warm, dry place and she's out of the weather."

A heifer having her first calf out of a big bull. And Phil didn't think there'd be any problems that a warm, dry place wouldn't solve. Ignorance was bliss—unless you were a heifer in trouble. Brett set aside the disinfectant and slowly eased his hand in to analyze the situation.

"Were you home?" he asked as he came into contact with a nose and a bent back front leg, which he gently worked into a better position.

"Close."

"What in the hell does that mean?"

"I was at Claire's place."

"And did you think the damn cow was going to call you if she had trouble?" Brett snapped, forcing himself to ignore the surge of jealousy that had just shot through him. "Get the chains," he said through gritted teeth. The heifer was obviously too exhausted to finish delivering this big baby on her own.

"The chains?"

"There." He pointed to the smooth stainless steel chains that hung near the pen. "Get them and get in here." A few minutes later he had a chain slipped over each fetlock, just above the calf's hooves. He handed the top one to Phil. "First, I pull, and when I get the bottom shoulder through the pelvis, I'll hold that leg in place and then you pull. But remember, we work *with* the cow, not against her."

Phil turned pale.

By the time the calf was delivered—alive, but barely—and the afterbirth had followed, Phil looked as if he might puke. Brett wanted to ask him how the hell he thought baby calves came into the world, and how he was going to handle his first prolapsed uterus, but he was too tired and angry to waste the time. He rubbed the calf with a towel and waited for the cow to recover.

Eventually the mother heaved herself to her feet and started showing interest in her weak little offspring, first sniffing and then licking it.

"I think we'd better tube the baby," Brett said. "Make sure it gets its colostrum."

"You mean, stick a tube…"

"Down its throat and into its stomach." Brett tilted his cap back. "How are you at milking?"

As it turned out, Phil wasn't all that great at milking, but the mama was cooperative, so Brett made him do it, anyway. Once the calf was tubed and showing signs of life, Brett zipped up his coat and started for the door. "You should probably check the other heifers before you go to bed. And keep an eye on this calf. We'll probably tube him again tomorrow, unless he's up and sucking."

"Yeah."

"Hey, this is one of sixty," Brett said, and then he headed for his truck.

It was only nine-thirty, but it felt like midnight. Brett was tired, mentally and physically.

And he still wanted to talk to Claire.

BRETT DID NOT run into Claire by accident, and they both knew it. She was coming out of the post office with a letter in her hand when he emerged from the bar, where he'd been waiting for her.

"I hear Phil experienced his first birth," she said when she realized he was heading directly for her and not the post office.

"Yes. He's probably an old hand at cow obstetrics by now," Brett said, thinking word had gotten to Claire mighty fast.

She smiled distantly, so he got to the point.

"I'd like to talk about…us." It felt so strange to say that word.

"Are you sure?" She tapped the letter against her leg.

"Yes," he said with a touch of impatience. He did. "I would have talked the other night, but you kicked me out."

"I kicked you out because you didn't want to be there."

"That isn't true," he said, even though he knew it was. He'd been uncertain as to his next move, and escape had seemed a reasonable option.

"Then next time you can stay," Claire said in that maddeningly calm way she had.

"Hey, Brett! Miss Flynn!"

They both turned as Jesse came pedaling up on his bike, Ramon balancing on the rear pegs.

"Brett, can Ramon come over and help with chores today?"

"Sure. Maybe I can even find a few extra chores for another guy, if he wanted to earn some cash."

Ramon smiled broadly and gave a big nod.

"We can go right now, if you want," Jesse said.

"I'll meet you there in a few minutes." He waited until the boys had pedaled away before looking at Claire.

"Can I come by tonight?"

"Sure," she said. "Any time you want." She gave him a brief smile, then turned and started walking back down the street to the school.

THE LETTER WAS WRINKLED. Claire had clutched it too tightly when she'd been talking to Brett, and now she smoothed it out on her kitchen table and read it again.

Apparently her decision to get real-world experience was going to pay off, because due to that experience she had been invited to take part in a two-year research project in conjunction with her graduate studies.

She'd originally planned to write a thesis on combined-classroom education in an urban setting, collecting data from the few schools that were experimenting with the idea, but she'd now be involved in a major study researching the same topic, working under one of her former professors who'd just received grant funding. She'd be helping to make decisions concerning class setups, age combinations, curriculum. It was an academic dream come true.

So why wasn't she more excited?

Because she was tired? Because she'd been away from college for a while and liked her job? Because she was falling in love with Brett Bishop?

All of the above?

She carefully folded the letter and put it back into the envelope.

All of the above.

CHAPTER THIRTEEN

BRETT DID NOT get a chance to talk to Claire. Phil made certain of that by calling with two more heifer emergencies. After the second young cow delivered on her own and was protectively tending to her calf, Brett looked at his watch. Twelve-thirty. Even if Claire was still up, he was too tired to have a decent discussion.

"There's more to this than I thought," Phil said, sluicing his hands in a bucket of cold water.

"Yeah." Brett fixed his tired eyes on his boss's face. "Wait until your first C-section."

"How do you know when you have to…?"

"Experience," Brett said quietly. "Unfortunately, you can kill cows and calves getting it." And Phil had expensive registered cows.

Phil nodded and leaned on the fence.

"You know," Brett said, "I'm going to have to get a job elsewhere." Wesley, if he could swing it. Elko, if he had to. Maybe one of the mines, even though he had no experience with heavy equipment. He was determined to stay in the area until Kylie graduated. He might not be able to claim her, but he was going to watch her finish growing up—from a distance, if necessary. "I can't get by on half a paycheck and still make payments on the homestead." And there were no other jobs in Barlow to supplement his income. Nothing dependable, anyway.

Phil hooked his fingers over the top rail of the fence,

focusing on the first calf born that night, which was now vigorously punching its mother's udder with its nose. "I hate to lose you, but it doesn't make sense to have two of us running the place."

"Nope. Not at all," Brett agreed, his heart somewhere near the top of his boots.

Phil turned to him, once again the businessman instead of the cowboy. "You are staying until June 1, aren't you?"

"I told you I would."

"I'll give you full pay until then. After that…" Phil's eyes went back to the cow and calf. "I'll have a better idea as to what I plan to do."

Brett nodded and headed for the door.

He had a feeling Phil was going to keep him on, that he was already figuring out that running a small ranch took a lot of work and there was a sharp learning curve. But nothing was ever certain with Phil, so Brett was going to have to live with an *un*certain future for another three and a half months, which was nothing new. It was the cowboy way of life.

So where was Brett? Did he think pulling a no-show was going to change things, make her start to think he wasn't worth wasting time over?

No, Claire thought, as she turned off the kitchen light before padding down the narrow trailer hallway to her bedroom, hurrying her steps just a little as she passed the washer in the dark. He wasn't the kind of guy to play games like that. Probably another calving problem and he was too busy to call. Phil's barn lights were on, so the theory made sense.

And she didn't mind that Brett hadn't stopped by, since she knew his mission. He was going to distance himself. Claire was still debating about how she was going to handle the situation. Should she let him go quietly or put up a tussle? She'd never dealt with a matter like this before—one where a man was walking away before she was done with him.

Claire Flynn, who'd never been able to settle on anything—career, hobby or man—felt as if she might have found a guy she wanted to stick with.

Now it was just a matter of convincing him it was a good idea.

BRETT WAS MAKING coffee the next morning, debating about his future and wondering if he should discuss the matter with Will at Kylie's game that day, when a rap sounded at his kitchen door. The top of Jesse's blond head was just visible through the window, and Brett immediately crossed the room to pull the door open. The Christmas bike lay carelessly abandoned on its side near the front porch.

"What's wrong?" Brett instantly asked. Jesse never dropped his bike.

"What happens if I can't come and do chores for Sarina's cat food anymore?" The boy blurted the question, his face close to crumpling, and Brett's heart gave an uneven thump.

"Why wouldn't you be able to do that?"

"I think we're going to move."

Another unpleasant jolt shot through Brett's chest. "You're moving?" Damn it, he didn't want Jesse to move.

"Yeah. And I can't bring Sarina."

"I'll keep her," Brett said automatically. "Where're you moving to?"

"Dunno. Some valley. Smoky Valley?"

"That's a ways away." And sparsely populated.

"I don't want to go."

"Are you moving because of your dad's job?" Although

Brett didn't see how, unless Tom Lane had hired on at a remote mine site.

"I don't know. My dad don't talk much anymore." Jesse pulled in a shaky breath. "And he didn't come home last night. I wasn't afraid to be alone, because of the dogs, but I was afraid that something had happened to him. And then when he came home early this morning, he said we were moving."

The kid was on the verge of tears. Brett had no idea what to do, so he went with his gut and knelt down, holding Jesse the way he wished his own dad would have held him after his mom had died. Finally Jesse stepped back, brushing his cheeks with the backs of his hands and then wiping his nose on his sleeve.

"The next time your dad doesn't come home, you call me, okay?"

"But I don't want to get him in trouble."

"I won't get him in trouble, Jess. I'll just come and stay with you or bring you here so you won't be alone. Okay?" Brett brushed the remaining tears from under the boy's eyes with the pad of his thumb. "Promise?"

Tears clung to Jesse's pale lashes. "Promise," he said solemnly. "I'm sorry I cried."

"What's wrong with crying?" Brett asked gruffly. "Everybody cries."

"Really?" he asked softly.

"Really," Brett said. "So what do you say we skip chores today and go over to the ranch. Phil needs some help with his calves."

"All right," Jesse said, wiping the back of his hand over his cheek again.

Even though he was supposed to go to the basketball finals that afternoon and watch Kylie play, Brett couldn't bring himself to abandon Jesse, so he stayed home and let Jesse help him first with chores and then with his biology homework. The boy tried to put on a brave face, but he was still upset about leaving, anxious about his cat and worried about being alone.

Finally, in the late afternoon, he told Brett his dad wanted him home by dinner. Brett refrained from asking Jesse who did the cooking. He had a feeling he knew the answer. He offered a ride home, but Jesse refused, and Brett's heart squeezed tight as he stood on the porch and watched him ride away.

If the kid moved, it was going to leave a big hole in Brett's life—which startled him, considering the fact that Jesse had only been *in* his life for all of five or six months. And he hated the idea of him living somewhere faraway, with no one there if his nut job of a father decided not to come home.

But there was absolutely nothing he could do about it.

LATELY, CLAIRE SEEMED to be spending most of her daytime hours at the school, and if the quilt display racks didn't start going together any faster, she'd probably be spending her nights there, too. But at least it gave her something to think about other than Brett.

The quilt show was being held over the long President's Day weekend. In addition to the display at the school, there was a barbeque dinner at the community hall, and the Wesley antique car club was putting on a small rally in spite of the fact that there was still snow on the ground.

"Something for everyone," Bertie said as she and Claire worked to assemble the wooden frames. "The campground is completely booked with RVs and lots of people will drive out just for the quilt raffle and the rally." She smiled wryly as she finished twisting a wing nut onto a screw. "We're quaint out here, you know, so people come for the day."

"Are they honestly going to get the lights hooked up over the quilts?" she asked. The school gym was dim, but Anne had promised light and rarely failed to deliver.

"The volunteer firemen are going to do it for us. Oh, look," Bertie added, "here comes the chief now."

But it wasn't the chief who walked into the gym, exuding charm and confidence. It was Phil, totally unaware that people were poking fun at him for cluelessly insinuating himself into an organization that was known for closing its ranks to outsiders. The firemen had no choice but to accept him, since he was landlord to many of them, but that didn't mean they liked it. Phil was oblivious.

"Hi, Phil," Claire called. She had a soft spot for the man, in spite of his self-importance. He simply didn't understand how the people in this town thought. In fact, he'd have been appalled if he knew *what* they thought of him. "Are you here to solve our light problem?"

"I'm here to take a look," he answered with a wink.

The man who'd come in with him rolled his eyes but said nothing.

"'Bout time," Anne grumbled, easing herself down off the stage. "Here. I've drawn up a plan."

Bertie took Claire's screwdriver out of her hand as the two men approached Anne. "We're going home," she said in a low voice. "It's late." She gestured toward the exit. "Quick. Before Anne sees us."

CLAIRE DID NOT go home. Instead, she went to Brett's house. It was time.

He didn't answer the knock on the door, but she heard noises coming from the barn, and she found him there, moving items around in the tack room. He turned, holding a saddle in one hand, looking every inch the hot cowboy and causing Claire's stomach to fill with butterflies as she remembered just *how* hot he'd been a few nights ago.

He'd been an amazing lover, tender and giving, yet demanding enough to bring an edge to things. And she knew he'd been surprised by his own response to her, which was part of the reason he'd shut down that night. They'd both gotten more than they'd expected.

He carried the saddle across the room and settled it on a wall-mounted rack, pushing it into place.

"I'm sorry I didn't make it over like I promised," he said.

"No problem." She wanted to step closer, touch him, but his body language made it clear that wouldn't be welcome. She ran her hand down the reins of a bridle hanging next to her, barely feeling the leather as it slipped between her fingers.

"The other night felt like more than just a one-time occurrence, didn't it?" she murmured.

"Yes."

"Does that bother you?"

"It raises issues," Brett said truthfully.

Claire studied him for a moment, trying to read the expression in his dark eyes before she said, "This is new territory for me, too. I'm more of a hit-and-run girl, but… I'm not ready to run yet."

She hoped she was imagining the color draining from his face, and she did her best to make things right. "It takes two, Brett, and if this isn't what you want then I'd like to stay friends."

He rubbed the tips of his fingers over his forehead. "I don't think we should sleep together—at least not until I work through a few things. That's what I wanted to tell you when I asked to come over."

"All right."

He gave a brief smile. "You could at least do my ego some good and fight me a little."

She took a step closer. "That's a mixed message, Brett. Very ineffective communication."

"I've never been all that good at communication, which is why I'm usually in so much trouble." She was close enough for him to reach out, touch her, but he didn't.

"I think you have some talents in that area that you may be underrating."

"And I think if I spend a lot of time with you, I'm never going to work through anything." He folded his arms. "Before we slept together, I thought we could fill a few evenings, have some fun. Go on with our lives, you know?"

She knew. She'd thought the same thing.

"I thought we'd just be two lonely people helping each other out."

"I think we were more like two horny people, helping each other out."

He laughed and it was a good sound, even if it was gone too soon. Claire's smile faded. "So what you're saying is that things have the potential to get more serious than you intended, and you need some time."

"That's what I'm saying."

"Okay. I can live with that."

Brett tipped his hat back. "Did you know Jesse was moving?"

"Actually, that's part of the reason I came over. He told me today."

Brett pushed another saddle farther back on its rack. "I worry about him. I met his dad at the bar, and I think I see a problem there." He quickly filled her in on the meeting.

"Unfortunately, there's nothing you can do about it."

"I know."

"You've been good for Jesse."

"I'll miss him." Brett swallowed, and Claire realized that Jesse's departure was going to be even harder on him than she'd imagined.

"You know," she said, "nothing in Barlow Ridge has turned out the way I thought it would."

"Amen to that," he muttered.

"But," she continued, as she took a few steps toward the door, "it still turned out right. Sometimes you just have to have faith."

BRETT SPENT A lot of time thinking about Claire that evening, amazed how when he was with her he could almost believe that maybe, magically, things could work out. Until he tried to come up with the words to tell her what he'd done so many years ago.

There was no way to sugarcoat the situation, and no way to continue seeing Claire, with whom he was halfway in love, without explaining. If he was serious about her, he'd have to come clean, but before he confessed to anything, he was going to get Will's permission. And for all he knew, his brother might not give it—not when it involved Kylie's peace of mind.

So what to do?

Brett was no closer to an answer the following day, when he drove to Wesley to stock up. He had just left the shopping center late that afternoon with about a month's worth of groceries when his phone rang. It crackled when he answered it, but he recognized Regan's voice.

"Great, I got you," she said. "Anne McKirk called, and she has a list of lighting supplies and general hardware she needs. Some quilt-show emergency, and she knew you were in town. Do you have a pencil?"

Brett glanced around the truck. No. And he didn't have

anything to write on, except a cereal box. "Do you have a list?"

"Boy, do I."

"How about I swing by your place and get it."

"Meet you there in ten minutes. Will just picked me up at school."

Brett was at the place in five. He'd intended to cool his heels on the porch and wait, but Kylie was home. She pushed the door open.

"I thought you were coming to the game," she said without a hello.

"Something came up."

Her eyes, so like his own, were hooded as she studied him, one hand still on the screen door.

"You want to come in?" It sounded like a dare.

"No," he said, spotting Will's truck down the road. "I'll be leaving in a second."

"You always do."

"Do what?" he asked.

"Leave. Either that or you don't show up." Her tone was more scathing than he'd ever heard—even after the big curfew incident. She sounded almost hateful.

"Maybe there's a reason I leave," he said, trying to think on his feet.

"You might have a reason *now*." Kylie emphasized the last word coldly. "But what I don't understand is why you left me in the first place. Didn't feel like having a kid?"

Brett's mouth went dry. She knew. He'd always wondered, but now he had the answer.

"Is that why you abandoned me and my mom? Left my dad to marry her and take over?"

She must have pieced the story together herself, since she didn't have the whole truth. Damn, he didn't want her to have the whole truth.

What a mucked-up mess.

He swallowed dryly. "You need to talk to your dad," he said, as the truck turned into the long drive. It felt like the coward's way out, but Brett owed it to Will to allow him to tell Kylie the truth in the way he thought best.

"No," she said adamantly. "I am not going to hurt him by doing that. I just wanted to tell you that I *know* what you did."

"You may not know everything."

"I know enough." She pressed her lips together, but her eyes never left his. "My boyfriend's parents used to rodeo with you."

"And...?" Brett prompted grimly.

"His sister heard them talking. About you and Dad and my mother. It wasn't a very nice story, but she thought I should know."

"Why would you believe it?" Brett asked softly.

"Because the facts fit," Kylie said bluntly, as Will pulled his truck to a stop next to Brett's rig. "And don't you dare talk to my dad about this." She stepped back into the house, letting the screen door bang before turning to speak through the screen. "And you know what? I kinda wish you'd quit hanging around, *Uncle* Brett. I really liked it better when you were gone." The wooden door closed in his face.

"I'm glad we caught you," Regan said seconds later as she came up the steps, looking so much like Claire it almost hurt to see her. "Anne says to put it on her account."

Brett squinted at the list, trying not to appear shell-shocked. "This'll take some time."

"Is something wrong?" Regan asked.

He glanced up, attempting to act normal. As if he'd ever feel normal again. "No. Just the usual stuff with Phil."

"What's going on with Phil?" Will asked, putting a hand on his wife's shoulder.

"He's trying to handle calving on his own, which means I spend most of my time rushing over there and saving the day. I think *he* thinks he's handling it alone." Brett held up the list. "He's in charge of lighting, too."

Brett had no idea how the words kept coming out in such a normal tone.

Regan laughed. "I wish I could attend the big weekend."

"You aren't?"

"I'm going to Las Vegas for a meeting that Saturday, and I'm going to try to pin down my mother while I'm there. Will and Kylie may drive out, though."

Somehow, Brett doubted that.

"I don't suppose you have time to come in for a minute?" Regan asked. Brett answered with a shake of his head, and she disappeared inside.

"You need to talk to Kylie," he said as soon as the door closed. "Her boyfriend's sister found out the truth about me and told Kylie, but she doesn't have all the facts right." He forced himself to hold his brother's gaze, wishing he had some way to make the situation right, because, damn it, Will didn't deserve this. "I'm sorry this happened," Brett finished lamely, halfway wishing his brother would take a swing at him, although that would have been too easy. Instead, he had to watch as Will's face went blank, the way it did whenever he was dealing with something that hurt.

It took a few seconds before he said, "Any idea what the kid told her?"

"That I abandoned Des when she got pregnant and then you stepped in to marry her."

Which was halfway true. Des had actually left Brett and gone back to Will as soon as she'd discovered she was pregnant. Brett had been well out of the picture by the time Kylie was born, and he'd stayed out of the picture.

Brett lifted his chin. "It's okay if she keeps on believing that."

"I'll talk to her," Will said in a detached voice, and Brett took it as his cue to leave. He started down the steps without another word, and was almost to his truck when Will said his name. He looked back, but his brother only shook his head, giving up on whatever he'd been about to say.

Brett sucked in a breath, got into his truck and drove away, leaving his brother to deal with a situation he had not created.

BRETT'S HEAD WAS pounding by the time he drove into his yard. Leave or stay? Shit, he didn't know. The only thing he was certain of was that he wasn't going to cause his family any more grief. He was through forcing himself into Kylie and Will's lives, through trying to be part of something he had no right to be part of.

He knew it would be easier on everyone if he left, including himself. Which was exactly why he was hesitant to make that decision. He was done being easy on himself.

The phone was ringing when he walked in the door, and he knew he had to answer it, just in case it was Will.

"I have some thoughts about our situation," Claire announced without even saying hello. "I'm coming over."

"Don't—"

But she'd already hung up. Her approach was like a blitzkrieg.

"What's wrong?" she immediately asked when he answered her knock.

"I tried to tell you not to come." Brett knew he had to look like hell.

"Why?"

"Because damn it, Claire, this isn't going to work."

She blinked at him. "Will you at least let me come in for a minute?"

"I think you'd *better* come in." It was time to set the record straight and end things once and for all. Otherwise, she would just continue to hammer away at him, and there was no way now he was going to have Claire tying him closer to his family.

"Have a seat," he said, waving at the kitchen chairs. "Do you want something to drink?"

"Will I need a drink?" She remained standing, watching him.

"Probably," Brett said grimly. "The reason I don't want to get involved is because of Kylie."

"Kylie?"

"She's my daughter."

Claire sat down abruptly. "Kylie is *your* daughter?" She looked up at him, seeking a denial to the scenario her mind was obviously piecing together. "So you and…"

"I had an affair with my brother's wife. She got pregnant."

Claire shifted her gaze to stare straight ahead. "Then why does Will have anything to do with you?"

Hell, Brett didn't know, but he made a guess. "Because I'm Kylie's biological father. In the age of DNA, I could always push for parental rights."

"Would you do that?"

"No. But I don't think Will is taking any chances. I haven't been the most trustworthy of brothers."

Claire stared at him.

"I'm sorry."

"So am I." Claire swallowed hard. "I need to go."

CLAIRE HAD NEVER been afraid to cry, and she indulged herself freely that day. She felt like a fool. Regan had known.

Will. Brett. Everyone in the equation had known but her. She'd sensed the weird undercurrents, but she'd chosen to ignore them. After all, if there was anything she needed to know, her sister would have clued her in. Right?

Wrong.

And the bitch of the matter was that she couldn't even blame Regan. This was a sensitive issue.

But they were sisters. And Regan obviously knew that Claire was getting seriously interested in Brett. Yet she hadn't said one word. Why?

Probably because Claire had never stuck with anything except teaching for more than six months. Regan probably figured she would have her fun with Brett, move on and no harm would be done. The secret of Kylie's paternity would be safe. Regan hadn't counted on Claire falling in love.

Claire hadn't counted on falling in love.

And now the big question was who had she fallen in love with? The real Brett Bishop, or some man she'd invented in her mind?

CLAIRE SPENT THE day numbly doing all the mundane tasks she usually put off until the very last minute, including her taxes. She sealed the IRS envelope, then walked the half mile to town to mail it. She needed to move, to breathe, to do anything but think.

She was standing in line behind two other people at the post office, willing them not to talk to her, when the bell on the door signaled yet another customer.

It was Marla. She stalked straight toward Claire. Claire drew herself up, ready to blast her out of the water if need be, but then her jaw dropped when the woman said, "I'm sorry," in a voice loud enough for the postmistress and the two patrons at the counter to hear. "What I did and said the other night was wrong."

Claire frowned, wondering if she'd heard correctly. It sounded like an apology.

"Toni told me that you didn't say anything about Deke, that you just told her to go home. I misunderstood. I hope there won't be any hard feelings." And then Marla held out her hand. Claire took it, shook and released. Marla glanced over at the postmistress, as if to say, *"There, I did it...Happy?"* Then she exited, as quickly as she'd arrived.

Bemused, Claire watched her go.

"Marla's business has fallen off some," the postmistress explained, when Claire stepped up to the counter.

"But she's the only game in town."

"Yes, but people aren't going to the bar quite as often as they used to. They're afraid that you might leave because of what she did. It's kind of a show of support, you know?"

"I'm going to leave, anyway."

"Yes." The postmistress smiled. "But people were kind of hoping... Well, you know."

Claire gave a slow nod. "I appreciate the support," she said. And she did. Now, if she could just shove Brett Bishop out of her mind, she'd be a happy woman.

"Uh, Miss Flynn."

Claire turned, marker in hand. "Yes?"

"You did that wrong."

"What?"

"You made a mistake in the equation."

Claire took a step back. Dylan was right. In her hurry to get through the problem, she had missed the decimal place.

She held out the marker. Dylan got out of his seat, took it and corrected her error.

"Thank you, Dylan." She spoke dryly, as she always did when the kids corrected her, but she felt a deep sense of satisfaction. The students were with her, paying attention, taking an active role in their education. Finally.

And as much as she would have liked to take all the credit, she knew that it was more a matter of consistency and expectations than any special ability—other than dedication—on her part. Any teacher could have achieved the same result. The trick was to actually work at teaching, unlike Mr. Nelson, and not to leave midyear as the two previous teachers had done. Kids could do amazing things, with some consistency and guidance. And they could fall to pieces fast without it.

"Hey, uh, Miss Flynn…?"

"Yes?" She looked up several minutes after taking her seat. Her desk was surrounded by her female students.

"Are you all right?" Ashley spoke, but Elena, Lexi, Rachel and Toni stood with her. "You seem kind of, I don't know. Weird?"

Claire couldn't help but smile. "Weird?" she asked, raising her eyebrows.

"Yes," Elena said seriously. "We think something's not right."

"I'm just tired."

She wasn't fooling these girls, who exchanged dissatisfied glances as they filed back to their desks. Not much she could do about it but continue to stonewall. She idly peeled the pink sticky note from the cover of her grade book, the one reminding her to email the graduate school admissions department at UNLV. She had to confirm her acceptance of their offer so they could send her the paperwork required to complete the arrangements.

She rolled the note between her fingers as she looked out over her own combined classroom, the members of which were now silently working on the science problems she'd assigned. What could she possibly research in graduate school that she hadn't already discovered through direct experience?

What would she achieve by leaving?

She was too honest not to admit that Brett Bishop factored heavily into the equation—it was very tempting to do the easy thing and hightail it away from this community because of him. But personal issues aside, she hated to leave these kids, hated to see their education handed off to someone who would probably take the position for a year in order to get into the Wesley school system and then transfer to town. Or worse yet, someone who was in Barlow Ridge because he couldn't get a job elsewhere—or who was being involuntarily transferred here, as Mr. Nelson had been. These kids deserved better than that.

These kids deserved her.

CHAPTER FOURTEEN

CLAIRE WAS A big believer in getting to the heart of a matter rather than edging around the periphery. She needed to make a decision, and in order to do that, she needed information, so she drove to Wesley Friday after school, when she knew Regan was on her way to Las Vegas.

Will was at the pasture gate, a halter and rope in his hand, when she drove in. "Hi," Claire said as she approached, thinking that was probably the last nonchalant thing she'd be saying in this conversation.

Will seemed to sense the same thing. He pushed his hat back. "What's on your mind?"

"Brett."

"What about him?" But a look of dawning comprehension had already crossed his features.

"Yes, he told me," Claire said quietly.

Will unlatched the gate and held it open. "I have to catch a horse. Come on."

They walked across the pasture toward the small herd in the far corner. "Regan knows, doesn't she?"

Will nodded. "You can see why she didn't tell you."

"Yes." And she didn't blame her sister. Not much, anyway. "How about Kylie?"

"She knows now. Her boyfriend's bitch of a sister told her an almost-true story she got from her parents. Kylie blindsided Brett two days ago."

Claire hadn't realized it had been that recent.

"It's been a rugged couple days for us here, but Regan's pretty good at this kind of stuff."

"She had a lot of practice with me," Claire muttered. "So Kylie's doing all right?"

"If she wasn't, Regan wouldn't have left. Kylie's pissed at Brett, and we're all pissed at the girl who told the story, but I think Kylie's doing better now that she's aware of the whole truth."

"She's lucky to have a strong family. How are *you* doing?"

"I always suspected this day was coming, and in a way I guess I'm glad it has, so we can deal with it." Claire nodded, and then Will amazed her by saying, "You know, this is harder on Brett than it is on me."

"How so?" she asked incredulously.

"I have Kylie. Brett has guilt."

"He probably should have." Claire couldn't quite erase the bitterness from her voice.

"There are circumstances." Will pulled a tall weed and bent it between his fingers as he walked. "Did he tell you?"

"No."

"Well, to begin with, our dad would never have won any father-of-the-year awards. He kept me and Brett in competition for most of our lives. He picked at Brett and doted on me. It wasn't the kind of environment where brotherhood thrived."

"Did you like each other?"

"I would have killed anyone who messed with my brother, but… We didn't exactly get along face-to-face. I used to try to talk to Brett about what the old man was doing, but he had a hard time listening."

"Regan and I were always close. Maybe too close. I depended on her for everything."

"That wasn't the case with us. And then Des and I got

married. We traveled on the rodeo circuit, and we had troubles." Will kept his eyes on the horizon. "Which wasn't that surprising for two kids still in their teens who'd had no home life to speak of. I wanted to settle down, get a real job and start building a future. Des wanted to party while we were young." He tossed the weed aside. "Then I got hurt and had to come home for a while, which made both sets of goals difficult."

"She didn't come home with you?" Claire guessed.

"Nope. She stayed on the circuit, angry that I wasn't there with her, spending money we didn't have. Brett was doing rodeo, too. She told him we were separated, and he believed her. She came on to him, and he finally had a way to be better than his brother."

"But still…"

"There are lots of small circumstances involved."

"But…"

Will stopped and turned toward her. "Brett made a mistake, Claire."

It took a moment before she could say, "You're remarkably forgiving."

"No. I was damn bitter about it—more so when Des decided she couldn't handle motherhood and hit the road. But—" his expression softened as he paused "—I found that bitterness fades when you have better things to focus on—like your kid."

There wasn't much to say in answer to that.

Will started walking again. "Brett has the right to insist on parental rights, you know. And he hasn't. I owe him for that."

"He thinks you're afraid he'll still do it."

Will shook his head. "I know he won't." The three horses didn't move as Will and Claire walked toward them. "I admit, I was worried when he first moved back from

Montana a few years ago, but we made our peace and I trust him. Now he needs to make peace with himself."

"So what do *I* do?" she said, more to herself than to Will.

"Damned if I know, Claire."

"I don't know, either," she said. "Part of me says do what he asks and leave him alone, but the other part… Well, let's just say I've never been known for common sense."

To her surprise, Will smiled as he ran a hand over the nearest horse's neck. "Which is why you're probably good for Brett. He needs someone who'll brush the bullshit aside and see things for what they are." He slipped the halter up over the horse's nose and ears, then buckled it. "I can see where he's avoiding getting involved with you because of Kylie and me. But—and I'm no shrink—I'd also bet he's doing it because he doesn't think he deserves to be involved with anyone who makes him happy."

"I think you might be right." Claire reached out to pat the horse. The animal bobbed its head as she stroked it.

"Brett's always been hard on himself. Add a mistake like Des and, well, you get the picture."

Yes, she did.

Brett was denying himself a future. And by doing that, he was messing with hers.

REGAN CALLED ON her cell phone just as Claire was pulling into her driveway an hour and a half later.

"You heard about my visit?" Claire asked as she got out of the car, slinging her purse over her shoulder and pushing the door shut with her free hand.

"I heard."

"I feel for Kylie." She tromped up the steps to the trailer as she talked.

"Yes, I know. But we have to play the hand we're dealt,

as best we can. I think Kylie understands that now. We talked about ways of dealing with the issue without totally shutting Brett out of her life. Now we'll wait and see what she decides." Regan paused. "Will told me you came to talk about Brett." She waited, and when Claire didn't say anything, she added, "I'd suspected there might be something going on between you two."

"Now you have confirmation." Claire dropped her purse on the sofa and then headed for the kitchen. "I've decided to stay in Barlow Ridge for another year."

There was a long, ominous silence. "Because of Brett?" Regan finally asked.

"No. Because of the job, but it gives me time to decide about Brett."

"You know, Claire—"

"Oh, yes, I know," she said, without giving her sister a chance to finish. The odds were great things wouldn't work out with Brett, but even if they didn't, she wanted to stay with her job. If Brett didn't want to live close to her, he could leave.

"So what are you going to do now?"

"The unthinkable," Claire said. "I'm going to call Mom. I'll talk to you later."

She grabbed a soft drink out of the fridge, took a deep breath and hit the dreaded number one on speed dial with her thumb.

Ever efficient, Arlene answered on the first ring.

"Hi, Mom. How's life?"

"Very good, thank you." She sounded suspicious, as well she should be. Claire never called out of the blue.

"I don't think I'm going to graduate school."

"Why am I not surprised?"

"Because you know me?"

Arlene sighed.

"Hey, I found something I like to do, and I'm sticking with it."

"Claire," her mother said with exaggerated patience, "you can teach anytime."

"I can go to graduate school at any time, too."

"The longer you wait, the harder it is. I have firsthand experience." And she did. Arlene had put herself through graduate school later in life, earning her MBA while Regan and Claire were in grade school.

"I know what I'm doing."

"Then why did you call?"

Claire could picture her mother sitting at her desk, her glasses pushed up into her dark blond hair. Why had she called? "Reassurance."

"Rea…"

"Reassurance," Claire repeated gently. "I'm going to do this, but I don't want it to be adversarial, like with all the other things I've done."

"You do remember that I was *right* on most of the other things?"

"But this time *I'm* right, and I want some moral support, Mom. I know we're different. I know we don't see eye to eye. But…"

"Why do you need moral support, if this is the right thing to do?"

"Because I just do. I'm not like you. I can't simply grab the world by the tail and give it a shake."

Arlene snorted. "Since when?"

"What?"

"You've been doing that since you were a toddler."

"But not with you."

"I'm glad to hear something scares you." Arlene let

out a breath. "All right. I will give you moral support. For now. Until I sense that you're making a major error. That should give you until next Wednesday."

A joke. Her mother had made a joke. Claire gave a silent sigh of relief. "Have you heard from Stephen?" she asked, changing the subject while she was ahead.

"Of course."

"But I thought…"

"We've come up with the perfect relationship. He stays in San Diego. I stay here. We visit once a month for five days, alternating locales."

"Mom!" Claire said, shocked.

"It works for us," Arlene said sharply. "You're always complaining about how I want you to be like me. Well, the same holds true for you. I like companionship in small doses. This works." And it also miraculously explained why Arlene had quit ragging Claire about her career choice well before the holidays.

"You're happy?"

"We're both happy. The only caveat is that during those five days I focus on us. No phones, no email, no faxes. The other twenty-five days of the month, I can focus on business."

"If it works for you, it works for me. I'm just glad this is the reason you've been incommunicado. I had some wild theories going."

"No doubt," Arlene said with a sniff. "You always were creative."

"You do take weekends off?" Claire asked curiously.

"Some," her mother allowed. "I've finally trained a decent manager. If she stays on, I may increase my days away. One at a time. I guess I have to retire someday."

"No, Mom," Claire said, smiling. "Not you. You'll always have your finger in the pie."

"Thank you, Claire. And…" Arlene drew in a breath, then said just a bit too briskly, "I hope things work out for you in your job."

"I'll keep in touch."

UNTIL HIS BROTHER had called earlier that day, Brett figured his last parting with Claire had been exactly that. A last parting. He should have known it wouldn't be that easy with her, and he wasn't completely surprised when her car pulled up in front of his house.

"Hi," she said, testing the waters.

"Hi," he echoed in a less-than-encouraging tone.

"I've been doing some thinking."

"And talking to Will."

She looked surprised. "That, too."

"He called." And although Brett appreciated his brother's intentions—especially during such a rough time in Will's own life—Brett had made his position clear. He'd caused enough family damage.

The conversation had escalated into an argument and had ended with Will hanging up on him. Brett always had been able to punch his brother's buttons, and he hadn't lost his touch. If Will was mad, Will would leave him alone.

"So, I'm wasting my time, if I came here to talk about us?" Claire murmured.

"I know what I have to do."

"So do I," she said quietly, a note of resignation in her voice. She gave him a long look. "Have you heard that I'm teaching here for another year?"

"No," Brett said, hoping against hope that she was messing with him.

"I like my job. I'm keeping it."

"How wise is that?"

"For me or for you?" she asked, idly twisting the ring on her left hand.

"Careerwise."

"Careerwise, it's an opportunity most teachers never get, so I think it's a fine move. I want to teach rural while they still *have* rural schools. And *we* still have some things to talk about." She tilted her chin. "Now we'll have plenty of time to do it."

"Claire," Brett said through clenched teeth, "I don't need a good woman standing by me in my time of need."

"But apparently you do need to be a stubborn ass about this."

Whatever got the job done.

BRETT DID NOT want to go to the quilt show and community dinner, but when Jesse asked if he would be there, he heard himself say yes. If he and Claire were going to live in the same community, they might as well get used to bumping into one another.

Hell, he was never going to get used to it, and he knew it, so he was thankful when he managed to meet up with Jesse and Ramon outside the community hall, about a half hour before dinner started, without running into her.

"Have you seen the cars?" Jesse asked, bug-eyed.

"Not yet."

"Come on," the boy said, heading around the corner of the building toward the parking lot in back. "They're cool, and one guy let us crank the engine. They used to *crank engines!*"

Brett allowed Jesse and Ramon to point out all the features of the ten cars on display in the frigid air, and he had to admit they were nice specimens. After the cars, he dutifully asked the boys if they'd seen the quilts.

"Yeah. They're at the school," Ramon said, unimpressed. "We've seen 'em. I'd rather eat."

"The only cool one is Miss Flynn's," Jesse added. "It's purple and green and black. If I had a quilt, that's the one I'd get."

"Purple, green and black," Brett echoed. "Cool."

"They're not selling them until tomorrow," Jesse added. "You have time to see them." The *without us* was implied.

Brett nodded at one of the firemen who was tending the barbecue behind the community hall as he and the boys headed for the entrance. "How're you getting home tonight?" he asked Jesse.

"We're dropping him at the end of his road," Ramon said. "And my mom wants to leave early, so we have to eat soon."

"Dad's home," Jesse added with a quick glance at Brett. "He had some work to catch up on, so he didn't come."

Big surprise. Brett followed the two into the community hall where a line was already forming. He'd grab a bite, then head home. Brett pulled his wallet out as they approached the cashier's table, where Bertie sat with a steel money box. "I'll pay for both these guys."

Bertie took the money and stamped their hands with ink smiley faces. The boys raced ahead, getting in line behind Marla and Deirdre.

"I heard she was staying," Marla said sharply. "And it's not my fault if she doesn't. I apologized."

"Well, I heard she wasn't staying," Deirdre responded.

The two women rounded on Brett, who hadn't even realized they'd noticed his presence. "You're her landlord. You should know. Is Claire staying or leaving?"

"Staying," he said abruptly.

Marla gave Deirdre a smug nod.

Brett ate dinner with the boys, and shortly thereafter

the Hernandezes collected Jesse and Ramon for the trip home. Brett was on his way to the exit when he spotted Claire at the corner table with Phil, who had apparently finished his barbecuing shift and was now trying to light a fire under her.

"Hey, Brett?" Anne McKirk's husband waved him over to the bar. "I need to run home for a sec. Can you watch things here? Fifteen minutes tops. The other firemen are eating or cooking."

Or flirting.

"Sure," Brett said, even though he wanted to escape. A little community service wasn't going to kill him, and the McKirks were always there when Brett needed a hand with Phil's wells.

Twenty minutes later Brett was still selling beer and surreptitiously watching Phil put the moves on Claire. He shifted his attention for the umpteenth time, wanting desperately to get out of there. McKirk was not very good at telling time, and no one who wasn't buying beer was stupid enough to wander close, as he had.

Phil swaggered up to the bar then, and since he was a fireman, Brett thought about abandoning ship. Until his soon-to-be ex-boss said, "Hey, no hard feelings. Right?"

Brett frowned. "About?"

"Claire. The best man and all that?" And then he had the audacity to wink.

Brett uncapped the beer and pushed it across the counter to Phil, who gave him a superior smirk and dropped a dollar in the tip jar. Brett felt like pounding him, but instead turned away and found himself looking into Anne McKirk's wizened face.

"How can you let that guy sniff around her like that?" she demanded.

"I think Claire can handle herself," Brett said in his best conversation-squelching voice.

"I know she can handle herself with Phil," Anne said, unfazed by his tone. "You're the one giving her trouble."

Damn it, had Claire been talking to *Anne?*

"She hasn't said a word," the woman snapped. "But I do have eyes in my head. That girl likes you. And, dumb son of a bitch that you are, you don't seem to be doing anything about it."

Brett scowled. "Maybe I'm not wild about her."

Anne snorted. "Maybe you think I'm stupid."

"Do you need a drink?" he asked. "And where's your husband, who stranded me here?"

"Give me a Pepsi." She plunked down a dollar. "And I don't know where McKirk is, but I know you'd better not let that teacher get away."

"You talking about that new teacher?" Justo Echetto, the sheep man, asked as soon as Anne had taken her Pepsi and stalked away.

Brett drew a slow, deep breath. "What can I get you?" he asked.

Echetto pointed at a bottle. Brett picked it up and poured a double, hoping the older man would shut up out of gratitude. The ploy failed.

"The kids are doing better in school, I hear. We should try to keep her." He looked at Brett as though he could get the job done.

Brett didn't know if Anne McKirk and Justo Echetto were serious or screwing with his head. And meanwhile, Phil was cozied up to Claire in a dark corner, and she was laughing at something he'd said. Neither Anne nor Justo seemed to notice that. They had to be screwing with him.

"Shift's up," McKirk said from behind him.

"Great." Brett wanted out of there. He glanced over at the corner where Phil and Claire had been sitting, and was greeted by the happy sight of him escorting her toward the front entrance, a smug smile still on the jerk's face.

Brett clamped his teeth together so hard his jaw started to ache. He kicked around for a few more minutes, then collected his coat from a hook in the crowded entryway, feeling as if he'd done his social duty for the next five years—which was a good thing, since he didn't plan on socializing again for a long, long time.

It didn't matter who Claire left with. It was none of his business. He was going home to work on his biology lesson, like any red-blooded guy would do on a Saturday night.

A few seconds later he was listening to the ominous clicking of a nearly dead battery. Muttering a few innovative curses, he popped the hood and checked the connections. All good. It was definitely the battery, which had been sluggish earlier that day. He looked around. The street was crowded with vehicles, but there were no people around to help him. Even Phil and Claire were gone. He'd have to go inside and bum a jump from someone....

Screw it.

He'd leave the truck and jump it himself tomorrow with the one-ton. It was a cold night, but it was also less than a mile home. No big deal. His breath showed as he shoved his hands into his pockets and started down the street.

He inhaled deeply, telling himself that this was the reason he'd moved here. For the solitude. He was a guy who needed to be alone. A guy who didn't do well in relationships.

So it therefore followed that seeing Phil's truck parked in front of Claire's trailer should have no effect whatsoever on his state of mind. And there was absolutely no reason for him to amble down the driveway to take the path across the hay field, instead of the county road. And there was even less of a reason for him to open the truck door and reach inside to hit the panic button on the keys, setting off the alarm before easing the door shut again.

No. It was a totally childish thing to do.

And it felt damn good.

The trailer door banged open as soon Brett started down the path. There was cursing as the truck rhythmically shrieked its warning. Brett resisted the temptation to turn around and see whether or not Phil was fully clothed. He really didn't want to know. He just wanted the SOB to know that not everything was easy in life. Sometimes, little inconveniences happened.

And just as Brett was justifying his actions, he tripped over the ladder, which Claire had apparently moved for some unknown reason, and he went down hard. He was shaking his head, wondering if anything was ever, *ever* going to go right in his life, when a pair of shapely calves in purple tights came into his line of sight.

"What in the hell do you think you're doing?" Claire demanded. Just when Brett didn't think things could get worse, a loud explosion lit up the night, and damned if she didn't give him an accusatory look, as if he'd somehow caused it.

But his mind wasn't on Claire—or Phil, who'd been striding toward him, probably with the intention of smacking him in the face—but on the horizon.

"That's Jesse's place."

Claire brought her hand to her mouth. Phil had already turned and was heading for his truck.

"We need to get over to Jesse's place," Brett yelled as he scrambled to his feet.

"I'm getting the fire engine," Phil called over his shoulder.

"Someone else will get the engine," Brett shouted back, but Phil was already in his truck, gunning the motor. He swung the big rig in a backward arc, barely missing Claire's vehicle.

Brett looked at Claire. "I need your car."

"I'm coming, too."

He didn't argue. They pulled onto the county road and turned in the opposite direction from town. Phil's taillights were distant red dots. Brett drove as fast as he could on the thickly graveled road. An orange glow was already lighting the sky.

"Does anyone else live out here?"

"Just Jesse and his dad."

Brett negotiated the corners as fast as he dared, then turned into the drive, bouncing over deep ruts. Claire's car bottomed out, but Brett didn't slow down. Right now, he had to get to Jesse.

The closer trailer wasn't on fire. It was the one fifty yards behind it that was engulfed in flames.

The big question was, where was Jesse?

"I'll check the house," Claire said, before Brett uttered a word.

He had never felt his heart pounding so hard as when he leaped out of the car and started running for the burning trailer. Two big dogs were instantly on him.

"Jed! Bully! No!" Jesse screamed from where he was crouched, too close to the burning trailer. He screamed the names again, and the dogs stopped.

Brett brushed by them, hoping they wouldn't sink their teeth into the backs of his calves as he approached the boy.

"Are you hurt?" he asked hoarsely, and then he saw why

the kid was so close to the trailer. His father was lying on the ground. Jesse looked up, tears streaking trails through the dirt on his face. "I can't move him."

All the first aid Brett knew—don't move an injured man—was negated by another small explosion. A ball of heat rolled over them, and Brett heard Claire shriek his name from somewhere nearby.

A second later she was there, her arms wrapped around Jesse. "Come on," she said.

"No," the kid choked out.

"Brett will get your dad. Come on." She started dragging Jesse away from the fire. The flames were spreading to a nearby tree, crackling and popping over their heads.

Brett grabbed Jesse's dad by the armpits and started to pull. The last thing he was aware of before the final explosion was the distant sound of a fire engine.

About time, Phil.

BRETT KNEW HE WAS all right—he'd only been knocked to the dirt and he'd hit his head—but Claire couldn't keep her hands off him. McKirk, who was one of the local EMTs, was checking his vitals, trying unsuccessfully to make Claire keep her distance. Brett squinted up at her. "Jesse?" he asked, his voice thick. He'd inhaled a significant amount of smoke.

"He's fine."

"You'll live," McKirk said finally. "I need to see where the sheriff is." He stalked off, and Brett grabbed Claire's hand. Instinctively, she helped him to his feet. He only swayed for a second or two.

"What happened?" he asked.

"Looks like a meth lab," Claire said.

Brett felt anger welling up from deep inside. Jesse was

sitting on the running board of a truck, a blanket wrapped around him, gazing at nothing. Tom Lane was stretched out on the ground, an oxygen mask covering his face. His eyes were open and he was staring straight up at the sky.

"Is he going to be okay?" Brett asked.

"He's coming out of it," an EMT said, "but I imagine he'll be doing some jail time. They're cracking down on these things."

Claire's hand closed over Brett's and he squeezed her fingers. Squeezed. Hell, he was hanging on to her for dear life. He forced himself to let go.

And then he made his way over to Jesse, who suddenly seemed to realize he was there. The boy tried to smile. He almost made it. And then he was plastered against Brett's waist, hanging on for all he was worth.

"You ready to go home?" Brett asked.

"You mean, your house?"

"Yeah."

"What about my dad?"

"The EMT says he's all right. You'll be able to talk to him tomorrow."

"He's really all right?"

"Yeah."

The kid drew in a shaky breath and nodded against Brett's side. "I want to go home with you."

"Do we need to tell someone?" Claire asked, as the three of them walked to the car. Jesse was in the middle, the blanket still wrapped around him.

"The sheriff knows where to find us."

The trailer was now a smoldering heap of twisted frame and melted aluminum. The fire crew was still hosing it down, and Phil was shouting orders, apparently forgetting he wasn't in charge. Both guard dogs were lying under Tom Lane's vehicle, growling at anyone who walked near.

Brett opened the car door and helped Jesse in. Claire automatically slid behind the wheel, and then Brett settled in the passenger seat, letting his head rest against the cool window. He had a hell of a headache, but at least his family was safe.

CHAPTER FIFTEEN

THEY SETTLED JESSE on the sofa, covering him with blankets to keep him warm. He still didn't seem to understand what had happened, but the fire chief had called to tell them that Tom Lane *was* going to be all right. Jesse nodded after getting the news, and then asked Brett to sit with him. He did, until the boy fell asleep.

Brett only went as far as the kitchen then, even though he could have used a shower. Claire was waiting for him, her arms wrapped around her middle. He crossed the room to take her into an embrace, hold her close, make certain she was really all right.

She hugged him tightly, then eased herself out of his arms. Her face had a smudge of dirt and he wiped it off with the back of his hand.

"What happens now?" she asked.

Brett didn't answer. He shifted his attention to the living room.

"I'm going to see if I can get custody of Jesse," he said at last.

Claire's mouth popped open. "What?"

"He needs a stable home. I can give him that."

"This may not be the time to make such a decision."

"Why not? I figure, if Jesse's dad does something decent, like try to find a proper home for his kid, then the judge may look at him in a more favorable light when it comes to sentencing." Or at least that was the proposal

Brett was going to make to Tom Lane. "And in the meantime, Jesse needs a place to stay."

Claire let out a quiet breath as she shook her head. "You can't make up for not raising Kylie."

"That's not it," Brett said impatiently. "I'm doing this for Jesse. I like him." Actually, what he felt was closer to love.

"So you have room in your life for a kid."

It sounded like a challenge, and Brett instantly rose to the bait. "Yes. I can raise a kid."

"Well, if you have room in your life for a kid, then you also have room in your life for me."

"Claire, it isn't a matter of having room."

"I think it is."

"Look," Brett said with an edge of anger in his voice. "It's about Kylie. You two are close, and every time you're together, it'll bug her, knowing you're hooked up with me. I won't do that to her. She's been through enough. Hell, I won't do that to you, either."

Claire started for the door. "You're not giving your family a chance."

"They don't want a chance."

"Yeah?" She turned to face him, her hand on the doorknob. "Have you asked them their thoughts recently, after they've had time to process all this? Or would that be too dangerous?"

"What do you mean, dangerous?"

She pulled the door open, letting the cold air whip in around her. "If they forgave you, then maybe you'd have to take the brave step of forgiving *yourself*."

She spoke quietly, then turned on her heel and disappeared into the darkness.

"BRETT!"

The hairs rose up on the back of Brett's neck as Jesse's terrified scream echoed through the house. He raced into the living room. The boy was sitting bolt upright on the sofa, his face pasty-white.

"I thought you were gone," he said.

"I was saying goodbye to Claire—Miss Flynn."

"Did she go home?"

"Yes."

"Will she be back in the morning?"

Probably not.

"I'm sure she'll come to see you."

"What about my dad?"

"We'll call the hospital in the morning and get a report." Or the jail, depending on circumstances.

Jesse just nodded. "He's not a very good dad."

Brett couldn't argue with that.

"I never saw him until Grandma left, you know. Then they found him and made him take me."

"I think maybe he just didn't know how to be a dad. He didn't have much practice."

"He wasn't trying too hard to learn."

"You tried to save his life, Jess. That tells me you care about him."

"I do. But I…"

"What, kiddo?" Brett brushed the boy's hair back from his smudged forehead.

"Nothing." His eyelids were at half-mast again.

"You lie down and go to sleep. I won't leave. If you wake up and I'm not here, I'll be close. I won't leave the house."

"What if Phil needs help with a calf?"

"I'll wake you up and you can come with me. You're a better rancher than Phil. Maybe he'll learn a few things from you."

Jesse smiled weakly and his head began to nod. Brett

eased him down onto the sofa and arranged the blankets over him again.

Their clothes smelled of acrid smoke, which meant that the sofa would probably have a wicked scent by morning. Brett settled down in a chair and watched the boy sleep.

Raising Jesse wouldn't make up for not raising Kylie. One had nothing to do with the other. Or very little, anyway. Jesse needed a father and Brett needed a kid. There was no *replacement* involved. It was simply something that needed to be done.

For the first time in forever, Brett began to have a feeling that maybe something in his life was going to work out right, after all. And if one thing could work out… His head slumped against the back of the chair, and the next thing he was aware of was a loud banging on his back door.

It was still dark outside. He jumped to his feet, and after checking to see if the noise had woken Jesse, he walked quickly into the kitchen. He'd expected to see Phil or the sheriff through the tiny window, but instead his brother stood on the other side of the door. Brett yanked it open with a frown.

"We heard about the fire," Will explained as he stepped inside. Kylie was right behind him. Her face was pale, and Brett was astonished to see tears in her eyes.

"She was pretty worried," Will said. "Claire called and said you were all right, but Kylie wanted to see for herself."

"So you drove all the way out here?"

"I kinda wanted to see for myself, too."

Brett bit the edge of his lip as he shifted his gaze from father to daughter.

"I'm fine," he finally said. "You could have just called."

"Is that the little boy Claire told us about?" Kylie asked, gesturing at the blanket-covered form on the sofa.

"That's Jesse."

She swallowed, nodded. An awkward silence ensued. "What happened?"

Brett indicated the kitchen chairs with a sweeping gesture, before closing the connecting door to the living room all but a crack. Then he settled into his own chair and told the story.

"What happens to Jesse?" Will asked.

"I, uh, I was thinking that I'd see if he can live here with me. No one else seems to want him."

Kylie stared at him, her mouth pressed into a thin line. And then she leaned her head against her father's arm.

She didn't seem entirely happy about Brett's decision, which made no sense at all, since she had Will. What more did she need?

Brett swallowed. "I'm trying to help make things right, by giving Jesse a place to stay."

Kylie gave a silent nod, then got to her feet. She walked quietly into the living room and stood looking down at Jesse's blond head. Brett had no idea what she was thinking, why she was there. He met his brother's eyes, and knew confusion and pain must be apparent in his own when Will said, "I think she's coming to terms with the fact that life is unpredictable."

"You mean, she'd better get to know me while she can?" Brett asked with a touch of bitterness.

Kylie came back into the kitchen, easing the door partially shut again. "Dad, can I talk to Brett for a little bit?"

"Sure." Will got to his feet and went into the living room, closing the door behind him, leaving Brett alone with the most frightening person in his life.

Kylie remained standing near the door, her arms folded over her chest. "You remember that time when I came to find you at the Friday Creek Ranch?"

"Clearly." After more than a decade of self-imposed

exile in Montana, he'd been laid off from his job and had moved back to Nevada to take the only ranch mangement position available. It was way too close to Will and Kylie for comfort, but beggars couldn't be choosers, and he had to admit he was curious about them, hoping they'd made good lives for themselves in spite of what he'd done. But he hadn't planned on actually seeing them. He had never quite gotten over the shock of riding in after a long day spent gathering cattle, wanting nothing more than a beer and a hot meal, only to be confronted by a younger version of Des, and realizing he was face-to-face with his daughter—who had hitched a ride to the ranch in a cattle truck!

Up until that point she'd been a shadow figure, but once he was in her presence, he was aware of one overriding emotion. Terror. This was his kid. She was real. And she wanted answers about her background. Like, why were her eyes brown and her father's eyes blue? Was she adopted? She'd figured Brett would tell her the truth without Will ever knowing, never guessing that she was actually talking to her biological father.

He had not responded well. Fear did that to a guy. He'd hauled Kylie back to her father—her real father.

"How could I forget?"

"You were pretty mean. You scared me."

"That's what I was trying to do."

"Because you didn't want me around?"

Yes. It was overwhelming. "I was afraid."

She chewed the inside of her cheek, pressed her arms more tightly around herself.

"I'd done a rotten thing to your dad. And to you," he said, gripping the back of one of the wooden chairs.

"Dad kind of…explained things."

Damn, he bet Will had enjoyed that. Telling the daughter who worshipped him about the mistakes he'd made. The mistakes her mother had made.

Kylie bit her lip, eyed him speculatively. "You were only two and a half years older than I am now when..." She faltered for a split second. "It happened."

"That's not an excuse."

"No. But it's an explanation." Tears were starting to well up in her eyes again and she looked at the ceiling. "Why did you move back?" she asked in a quiet voice.

"I got tired of being alone. I never found anyone to hook up with, have a family of my own." And looking back, at the women he'd dated, the choices he'd made, he wondered if he would have let himself do that. "I missed your dad and I was curious about you—even if I was afraid to admit it. So when the Friday Creek job opened up, I took it. I thought I could at least find out about you two, without intruding in your lives."

"Regan said you asked her whether or not we were happy, when she first met you—back when she and Dad were dating."

"I did."

The girl pulled in an uneven breath. "Now you have a kid to replace me."

"I can't replace you, Kylie. You were never mine."

She pressed her lips together. "I think Dad misses you."

"You think?" he asked solemnly, but his heart started beating faster, and he knew his eyes were probably getting damp around the edges.

"I know," she said. And then she walked into his arms, and for the first time ever, Brett Bishop got the chance to hold his daughter tight.

ALMOST AN HOUR LATER, Brett left his seat at the kitchen table to brew his world-famous instant coffee, leaving

Kylie chatting quietly with her father. The three of them had talked for over forty-five minutes about…things. Nothing serious, just talk, and even though Brett knew they were all still working through issues, the fact that they could discuss everyday matters, like Kylie's grades, and Phil, made him realize that he'd honestly turned a corner in his life. Finally, after more than fifteen years, he no longer had the burden of living a lie. No more secrets to be kept, other than those that belonged in the family. And his daughter didn't hate him, which made his heart swell with happiness every time he thought about it.

But he couldn't help glancing out the kitchen window at the trailer. There were other things he still had to deal with. He wondered if it was too late.

After stirring coffee crystals into the hot water, he grouped the three cups together and carried them to the table without spilling. Kylie automatically reached for the blue cup. His cup.

She waited until he'd taken his seat before announcing, "Regan says Claire's probably in love with you."

Brett almost choked on his coffee. "Yeah?"

"That's what I hear." She took a sip. "So, what are you going to do about it?"

"I don't know." Brett glanced toward the living room.

"We'll watch Jesse," Will said.

Brett gave him a surprised look. "It's after midnight."

"Her light is on."

"Jesse might be kind of scared if he wakes up alone."

"Don't worry," Kylie said. "I'll talk to him."

"Thanks," Brett said softly. And then he grabbed his coat.

He was at Claire's door less than five minutes later. He hesitated only a moment before he knocked. The trailer had gone dark just as he'd trotted down his own porch steps, but he didn't feel like waiting for morning.

He knocked again, and was posed to rap a third time when the door swung open. Claire stood with her kimono gathered at the neck.

"Is Jesse all right?" she asked, looking alarmed.

"He's fine. Kylie and Will are watching him." The emotional speech he'd practiced on the walk over suddenly evaporated from his mind. "Claire, I'm so damn tired."

Without a word, she opened her arms and he stepped into them, gathering her close, burying his face in her neck.

EPILOGUE

Six months later

"So you see," Jesse explained to Kylie with a serious expression, "we talked to the judge and then Brett explained to me how my dad giving him custody was a way of showing love, since he didn't know a lot about being a dad, and Brett does."

Kylie reached out and ruffled Jesse's hair. "I coulda told you that."

"But you didn't."

"Hey, some things you got to work out on your own or they don't mean a thing." She looked up as a truck pulled into the drive. "Shane's here. See you, Junior."

Jesse made a face at her, then scampered off as Ramon hailed him from the reeds near the creek.

Claire leaned closer to Brett as they watched the kids go in opposite directions. "Kind of warms your heart to see her picking at him like that."

Brett didn't answer, but his arm tightened around her.

"There's Phil," he muttered as a truck approached from the direction of the Ryker ranch. "What now?"

Brett was full-time manager of Phil's hobby ranch again, since Phil had forgotten to release the bulls on time for an early calving, due to an impromptu trip to Cancun, and then the hay crop had been disastrously harvested by the temporary help. After those two incidents, Phil had decided it was more cost-effective to simply keep Brett on. Apparently there was a limit to how much of a loss he was willing to take for tax purposes, especially when his neighbors were all snickering at him.

"Nothing. I invited him," Claire said.

"To a family barbecue?"

"The whole school is here," she reminded him.

"Yes, but how many were invited?"

Claire smiled and reached up to brush a bit of wind-blown dandelion fluff from her husband's hair. "All of them."

"I think you need to reevaluate your definition of family."

"Family, my love, is where you find it and what you make of it." She pulled his mouth to hers briefly. "Don't you agree?"

He smiled down at her. "Wholeheartedly."

* * * * *

We hope you enjoyed

HOME ON THE RANCH: NEVADA.

If you liked these stories, then you're in luck—Harlequin has a Western romance for every mood!

Whether you're feeling a little suspenseful or need a heartwarming pick-me-up, you will find a delectable cowboy who will sweep you off your feet.

Just look for cowboys on the covers of Harlequin Series books.

Available wherever books and ebooks are sold.

SPECIAL EXCERPT FROM

HARLEQUIN®

SPECIAL EDITION

Cecelia Clifton came to Rust Creek Falls hoping to find true love. Then she fell for Nick Pritchett, the commitment-phobic Thunder Canyon carpenter she's known all her life. But when Nick agrees to give his best friend boyfriend-catching lessons, he discovers that there's more to Cecelia than meets the eye—and that he wants her all for himself!

***

"I know these are for the charity auction, but if I give you twenty-five bucks, will you give me a bite of something?"

He must be desperate, Cecelia thought. Plus there was also the fact that she knew that Nick did a lot of charity work. He was always helping out people who couldn't pay him. Her heart softened a teensy bit. "Okay. Two apple muffins for twenty-five bucks. Frosting or not?"

"I'll take one naked," he said and shot her a naughty look. "The other frosted."

His sexy expression got under her skin, but she told herself to ignore it. She handed him a hot cupcake. "It's hot," she warned, but he'd already stuffed it into his mouth.

He opened his mouth and took short breaths.

She shook her head. "When will you learn? When?" she asked and frosted a cupcake, then set it in front of him. "Now that you've singed your taste buds," she said.

He walked to the fridge and grabbed a beer then gulped it down. "Now for the second," he said.

Where's my twenty-five bucks?" she asked.

"You know I'm good for it," he said and pulled out his wallet. He extracted the cash and gave it to her. "There."

"Thank you very much," she said and put the cash in her pocket.

Within two moments, he'd scarfed down the second cupcake, then pulled a sad expression. "Are you sure you can't give me one more?"

"I'm sure," she said.

He sighed. "Hard woman," he said, shaking his head. "Hard, hard woman."

"One of my many charms," she said and smiled. "You always eat the baked goods I give you in two bites. Don't you know how to savor anything?"

He met her gaze for a long moment. His eyes became hooded and he gave her a smile that branded her from her head to her toes. "There's only one way for you to find out."

***

Enjoy this sneak peek from
MAVERICK FOR HIRE
by New York Times *bestselling author Leanne Banks,*
the newest installment in the brand-new six-book continuity
MONTANA MAVERICKS:
20 YEARS IN THE SADDLE!,
coming in September 2014!

⬩HARLEQUIN®

ₛPECIAL ᴇDITION

Life, Love and Family

NOT JUST A COWBOY

Don't miss the first story in the
***TEXAS RESCUE* miniseries**
by Caro Carson

Texan oil heiress Patricia Cargill is particular when
it comes to her men, but there's just something
about Luke Waterson she can't resist. Maybe it's
that he's a drop-dead gorgeous rescue fireman
and ranch hand! Luke, who lights long-dormant
fires in Patricia, has also got his fair share of secrets.
Can the cowboy charm the socialite into a
happily-ever-after?

Available September 2014
wherever books and ebooks are sold.